Santa

A book in the series Latin America in Translation /
en Traducción / em Tradução

Sponsored by the Consortium in Latin American Studies at
the University of North Carolina at Chapel Hill and Duke University

Santa

A NOVEL OF MEXICO CITY

Federico Gamboa

Translated and edited by John Charles Chasteen

The University of North Carolina Press Chapel Hill

Translation of the books in the series Latin America in Translation /
en Traducción /em Tradução, a collaboration between the Consortium in
Latin American Studies at the University of North Carolina at Chapel Hill
and Duke University and the university presses of the University of North Carolina
and Duke, is supported by a grant from the Andrew W. Mellon Foundation.

© 2010
THE UNIVERSITY OF NORTH CAROLINA PRESS

Library of Congress Cataloging-in-Publication Data
Gamboa, Federico, 1864–1939
[Santa. English]
Santa : a novel of Mexico City /
Federico Gamboa ; translated and edited by John Charles Chasteen.
p. cm.—(Latin America in translation/en traducción/em tradução.)
ISBN 978-0-8078-7107-2 (pbk. : alk. paper)
I. Chasteen, John Charles, 1955– II. Title.
PQ7297.G3S3 2010   863'.62—dc22   2010004478

cloth   14 13 12 11 10   5 4 3 2 1
paper   14 13 12 11 10   5 4 3 2 1

TO PROFESSOR BILL BEEZLEY,

who inspired this translation and who has
done so much to promote the historical study of
Mexican popular culture in the United States.

Contents

Introduction

WHY READ *SANTA*?

Why read *Santa*, a novel written more than a century ago? Because of its quality, above all. This is a sophisticated and beautifully executed novel. Santa, the paradigmatic prostitute of late nineteenth-century naturalist fiction in her Mexican incarnation, is rendered by Federico Gamboa with carefully researched veracity, a cinematic eye, and, it must be admitted, not inconsiderable lust.

No wonder that Mexican filmmakers have done so many movie adaptations of the novel, no fewer than four. Though the novel immediately attracted an avid readership when it was published in 1903, it is the cinematic and other nonprint versions that have given *Santa* its enormous projection in Mexican popular culture. There was a silent *Santa* film in 1918. Then, in 1932, *Santa* became the first Mexican "talkie," with notable box office success and a soundtrack hit song, "Santa," by the immortal Agustín Lara, who might be described as Mexico's Cole Porter. A bit later, *Santa* also became a pornographic comic strip. Historian Katherine Elaine Bliss has found that some young Mexican prostitutes of the 1930s told their life stories to social workers in terms that sounded much like Santa's and that, in doing so, they often mentioned the 1932 film version starring Lupita Tovar, Mexico's first glamorous movie actress. Meanwhile, *Santa* found its way into a steady stream of stage productions and returned to the big screen in 1943 and 1969. In 1978, it became a primetime television series, or *telenovela*. An analog to *Santa* in the United States would have to be a novel like *Uncle*

Tom's Cabin or *The Adventures of Huckleberry Finn* because of *Santa*'s familiarity to the nation at large, rich and poor, readers and nonreaders over several generations.

But *Santa* is a very different sort of novel from those two American classics. *Santa* is a naturalist novel that one might also compare to Upton Sinclair's *The Jungle* or Theodore Dreiser's *Sister Carrie*. Literary naturalism supposedly made novelists into literary scientists studying human behavior much as naturalists might study a colony of birds, that is, through systematic observation. Literary naturalists more or less went out with notebooks to observe the social environments in which they planned to place their fictional characters. Federico Gamboa kept a detailed journal that reveals his observational notes for various scenes in Santa. He never recorded details of a Mexico City brothel, but this does not mean that Gamboa did no participant observation in that department, because he most certainly did. Here is the point: literary naturalists created quasi-documentary historical sources from detailed re-creations of social environments in crafting the settings for the stories they wanted to tell.

A surprising lot of naturalist novelists wanted to tell stories about prostitutes. Émile Zola, the leading exponent—and more or less the inventor—of naturalism wrote about a girl named Nana in his widely influential 1880 novel that takes her name. Gamboa even visited Zola in France, where he became linked, for a time, to a prostitute of the Moulin Rouge, whom he used as something of a nonliterary model for Santa. Likewise, a brothel piano player that Gamboa knew in Mexico City became the model for Santa's blind admirer, Hipólito. In their desire for an unsentimental, scientific understanding of human behavior, naturalists wanted to strip away the clothing of civilization to expose the human animal. That led them to portray socially marginal characters, whose animal instincts were thought to have been laid bare by corrosive poverty, pathology, and exploitation. Naturalists were particularly interested in showing how social environments determined their characters' behavior, how a nice girl like Santa, in other words, could end up as she did. Naturalists wanted to demonstrate in their characters and plots that sex—supposedly among the most animal of instincts—was a mainspring of human behavior.

The naturalist aesthetic, out of style for several lifetimes, is not itself a reason to read *Santa* now, of course. For most readers, the appeal of *Santa* will come from the fact that naturalist novelists really did know the everyday sorts of places and people portrayed in intricate detail in their novels. Following his French influences, Gamboa believed that a novelist's mission was to tell the composite stories of people whose lives were never recorded individually as biographies, to become, in words that he himself used, a historian for people without a history. This makes *Santa* an interesting lens through which to view life in Mexico City circa 1900.

Readers need a sense of the author and his historical moment in order to interpret *Santa*. Gamboa was born into Mexico's upper class in 1864. In his youth, he wrote the society column for a Mexico City newspaper. He then spent much of his life as a career diplomat in a variety of foreign capitals, eventually returning to Mexico to become a literature professor and a government minister. He lived in the United States several times in his life, including a year in New York, a stint at the Washington embassy, and a brief political exile in Galveston. He knew English well, but he was distinctly not an admirer of the United States. In keeping with a proud conservative tradition in Mexico, he warned against U.S. influence.

Gamboa was a strong supporter of Porfirio Díaz, the famous Mexican dictator whose decades-long reign was at its zenith in 1900. Díaz was a *liberal* dictator, meaning that he postponed the introduction of democracy on the theory that average Mexicans would require decades of tutelage before they could govern themselves. Gamboa, on the other hand, was a true conservative in that he abhorred the very idea of democracy. He preferred a monarchy or, in its absence, a dictatorship. Gamboa supported Díaz partly because of this preference for law-and-order authoritarianism and partly because of personal loyalty to someone who was a friend of his family. But Gamboa was out of step with the Europhile, positivist ideological tilt of the Díaz regime. Gamboa was an outspoken opponent of the Científicos, the technocratic advisers who surrounded Díaz. In *Santa*, Gamboa adopted a nostalgic, traditionalist view, skeptical about the power of science and the benefits of untrammeled Progress.

Catholicism is at the heart of that traditionalist view. Gamboa's religious attitudes make him a highly atypical naturalist novelist and suggest comparisons to Tolstoy, whose novel *Resurrection* (1899) Gamboa read just as he was about to begin work on *Santa*. The church seldom enters the story and, when it does, in a negative light. Religious language pervades the book, however, providing many of Gamboa's favorite metaphors. Furthermore, the structure of the plot—with Santa's fall from grace, judgment, penitence, and redemption through suffering—is strongly Christian. Most naturalist novels are bleaker than *Santa*, offering no hope of redemption.

Gamboa ran unsuccessfully for president of Mexico as the candidate for the Catholic Party in 1913, and during the 1920s he sided with followers of the "Cristero" insurrection, a religious reaction against the Mexican Revolution. Being politically pro-Catholic was part and parcel of Gamboa's larger conservatism, his nostalgic, pro-Spanish attitude toward Mexico's colonial heritage. *Santa* was written during the U.S. occupation of Cuba, which occurred in the wake of the 1898 war on that island, and Gamboa became one of the prominent Latin American intellectuals waving pro-Spanish banners and standing against Anglo-Saxon materialism and aggression. Spain's trouncing by the United States awakened traditionalist feelings of cultural kinship from Mexico to Argentina. For example, *Santa* gives loving attention to bullfighting, a tradition powerfully emblematic of Spain. (By way of contrast, one could point out that by 1903 Cubans, whose bid for independence distanced them from Spanish traditionalism, already preferred baseball to bullfighting.) In addition, most of the novel's secondary characters are Spanish, including almost all the women other than Santa herself.

Naturalist authors tended to write with a didactic purpose. What lessons did Gamboa want to teach in *Santa*? A Christian lesson about sin and personal salvation, clearly, but beyond that, what message about Mexico? How does the political order called the Porfiriato appear from the perspective of the street in 1900? What is Gamboa signaling about Mexico's incorporation into what was already, by that time, a process of rapid globalization? And what on earth is Gamboa saying about women in this story? Can he really be defending the traditional honor ethic that turns Santa's sexual "slip" into her inevitable doom? (Gamboa's men, by the way, resemble nothing so much as a pack of baying hounds, and this is clearly self-critical on the author's part. After all, as a young man he had been just like the novel's fashionable clubmen who flock around Santa in her heyday as "queen of the night.") And where, oh where, in this novel, is race? Racial descriptions are not applied at all, aside from a few glowing references to Santa's soft brown skin. Finally, if one reads Santa's story as a metaphor for Mexican history, as Gamboa probably intended, what is the lost paradise, what the perdition, and what the redemption? Questions to ponder.

Meanwhile, you will not be bored. However one regards Gamboa's social and political attitudes, one cannot doubt his skill as a storyteller. The Spanish-language original is a spectacular achievement that can be only partly re-created in English. *Santa* contains a notable range of styles, from quite formal to quite colloquial. Formal descriptive set pieces like the courthouse scene deploy elaborate syntax and bombastic diction in sentences half a page long. On the other hand, Gamboa's dialogue is quite colloquial, capturing people talking in a variety of accents. So when the bullfighters or the madam of the brothel open their mouths, they sound Spanish, not Mexican. Alas, such distinctions disappear in translation. In the absence of dialect, I have transferred the natural, colloquial quality of the dialogue to a contemporary U.S. idiom. Likewise, I have tried to reproduce the elaborate syntax and bombastic diction of the tour-de-force descriptions only within the limits of what works naturally. As editor, I have reduced repetition and privileged reader comprehension above all else. As translator, I have worked to maintain the polish, poise, and vividness of Gamboa's prose.

One of the delights of *Santa*, should you give in to the guilty pleasure it affords, is its sentimentalism. It may seem odd, and it is quite out of keeping, really, with the naturalist aesthetic, but sentimentality is powerfully present. The scenes of Santa's girlhood in Chimalistac are particularly lyrical and sun drenched. In contrast to the rest of this rather dark novel, these childhood scenes read like sentimental local color meant to idealize small-town life, a chapter of *costumbrismo* amid the *naturalismo*. I confess to liking that chapter best. And then, of course, there are the wrenching final scenes during which, as I dutifully strived to reproduce Gamboa's tear-jerking intentions in English, I found myself having to wipe my eyes in order to see my text. Readers impervious to sentimentalism may prefer to concentrate on how a high-class brothel, a low-class dive, or a modern hospital or police station operated in 1900 Mexico City; or they may even turn, and pardonably so, to Gamboa's leering descriptions of our protagonist's firm brown flesh and the rippling muscles of the bullfighter who really loved her.

Santa, indeed, has something for everyone.

JOHN CHARLES CHASTEEN

Santa

Part One

One

"This is it," said the coach driver, suddenly stopping the horses, who shook their heads in protest at his roughness. The passenger stuck her head out the door of the coach, looking to the left and right, and hesitantly, not recognizing the place, she asked in surprise:

"Here? Where is it?"

The driver, contemplating her with a wicked expression from his high perch, pointed with his whip:

"There, straight ahead. That closed door."

The woman climbed out of the coach and reached back to extract a small bundle, her luggage. Then she stuck her hand in the pocket of her petticoat and handed a peso to the driver.

"This should cover it, sir."

Very slowly and without taking his eyes off her, the driver stood, pulled several coins out of his pants pocket, put them on the roof of the vehicle, counted them, and finally returned the peso.

"I don't have change. You can pay me some other time when you need me. I'm at the cabstand with a red flag at 317 San Juan de Letrán. Just tell me your name."

"My name is Santa. No, but go ahead and charge me. I don't know if I'll be staying here. Keep the whole peso," she added as an afterthought, anxious to get away.

And without waiting for a reply she set off quickly, looking at the ground, her body half hidden by the shawl that barely clung to her shoulders, as if she were embarrassed to be seen in that place at that time of day, with so much light and so many people who surely observed her and knew where she was going. So, hardly noticing the anemic, unkempt little garden to her right or the unsanitary-looking eatery to her left, she walked straight ahead to the closed door and knocked on it. She did get a vague impression of patchy grass, stunted bushes, a few tree trunks. She did get a whiff of food and cheap liquor, a rumor of men's conversation and laughter. She even sensed, without daring to stop or turn her head, that several men had gathered in a doorway to stare brazenly and make loud, mocking comments about her. Agitated, she vented her feelings repeatedly on the door knocker, giving it three hard knocks each time.

The truth is that nobody, aside from some loiterers in the cheap restaurant, paid any attention to her because, although it is the domain of prostitutes and their clients by night, by day this neighborhood is as honest and hard-working as any other in the city. It has many small industries: workshops producing gravestones and Italian copper work, a French dry cleaner's shop with a big sign and an enormous brick chimney in the courtyard, a charcoal seller's shop always covered with a fine black dust that attaches itself stubbornly to pedestrians, making them snort, dust themselves with their handkerchiefs, and pick up the pace as they pass by. On one corner stands a modern and neatly painted butcher shop, La Giralda, with three open doors, smooth artificial stone flooring, and a counter of marble and iron, the ceiling supported by quite narrow pillars to maximize ventilation. La Giralda's large scales sparkle with cleanliness, and from its range of heavy meat hooks hang huge, headless, beef carcasses split down the middle to display their dirty white ribcages and the revolting, bloody redness of their fresh, recently killed flesh. The butcher shop attracts clouds of unquiet, voracious flies and one or two stray dogs with rough fur who lie heavily on the sidewalk without quarreling with one another, dozing or nosing after fleas with an intent gaze and erect ears, patiently awaiting scraps. On the opposite corner, advertised by its traditional banners, stands a pulque shop, its walls painted with primitive murals, a small tin roof over each of its doors: The Corner of the Magi, trusty dispensary of the famous Santa Clara and peerless San Antonio Ometusco brews. In addition to the garden, with its small circular fountain, its primitive fountainhead forever welling over without ever running out of water despite the furious assault of the water-carriers and of the neighbors who carelessly spill more than they ought to, so that the edges of the fountain and its surroundings are always soaked—in addition to that garden, the block can boast no fewer than three electric streetlights and as many as five houses with fine fronts, three or four stories tall, with whitewashed balconies and plaster cornices. The pavement is of compressed-cement blocks, traversed by streetcar rails. And on the other side of the garden that helps hide the brothels there is a public school.

Given such diverse elements and being, as it was on that day, very close to twelve noon, the street was fully in motion, fully alive. The summer sun of late August drenched everything, extracting flashes from the gleaming rails and a slight haze of evaporation from the gutter damp from the rain of the previous day. The streetcars, pulled by mules with jangling bells around their necks, their drivers perpetually sounding the raucous warning horns, glided by with muffled stridence, painted bright yellow or green depending on the class of service, packed with passengers whose hats and heads could barely be glimpsed bent over some newspaper, turned toward their seat mates, or distractedly contemplating the passing buildings.

The stone cutter's shop, the copper works, and La Giralda alternately emitted the chink chink of chisels on marble or granite, the rhythm of hammer blows falling on copper pots and pans, or the thump of butchers' meat axes cleaving flesh. Street vendors passed, calling out the nature of their merchandise, or stopped in the middle of the stream of people and animals, turning to look in all directions, their hands at their mouths to direct their voices. Pedestrians contorted slightly this way and that to avoid bumping into the street vendors or each other. From the open windows of the school, rumors of children's voices occasionally came floating in chorus on the air; they chanted, "a, b, c, d, e, f, g . . ."

Because the door did not open for a long time, Santa eventually turned to look at the street scene. But when the Cathedral bells loudly struck twelve, the French dry cleaner's steam whistle thrust its anguishing shrillness into the air in a straight, white column of steam, and the workers there and in the other shops lighted cigarettes with rough hands, tucked their filthy blue shirts into their pants, and began to pour onto the sidewalk and obstruct it, shouting their vulgar goodbyes to each other or, with arms around each other's shoulders, heading up the street to the Corner of the Magi. Crowds of schoolboys joined them on the sidewalk, shoving each other, knocking off each other's caps, and raising Cain, their books and slates tumbling, their ink-stained fingers wiping away momentary tears, each impish face soon recovering its mask of mischievous high spirits. Urgently, Santa turned and redoubled her pounding on the door knocker.

"What the devil is the big hurry?" came the answer, finally. "Doña Pepa, the manager? Yes, she's here, but she's still asleep."

"Fine, I'll wait," said Santa, quite relieved to have escaped the curious looks from the street. "I'll wait for her here in the stairwell."

And she sat right down on the second step of the stone stairs that curved up in a half spiral beginning a few feet from the door. The woman who had opened the door, softening at the sight of Santa's beauty, first smiled a somewhat simian smile and then subjected her to a knowing interrogation. Did she intend to stay here, in this house? Where had she been previously?

"You're not from Mexico City . . ."

"Yes, I am, that is, not from the capital itself, but from very nearby. I'm from Chimalistac . . . not far from San Angel," she added by way of explanation. "You can go by train. Have you ever been?"

The woman knew of San Angel because of its annual fair, which she had on several occasions attended in the company of her employer, who was an avid player of monte, a card game much played at the fair. Captivated by Santa's face and simple candor, the woman moved forward, resting her elbow on the banister, feeling pity, almost, to see Santa arrive in the same hole where she herself earned a living, a hole that would devour that beauty, devour that young flesh still ignorant, no doubt, of all the horrors that awaited it there.

"Why are you starting this life?"

Santa did not answer, because at that very moment there came the loud sound of a glass door opening suddenly and a woman's voice with a strong Spanish accent:

"Eufrasia! Go ask for two large glasses of anisette and soda water from Paco's store. Say that they are for me."

Santa's interlocutor shrugged in the manner of someone resigned to suffer an incurable illness. She let the "new girl" into a small waiting room, and without further ado, went to do the errand, though she did slam the street door to signal her displeasure at being sent without a coin in hand.

As if the order for the two drinks of anisette were a bell ringing, the entire house now began to rouse itself, a very little bit at a time, amid an odd mixture of songs, laughter, and shouted commands, the doors of glass cabinets opening and closing, water pouring into unseen basins, masculine-sounding guffaws coming from women's throats along with some brazen, hoarse obscenities that punctured the air unabashedly . . . Santa listened in confusion, and it was only confusion that kept her from following her impulse to escape and return, if not home—for that was now impossible—then anywhere else that people did not speak that way. But she did not dare even to move for fear that she might be noticed, that a creak of her chair might give her presence away to the men and women in the upstairs rooms, whom she imagined tangling naked with one another. She did not even notice the return of Eufrasia, who startled Santa when she approached and said:

"Do you want to go in to see doña Pepa? She's awake now."

Still confused, she followed the servant upstairs, through two dark, foul-smelling hallways, then into a parlor with two makeshift beds—belonging to servants, perhaps—still spread out on the carpet, the atmosphere acrid with the smell of alcohol and tobacco. In one corner stood an upright piano, its keyboard looking, in the dim light, like a monstrous set of teeth. Down another corridor, Santa heard, somewhere nearby, the crackle of grease in a frying pan. They went down a staircase and emerged in a small interior courtyard at one corner of which was a door of frosted glass panes.

"Señora," called Eufrasia, rapping on the glass with her knuckles, "here's the new girl." A thick voice answered from inside the room:

"Just push, *hija*. It's open . . ."

Eufrasia pushed, the door opened, and Santa, who could not see a thing in the darkness of the room, stepped through the door.

"Come closer, doll . . . Watch it! That's a table. But come closer, over there, to your right. That's it. Come to the bed . . ."

Santa could hardly see anything, but she found the bed by following the instructions and moving with extreme care. To her dismay, behind the voice of the strange woman she detected the snore of a man, a corpulent man, by the sound of his snores, which did not cease even when Santa's knees bumped into the bed.

"So you're the country girl," inquired Pepa, raising herself up on pillows so clean and stiff with starch that they sounded almost brittle. "What's your name? No wait, I know, don't tell me. Elvira told us . . ."

"My name is Santa," she said with the same slight mortification as earlier when she declared it to the coachman.

"That's it, that's it," laughed Pepa, "that's pretty funny! Quite a name. It'll make money, too, I bet."

The bedsprings squealed in time with her laughter, and the snores abruptly stopped. Pepa's spontaneous laughter did not bother Santa, who even smiled in the darkness, quite used to reactions of incredulity or astonishment when people first heard her name.

"Hey girl," exclaimed Pepa, who had put her hand on Santa carelessly, "you're firm as a saint's effigy, a santa indeed!" Pepa's expert hands, the hands of a courtesan grown old plying her trade, lingered appreciatively on the body of the newcomer, who jerked defensively. Santa's face burned, and she felt like crying or lashing out at the woman who examined her so degradingly.

"What's going on?" asked the man lying next to Pepa.

"The new girl is here. Go back to sleep."

"The new girl, the new girl." He stretched and turned over, and Santa could distinctly hear him chuckle softly.

Pepa jumped out of bed and, with the sureness of someone moving through a familiar space, went in the darkness to unshutter a window. Light filled the room.

Ah, the grotesque figure of Pepa, in spite of the long nightgown that covered the imperfections created by a lifetime of vice! Her wilted flesh, exuberant in the places that men love to grab, hardly seemed to belong to her, so damaged and needful of replacement, so useless for the bitter, daily battles of a brothel. Whenever she stooped to pick up a stocking or lifted her bare arms to light a cigarette or plunged her head and neck into the wash basin, her enormous old drinker's gut and her bulky, flaccid breasts of a Galician peasant oscillated disgustingly, with something bestial in the oscillations. Without the slightest hint of modesty, she did her personal morning routine, chatting loquaciously with Santa who replied, now and again, with monosyllables. Pepa liked her, of course, as did everyone in the face of Santa's provocative beauty, a beauty made all the more provocative by the obvious and sincere sweetness that her semi-virginal, nineteen-year-old body seemed to exude.

"I bet they've told you horrors about us and our houses, right?"

Santa shrugged her shoulders and gestured vaguely with both extended arms. What did she know?

"I've come," she added, "because there is no place for me at home anymore, because my mother and brothers have thrown me out. And because I don't have a skill, and above all . . . because I swore that this is what would happen to me, and they didn't believe it. I don't care if these houses and this life are the way people say or if they're worse . . . the sooner that it's done with, the better. Fortunately, I don't have anyone."

She began to examine the colors of the rug, her nostrils flaring slightly, her eyes tearing.

Pepa, busy sponging cheeks and neck, assented without formulating a word. An experienced woman of the world, she easily recognized in the protesting girl, who was no doubt still reeling from her recent abandonment, yet another jilted victim of men's deceptions. It was the cruel, eternal story of the sexes, the coming together with a kiss, a caress, and a promise, only to separate soon enough, with ingratitude, disappointment, and tears! Pepa knew that story backwards and forwards. She had not always been like this—with a gesture toward her extinct charms, barely sufficient anymore to attract a beast like the one still lying in her bed, a total drunk, an ex-convict or escapee from God-knows-how-many prisons, who was finishing his miserable, shiftless life with the subsidy that Pepa earned, coin by coin, doing . . . all sorts of things.

"Want to have a drink with me?" she said, pulling a bottle of clear aguardiente out of her dresser. "Here, don't be silly. This is the only thing that keeps us going . . . No? Well, you'll get used to it."

Pepa downed her brimful glass while standing quite close to Santa, who was watching her closely, and she continued her sudden burst of confidences, initiated to impress the neophyte, no doubt, but extended by her own need to give vent, from time to time, to what she had seen and suffered. By expressing these things, she expelled a bit of the stagnant, putrid water that drowned her own spirit, so to speak, and splashed it on other hearts and other women who did not give a damn about her, as she well knew.

"You wouldn't appreciate it yet, anyway," Pepa went on, "sitting there with that expression of shock. You feel young and healthy, with a wounded heart that you can't accept, and you want to take it out on your body. Well, it won't be the last disappointment, *hija*, and our bodies eventually wear out and get sick. Eventually they won't want you, anymore, and you'll be like me, a sorry sight, look . . ."

And with a tragic attitude, she unabashedly lifted her nightgown to show Santa her sinewy, undefined calves and withered, deformed thighs, her hanging, discolored belly split from side to side by deep folds, like the furrows left by the repeated plowing of a field that had once produced harvest upon harvest to enrich the landowner, but now lay exhausted, its fertility gone, leaving only the perpetual, shameful trace of its long exploitation.

"I was pretty, if you can believe it, as pretty as you, or prettier. And now I'm a hag taking care of a brothel, and glad to have the work. Now I'm reduced to accepting the tolerance and supposed affection of something like *that*, something that's not even a man anymore, that's not nothing, just another ruin like me . . . But here I am going on and on about things that don't matter. Don't mind me. What foolishness! And don't tell the others I've been preaching at you. Just a second and I'll put on my dress, some street shoes . . . there we go . . . and a scarf . . . and we're off, the both of us. Wait a second . . . Diego! Diego! I'm leaving. The bottle is there in the wash basin."

"You're leaving, what for?" blubbered the recumbent figure, wrinkling his eyes shut tightly against the light flooding in through window and doorway.

"Because I've got to get this kid officially registered and bathed and ready for tonight. Haven't you seen the same thing a hundred times?"

"Get out of here, then, and to hell with you and your new girl," replied the man, chuckling softly a second time. "But hand me the bottle first, honey . . ."

Santa followed Pepa as if sleepwalking. They exited by a street door different from the one by which Santa had entered, walked around the garden she had noticed earlier, and ducked into a coach that appeared to be waiting for them. Pepa gave instructions, and the coach tore down various streets, pulled briefly alongside a street car, stopped suddenly to avoid another coach, then careened around a corner, the coach always amid many vehicles, many people, much sun, and much noise. Pepa smiled and smoked a cigarette, hardly paying attention to Santa, to whom she had so recently confided a portion of her hardened sinner's sorrows. The coach halted unexpectedly at another small garden between two churches and beside a larger park, which Santa believed to be the city's tree-lined avenue, or Alameda, and Pepa warned with sudden seriousness:

"Don't contradict me, hear? I'll answer whatever has to be answered, and you let them do whatever they want to do to you . . ."

"Whatever they want to do to me? Who are you talking about?"

"Don't worry, dummy! It's nothing bad, just some doctors who might insist on examining you, understand?"

"But I'm completely healthy. I swear."

"Even if you are, silly, there's a law. I'll try to keep them from examining you, but you have to let them do it. Now out, let's go!"

From there until the hour of the nighttime meal, everything was a jumble in Santa's mind. Her poor memory, as if bruised during the proceedings, retained precise details concerning certain things of scant importance but tended to garble her recollection of other more crucial things. Lying in the bed that they had given her for her own, a soft double bed of bronze posts and rails with more gold plating than the chapel of the church in her village, Santa's head split with a tremendous headache that kept her from opening her eyes for two hours. She tried to remember what the doctors had done to her during the exam that, in the end, they had absolutely insisted on doing. She remembered a lithographic portrait in a varnished wooden frame, an odd-looking man wearing a military uniform but with a handkerchief covering his hair and knotted at the back; she remembered the eyeglasses of one of the doctors that kept slipping down his nose; she remembered the vulgar physiognomy of a male nurse who stared at her as if wanting to eat her. About the exam itself, however, she remembered nothing, only that they had made her lie on a sort of table covered with rather filthy oil cloth, that they had probed her with a metal apparatus, and . . . nothing else, no, nothing else. Also that the room smelled very bad, of that stuff that they put under the bed when they lay out dead people . . . What's it called? Iodu, iodi . . . iodoform, something like that, sickly sweet stuff, the smell of which makes you dizzy and want to gag.

What she remembered very well, indeed, was that when she sat up and was straightening her dress, the doctors addressed her familiarly as *tú* and even made some abusive jokes that provoked loud laughter from Pepa and flashing anger in Santa, surprised that such gentlemen feel they can casually mock a woman . . . like her.

The word that came to her mind in that moment, the vulgar term that from now on would be applied to her, made her squeeze her eyes more tightly shut and press her hand over the ear not sunk into her pillow as she lay on her side, flexing her knees to draw up her legs; and yet the word came and lashed at her temples and the interior of her entire skull, making her headache even worse. She was not a woman now, but a . . .

For the second time in that tragic day, she felt an overwhelming desire to get out of there, to flee back to her village, to her own little corner of the world, to her family, her birds, her flowers . . . where she had always lived, a place she had never expected to leave, much less be chased away from by her brothers. What would they do without her? Could they have forgotten her so quickly? The anguish of fearing herself forgotten made her sit up abruptly on the edge of the bed, her hands falling to the hollow in her dress between her half-opened legs, her feet not reaching the floor, swinging unconsciously, mechanically backward and forward, her eyes fixed on a vision of her village, her humble but cheerful abode, adorned with ivy, heliotropes, and bellflowers, a home she had disgraced and to which she could never, ever return.

She felt so miserable and abandoned that she hid her face again in her pillow, still tepid where her head had lain, and she cried her heart out with deep sobs that shook her beautiful, curled-up body; she cried a torrent of tears from varying origins—some from a touch of hysteria, childhood memories, and a secret mourning for her lost purity.

The release of nervous tension that weeping brings and the exhaustion of her energies over the course of the whole day combined to make Santa drowsy and offered a sort of imitation slumber similar to what one sees in afflicted children: a few final sobs and delayed, intermittent sighs surfacing occasionally, only to fade and then evaporate, as if hurrying off to rejoin the pain that had originally engendered them but that was now finally receding. Therefore, she was not fully aware of the mysterious noises that filled her new residence in the afternoon, nor of the visitors who arrive at such houses at that time of day: dealers in jewelry of uncertain provenance; bullfighters who are not admitted during the evening hours because better-paying customers (who believe every bullfighter a potential murderer) might become alarmed; young men of good family who are taking their first steps on the path of sinful pleasures; model husbands and family men who cannot resist another taste of the piquant fruit they learned to relish when young; and finally, true aficionados who long to be alone with the prostitutes and imagine themselves their only lovers, even though the acts they desire and the pallid, sleepless appearance of the objects of their affections both clearly signal their lascivious nightly commerce.

A murmur arose from the street below, confused and somewhat distant, thanks to the garden that separated the house from the streaming traffic; thanks, as well, to Santa's high window with its lacey curtains facing away from the street and towards the irregular panorama of the city's roofscape: tiles and terraces, a fantastical immensity of chimneys, water tanks, flower pots, clothes hung out to dry, unexpected ladders and doors, church towers, flagpoles, signs with monstrously huge lettering, and remote balconies with windows that, at such a distance, seemed shattered into sparkling fragments by the oblique rays of the sun, a sun already descending between the crests and plumes of the mountains on the backdrop of the horizon.

Santa's drowsiness was interrupted by someone knocking imperiously on the door.

"Who is it?" she asked, annoyed, lifting herself on an elbow without leaving the bed. But then recognizing the voices of Pepa and the owner, she got up to open the door.

The owner, Elvira—whom Santa had not seen since the fair at San Angel, when Elvira had affectionately invited her to come live at this house—had something mannish in her intonation and gestures. She wore a loose dress, held a cigar in her teeth, and sported diamond earrings the size of hazelnuts. Much bossier even than Pepa, she leaned in Santa's face.

"So you refused to eat lunch, and you shut yourself up in here all afternoon, huh? I'll forgive you this time as long as it never happens again, understand? We're not here to do whatever we feel like, and you don't make your own decisions any more, or why did you come? They're going to bring you a silk gown and silk stockings, too, and a blouse so fine you can't imagine, and embroidered slippers . . . Has she bathed yet?" she asked, turning to Pepa, then back to Santa: "Magnificent! But it doesn't matter whether you've bathed already, *hija*. Every evening when you get dressed to go down, wash yourself again, and use plenty of water, *hija*, plenty of water!"

And she went on in that half-scolding, half-advising manner, detailing for Santa the hygienic measures indispensable in minimizing the risks of the profession. She said everything with extraordinary knowledge and aplomb, without allowing herself to be interrupted, even when she had to pause for breath, on which occasions she maintained Santa's silence with a look or gesture before resuming her discourse. Without hesitation or embarrassment, she called the most incredible things by their exact names; this should be done in such and such a way, that in another way; some men have this weakness, some that one; there are a thousand sorts of fakery that, although repugnant at first, should definitely be cultivated. And so on, in a complete catechism, the perfected manual for the resourceful, modern prostitute in an elegant establishment. Elvira's recommendations and mandates were so naked that they almost lost their immorality. She presented her dicta in such a natural and straightforward manner that one could easily mistake her for an austere English governess correcting a clumsy pupil. Only once in a while did a casual, energetic expletive, which Elvira pronounced without the slightest self-consciousness, break the spell. Some governess, indeed! Only an old prostitute, rotten in mind and body, could formulate such theories, argue their utility, and encourage their practice! In the course of her peroration, she sat down beside Santa and, noting the girl's shock, used her inveterate dissembler's skills to present the other side of the coin: heck, it wasn't so scary as all that, and to the contrary, one found it a more acceptable and comfortable way of life than many others.

The ones who end up in the hospital are just *lipendis* . . . that is, scatter-brained and silly," she explained, seeing Santa's expression upon hearing her southern Spanish slang, "but the girl who doesn't mess around and learns the ropes early on, well . . . doesn't have to worry about hospitals and jails. Somebody put together like you are can go a long, long way, get it? Jewels, a carriage, and money, money, money, as we say. Right? As for men, they're a bunch of miserable pigs. They can pitch their little fits all they want, but they can't go without their nooky . . ."

Then, after a pause, she continued more reflectively:

"The meaner we are to them, the more they adore us, and the more we lie to them, the more obsessed they are with us. Do you know why they'd rather be with us than with their wives and girlfriends, why they're after us and not them? You don't know? Well, it's precisely because their wives and girlfriends are sweet and modest (some of them, anyway) and we're not. That's why. We taste really different, you could say, spicy, sometimes too spicy, while the other ones always taste the same, bland, and they get tired of that . . ."

Elvira fell silent. Pepa leaned back against the wardrobe, and Santa, her heart in her throat, hung her head. What she was seeing and hearing discouraged and disgusted her completely. She had to get out of there.

"Well, I've decided I'm leaving," she declared gravely, standing up.

"Leaving . . . where to?"

"Anywhere, out of here," she answered more energetically, pointing, with firm resolution, toward a patch of blue sky visible through the windows.

Pepa walked over, Elvira stood up, and, as if in a trance, both women peered where Santa was pointing, a patch of sky that grew slowly paler in the dusk as a flock of swallows zigzagged across it chimerically in flight.

Elvira immediately recovered her demeanor of a dress-wearing slave driver who refuses to tolerate the slightest hint of rebellion. Her hands on her hips, her face twisted, her look irate, she turned to Santa in fury. Nobody kidded or tried to fool her!

"Keep your dignity for another occasion, got it? You're already registered and have a number, like the coaches out there for hire on the street, let's say. You belong to *me* and the police and the public health department. So you're leaving, huh? So full of herself, this little tart! So where are you going to, jail? Don't try me, because it will cost you, hear? I give the orders, and everybody else takes them! And tonight you'd better be nice and sweet with the paying customers, and there'd better be no silliness, no tears, and no fainting, because the police will be here to take you when you wake up.

The more exasperated Elvira became, the more Santa's spirits sank, as if her earlier energy had been diverted or broken. Mesmerized by the wrath of her new patrón, she retreated until her back was against the wall, Elvira following her step by step, waving her hands and breathing her insults in Santa's face, huffing and puffing with the stink of tobacco and her recent meal.

Pepa smoked a cigarette.

Her eyes wide and her throat dry, Santa submitted to the avalanche of ugly words, to the tongue-lashing that curled around her body, to the hydra that harassed her, ready to rip her with its claws. She felt herself crushed, defeated, unconditionally at the mercy of the unbelievably cruel, bejeweled Spaniard who belched obscenities and threatened her with fist, visage, and attitude.

"Alright, señora," she murmured in surrender, "easy. I'm not going anywhere. Where would I go, anyway?"

Pepa saw an opportune moment in which to intervene, and she approached the other two women, taking Santa's arm reassuringly.

"Let's do something about that mop of hair, *hija mía*. We need to get it trimmed. Now take a deep breath and dry those pretty eyes."

No doubt Elvira was waiting for the intervention, because instantly she softened, relit the half-cigar between her fingers, put her arm affectionately around Santa's waist, led her to the sofa, and, with surprising delicateness, dried her tears.

"She's right," declared Elvira, indicating Pepa. "We've got to fix you up. Just look what crying will do to you. And what for? I don't dislike you, silly! To the contrary, I'll make sure you get everything that I promised when we talked at your village, remember? Isn't it enough for you? And this evening when you come down to dinner, if there's anything not to your taste, just tell Pepa, and we'll cook you whatever you like. Pepa, be sure nobody pulls her leg at the table, and give her some wine from my personal stock. That'll calm the nerves of this pampered girl. Now, lazy thing, lift your face and give me a kiss to show we've made friends. I want to see you dressed for battle! Have them bring her chemise, dressing gown, and slippers, Pepa.

There was nothing else to do. Santa smiled and allowed herself to be dressed by Pepa and two or three other girls attracted by all the fuss, a thoroughly decent operation supervised and applauded by Elvira, who, with silent nods, seemed to approve the rapid and fragmentary displays of Santa's nudity—a shoulder, an undulating breast, a glimpse of thigh. There was the provocative pink with just the slightest shadow of fine down, except when her dressing gown slipped, and to catch it Santa moved violently, exposing for a just a second, the jet black growth beneath her arm . . .

That night, the eight-o'clock meal, often silent and gloomy because of the approaching fray, seemed more like a party. Nobody reproached anybody, nor did irreconcilable jealousies and mortal rivalries flash in carefully made-up eyes. The usual obscene phrases and insulting nicknames were not bandied about, and for once nobody made fun of the servant. Under the benevolent gaze of Elvira—who granted her livestock the honor of her presence to celebrate the herd's new addition—moderately good spirits and exaggeratedly good manners reigned throughout the meal. The jokes were inoffensive, the laughter truly feminine, and the clink of the silverware unobtrusive. Indeed, the dining room resembled the ultra-modest refectory of an educational establishment for fashionable young ladies, and Elvira was moved to offer everyone a glass of her personal stock of wine, which had been brought out in Santa's honor. Very dignified in her responsible, managerial function, Pepa drank water as usual, and the poor girl nicknamed "Mosquito," who looked though she might have tuberculosis, refrained from playing with her dessert the way the she normally did every night.

Suddenly, from downstairs, the strident, dissonant voice of Eufrasia called them back to reality:

"Doña Pepa, some gentlemen are here!"

Santa observed a horrid transformation, as the group of eight or ten women rose from their places as one, toppling their chairs, lighting and puffing on cigarettes to mask the smell of food, and hurriedly rinsing their mouths with water, some of which they spilled on the table cloth, some of which they spit on the floor. All then plunged down the steep staircase shouting and shoving, charging toward the money, smoothing their hair, chewing on their lips to make them bright red, and pulling their elbows close to their waists to make their breasts more prominent. All purposely made their high heels clatter on the steps, and, reaching the bottom, all stepped out with swaying hips like a line of bullfighters entering the ring.

Pepa went down slowly.

"You go down, too!" Elvira commanded Santa, "and order beer or champagne for the clients, depending on who they are, but make sure they order something. And if they come up to a room with you, no dumb stuff, eh? We talked about that already."

Santa did not even hear the last part of these instructions, because the first part, the awful "you go down, too," had made her tremble like a leaf, but she knew that she had to go down, to fight and fawn over the visitors, and oblige them to spend money.

She went down rigidly, more disposed to refuse than to offer anything, experiencing an unconquerable physical revulsion. Standing in the doorway of the illuminated salon, she saw the customers still wearing their hats and joking around with her colleagues, who not only consented to their foul language and their rude, lascivious caresses, but actually provoked them on purpose and asked for them to continue, in a greed-inspired effort to enflame the beasts.

A great peal of thunder, announcing the rain that just then blanketed the city, rattled everything, and turning her face to the street door only a step away, Santa lifted her skirt and strode toward it, guided by an instinctive desire to escape, to run as far as she had strength to run, to run wherever the danger that seemed so imminent could not reach her. But just as she reached the door the skies released a furious deluge that lashed walls, windows, and pavement with huge raindrops that landed with a sharp, metallic splatter, exploding with the force of their trajectory. Santa looked at the street, down the middle of which the shower unfurled like a high, thick curtain of gauze blowing at an angle. The wind shook the electric street lamps, their rays magically interweaving with the silver threads of water that disappeared ultimately into dark, noisy puddles on the pavement.

Against that dreamlike backdrop and in the sudden, stark brilliance of a bolt of lightning, one among many that cracked the sky, Santa saw a small boy leading a man by the hand, neither of them protected from the storm by an umbrella or coat, both of them leaning toward the house, heading in that direction. At first, she couldn't believe it. How could they be coming there? Yet the couple continued approaching, the man furious when his cane and the little boy together failed to keep him from stepping in a pothole, the kid impassive despite the rain that fell from the clouds to drench his back and the rain of insults and swear words showered upon him by the blind man he served.

Santa had to step aside so that the two apparent vagabonds could enter, and she hardly replied to their hello, too worried about getting her clothes wet if they came close. She was expecting to hear Pepa scold the new arrivals, but instead, the blind man calmly let go of the boy and moved ahead with only his cane to guide him, ragged and dripping wet, but smiling, hat in hand, and looking sightlessly around with the horrid whitish eyes of a bronze statue without patina. He stepped right into the salon, where Pepa and the other women greeted him warmly and addressed him familiarly as *tú*.

"Hello, Hipo, did you get wet? You're soaking, man! Go shake that water off outside or you'll ruin the furniture, and then come play."

Come play? Santa watched amazed as the blind man they called Hipo felt his way to the interior courtyard where he did, in fact, brush the water off his clothing and afterward dry his hands with his handkerchief. Next, she saw him go straight to the piano, open it, and begin to play. Forgetting all about escape, she too entered the salon and leaned her elbow on the top of the piano to contemplate this prodigy, a blind man who played the piano so well.

How beautifully he played, and how ugly he was, his face pockmarked and unshaven, his grey mustache droopy, his forehead wide, his jaw powerful, his neck thick, his shirt filthy and in want of mending at its frayed collar and cuffs, his tie crooked and hidden, for the most part, by his vest. The blind piano player's long fingernails were yellowed by cigarette smoke, and his hands were boney, but they were also agile and expressive, sometimes flitting back and forth between the black and white keys so rapidly that, to Santa, his fingers seemed to multiply, sometimes lingering on a single key so lovingly that its note stood out from the rest, as if sounding more vigorously of its own accord.

With a blind man's instinct, the musician sensed the presence of someone at his side, and in spite of the noisy dancing that had begun, he half turned his head toward Santa, who felt repelled by the unseeing gaze of his horrid whitish eyes, orphaned without sight.

"We're not going to make much tonight if it keeps raining," he said, not hesitating to equate himself professionally with the women. "Who's dancing?"

"I don't know them," replied Santa, trying to avoid the eyes that, although blind, nonetheless appeared to look intelligently around the room, with expressive inflections of the eyebrows.

"Pardon me," he said, "I thought I was speaking to someone of the house."

"I just got here today. Hey . . ." began Santa, but stopped with a cry, feeling arms slide around her waist from behind.

It was nothing, just one of the gentlemen mentioned earlier, who, incited by the delicious lines of Santa's hips, had come from behind to examine them, hugging her waist and sinking his chin into one of her soft shoulders . . .

"What's the fuss about, good looking? You'd think I was hurting you! Come dance and have a drink with us."

"I don't want a drink, and I don't know how to dance," answered Santa dryly, after extricating herself from the grasp of the not-so-young man, who was well-dressed and seemed well-respected by his companions.

"Goodbye! And what if I pay you to get me drunk and dance naked with me if that's what I want? Do you think I'm begging? Do you think that any slut can give me orders? Well, you're mistaken! I've got enough money here to buy you all!"

The mood of the gathering suddenly changed. The piano player terminated the dance with an artful transition to a couple of resolving chords that softened the brusqueness of the interruption, and, aided only by his sense of touch, philosophically lit a cigarette. Santa, who did not yet have other weapons with which to defend herself, resorted to tears, but her comrades, and one, above all, called la Gaditana because she was from Cádiz, leapt to Santa's defense:

"Hey, buddy, who do you think you are? What makes you so special that we should put up with you, huh?"

Pepa, her cigar hanging from her lip and her money bag from her wrist, intervened. She spoke to the companions of the man—who persisted in his affirmations that he had a lot of money and exhibited various denominations to prove it—and his companions, while mortified, declined to recognize their friend's rudeness and insisted on his behalf that he ought to be pardoned because he had drunk a bit too much and because he was, after all, the governor, no less, of a rich and distant state of the republic.

"More champagne!" ordered the drunk governor, as if to make up for his drunkenness, "more champagne and more dance music, maestro!"

The piano again filled the air and the girls again danced with the friends of the inert state executive who sat collapsed on the sofa with his eyes riveted on Santa who, in turn, was having an extremely animated chat with Pepa. The most diplomatic member of the governor's entourage produced a pile of bills, and having cleared the idea with Pepa, ordered that, in light of the continuing deluge, the door be locked and announced that his friends were paying for the whole house that night.

The rain outside continued intoning its monorhythmic melody, its high-pitched drumming on the window panes and dull drip, dripping from the exterior railings and cornices, the sharp splatter of downspouts vomiting torrents on the sodden pavement. At the drain in the middle of the courtyard—a tile perforated by five holes in the shape of a cross—the water hurriedly and noisily hurled itself as if escaping, hiding itself in the darkness, not wanting to witness what went on in the building.

At that point, Elvira had come to say hello to the governor in the manner of greeting an old friend, unconstrained by social formalities:

"When did you get here, *hijo*? Seems like it's been centuries since you've come our way!" And, lowering her voice: "Have you seen my new girl?"

The governor, in an alcohol-driven fit of touchiness, and without understanding Elvira's question, commenced a litany of complaints about one of the girls, yes, that one over there by the piano . . .

"She got all mad just because I touched her, and she and another one, too, talked to me worse than a dog. You know me, Elvira, you know that I'm not stingy . . . but now I'm not staying, you better believe I'm leaving! No, let me go, let go of me . . ." he growled, wobbling and failing to stand up because Elvira kept him from doing so—although the greater impediment, it must be said, was his own drunkenness.

"So that's the one you like, you old dog? That's my new one! She hasn't been with a soul in this house, I guarantee that, and she's one in a million. You want her?"

"Of course I want her . . . that one or none at all."

"Santa!" shouted Elvira without interrupting her focus on the rich client, certain that she would be obeyed. "Santa, come have a drink with this old ruffian. He's a general, after all, and, do me a favor, treat him right . . ."

As the governor and his friends laughed at Santa's name, supposing it feigned, Santa, impotent in the face of Elvira's irresistible influence, moved away from the piano and toward the distinguished personage.

"No, not there," intruded Elvira, "in his lap, honey. You've won the lottery because he likes you. Pepa, more champagne! The general is offering me a glass."

A bit shakily, Santa did as she was told, and the piano player swung into a waltz which mixed with various other sounds: laughter, sweet talk, the smack of a kiss, and the pop of champagne bottles uncorked by a servant. The governor, in his cups, was waxing sentimental. Displaying an elaborate courtesy toward Santa, he asked permission to whisper in her ear: Did she forgive him?

"I just wanted to teach you a little lesson, I swear, and if you can't stand me, I'll let you go and pay you anyway, okay? I've got a lot of money here, and it's all for you if you sleep with me tonight. What do you say?"

"Okay," murmured Santa, intimidated by the look that Elvira gave her before leaving the room.

"Another round, then, on me! Great balls of fire!" roared the governor, and to Santa: "From now on you give the orders. You're the queen, baby!"

Even the piano player benefited with a gift of ten pesos that for him were like ten thousand, and for which he gladly would have played for a whole week.

Champagne flowed and spirits rose higher than perhaps they ought to have risen. The party became vulgar, an orgy of obscene words and gestures, shrieking laughter, and bestial propositions. The desertions began as couples went upstairs without the slightest effort to dissimulate their intent.

"We're off. To bed, children!"

As they climbed the stairs one could hear kisses, drunken stuttering and stumbling, the squeals of women being tickled. With Santa at his side, the governor downed glass after glass, and from time to time he rested his grave, taciturn, grey-haired head on Santa's shoulder.

"What do you want me to give you when you die?" he asked suddenly.

Santa shrugged her shoulders, not knowing how to respond to such a gloomy and unexpected question; she was somewhat shaken, deep down, by the words that drew the attention of everyone who heard them, including Pepa and the piano player. The governor himself, on the verge of passing out, seemed taken aback by what he had said. The four of them fell silent, as if thinking that death might be close by, just waiting to grab anyone who spoke its name.

"Don't answer him," offered Pepa, finally. "He doesn't know what he's saying."

"Have some masses said for my soul," said Santa to the governor, and to Pepa: "What else?"

With visible effort, as if noting a serious matter, the governor wrote down Santa's request and ordered more to drink:

"I'm the one who's dying now . . . of thirst! More drinks over here!"

The drinks that were served at that point finished off the governor, who spilled half of his and fell asleep. Santa breathed a little easier. Though slightly dizzy, she thought that she was safe. Could she go to bed alone?

The benevolent Pepa corrected her error in confidential tones that even extended to the piano player:

"No, *hija*, the general sleeps with you. Don't you think that's right, Hipo? But fortunately, he's unlikely to bother you, in the condition he's in."

The two women and a servant awakened the old man and helped him upstairs to the room that now belonged to Santa, who carried her temporary lover's hat, coat, and umbrella, as she had seen others do. The piano player, whose young guide was curled up asleep by the door, took his leave of Pepa for the evening.

The governor fell like a log into the soft bed, where his shoes, jacket, vest, and previously unbuttoned shirt were laboriously removed.

"You think I'm drunk, huh? No, I'm only a bit fuzzy is all, and I'll be fine in a minute . . . The proof is that I hear it's raining and that I'm asking you to undress completely, completely except for the stockings . . . and tell the truth . . . you're name's not really Santa, is it? Tell me . . . your story . . . how you came here . . ."

Santa did not need to refuse his demands or answer his question, because no sooner had the governor said these things than he fell asleep again, this time like the drunk who is out until tomorrow. On tiptoes so that she wouldn't awaken him, Santa turned off the lamp and began to undress in the darkness, overjoyed to think that no one would have her that first night. Suddenly in the darkness she put her hand to her neck and stealthily, as if she feared being seen in spite of the darkness, reached into her chemise, paused for a moment until reassured by the governor's steady breathing, and then pulled out a scapulary that she could no longer wear, that she had to hide. Poor little rag, faded and tattered like her own purity, witness to happier times, a keeper of relics that, in the end, had not protected her, a companion to her maidenly sighs and the palpitations of her first love! She kissed it chastely and repeatedly, the way we kiss a thing we will not see again, and hid it in some mysterious place in her sinner's boudoir.

Outside and far away, the sound of string instruments floated on the night air as somewhere, no doubt, a party continued, defying the bad weather, playing music as sad as her own story. Her story, which the old drunk had wanted to hear . . .

It had stopped raining, but the dull dripping from railings and cornices could still be heard outside. And at the drain in the middle of the courtyard, with its tile perforated by five holes in the shape of a cross, the water still hurled itself down as if escaping, as if hiding in darkness, not wanting to witness what went on in the building.

Two

Her story . . .

It was the old story of poor girls who are born in the country, and grow up in the fresh air, amid breezes and flowers, ignorant, chaste, and strong, cared for by our eternally affectionate mother earth, with wild birds for their friends, and with dreams as simple and pure as the violets that grow hidden along the banks of a river, the sort of small river that rocks the cradles of these girls so softly, so lovingly, running behind the rustic little houses where they grow up, before slipping away; rivers that run angrily in autumn, turbulent and foaming, but pensive and blue in the springtime, as if concerned that so much aquatic wealth that might move mills, power factories, and irrigate fields will instead flow unrevealed away, away to the sea. Imagine that, the sea!

Santa tried to drive the memories away by waving her hands in front of her, the way that back in her good times as a decent girl she had occasionally waved away the bees upon approaching their hive or fended off the most amorous doves when visiting the dovecote. But her memories did not go away. To the contrary, as if provoked by the snores of the drunk beside her, they rioted all around her, flitting in and out like fairy workers busily trying to reconstruct the temple of her innocence and the stronghold of her adolescence, both desolate and in ruins, but they only managed to make a knot in her throat, fill her eyes with tears, and wound her heart, a heart still much more virginal than her splendid young prostitute's body.

And that is why the sad, dark room was suddenly inundated with the light of her memories.

There it is . . . the little white house, hidden away on one of the narrow, unpaved lanes of her village, lanes flanked on both sides by thick foliage, flowers, and ivy that scales the high walls constructed here of brick and mortar, there of gently crumbling adobes. One enters—through a rustic wooden gate that presents no resistance to the slightest push—into a yard adorned only by the overarching sky and six orange trees, their boughs bending under their load of golden fruit or covered with white flowers that swoon with the power of their own fragrance. There is the well, deep, dark, echoing faintly with tiny mysterious sounds like a fairy cave, its water crystalline to the eye and icy to the taste, the nooks and crannies of its ancient stone rim colonized by daisies, its pulley whining terribly whenever the bucket descends into the depths. On one side of the smoky kitchen, with its wide-mouthed little chimney, is the bee hive, and on the other, higher up, the dovecote, although the doves prefer to spend their time in the branches of the nearby woods or the ruined tower of the chapel of San Antonio, also nearby. In back, a fat pig lies wallowing lazily in the mud, tethered by a leg; hens and their chicks scratch the dirt, looking up at the sky with a single eye, from time to time, by tilting their heads almost horizontally to the ground; and a large yellow and black dog, Coyote by name, dozes tranquilly in the thick shade of the orange trees. On the covered walkway that runs along the side of the house, to the left of the entrance, are various rustic chairs and stools, and there, too, hang the cages of various songbirds that fill the air with their harmonies and arpeggios each day from the first glimmer of light. On the wall, bull's horns serve as hooks from which to hang the bridle and other riding tack of the family's only horse, taken out each day to pasture along with cows and calves belonging to the owner of the local store. Tied to the posts that support each extreme of the covered walkway are two fighting cocks, one of them jet black and the other sporting yellow feathers on its wings and around its neck, both crowing and flapping their challenges to each other when not sharpening their beaks on the ground always wet, sooner or later, with drinking water from the rusty sardine can placed beside each bird, the can overturned in the course of some abortive practice attack.

Inside the house, only four rooms:

First, the living room, which is also the dining room, judging by the square table in the center of it and the massive water jug along the wall under shelves crowded with plates and dishes, cups, and glasses of the most ordinary sort of materials. Along the other walls, wicker chairs. In a corner, a somewhat worm-eaten triangular piece of mahogany furniture that displays—along with a conch shell, a ceramic piggy bank (though shaped like an apple), and a pair of vases with silk flowers—the family's most treasured possession: a sculpture of middling quality representing the Santo Niño dressed in sequins and fringed silk, his right hand raised in blessing, seated on something one cannot quite see, and imprisoned in a large niche of leaded glass. On the floor, straw mats of various sizes; and hanging from a large nail beside the window, a guitar whose lack of dust and full set of strings testify to regular use.

Next, the bedroom of mother and daughter, who sleep in the same bed, a bed without springs or headboard, but spacious and spotless and defended by three things on the wall above it: a monochrome lithograph of the Virgin of Soledad fixed with four tacks; a colored one of the Virgin of Guadalupe in a frame that was once gilded; and a yellowed palm leaf that is replaced every Palm Sunday, whose Christian virtue protects the humble home from lightning strikes. During the day, the bed is the domain of a cat that passes the hours there, curled up in a ball.

Then, the bedroom of the two grown brothers—the bread-winners of the family, Esteban and Fabián—with two ordinary cots, a seed bin, two large trunks covered with half-cured cowhide, a piece of furniture always hung with recently and not-so-recently worn clothes, and on the walls, an infinite number of small, colored images arranged with certain care, celebrity portraits including dancers, circus performers, and professional beauties, that come in packages of La Mascota Cigarettes. Leaning in a corner, the shotgun, with powder horn and a bag of shot small enough to use for hunting in the woods and large enough to defend the house with or to patrol the village on the nights when the brothers were assigned to do so with other young men of the village.

At the end of the house, the kitchen, with its interior cooking area and small brassier closer to the door, between two rough stone *metates* on which mother and daughter grind corn to make tortillas.

Everywhere there is pure air, the perfume of the roses that peep over the walls, the sound of wind rustling leaves in the trees and water spilling softly over the village's two mill dams. During the day, the hum of insects in the sun; during the night, fireflies lit up by love, pursuing each other until, meeting, they go dark. Behind the house, myriad maguey plants, with their unvarying shade of green; on both sides, gardens and orchards; across the way, the property of their parish priest, Padre Guerra; and a few paces away, the chapel, tiny and poor, but furnished with saints who comfort the farmers in their grief and, occasionally, grant their wishes. A bit further on, the cemetery, open and silent, without marble statuary or poetic inscriptions, but offering a comfortable, protected spot for eternal slumber with its carnations and heliotropes that greedily cover the gravestones, the names of the disappeared, and the dates of their disappearances. And there is the bank of the small river, flanking the village square, shaded by ancient ash trees, the bridge hewn from a single enormous trunk, the three wash stands of crude tile where village women do laundry, and starting at the edge of the two mill ponds and their big dam, the road paved with fat, deeply seated stones leads to the lava flow called the Pedregal.

Here, Santa is a young girl, and later, a young beauty. The little house belongs to her, the pampered daughter of old Agustina, at whose warm side she sleeps night after night. She is the idol of her brothers Esteban and Fabián, who watch over and protect her, the pride of the village, the ambition of its young men, the envy of its young women, healthy, happy, and pure. What innocence in her spirit! What loveliness in her nubile body! But why have her hips grown broad and her flesh grown so silky soft? Why have her bosoms—oh, so much more marked than they were, and not so long ago—grown these rosebuds, and why do they tremble and ache with the curious explorations of her own fingers? Why does Father Guerra not allow her to describe these worries to him in the confessional, but instead, only counsel her not to look at her own breasts?

"You don't worry like that about the flowers, do you? You don't examine them every day to see how much they've grown, do you? Well, be like them, grow and become more beautiful without even realizing it. Be fragrant without knowing it. And so that you won't lose your virginal beauty and purity, pray, confide in me, adore your mother, take care of your brothers . . . and *live*, breathe deeply, laugh by yourself, and above all, love your guardian angel, the only male who will never deceive you."

The dawn of Santa's young adulthood simply prolonged her childhood, without troubles graver than the death of a favorite hen or a plant that she tended and watered, such as the carnation that she found withered one morning after a hard frost, its stem broken and its petals strewn—hemorrhaged like strange drops of blood—on the ground. Aside from these small sorrows and others like them, hers was an existence without dark clouds, as she grew and developed, becoming more beautiful, adoring her mother, taking care of her brothers, and breathing deeply, but not laughing by herself, because the birds, envious no doubt, laughed with her, as did the orange trees and the river and—why not admit it?—even the bell in the little chapel laughed with her when announcing mass at 6:30 on Sunday mornings, the mass attended with equal devotion by the villagers and by the rich families from the capital who came to summer at San Angel, and attended, too, by various officials and personages of local importance such as the pharmacist, who sometimes entertained the villagers in the evenings by employing who-knows-what mysterious arts to set several large bottles aglow with purple, red, and yellow lights . . .

How lovely to awaken on work days before the early rising sun! In a moment, the impotent silence of night, which is soothing in its way, would be interrupted by the crow of a rooster to which other roosters would respond, and then others and still others, ever farther away, in locations impossible to know exactly, and Santa would half open her eyes but see only her mother, toward whom she had moved, timidly, ever closer in the darkness. Half asleep, she felt herself caressed and sensed her mother's warm breath under the sheets:

"Go back to sleep, *hija*," the soft voice says. "Go to sleep. It's still dark!" It takes a while for sleep to return, and in the meantime she cannot really hear or see straight, and everything is confused, impalpable, except for a physical well-being so intense that it totally immobilizes her. She perceives that above, on the roof, the doves are fanning their tails and cooing, that the pig is grunting outside, and that in the next room Esteban and Fabián are out of bed, pouring water in the washbasin. They cough and strike matches to light a cigarette or the stove for breakfast. Santa is going back to sleep now, losing a sense of the passage of time between noises that she hears, and she barely registers the entrance of her brothers into the bedroom, on tiptoes so as not awaken her, for which she smiles in somnolent gratitude. They have come to say goodbye, to receive the daily blessing that will protect them and give them, the family breadwinners, strength to continue as workers at the Contreras textile mill miles away from their house. The brothers remove their hats, kneel, and bow their heads very low so that their mother will not need to sit up and can stay under the blanket, and, following the ancient custom, they reverently implore:

"Your hand, mother . . ."

Agustina's outstretched hand blesses each of them, and feeling blindly, she pulls them to her together and embraces them together, confusing the two heads that she loves equally, and the two big men softly kiss the old hand that makes the sign of the cross in the air. They leave, on tiptoe again, and in the yard Coyote barks at them jubilantly. They close the front gate, and in the silence that covers the sleeping village, the sound of their foot-steps, loud at first, disappears little by little, like the rhythm of a distant pendulum. Santa's mother sighs and raises her voice as though to be better heard by the Almighty:

"Lord, take care of my sons!"

Rays of pallid light begin to poke their way in the cracks around doors and windows, the noises get louder, and the bells of dawn begin to ring at the old Carmelite convent, and ding dong, ding dong, their music flies down the roads, by houses, orchards, and newly sown fields. Agustina rises and tucks the blanket carefully around Santa, who, reconquered by slumber, sleeps for another hour and dreams that life is good and that happiness exists.

Overflowing with health and tranquility, Santa rises and sings in the early morning as she cleans the cages of her birds, draws chilly water from the well, and washes her face, neck, arms, and hands with soap suds that caress her skin as they slowly slide off it, making her smile with contentment. Her young blood races through her veins, colors her cheeks, and fills her red lips, as if kissing them gluttonously. Soon she is dressed for the day and has fed the chickens and doves, who crowd around her and follow her gently like devoted subjects. The pig, grunting with satisfaction, has buried his snout in the little pile of corn that she carried to him in her apron, and Coyote has greeted her, bounding and barking. The store owner's young helper has come to take their old horse out to pasture with the animals belonging to his master, don Samuel: melancholic cows, recently milked, their calves ravenous, turbulent, and protesting. Cows and calves depart down the lane in a slow procession, sticking their faces into the leaves and flowers on the walls, examining the maguey plants, even swirling into the always-open cemetery, where graves thick with green offer them a delicious breakfast.

"Santa! I'm leaving, get the chestnut horse out here!" shouts the boy from the lane, without looking at her or at the cattle, who continue their lazy march, because he is so intensely occupied untangling his sling with teeth and fingernails. Santa shoos the chestnut through the gate, unencumbered by saddle or bridal, and says to the boy:

"Careful, Cosme! Don't gallop him or get him too hot . . . Want some milk?"

"Just give me some and you'll see! Don't you have any honey from your bees? It makes stale bread taste wonderful," says Cosme, as he takes a length of cord from around his waist to improvise a lead for the horse.

Santa goes to the house and returns with a glass of frothy milk in one hand and, in the other, a slice of bread spread with honey that hangs off its edges in transparent threads that never reach the ground. Cosme drains the glass of milk, runs his tongue around his lips, seizes the honeyed crust of bread, and throws himself onto the chestnut horse, squeezing its flanks with his bare heels. The old horse responds with a canter despite its years, and the boy, prodigiously balanced atop the bounding animal, twists his upper body back toward Santa as he takes a bite of the bread.

"Don't get mad, Santa. I'm only going fast now because the cows are getting away from me. As soon as I catch up . . ."

The rest of his sentence is inaudible as he disappears around a bend in the lane, the horse now at a full gallop, Cosme leaning far forward the way circus riders do in the ring.

It is not yet seven o'clock, and yet, the sun leaning over the mountain ridge turns the tree tops golden, peers here and there into the houses, and casts absurdly long shadows of everything that it finds, making a rose bush seem antediluvian, an ordinary dog appear a hulking dinosaur, and a tree trunk many leagues in length. With the glinted reflections of the river and the floral aroma exuded by all nature—even leaving aside the ripple of water, the singing of birds, and the rustle of the wind in the trees—there is something impalpable that floats on the air and rises like a wordless prayer that the earth, eternally wounded, thinks and utters upon awaking each morning, a profound prayer of thanksgiving for having escaped, for one more night, the cataclysm that hangs over it and that will finally, treacherously come to mutilate it and annihilate its sacred, infinite, maternal fecundity . . . Full of these impressions, Santa lifts her eyes to the heavens, her nostrils flaring, and stands motionless, almost ecstatic, herself an unconscious part of the earth's wordless prayer of thanksgiving.

During the day, there were always chores to do, whether at home helping old Agustina, or by the river washing clothes and shopping at don Samuel's store that "has everything." As evening came, Santa and other girls her age would take over the village square, where they frolicked and romped without machos around to make fun of them at that hour, unless one wanted to count the small boys emerging from Father Guerra's catechism class or, even less probably, Father Guerra himself, who, upon bidding farewell to his pupils and turning to the girls, normally fussed at them amicably:

"On your way, out of here, let's go, get on home, bunch of tomboys!"

And, clapping his hands, he would scattered them exactly as one does a flock of chickens.

Sometimes, having first gotten Agustina's permission, Santa would go by herself to the edge of the Pedregal, a marvelous place, still only half explored, unique in the Mexican Republic. A volcanic landscape dotted with bushes, colossal monoliths, and sloping stones so smooth that not even goats could pause when crossing them, the Pedregal possesses serpentine, crystal-clear streams that flow from unknown springs, disappearing occasionally, only to reappear some distance away, then plummet silently and permanently into cavernous openings that the weeds disguise with seemingly criminal intent. There are dark grottos full of brambles and wide, misshapen leaves, and crevices so deep as to seem bottomless, their rocky, vertical walls covered with twisting, fantastical cactuses. Out of the mysterious depths of these crevices, when one drops a stone into them, fly corpulent, sinister-looking birds that rise into the sky in slow, wide spirals. One discovers low areas, accessible at the cost of only a few bumps and scratches, that some farmer has been able to sow with corn or barley, or even with elegant sprigs of wheat that bend flirtatiously in the breeze. Here and there: a maguey plant, and, overlooking the cliffs and precipices, leafy pirú trees that beckon with their delicious but dangerous shade, which some people say causes a headache or even madness in those who shelter there. Teeming anthills poke up in places, their busy comings and goings quite perceptible, and from cracks in the frozen lava flows emerge fishhook cactuses that defend their tasty fruit with bloodthirsty spines. Everywhere, there is dense brush that tears one's clothing, a home to vipers and tarantulas, harboring even mountain lions and the threat of death. Everywhere, there are haunted places, suffering souls that restlessly wander the tortured earth after dusk. Everywhere, enchanting spots, colorful names—*the lovers' fountain, the sparrow hawk's nest, the skull, the deer.* There is a road, or at least, a path widened by the passage of an occasional cart that has spurned the camino real and seeks a shortcut to San Angel through this lonely, out-of-the-way location. Over toward Tizapán, there is a hacienda lost in the solitude, its buildings surrounded by small herds of cattle and sheep that graze tranquilly in the primitive peace of the place, untended except by fierce shepherd dogs who lunge furiously at anyone who approaches. There are also stallions standing by themselves and mares escorted by their playful colts, who occasionally race away only to return, before long, to nip at their mothers and, then, brusquely nurse with half-hidden faces. At certain points, lovely, poetic panoramas:

to the west, the tile-covered domes of the old Carmelite convent; to the east, the Ajusco volcano, as blue as a deep, calm bay, standing above the other mountains on the horizon. And over this entire, colossal volcanic desert, this petrified ocean rippled by stony waves, hang the legends everyone has heard: tales of homicides never solved or punished; of patriot hideouts during the wars of independence; of French and Yankee invaders who entered and wished they never had; even a scientific legend whereby the Pedregal was produced in a single cyclopean eruption, evidence of which extends all the way to distant Acapulco . . . and who knows how many others! A confusion of real events and old wives' tales, of truths and inventions, that, after so many years, have become totally mixed together, so that it is now impossible to discover where fact ends and fiction begins.

On the afternoons when her mother had given permission, Santa would remove her shoes by the bigger of the two mill dams, and carrying them in her hands, with the current lapping avidly at her bare brown feet, she crossed the river on stepping stones placed there for that very purpose, and she reached the other side holding her breath for fear of the slight danger that she might slip and suffer, at most, an unintentional little splash in the water. At the edge of the Pedregal, she stopped, frightened a bit at the thought of its breadth and desolation. It was beautiful, certainly; but, my Lord, how deserted! One late afternoon when Santa had entered into her chaste and meditative communion with nature, a sudden melancholy invaded her spirit, a pressure in her chest that made her want to cry, and she burst into tears. Cosme, who was returning from pasturing the cows, came upon her in that situation, and neither he nor she could find an explanation for her sadness:

"Couldn't it be that you've done something wrong at home and you're afraid that your mother will punish you?" inquired the boy, dismounting from the chestnut horse and sitting down next to Santa, who was crying with her back against a tree. "Because that's what happens to me. I get very afraid before a whipping, and I feel like running away . . . look, way over there . . . where they can't whip me."

No, that was not it. Everyone in Santa's house was always kind to her.

"My sadness is a sadness that comes from inside, from my body . . ."

"Ah . . . it comes from your body? Think it's the pox?"

The sadness lasted for several days, complicated by fatigue and a predisposition to weeping. Yet her mother and brothers did not seem to be surprised, and they redoubled their affectionate pampering of her, until one early morning, when Santa awoke with the farewell of Fabián and Esteban, the enigma was clarified.

"Mother," she said to Agustina as soon as they were alone, "I must be really sick, because look how I've been bleeding in the night . . ."

"Shhh . . . ," replied the old woman, kissing Santa's forehead. "We don't talk about those things or show them to anybody . . . It's the way that God blesses you and makes you a woman!"

A woman, indeed, and a handsome one, better looking as she matured and developed, day by day. Her mother and brothers now began taking excessively good care of their little "queen of the house." They began taking her for day trips into Mexico City, so that she would be familiar with the capital, where they could buy her treats using the tiny savings they had gleaned from secret economies done in her name. They began taking her on Sunday outings to nearby San Angel, to hear the military band that played in front of the town hall and see the metropolitan street cars arrive from the capital, full of well-dressed people eager for diversion. The whole family piled into the cart on those days: Coyote reconnoitering; Fabián and Esteban driving in their broad, gold-trimmed sombreros, tight-fitting pants, black jackets, fluttering red ties and blindingly white shirts showing in front, silk sashes around their waists, and new shoes of yellow suede on their feet; Agustina and Santa, their elegant passengers. Agustina dressed in the now old-fashioned style of her youth: soft wool petticoat; loose-fitting jacket; high shoes of fancy fabric; scarf pinned around her neck, extending in a triangle down her back; rebozo of English fabric over her head, smelling like quince, which was the perfume of her clothes chest; thick filigree earrings; and, on the hand that held her parasol, several simple gold rings, dulled and burnished by long wear. Santa, adorned by little more than her fifteen years, a tapered cotton dress just short enough to reveal her small, well-shod feet, rebozo over one shoulder, and her gleaming, velvet-black braids bare except for a single carnation.

And off they go on the wide road to fashionable San Angel: to their right, the thick adobe wall of the Hacienda de Guadalupe, to their left, a string of country houses belonging to rich families from Mexico City—the Casa de Sanz, the old and aristocratic Casa de Cumplido, and many others. If they have time, they drive through the small squares of San Jacinto and Los Licenciados, stopping, on the way back, to enjoy the shade of the fresno and wax trees in the company of well-to-do families who are spending the summer in San Angel. Agustina and Santa sit on an iron bench, Coyote curled up at their feet and Esteban and Fabián apart, to one side, leaning on a tree trunk, all of them silent and filled with the inhibitions that humble people feel in the presence of the rich. If it is getting late, they go no further than the Plazuela del Carmen and listen to the music under the arches of the city hall, and they buy sweets that they are too embarrassed to eat in front of so many strangers. Normally, they stay until the departure of the seven o'clock train back to the capital, its cars brightly lit and full of shouting people who laugh and call to one another. The train pulls out with a thunderous sound, as if a glass building were crashing to earth, and it rolls away down the darkening track, leaving behind it snatches of song, an echo of children's wails and women's laughter, and thousands of sparks that whirl drunkenly in the air until finally disappearing in the fields on either side. Then Santa's family begins the trip home.

It is a moment for melancholy . . .

The countryside spreads out measurelessly, inundated by a sea of shadows. The contours of the things around us grow larger in our eyes and the quiet of our surroundings penetrates our spirit. Our immediate sorrows seem to diminish, while our hidden yearnings, our unconfessable, utterly unrealizable desires, rise up close at hand, with the face of imminent possibilities, mixed together in the shadows with all that has been but never more will be. An angelus played by the poor bells of the secularized Carmelite convent hangs so tenuously in the sky that its call to prayer lacks the power to interrupt the landscape's solemn preparations for sleep or our own mystic meditations.

It is a moment for melancholy . . .

Fleeing from the reality of their lives, Fabián and Esteban dream aloud about how they might take over the factory where they work, the factory that, like a gigantic vampire bat, dulls their senses as it sucks away their health and freedom. At that moment, the solution to the problem seems obvious and simple:

"Look," they say, drawing grand forms in the dark air, "if we save such and such, and do so and so, why, at the end of one year we'll have . . ."

They are not disheartened by their pitiful wages, truly exiguous when compared with the mountain of sacks of silver pesos that the factory must be worth. It would take a lifetime, both their lifetimes, the lifetimes of their whole village working and economizing incessantly, to amass a sum sufficient to try to buy that cruel and insatiable monster, the devourer of workers who are attracted to it from a young age, used up, and thrown away injured or old, when not actually dead, and forgotten, just as the factory jettisons its industrial detritus and the waste water from the steam engines that power its machinery. Not disheartened, Fabián and Esteban resolve to continue like tame beasts of burden, slaves who virtuously deny themselves in the impossible hope of getting ahead, and turning their minds away from temptation, they huddle close to Agustina and Santa. Alerted by the angelus recently dissipated among stars and clouds and compelled, too, by inveterate custom, Agustina has begun to say her rosary automatically. Coyote, tongue hanging out and tail swinging low, trots along, senses something from time to time and stops and growls, sniffing the shadows. Santa sighs, waits, and wishes for . . . what? What all girls wait and wish for, of course, when they are fifteen years old. Lovers with golden swords and capes of moonbeams, a chaste caress, an infinite passion, kisses that are not a sin, fairies and wizards . . .

It is a moment for melancholy.

NO ONE IN CHIMALISTAC concerned themselves much about the change of the military detachment in San Angel. People merely shrugged upon learning that the mounted municipal police would replace the rural mounted police who preceded them. At most, the villagers would miss seeing the chaps and leather jackets of the *rurales*, clothing more familiar to them than the European-style gear of the municipal police. Other than that, if the wind was blowing from the right direction, the bugle calls sounded just the same, and the washer women down by the river still watched the detachment bathe by the smaller mill dam twice a week, and storeowners like don Samuel and don Próspero still sold drinks of tequila and pulque to the valiant defenders of the peace, supposedly on credit, but with little chance of ever seeing the debt paid, as they well knew.

Only Santa, two years older by the time that the new gendarmes arrived, expressed a different opinion. The *municipales* were not at all like the old *rurales*, not even close, particularly the second lieutenant! The second lieutenant truly was a dashing fellow, with his wide back and outthrust chest, his twinkling eye and easy chuckle in which his shaven brown cheeks parted to reveal white, even teeth that shone as if made of enamel. He was young and strong, tall when afoot, and graceful when mounted on his fiery spotted horse. He always wore his uniform, and it was always spotless, with his kepi tipped slightly back on his head, giving him the air of a swashbuckling lady's man.

The two met on a certain afternoon at the edge of the Pedregal. The second lieutenant, escorted by a number of dragoons, was emerging from the rocky wasteland and Santa, looking for Cosme, had just crossed the river barefoot on the stepping stones and, thinking herself unobserved, she had sat down on the ground to rinse off her naked feet and put her shoes on. The sand muffled the riders' approach, and by the time that Santa realized it, the dragoons had gotten a very good look at her ankles, as their sheepish expressions clearly testified. The second lieutenant, for his part, was totally entranced.

"May God turn my heart into the sand you walk on," he declared, reining in his mount abruptly.

From that moment began the siege, a campaign characterized on the second lieutenant's part by tenacious insistence, and by only weak resistance on the part of Santa, who did not defend herself the way she had earlier against Valentín, the lovesick troubadour who worked at the factory with Fabián and Esteban and could only sigh in Santa's presence. The second lieutenant, on the other hand, worked fast and knew all the tricks in the book. He found a dozen excuses to meet the girl as if by chance, and, clean shaven and smiling, he knew just how to chat with her, jokingly most of the time, tapping his high boots with his riding crop or petting the neck of his horse when he said something more serious. At first, Santa had acted sullen or arrogant and had clammed up or run home so as not to lend an ear to his gallantries, but little by little she softened. She stopped in front of the mirror to look at herself more often than she used to do. She began to recognize the gait of the spotted horse from far away, and she took to sitting beside the road to San Angel in the afternoons, anticipating that the young officer might pass, alone, and she was not often disappointed. Neither her mother nor her brothers noticed these changes, and the girl was drawn like a moth to the flaming passion simulated by the corrupt and careless suitor whose ardor came not from true love but merely from the desire to taste that delicious, ripening fruit, because he found it within reach of his heedless youth and his handsomely smiling teeth. Like so many soldiers stationed now here, now there, whose rank and sword confer a bit of authority, he did not care if he happened to knock down someone's fence or transform passionate kisses of greeting into desperate tears of parting. What did it matter? He did not make the world and its sorrows. He was an ignorant, irresponsible macho of the common sort, looking for an amorous adventure where it would cost him least and afford him most pleasure. Like so many, he showed little interest in the children whom he engendered unconsciously, a transient soldier incapable of repairing the damage he did to the country maids who gave themselves to him, just as he could not mend the unraveled seams that, from time to time, marred his uniform.

For that reason, when, during one of their daily and supposedly casual conversations, Santa told him quite urgently and seriously that he must speak to Agustina about their relationship, Second Lieutenant Marcelino Beltrán simply laughed his frank and impudent twenty-two-year-old laugh and caressed the girl's chin, while simultaneously slashing through the stems of various inoffensive flowers with a sidelong swipe of his riding crop:

"And why should I say anything to your mother when I've already said everything directly to you?"

He had, indeed, said everything to Santa, from the innocent and apparently candid words with which such men normally commence their love-making, to the ardent expressions that come later, pronounced in a murmur, with hands clasped, faces close together, eyes locked, lips parched, and spirit ravished. Eventually, by tacit agreement, as soon as Santa glimpsed Marcelino's spotted horse approaching on the wide road to San Angel, she would duck into the back lanes of her village, and hurriedly, without pausing to return the greeting of anyone she met, she would take the longest but most deserted route to the edge of the Pedregal. Marcelino would join her there, and looking frequently back to see who might be spying on them, they would enter the wasteland together. Once within the Pedregal, of course, there was no one to spy on them. The birds that flew up at the couple's approach did not look at them twice, nor did the bushes or the trees that whispered God-knows-what confidences to one another in their secret language of rustling boughs, known to the Druids, perhaps, but to no other human beings. Her instincts of self-preservation led Santa to keep Marcelino at a distance that her crafty lover respected at first, while he swore by all that was holy that no wicked intention or appetite motivated him, while he simply repeated in a soft monotone, the sweet, familiar song:

"I love you so much, Santa . . . so, so much, in a way I've never loved before and never expect to love again . . ."

Santa did not answer. How could she have answered? Her blood seemed to drain away from her head, her heart felt ready to burst out of her, and her voice formed a knot in her throat, so that, were it somehow to find its way to her mouth, it would surely be transformed into little more than sobs of happiness? What she did do was simply close her eyes to keep the world from spinning around her and breathe quickly, quickly, in order not to suffocate. If she had answered, it would have been to beg him to say it again: the ancient lie that men always utter and women always believe, the never-kept promise of eternal love and fidelity!

The Pedregral itself was the couple's discrete and cooperative accomplice, with its remote corners and hiding places that offered unsurpassed protection from prying eyes, unlike any of the other places around Chimalistac ordinarily employed for lovers' trysts, where a suspicious passerby, the sudden approach of the Churubusco streetcar, or any other trivial but unexpected circumstance might betray them. Only the Pedregal itself witnessed Santa's slow, inexorable surrender. First, she let Marcelino hold her hand, then let him put his arm around her waist, then put his head in her lap in order, the rascal affirmed, "the better to look at her." Finally, the kisses: first, she let him kiss her hands, "just her hands, nothing more," then, her neck, with soft, diabolical kisses that barely brushed the skin, then her mouth, the moist, parted lips of the girl, who shuddered with the feeling of pleasure and, abruptly, tried to escape, trembling and imploring:

"Let me go, Marcelino, let me go, oh God . . . I can't stand it!"

Without replying or ceasing his kisses, Marcelino deflowered Santa in the enchanting hideaway where the two had ensconced themselves. And Santa, who totally adored him, stifled the cries that normally accompany the loss of virginity. Sighing spasmodically as the tears rolled down her cheeks, she continued to kiss the man who had sacrificed her virtue. In idolizing feminine renunciation, in sovereign, primitive holocaust, in loving payment for what he had made her suffer, she gave him everything. She vibrated with him, submerged herself together with him in an unknown ocean of unparalleled delight, a sensation comparable only to a perfect death, so immense and extraordinary as to be worth all her blood, tears, and future hardship, or so she believed.

Once the catastrophe was consummated, they contemplated one another, mute, sweaty, and panting. Marcelino rose awkwardly to his feet. Santa, half sitting up on the green carpet, pulled up handfuls of grass and nervously tore it to pieces between her trembling fingers. Evening descended peacefully on the scene. In the majestic silence of the heartless volcanic wasteland, one could occasionally hear—from far, far away, who knows where—the sorrowful bleating of sheep who were lost or being shorn, and also, the off-key singing of a child, possibly Cosme, mounted on the house belonging to Fabián and Esteban, returning cheerfully from a day spent pasturing the cows.

"We should get going, don't you think?" proposed Marcelino, to put an end to the embarrassing situation.

"Where do you want me to go like this?" replied Santa, unsteadily, alluding to her murdered virginity.

Marcelino could not comprehend such peculiar squeamishness, so he answered her curtly:

"I suppose you should go home, you don't want me to take you to the barracks, right?"

"Take me wherever you want to, I don't care, but I'm not going home."

"Santa, don't act crazy. Just go on home, and tomorrow, when things settle down, we can decide what to do, okay? Now, come on, let's go!"

And, taking her arm, he pulled her to her feet, put his arm around her, and steered her out of the Pedregal, trying to console her and, especially, calm her down. There was a way to make everything right:

"Don't say a word to anybody, not even to your shadow, and here's my offer, okay? As soon as I can, . . . soon, I'll marry you, okay? We'll be poor because I don't have a thing, but if it makes you happy . . . Don't you have anything to say? Where is your affection?"

"Where's my affection, Marcelino? . . . I love you so much that I'd give you a thousand virginities if I had them . . . and any way you wanted, one by one to make it last longer, or all at once, so that my body would give you more pleasure than all the other women who could fall in love with you . . . Just don't abandon me! Oh, Nuestra Señora del Carmen, please, don't abandon me, Marcelino . . . If you knew my mother and my brothers . . . they'll kill me if they find out . . . So swear right now! Swear you won't abandon me! Swear you still love me as much as before . . ."

"No, no, I swear I won't," exclaimed Marcelino, none too happy with the tenor of events. "Don't act so upset, woman, anybody who sees you will think that they've already thrown you out of the house, as if everybody were already pointing a finger at you . . . Nobody knows, you little coward! Nobody saw us, right? And anyway, what's happened to you isn't so terrible, I mean, we can make it right, so there's no reason to tell anybody yet. Go on, Santa," he added, pulling her softly against his chest, "go on home as if nothing has happened, and tomorrow we'll see each other again, just the two of us, like today, and I bet you'll be laughing about these fears by then."

The evening flow of water had started over the big mill dam and darkness was gathering everywhere. It was almost nighttime. Three or four workers returning from the maguey fields, bent over under their heavy burdens, bustled past the couple without recognizing them.

"Buenas Noches, God willing," they murmured without even slowing down.

"Buenas Noches," answered Marcelino, altering his voice slightly, as Santa tried to hide behind his back.

At this hour they could no longer cross the river on the stepping stones, because when the mills that divert part of the river's current to power their machinery during the day cease to operate in the evening, the volume of the river's flow returns to a higher level. The stones were under water, so the couple had to take the narrow path along the bank and climb across the dangerous bridge hewn from a single tree trunk, without any rail or place to recover one's balance, impossible to traverse without agility, firmness, and practice. The river looked black, more like ink than water, as it passed below them with a raspy, frightening, interminable sigh. Village dogs barked invisibly in the middle distance.

"No, you go first," indicated Marcelino, who, upon reaching the beginning of the bridge, stepped back to let Santa cross first. "You are used to it, so show me how. This isn't really a bridge, anyway, it's just a log and must be sixteen feet long . . ."

"Give me your hand," said Santa. "Don't look at the water and let me guide you."

"Reaching the middle of the trunk, Santa stopped, and with a decisiveness made more solemn by the abyss beneath her feet, the darkness of the night, and the hoarse moaning of the water, unable to turn around or even look back for fear of losing her balance, she said:

"Marcelino, tell me again, swear to me again, that whatever happens you won't abandon me, swear, or I'll jump right now!"

And she tried to let go of his hand.

"I swear, I swear, for God's sake, Santa, don't act crazy, we'll fall," replied the second lieutenant, absolutely terrified. Barely had they reached the opposite bank when the ferocious village girl spied two approaching shapes in the twilight.

"Quick, get out of here, my brothers are coming."

She was right. And together with Fabián and Esteban, Santa went home and made up some sort of story about being lost in the Pedregal, being really frightened, calling for help . . .

"Who were you talking to?" asked Fabián darkly.

"I was talking to myself. Who else would I be talking to on the bridge? You didn't see that I ran your way as soon as I recognized you?"

They say that nobody slept a wink that night in the little white house. Fabián kept lighting cigarettes, and Esteban got up around midnight, going first to the corner where they kept the shotgun, then outside for a few minutes, but the brothers did not speak, although each knew that the other was awake for the same reason. Agustina, as if she sensed that some evil magic was about to wilt the treasured lily of her old age, touched her daughter softly with the pretext of pulling up the blanket or arranging the pillow. And Santa, trying to control her heart, which occasionally pounded as if it had grown instantly so large that it hardly fit in her lovesick bosom, lay very still indeed, and pressed her legs together so that her mother would not somehow sense her shameful and incurable wound . . .

Marcelino failed to materialize as promised the next day, and nothing was heard from him for the next week. Santa made the drastic decision to go in person and confront him with his abandonment of her. Although the harmony of her family had recently become clouded, nothing impeded her from going to San Angel with the pretext of attending the famous Fiesta de las Flores held there annually.

Without paying the slightest attention to the crowd in the town square, in which, besides the temporary bull ring that carpenters were erecting by order of the town council, she encountered a profusion of tents scattered everywhere in the style typical of country fairs, offering the chance to try one's luck at a roulette wheel (or other similarly edifying diversions), to sample various delicacies, or to drink pulque in the open air, Santa headed straight for the old Carmelite convent, crossed its spacious enclosed atrium, and before entering the church proper, looked in the direction of the police barracks that now occupied the former cloister. She did not see Marcelino. A sentry dressed in fatigues stood guard inside a crumbling brick structure, and Santa could see through the wide windows with worm-eaten wooden bars into a space that had formerly been a semi-gothic walkway but whose vaulted ceilings now sheltered a military check point with ten carbines reclining in a rack on the wall.

Standing in the church door, Santa vacillated; she had no intention of praying, so why go into the sanctuary? She blushed, tried to conceal it, and approached the sentry.

"Excuse me, could I talk with Second Lieutenant Beltrán, please?"

"Corporal!" called the sentry by way of reply, winking at Santa.

Blushing redder than before, Santa had to repeat her request to the corporal, a good-humored little man who first played dumb in order to prolong the conversation and then identified himself as the best friend and great uncle of Beltrán, whom he was prepared to represent in the matter at hand.

"Tell me what's troubling you, sweetie pie, and you won't be sorry."

Just then Marcelino appeared with angry looks for both Santa and her interlocutor, who abruptly stepped back, did an about-face, and vanished into the building.

"What are you doing here, Santa? What do you want?"

"How dare you ask me what I want?"

"Okay, okay, let's not talk here," interrupted Marcelino. "Go someplace else, any place you want, and I'll follow you."

Like an arrow, Santa crossed the square crowded with partiers, descended the ramp by the streetcar stop, passed a gambling den beside which musicians and curious onlookers stood around in the shade, and, reaching the street, turned left toward the open countryside, in the direction of Tlacopac. But, instead of the recriminations that she had rehearsed over and over, instead of the apologies that Marcelino ought to have offered her, what occurred was the normal thing when a woman who has given herself for love confronts the rascal who has seduced her with cynical expertise. The recriminations become entangled and lose their force among tears and kisses. The seducer gains the upper hand, swears and promises yet again. The two young bodies attract each other with a secret, irresistible force, and the woman surrenders herself once more, this time experiencing even greater pleasure, the more lasting and intense precisely because it is increasingly alloyed with remorse.

Consequently, they resolved to continue their love, which is to say that they resolved nothing at all . . .

Santa returned by the route she had come. As she passed the gambling den a second time, a heavy-set, jewelry-encrusted older woman stepped away from a group of gentlemen with whom she had been conversing and spoke to Santa.

"Where are you going so fast, little one? Let me look at you . . . My, aren't *you* pretty!"

Against her will, the taste of the forbidden fruit still in her mouth, Santa stopped and let herself be examined. Vaguely, she heard herself being praised, being asked jokingly if she had quarreled with her boyfriend, and then being told, much more seriously and, as it turned out prophetically, that if her boyfriend were to break up with her, well, she could earn twenty pesos a day at an easy job in the city.

"Just ask for Elvira, la Gachupina they call me." Plaza such and such, street number so and so. "You won't forget? I promise I'll make you a princess!"

Santa went home, where she arrived with a certain officious cheerfulness by which she hoped to allay the growing suspicions of her mother and of Fabián and Esteban, who were off working for three days because of the Fiesta de las Flores.

The end of the festival coincided with the full onset of Santa's misfortune. Marcelino was clearly getting away from her and, by the end of a month of desultory courtship showed himself clearly fed up, more likely to avoid than to seek any sort of encounter with her. And one fine day, early in the morning, Marcelino paraded down the wide road from San Angel at the head of his detachment, on the way to Mexico City and then, ultimately, to some other destination, without notifying Santa, who knew nothing of his redeployment. There were no trumpets or high-spirited horseplay that morning, as the horses filed past, their hooves sinking quietly into the loose sand of the wide road through the village. Were it not for the cries of a boy who saw the detachment passing through, Santa would have had no idea at all that Marcelino was leaving. She joined the boys who were running toward the shrilly shouted announcement:

"Come see! The soldiers from San Angel are leaving!"

They ran in vain, because all they were able to see in the end was a cloud of dust that rose from the unpaved road to defend horses and riders like an impenetrable shield from the curious gaze of the villagers. Only at a single moment, as the detachment climbed the paved approach to the high bridge at El Altillo, did the dust dissipate enough so that one could glimpse the backs of the dragoons who rode in the rear guard, their carbines slung across their backs, their horses' rumps twitching and tails whipping back and forth furiously because of the flies. Santa realized at last that she was the victim of the cowardly, eternal abandonment she had most dreaded, she leaned against a high wall of cut stone—softer stuff, it now seemed to her, than her fugitive lover's heart—where she raised her apron to her eyes and, Virgin Santísima, how she cried! For her broken heart and her broken body, for the ingrate who was leaving her and for the innocent life that was already making its presence felt inside of her . . .

Here Santa's memories became confused, cutting off the involuntary evocation of her story. One thing that she did remember, however, with admirable and painful precision, was her miscarriage more or less four months into her sinful, clandestine pregnancy. She had one foot on the rim of the well and was pulling up a heavy earthenware jar of water that chanced to spill, throwing her off balance. She felt a bolt of lightning: a sudden, copious sweat, a horrible sensation in her hips and groin, and in her lower back a stabbing pain so powerful that Santa dropped the jar, let out a scream, and collapsed on the ground. Then came the hemorrhage, as abundant and loud in her memory as the water that had spilled from the jar as it fell and shattered against the moist walls of the well. Then Agustina was there, bending over her, discovering the secret, wavering between the impulses to curse and slap her, on the one hand, or to forgive and care for her on the other. Then Coyote was licking at the blood that sank into the mud, and one of the fighting cocks started singing for no reason. What happened next? Somber faces, the hushed silence that accompanies catastrophes, an intense fever, the whispered gossip of the villagers as they sniffed around for clues about what had occurred, inventing their own distorted versions of it.

Finally, twenty days after the doctor pronounced Santa all better, Agustina—older and more bent over since the accident, her eyes sunken and her hands shaky—convened an implacable family tribunal to sit in judgment. The accusers were Fabián and Esteban, harsh, sorely ashamed of their sister, and determined, like avenging storybook heroes, to reclaim and cleanse the family's stained honor, its rustic and humble, but much-prized honor, which they had always upheld. Santa, pale and with dark circles under her eyes, faced this tribunal in the yard in front of the little white house, under the orange trees laden with fruit. High above her, the heavens hung limpid, impenetrable, and serene. Below, from behind the house, came the sound of the river, condemned to its endless voyage, grasping perpetually at the rocks and trees along its banks, as if trying to stop and rest if only for a moment, but always failing to hang on, always continuing its voyage of exile, leaving only bits of foam that finally burst with a sigh to sprinkle flowers and leaves with glistening tears.

Unable to prolong her deception, Santa had told them the story of her tragic idyll, but she refused to pronounce the name of her lover on any condition. Let them find it out if they could.

"I won't tell you, not to save my life! No, no, no!"

Faced with Santa's stubbornness and the fury of her brothers, who were hardly able to contain themselves, who knows what heart-rending words were uttered by the old Agustina as she sat with her hands on her knees, her arms rigid, her body erect, her head thrown back so that her immaculate white mane, falling in disorder on her poor, thin shoulders, resembled the imprecise radiance of a holy image in a dimly lit sanctuary. Whatever she said, her eyes half closed, they were things that weighed heavily in Santa's heart, things about her honorable birth and upbringing, about the sacrifices made by her parents, about her first steps and her first communion, about how "if her father were alive, this would kill him." Her mother's bitter, candid lamentations in the face of the inevitable sounded childish and sarcastic on the lips of a woman who had lived so long. Agustina did not curse her. No matter how impure, Santa was still her beloved daughter for whom she implored God's infinite mercy. But her mother did repudiate her, as must be done when a virgin leaves the path of righteousness and allows her cloak of innocence to be torn asunder; as must be done when an unworthy daughter stains the honor of an aging mother soon to meet her maker; as must be done when an ungrateful sister dishonors the brothers who labor, day in and day out, to support her. In such cases, she who is no longer a virgin, the unworthy daughter, the ungrateful sister threatens to corrupt all that surrounds her, and she must be repudiated, cast out, and regarded from then on as if no longer alive, may God have mercy on her soul.

And with a supreme effort—the energy that she feigned to possess now totally exhausted—Agustina rose to her feet, exalted and sacred.

And as she rose, Santa shrank in humiliation, lower and lower, falling at her mother's feet, pressing her beautiful, sinful face against the ground.

And Esteban and Fabián, imposing, healthy, and strong as ever, stood and took off their hats as if awed by the priestly solemnity of Agustina's utterance.

"Go, Santa!" ordered the aging mother. "Go! I can't stand any more . . ." It was true that she could not stand any more. Like an old oak split by lightning, she collapsed into the arms of Fabián and Esteban, who hurried to her assistance.

Meanwhile, Santa, without resisting her mother's final mandate, cast a final anguished look of farewell toward the little white house and its inhabitants, and walked unsteadily to the gate. There she stopped, hoping against hope that they might call to her. She turned to see her mother for the last time, in her brothers' arms, as if in a tableau representing the austere justice of biblical patriarchs. Agustina's right hand was still raised from the moment when she had ordered Santa to leave.

A movement of Santa's bedmate, who was moving brusquely in his sleep, interrupted her protracted remembrance of things past and brought her back to the present. For an instant, she considered leaving the bed to finish the night on the sofa or the carpet, but she changed her mind for one reason. Since she had lacked the courage to throw herself into the river back home—which had promised death, oblivion, perhaps even purification—she would punish herself by drowning, instead, in the mud of this stinking, shameful flow of filth!

Three

"Bravo, Hipólito, well done! What did you say it's called?"

"'Welcome,'" said the blind piano player, without getting up.

"Let's hear 'Welcome' again, then, come on!" shouted the brothel's clientele with one voice, continuing to dance with the girls.

The dance called "Welcome" was passionate and, in spite of its saucy syncopation, truly beautiful. The first part, above all, moaned with a deep emotion that obscured the workings of the chords and bass line; then, in the second part—the up-tempo, danceable part—sadness and inhibitions evaporated in a harmonic transition, leaving only fiery notes in a racy, provocative rhythm meant to draw a dancing couple closer together. The dancers had Hipólito repeat his new composition as many as four times, amid explosive, rowdy applause.

"That song is for me . . . right, Hipo?" said Santa to the musician when she went to the piano to get his hat.

"Yes, Santita, this one and two others that I'll play when the visitors leave. All three are for you," declared Hipólito gravely.

Santa worked wonders with the musician's hat as she passed it around. Her exceptional take amounted to almost half a dozen pesos. And, jingling the coins with glee, she stuffed them by the handful into the jacket pocket of the composer, who continued at the piano, rolling a cigarette with the amazing manual dexterity common in the blind. Close to his ear, she murmured:

"Don't think that I'm trying to repay you with a few coins, Hipo. It's only right that these guys pitch in for the music. I really appreciate your thinking of me . . . Believe me, I really appreciate it."

The blind man smiled, his eyebrows twitching, and said nothing. And since he put the lit cigarette in his mouth as he began the introduction of another piece, requiring all fingers on the keyboard, it would be hard to say for sure whether the tear that he quickly wiped away with the back of his hand responded to Santa's thanks or to the smoke that wafted into his horrid whitish eyes.

By an odd mutual attraction, Santa and Hipólito had become friends immediately. It was a timid and unconfessed friendship, of course, because of the setting, a place where nobody believed in platonic friendships. The brothel admitted only love, whether real or feigned, and many times—perhaps usually—neither the poor women nor the men who communed with them in relative intimacy could be sure when their love was real and when it was feigned. Hipólito and Santa had become friends, but as soon as they realized it, both hid their friendship in mutual self-interest. If the others found out, Hipólito was likely to lose his job in one of the best houses in the city and Santa would no longer enjoy the special consideration that she received from Elvira and Pepa, delighted at the avid, growing enthusiasm that her fresh flesh awakened in both the established customers of the brothel and the new ones attracted by her sudden reputation.

Because Santa was decidedly a hit, her triumph had required only that she allow herself to be undressed and bathed in champagne in a closed room of the Maison Dorée Restaurant, on a certain night when the richest members of the city's Sport Club arranged an orgiastic dinner to celebrate her, like a modern, olive-skinned version of a legendary Greek concubine.

That edifying spectacle marked Santa's transformation from withdrawn, half-wild "new girl" to stylish courtesan, whom all the males able to afford her substantial price yearned to try for themselves. More than a sensual appetite, theirs seemed an urge to vent some dark desire, to crush and bruise that spicy, delicious, unresisting flesh whose owner was bound for hell and with whom each customer could act out his desires with impunity. And even though these extremely numerous gentlemen included respectable fathers and husbands, upstanding citizens, the cream of society, some of them Catholic, some freethinkers, men both lighthearted and solemn, men who represented public authority and worthy causes—none of them considered rescuing this poor girl from her fate. So it is in this Vale of Tears where each of us mortals has a cross to bear! Is someone's fate particularly cruel? Too bad! These decent, respectable men pursued the recently fallen girl like a galloping herd of stallions that, on fire with bestial lust, respect nothing and will stop at nothing. One could say that the most lascivious denizens of the entire city passed through Santa's bedroom, hardly giving her time to change position. The fallen woman! That is exactly the way they wanted her, the way they dreamed of her—the supremely attractive forbidden fruit.

Santa, deep down, felt flattered in her womanly vanity by this seemingly infinite adoration. Rather than bruising, she smiled—in her perpetual, shameless nudity, fleshy arms folded behind her head, her black mane spilling over them—at the ceaseless parade of men who approached her tremulously and mashed her lips with their kisses, who deafened her with their whispered, fleeting promises only to depart, soon enough, embarrassed at their own words and actions, leaving a few coins on the table and, in Santa's heart, a mixture of disdain and anger. They wanted, asked for, demanded that she offer them not only her lovely body but also her affection, her love!

"Love me," implored their banknotes and furious caresses. "Love me for an instant at least!"

Love them . . . how could she love them, when the first rascal she had come across had left her without the slightest desire for a repeat performance? Are there men who deserve to be loved?

As she looked for the answer to that question, the parade of machos, the rain of money and caresses, continued, and somehow her health withstood it marvelously. Santa became even more beautiful. Like diabolic magic turned to a perverse purpose, far from making her haggard, her late-night excesses added a sultry pallor, a mysterious allure to the formerly innocent face of a country girl. What she did lose—and unfortunately, very quickly, indeed, she lost it all—was a moral sense of what her beauty meant. So quickly did she slip into synch with her degrading new environment, that she presumably had something in her blood, some infection of ancient lasciviousness inherited from some great grandfather, manifesting itself anew, full blown, in her present behavior. Her speedy adaptation clearly shows that this girl was not born to be good, not unless she had someone to keep her on the straight and narrow path, someone to lend a hand when she stumbled. At the moments—and these were rarer every day—when waves of remorse came over her and saddened her, she gave herself brief pep talks about making a change, but no matter how much she looked around, like a drowning person asking for help, all she found were people who shrugged their shoulders or who tried to drown her faster in order to rid themselves of the temptation and torment incited by her too-beautiful body. And so the remorse faded, as did the fragmentary recollections of her catechism, her childhood, and her mother, and Santa fell victim to her bad instincts, indolently abandoning herself to what she now considered to be her fate. Where would such a life end? In the hospital and the cemetery, of course, the last port of call in every life's voyage, whether virtuous or sinful. But between now and then, she reckoned that she had at least a decade of health and beauty—qualities that she fully appreciated, having bathed them, shown them, and sold them so assiduously. This is the way that she behaved, at any rate, but deep down inside, while she considered herself as guilty as could be, she was counting on the opportunity to make last minute amends on her death bed and gain some forgiveness from Him whose laws she so egregiously violated, He whose name she refused to pronounce even when she was alone, because of her superstitious fear.

"Isn't it true, Hipo, that girls like us shouldn't say it?" she asked the piano player on an occasion when one of the women of the house, awash in tears because of the terrible affliction that she experienced, incessantly invoked the holy name.

"Well now, Santita, listen. That's hard to figure. You've got María Magdalena to think about . . ."

"María who?"

Hipólito was unable to make a further display of erudition because some inebriated customers interrupted the consultation. However, nothing would have changed Santa's mind, and she remained determined never to mention the holy name so as not to profane it with her impure lips.

On the other hand, with the feminine instinct that rarely fails to indicate who are potential friends here on earth, Santa got closer and closer to Hipólito. It was an odd sort of affection, more than just sympathy, much less than love. His appearance made her suffer: his twitching eyebrows, his horrid whitish eyes of a bronze statue without patina, sightless eyes that one would say appeared to see, eyes that seemed to look particularly at Santa, to stare at her with astounding fixity, as if trying in that way to accomplish the miraculous recovery of his vision or record forever the features of the woman that he knew to be so young and beautiful. Santa felt repulsed, and yet, she still stood and sat close to him, trying to avert her own eyes in order not to see those monstrous orbs that gazed at her in supplication, all the more mournfully because they could not see her. As for conversing with the blind man, that she did very happily, even submitting to his experience, old libertine that he was, certain complex or intractable problems that she faced as a novice prostitute.

Thus began their good, mutual friendship, with Santa consulting and Hipo advising her from his substantial fund of dubious knowledge. Santa's activities left her little free time, but what she had was normally dedicated to chatting with the piano player. In a low voice when he was not playing the piano, and in a louder voice when he was, she asked him questions, answered his, and listened attentively to his wise counsel and his timid admonishments. Their conversations were always discontinuous because Santa was perpetually in demand, because Hipo had to play the piano for hours at a time, and because nosy people often approached them, interrupting their colloquy, making them disguise it in meaningless chatter. When they found themselves alone again, they would simply take up where they had left off, the way friends do. Santa felt sorry for her mentor, who did not seem to suffer as much as his circumstances suggested, and the mentor felt fleeting shudders of delight when his new companion came a little too close or leaned her shapely arms on his back after passing around his rumpled and dirty hat to collect monetary contributions from the clientele of the house. The girls joked that old Hipo could keep up with the best, that he was an unrepentant satyr from way back, and they pulled his leg mercilessly:

"Oooh, nasty boy, so now you're sweet on Santa?"

"On *all* of you . . . so tasty! I could eat all of you up in a single bite, ahhhh!" And he made a fantastically frightful face with his mouth wide open, as he had done for them a million times, provoking laughter, swearing, and delighted cries of horror from the prostitutes.

One night, when business was slow and the girls were lying around on the sofas, playing solitaire, or dosing in the corners and generally waiting to get "off work," Pepa knitting a scarf for her Diego in the manner of any respectable matron, and Hipólito and Santa at the piano, as usual—the two began for the first time to tell each other their stories.

Santa has told every bit of hers, at this point, and she is stubbornly insisting that Hipo tell his. But he is resisting:

"No, it's not that I don't want to, but because it'll make you sad, and me too, in the bargain . . ."

"Fine, don't tell me anything" said Santa, acting angry, "but tomorrow don't expect me to talk to you at all."

"Don't be mad, Santa . . . Okay, but come closer because I don't want anyone else to hear . . ."

After sitting silently and smoking nervously for a moment, he began:

"Imagine, Santa. I've seen neither light, nor father, nor mother." And he paused for a long time, his brow knit, puffing on his cigarette so hard that it singed his moustache.

"Neither father nor mother? Why?" asked Santa, disturbed.

"My father never concerned himself with my existence at all, I suspect. And I never saw my mother because of this damned blindness, but even if I had seen her, I guess I would have forgotten her by now. I lost her when I was a child and she had to leave me, God knows why, at the School for the Blind."

"Your mother abandoned you when you were little and already blind?"

"Oh, but I forgave her . . . when I took my first and only communion."

There was another long pause in the quiet conversation. Santa went to the window and pushed aside the curtains. Hipólito shut his whitish eyes.

"Hipo, you old son of bitch, play something. This ain't a wake, is it?" complained the girl they called la Gaditana, in a bad mood because she kept losing at solitaire. The piano player automatically began the introduction to a waltz.

"How old were you when you lost her? Do you remember?" asked Santa, over his shoulder.

"Six or seven at the most. I still cried a lot then, about anything . . ."

The first part of the waltz flowed out of the blind man's hands, into the air, slowly and voluptuously.

"Where did this happen, Hipo?"

"You'll see. Because I was already blind when I was little, I never left my mother's side, not even to go play. She would sit me on her lap to feed me, spoonful by spoonful, and before she gave me each one, she told me what I was going to eat . . . and I was so clumsy, because I was so little and couldn't see, that I often spilled the soup or got my directions confused and took a bite of air . . . and she . . . I guess, she cried . . . but so quietly that I didn't hear her, and so I would ask her what those warm drops were on my cheeks. She took a long time to answer, and the drops increased, getting my cheeks all wet, and it made me so sad, Santita, that I would stop eating and—I still remember it perfectly—I'd ask her a lot of childish questions, wanting to know more about her than I could know from her voice and her tears: 'Tell me, mamá,' I'd say, 'what you look like and what I look like.'"

Santa, her eyes bright with her own tears, blew her nose loudly and uttered not a word.

The second part of the waltz, much faster and more cheerful than the first part, was now escaping from the piano player's tobacco-yellowed fingers, which pursued it artfully all over the keyboard.

"One day," he continued, "my mother kissed me a lot, much more than usual. She changed my clothes, and picked me up to go out, but she started sobbing so hard that I got scared and, hiding my face in her shoulder, threw my arms around her neck and whispered in her ear, asking where she was taking me . . .

"'I'm going to take you to a school, where you can learn things, and where . . .' and she couldn't go on, and she hugged me harder than I was hugging her, and she sobbed openly and her tears drenched my face. And Santa, if you could see what I felt, as if something were breaking inside, an unknown sensation of pain and fear . . .

'You mean I'm not going to live with you?' I couldn't believe it.

'No, but I'll come to visit you twice a week, and I'll bring you toys and money to buy candy.'

'Then you don't love me anymore. Without your hands, how can I move around or eat? My hands are no good!' And I cried, too, since I didn't have eyes to see her, I smelled her, I sniffed her like a little dog, and she begged me to stop crying . . .

'Hush, for God's sake, my baby, people will hear you . . .' and I swear that she was crying more than me, and we walked and walked until we got to the School for the Blind . . . and mother sprinkled these blind eyes with kisses and leaned against the wall.

'If you only knew why I'm bringing you,' she said, 'if you only knew, you'd forgive me . . .'"

Santa was trembling. One of the girls had the servant bring some hot rum punch, good and strong. The third part of the waltz—slow, languid, melancholic—drifted through the rooms of the brothel.

"And then?" inquired Santa, gazing as if in a daze beneath the open piano lid at how the hammers hit the metal strings.

"Nothing, at school I learned to read, but not books. I learned to read with my fingers . . . running them over raised letters. I learned to play the piano, and I learned to suffer, because I never really suffered before, even from my blindness. Being with my mother, her voice, her touch, was my universe. True, I couldn't see, but she saw for me, even better! In her way, she explained things to me, animals and people. She talked to me about colors, described flowers, the countryside, even the clouds! And better than the clouds, the sun itself! Because of her I know that the sky is blue and the countryside is green, and even though I don't know what blue and green are, here in my head I make up my own colors, and it could be better than reality . . . because when I imagine colors, I bring back my mother, who was, and still is for me, prettier, so much prettier than all the sky and countryside in the whole world. Even though my mother hardly visited me. During the first four or five weeks of my captivity, there she was, even early, every Thursday and Sunday, full of sweets, and tears, and affection all for me. I'd tell her, once we'd finished crying, about my progress in reading, music, and lace making. She would listen to me, hugging me to her bosom, and it was oh so hard to tear myself away when the bell rang to end visiting hours . . . Then she missed a Sunday, a Thursday, and another Sunday. How anxiously I awaited her, Santa, sitting in a corner of a courtyard, the one with the fewest people, where I wouldn't suffer more from overhearing the laughter and conversations of my schoolmates' families. Silly me. When I cried, I even tried to save my tears in my handkerchief to show her, when she returned, how I idolized her. But guess what! They evaporated! All tears evaporate. Ask anyone who knows about them . . . What I know is that the pain finally evaporates, too."

The coda of the waltz extended itself softly and rhythmically across the keyboard, the girls sipped their rum punch, and Pepa, "the manager," counted a pile of banknotes in her lap. With one finger, Santa was drawing odd shapes in the fine dust on the piano lid.

"Then," Hipólito forged ahead, "until I was fourteen years old my life was colorless . . . dark, as sighted folk say. My four senses became well educated, the sense of touch, particularly. But my heart became callous, used to beating without caring. Why should I care about anybody if nobody cared about me? In my memory, my mother. In my hand, a cane that guided me and defended me and that I came to consider my only friend. Behind, total blackness. Ahead, total blackness. Invalid, miserable, poor, without hope, without affection. I was condemned to life imprisonment in public institutions, or to starvation if I tried make it on my own . . . unless some charitable soul took me out of the school with the idea of applying my skill at music or the manual arts. And that's what happened. A man named Primitivo Aldábez who owned the neighborhood upholstery shop, pitying my blindness and impressed by my manual dexterity, fulfilled the legal requirements and took me out of the school after getting my consent, which I didn't hesitate to give, anxious for a new direction . . ."

"Thank God!" exclaimed Santa, as if a great weight were removed from her.

"Not so much, Santita, not so much, because it wasn't long until ..."

And just as the waltz, returning to the initial motif, died and was buried among the keys by Hipólito's hands, softly accentuating its final measures, a cloud of visitors descended on the house, so that the piano player reserved what remained of his biography for a better occasion, and Santa, still burning with curiosity, had go greet the recent arrivals. The parlor awoke.

That night marked the beginning of the friendship between Santa and Hipólito, the daily chats, her consultations and his advice, and his dedication to her of the three songs—"Welcome," "I Was Waiting for You," and "If They Looked at You"—that augmented the musician's reputation and Santa's affection for him. Therefore, when Santa's first serious lover entered the scene (Señor Rubio, by name and also hair color, since he was blond, the sort of man that the other girls of the establishment wanted for themselves), no one became aware of the occurrence faster than Hipólito.

"Hipo," Santa asked him, "Rubio is offering to rent a house for me if I will go with him, what do you advise?"

The musician almost had a fit of nervous trembling when he heard this.

"Well, Santita, there's no advice for that ... Do you like him?"

"He is a fine gentleman, Hipo. You know how he treats me in front of people. You should see how he treats me when we're alone!"

"And what the heck can I see? But it's just as well because ... I mean ... Do you love him, Santita?"

"Love? ... There are lots of ways to love ... even though you're shaking your head, Hipo ... there are lots and lots of ways!"

"Well, all right, go with him then. Sooner or later it had to be somebody, that's for sure."

"What's for sure?"

"Your leaving the brothel. Except that the brothel is like jail, the hospital, or hard liquor. It's rough at first, but once you've got a taste for it, nobody can take that taste away ... You'll come back to this house, Santita, to this one or a worse one ... God forbid, don't get me wrong, I hope it won't turn out that way for you, but sometimes one just doesn't know ... Why don't you wait a few more months? Far from missing something, maybe it'll be better, and if Señor Rubio gets tired of waiting and turns his back on you, that will show it wasn't serious. He who truly loves never gets tired of waiting! And, right now, what do you lack, anyway? You've got fabulous health, plenty of customers, Elvira and Pepa treat you well—why not hold out longer, maybe you'll hit the jackpot."

And, for a while, at least, the twisted theorems of professor Hipólito held sway, reproducing the conventional wisdom of the underworld that had been his academy, preaching shameless atrocities with a straight face. So great was his influence over Santa, that the fellow, Rubio, in spite of the countless advantages in his favor, had to content himself with what the girl deigned to grant him: her manifest preference in public; two full nights a week, starting early, with dinner and the theater. It was the make-believe committed relationship so common among such women in their heyday, so common among all men when their heyday is past. And Hipólito, like the hidden prompter at the theater, slyly directed the action on stage, but because he had to remain hidden, he was unable to counter the well-planned advances of another suitor, the famous and valiant matador, el Jarameño, star of the city's bullring, who had been contracted directly from Spain to delight Mexico's City's bullfight fans every Sunday at the Bucareli bullring. El Jarameño's big spending and amusing conversation got him past Elvira, who preferred not to admit *toreros*—"guys with pig-tails," as she called them—to her establishment.

"They take a lot and pay zilch," she explained to the girls, who had the most to lose by nonpayment, "and worse, they scare away young gentle-men."

With el Jarameño, it went differently. To begin with, it was young gentle-men, precisely, and of the most excellent sort, who brought him to the house; and secondly, he treated the girls like silver pesos, and pesos, like grains of anise, spending just as much as his rich friends did and giving generous tips to the servants, not to mention the piano player. But he really consummated his triumph when he played guitar and sang, and the girls, most of whom were Spanish, clapped along and rewarded him with kisses that seemed aimed more at their distant homeland than the clean-shaven face of this particular young man from southern Spain. El Jarameño no-ticed Santa immediately, of course, not only because she was eye-catching but also because the rich kids swarmed around her. A lightning bolt of de-sire ran through him, making his macho, southern Spanish blood boil.

"Hello, good looking," he said in his marked Andalusian accent, "you've got no *beau*?"

Holding her wrist in his powerful grip, not hurting her at all, but, to the contrary, almost caressingly, yet with a touch suggestive of a Herculean, primitive, animal power kept totally in reserve, the torero awaited her an-swer, staring hypnotically at her until Santa, subjugated by his will, finally stared back, extremely flustered in spite of the forced laughter with which she tried to respond.

"What's it to you whether I do or not? And what's that about a *beau* anyway?"

El Jarameño let go of her calmly, without anger, as one might put down some delicate object that looked good from afar but has lost all appeal on close examination, and took up the guitar again. In true Flamenco style, amid the whirl of drinks and rhythmic clapping, he poured out his heart in melancholy lyrics: *Two things in the world / Can cost your life, oh* . . .

Santa was miffed by the behavior of the torero, who paid no further attention to her, and she felt the impulse to make him suffer by lavishing her affection on the young men around her. She sat on this one's lap, drank from that one's glass, allowed this other one to take her shoe off, and grimacing a thousand times, she took two puffs on some fellow's cigar. As the party really got going, she broke open an uncorked bottle of wine. Some of the guys proposed that Hipólito play for them in their private dining room, and they sent two of their fairly inebriated number to parlay with Elvira, whom they convinced to put aside her air of lofty detachment as mistress of the harem and drink a glass of whatever she wanted in good fellowship. Amid the increasing disorder, someone proposed an outing for the next day, an outing with the girls in rented coaches:

"Elvira will go along, I guarantee. And we'll take el Jarameño . . . hey, want to go with us to hear the Cry?"

"What cry, man? You haven't heard cries enough?"

Laughter, ignorance, explanations, hiccups—it was not just any cry, but the Cry of Dolores, which for the people of Mexico, commemorates the country's independence from Spain.

"It's the Cry with which we threw out Spaniards like you," suggested the piano player, a bit aggressively.

"And since when were we thrown out of anywhere?" replied el Jarameño proudly.

"Since when? Since we threw you out of Mexico . . . years ago!" pronounced the house wise man.

"Yeah? Well, I never heard those cries, and you can tell me about 'em later . . ."

"Jarameño, take it easy, don't quarrel over matters of no importance . . . all that stuff's over and done with. And here are guys like you, in Mexico, and it's gone well for you, right? I mean, plenty of applause, plenty of money, no? Aren't there thousands of your compatriots whom you couldn't drag away, because they like it here that much?"

"Now that's the truth . . . so okay, we're square . . . and I'll drink to that! My good woman," said el Jarameño to Elvira, "bring out some manzanilla, because this Spaniard invites everybody to join him in a toast to Spain!"

Tensions dissipated in rowdy good spirits. Hipo tried to provide music for reconciliation by playing bullfight marches, the best known of which had Elvira and her girls all singing in chorus: "Viva España, and long live her valiant sons . . ."

El Jarameño covered his beer glass, bumped it against his chest, changing its liquid into a thousand gold bubbles, and shot them in the direction of Santa, saying:

"Drink to my country, gorgeous, because I'm drinking to yours, and to you!"

Plans for the next day's outing were finalized, and Elvira was paid in advance for the girls who would go. They calculated the number of rental coaches they would need, with two couples in each coach. It was already light and the drunkest of them decided to stay at the house and sleep that day, but el Jarameño and another fellow who was also leaving said their goodbyes. What instinct inspired Santa to accompany him to the front door? The torero, without removing his arm from the shoulders of his friend, asked for a friendly goodbye kiss, and it was granted.

"When are you going to sleep with me, Santa?" he asked in her ear, very seriously.

"With you?" she said and, after reflecting for a moment, concluded: "Never!"

"You hate me that much?"

"I don't hate you at all. I'm scared of you."

Blind Hipólito, who was going out the door after them and overheard Santa's declaration, could not restrain himself.

"Congratulations on your new suitor, Santita," he said as, with the tip of his cane, he woke his little guide, who was curled up sleeping in the usual place on the floor. "These guys with pigtails are the biggest men around . . ."

Santa resented the way that Hipólito vented at her, as if he had a claim on her and had just surprised her in a flagrant infidelity. Why should he taunt her about el Jarameño, whose proposals she had rejected and whom she really did fear, with an odd and merely physical fear, an organic desire for self preservation? And, after all, what claim did Hipólito have on her? She had not granted him any, and felt less inclined to do so now! If she did not belong to herself, if she was everybody's slave, then she would at least hold onto her heart—if any of it remained, which seemed dubious—and force the men to be content with her magnificent body, strong and stripped of both clothing and affection. Let her body satiate their immense, fierce, limitless lust; let some bless and kiss it while others cursed and bruised it . . . But let them leave alone her heart, her tears, her memories, the things that she carried hidden inside, things that came bubbling up on occasions, and that night was one, when she had too much to drink . . . And as for Hipólito and el Jarameño, she would not rent them her body, not even if they offered her double or triple, not for any price. Not Hipólito, because she might love him a little just because she pitied him so much. Not el Jarameño, because fear made her love him already. And, trying not to spill any hidden tears (or hidden memories, or her hidden heart) as she walked, clumsy with drunkenness, back up the stairs, Santa clumsily drank even more, allowing herself to be escorted to her perfumed cubicle of a worshipper of Bacchus by one of those rich young gentlemen, who smelled of wine, groped her breast, and blathered obscene gallantries.

That morning, 15 September, was overcast and lugubrious, so when Santa and her customer awoke—around midday—they assumed that the evening's planned expedition would be canceled on account of rain. Faced with the prospect of being together alone for so many hours without an iota of love or even friendship to help the time pass, they did not attempt to conceal their displeasure and, to the contrary, showed it plainly: the customer by stretching, tossing, and turning under the warm, rumpled, evil-smelling sheets; Santa, by rummaging in her dresser drawer, where she was certain to find nothing since she was not looking for anything. They said little, and when either of them spoke, it was only to make little jabs or insulting allusions toward the other, as if they had both remembered after a night of commercial caresses that, except for the fellow's now pacified lust, there was nothing between them, only the eternal rancor that separates the sexes. A mutual repugnance was visible in their looks, audible in their words. On their tongues, both had the queasy aftertaste of too much alcohol and venal pleasure, which make us feel depressed and embarrassed once their titillating effects have evaporated. Santa did not care that her nightgown, slipping and revealing portions of her brown skin, allowed her brief lover to see her body. She had no interest in exciting him, and the truth is that he did not even look at her, satiated as he was with that flesh that everyone had tasted, and he turned to face the window and lay looking up at the clouds through the curtains.

"If you get me a cup of coffee," he exclaimed, finally, "I'll take you to Tivoli for lunch."

Santa vetoed the idea, saying that she had to bathe and visit her seamstress.

"You go with a friend, and we'll get together tonight. Let's go, time to get moving . . . up!"

The client got dressed in a flash, overjoyed to be set free so easily, and Santa passively accepted his goodbye hugs and kisses. By herself, finally, she opened a window, draped a shawl over her shoulders, and sat down on a sofa, crossing her legs and nervously swinging her foot in the air.

Always the same! Always the same horribly cold, disheartening awakenings, in which she could feel the protests of her tired body and of something else that was not exactly her body but that she could feel protesting inside of it . . . Always the same feeling of disenchantment, of disgust with the idea of continuing this exhausting, insipid, cruel life—a life that forced her to share sexual pleasure with men who did not appeal to her at all. Always these pangs of repentance, but only at awakening, pangs that dissipated thereafter in the course of the day as she slowly got used to the idea of this life again and convinced herself, again, that she could not aspire to any other, and even lost the desire to try, settling into it, one could say, almost physiologically, as if this fate belonged to her. Lately, the scary stories about threats to her health seemed just that, scary stories. A little while longer, and she'd be just like the other girls. What she really needed was a *lover* to take special care of her, but a lover that she really loved . . .

She did a quick mental survey of the legion of men who had sworn they loved her. Why had el Jarameño won her heart so easily, when she had only just met him? Why did Rubio, the "decent gentleman" who promised to rent a house for her, attract her at the same time? Why did Hipólito, who had never uttered to her a syllable about love, try to get between her and her suitors, looking and looking at her, sightlessly, with those horrid whitish eyes of a bronze statue without patina?

The organizers of the outing appeared that evening, as punctually as creditors collecting a debt, in the company of el Jarameño. At the same time, four common yellow-flagged rental coaches parked themselves along the curb in front of the house of ill repute.

What a scuffle took place inside the house! Now all the girls wanted to join the merry band and, amid jokes and laughter, a number of hard bargains were driven and the caravan expanded. The expeditioners sent for another coach which, when it arrived, turned out to be dirty, rickety, squeaky, and pulled by two old nags that, according to the authoritative pronouncement of el Jarameño, were not even good enough for a bull to gore.

The coaches set out in a straight line, one after the other, as soon as the lighting for the celebration began.

The enormous municipal arc lamps that hung over the middle of the streets, the elaborate electric lighting that capriciously covered the façades of expensive stores, and the humble little lanterns of glass or paper lit by the common people combined, on that evening, to give the city the magical appearance of an elaborate theatrical set. As soon as the caravan turned onto wide Juárez Avenue, they could see San Francisco and Plateros Streets overflowing with light, closed to vehicle traffic, hardly big enough to contain the surging flow of pedestrians that moved toward the Plaza de Armas. Above the sea of heads one could see, here and there, little children riding on their fathers' shoulders and guitars that appeared to float along by themselves on the ceaseless, roiling, multicolored waves, as if they had fallen from on high. The coaches advanced slowly until, on arriving at the corner beside the San Francisco bridge, the impenetrability of the human masses and the signal to halt given by the mounted police forced them to stop and decide how to proceed. Santa—a daughter of the common people of Mexico, after all—wanted to continue on foot, mixing with the multitude that almost overflowed the street. But her colleagues, who were Spanish and frightened of the crowd—a monster whose whistles, exclamations, shouts, and laughter gave the impression of a hurricane—were totally against going on foot, preferring, in that case, to call the whole thing off. The men did not approve Santa's proposal, either. They did not like the idea of going to the Plaza de Armas so early, nor of sitting cooped up in the small, uncomfortable coaches as every military band in the whole city played between nine and eleven o'clock. They proposed going for a quick dinner first, and then to the celebration afterward, just in time to hear the Cry.

"To the Café de Paris, fellow," they ordered the driver of the first coach in the caravan.

The tide of people was rising. The coaches now seemed like rudderless boats, laboring along, occasionally detained (to the noisy protest of their occupants), occasionally racing ahead for short distances when an opening presented itself, leaving in their wake strips of open pavement that the crowd reclaimed immediately amid whistles, angry gestures, and shouts:

"Coaches off the street!"

Only the mule-drawn streetcars—bursting with passengers, colored lanterns, and metallic clanging—were able to plow implacably ahead, straight through that human ocean, as majestically as battleships, their horns startling people with their sound, loud, hoarse, and uneven, the bells around the necks of the mules supplying a gratuitous note of playful high spirits. In the atmosphere that hung over the crowd, there was a neutral marriage of odors: the bitter smell of the people themselves, the resinous aromas of fire from the street vendors, and a soft warm breeze that purified the air, gently agitated the flags, banners, and torches, and seemingly in a hurry, swept away the clouds to reveal the sky with all its stars, making its own voluntary contribution to the patriotic independence-day illumination of this ancient metropolis of América.

They finally made it to a private dining room of the Café de Paris, where, as practiced libertines who understood the special properties of shellfish, they ordered a seafood dinner for everyone, and the girls, being who they were, believed that they had to find the food delicious, even though they had little experience with crabs, shrimp and other such creatures, so difficult to eat and so unpleasant to the unsophisticated taste buds of ordinary—and beneath it all, still quite uncouth—young women such as they. El Jarameño ordered pork ribs and a salad, apart.

"For me, some of them nice ribs," he said to the waiter, and turning to his friends, he added:

"Don't you laugh, see, because whenever I eat one of those things," he pointed to a gorgeous lobster whose long antennae extended out of the serving platter, "I get the idea that it's still alive inside me, pinching my guts with those claws." He looked a second time. "What an ugly bug . . . yuck!"

The murmur of the street was growing as, little by little, people filled the wide Plaza de Armas. Carriages passed more frequently now beneath the restaurant's dining-room balcony, onto which the members of Santa's party occasionally stepped to look in the direction of the plaza, which truly blazed with light.

Next, they heard the sound of fireworks, followed by a tremendous "aahhh" from the multitude, and the monster-concert began in the plaza. At the table in the Café de Paris, they served the food and uncorked the Pommery champagne, which inspired them to go so far as to speak of the Patria, without any of them being too sure of the true meaning of that abstraction. But it seemed disrespectful to have such a conversation in such a vulgar locale, with its stained carpet and vulgar, cushion-studded sofa, its electric light sprouting from a defunct gas fixture, its swaying bell cord with which to call the waiter, and its mirror scratched with a tangle of initials and dates, left there in unfortunate perpetual commemoration of alcoholic enthusiasms and love affairs unconfessable in any more transparent medium. And the behavior of the waiters, who never entered without knocking and never exited without carefully shutting the door behind them, seemed to make idealistic talk of the Patria even more hypocritical.

The revelers could not agree on a definition of the concept, hashing over formulas learned at school and various false notions heard or read somewhere or other. There were, of course, romantic toasts of a patriotic character over dessert: Everything for the Patria! And there were toasts from skeptics, too, strong-minded individuals in elegant tailcoats, who believed that in this modern age, New York City, with its elevated train, and Mexico City, particularly its central business district, why, they're basically all the same thing.

"What's your opinion, Jarameño? Is your Patria simply Spain, or is it the entire world?"

The women sat gravely, getting bored. Intermittently, random bits of music from the nearby Plaza de Armas floated in the balcony doors as did the awesome, breathing roar of the audience.

"Oh, it's got to be Spain, you know! But without any of those islands or overseas territories . . . and not even all of Spain, 'cause I never seen most of it. My Patria," continued el Jarameño, counting on his fingers, "let's see . . . Andalusia, my house, the grave of my parents, may they rest in peace, and the window with carnations and geraniums where I go to visit my sweetheart . . . that is my Patria!"

Applause and more Pommery greeted el Jarameño's simple, picturesque definition, and the torero, for his part, feigned exaggerated care with the ash of his cigarette, the better to view the effects of this peroration on Santa's pensive face. And their eyes met, and as always, his emerged victorious from the encounter and her eyes fled—in this case, to the mantel, which they had already thoroughly examined, and no doubt they called her long eyelashes down to defend them, because down they came, and Santa, slipping some in her seat, closed her cowardly eyes and rested her head on the back of the chair.

"Who'll let me bum a smoke? I'm the only one not smoking . . ."

After looking at watches, the party called for the check, which they more than covered with exaggerated shows of generosity, much pulling out and pocketing of wallets bulging with bills, and each man vying for the honor of paying by himself. El Jarameño offered Santa his arm with a decisive air.

"Be my date tonight, country girl, until after "the cries." Then you go your way, with whomever, and I go mine . . . deal?"

The jolting of the coaches ended up putting the two in close and prolonged contact that would have been difficult to avoid, had they tried, because every jolt was followed by another, worse one, and they ended up simply remaining in whatever position resulted, "not noticing" how much their bodies were in contact, his steely muscles and her provocative flesh. The lit tips of several cigarettes glowed in the darkness of the closed coach, resembling fireflies that had not managed to escape before the doors closed, and that, now trapped, whirled in desperation, periodically diving into the smokers' laps.

Meanwhile, the drivers found a way to enter the ocean of people that completely filled the Plaza de Armas. They followed the arrival of two marching groups, a teamsters' guild, and a company of firemen who began to penetrate the crowd four abreast, carrying flags, banners, and blazing torches that gave the impression of mythological beings, so furiously did they shake their heads, so copiously did their hair of flames spray sparks that floated, twisted, and finally died in the air. The coaches inched into the plaza behind the parade to a certain point at which all progress stopped. It was materially impossible to advance any further. Yet, from that forced anchorage, they had an excellent view of the great spectacle.

In the center of the plaza are the shade trees hung with decorative lanterns and the central kiosk emitting brilliant electric light. Next, along the tree-lined walk that leads to the palace of government, more lanterns strung along like illuminated garlands. Then, the old palace—severe, irregular, enormous. Only the sumptuous curtains of its balconies and the countless hydrogen gas jets inside glass bubbles that line the railings relieve the austerity of its façade. And on those same balconies, the heads of women in elaborately decorated hats intermixed with those of gentlemen without hats, moving in inaudible conversation. On the women's hats, the bird feathers flutter as if they longed to take to the air, and the artificial flowers tremble as if dreaming of flying away to take root elsewhere. These are the balconies of the celebrated Ambassadors' Room, which is absolutely bursting with blinding light, spilling torrents of excess illumination out of every opening, and the heads on the balcony belong to the privileged few who attend the great celebration in utmost comfort, by special invitation of some high official.

Only the middle balcony—the historical one with a bronze railing—although open—remains dark. A clock above it gives the hour, a quarter to eleven o'clock, and above the clock, high in the air, the flag pole and the national flag of Mexico flapping in the breeze under the stars. Beneath the middle balcony, a clearing in the crowd, several rows of seating occupied by ladies and gentlemen, and a pavilion for the gigantic military band, with more drummers and trumpeters lined up offstage to the left.

"Wow," declares el Jarameño, hanging half his body out the coach window, "this is really something."

Behind their coach is the old row of portals called Mercaderes, the historic venue of buying and selling, now interrupted by a new construction, the almost finished Mercantile Center, which has decorated its two completed floors with incandescent lights for tonight. To the right, the ancient city hall, massive, harsh, anachronistic, like the palace showing curtains at its balconies and extremely lit up without escaping the wrinkled and somber appearance of great age. Across from the city hall, defining the north side of the great square at the heart of Mexico City, the metropolitan cathedral: monumental, eternal, imposing, with its high towers, gray walls, and bold dome, a colossus of stone, which time and human passions cannot budge. The cathedral, too, is draped with colored fabric and hung with decorative lanterns, all of an old-fashioned, even antique variety, the lamps fueled by oil, the hangings faded, venerable, smelling of incense, who knows how many years old! To one side, the sacrarium, full of sacred relics and studded outrageously with architectural ornamentation of a century long past.

And everywhere around the Plaza de Armas, where temporary stalls have been erected to sell food and wine, there is the sound of frying and the smell of many fruits and the mass of bodies. One hears fragments of conversation, guitar arpeggios, babies crying, free-floating laughter, occasionally, a sinister outbreak of oaths and threats, finally, fights and reconciliations. There are no holes in this wall of sound, only the human herd, packed together, stamping its feet, explosively eager for the moment when it will shout its tribute to national independence.

Suddenly, a vibration runs through the restless multitude, agitating it even more. Then, a silence, frightening and exciting because it is so universal, the sort of silence that precedes something extraordinary. Inanimate objects seem to withdraw into themselves at this moment. One would say that the hundred thousand souls that fill the Plaza de Armas have fused into a single soul. Everyone, everything, is hushed—the musicians, the privileged guests in the balconies, the herd that floods the square. The crowd holds its breath watching the clock on the palace façade, eyes glued to the moving gears, hearts beating impatiently . . .

And, together, the clocks of the palace and the cathedral break that silence, first with bells indicating the four quarters of the hour, and then, with mechanical ponderousness, each clock tolls eleven o'clock. This process has hardly begun, however, when all at once the historical balcony with the bronze railings lights up and the president of the republic steps onto the balcony in a blaze of illumination, wearing across his chest the tricolor presidential sash, symbol of his anointment by the people. With noble gesture, he takes hold of a hanging bell cord and pulls it once, twice, producing a marvelous ringing, just like the bells of Dolores village must have sounded in days of yore when calling our forefathers to die so that our nation might live.

Golden confetti rains from the cathedral towers, their bells tumbling with jubilation. Fireworks fill the air, all the bands strike up our national anthem, and far away, in the armory, the cannons salute our national honor. The stars in the heavens blink as if holding back cosmic tears, moved by the spectacle of an entire people deliriously in love with their native land, a people who, at least on one night of each year, truly believes in itself and remembers that it is sovereign and powerful.

Some mothers hold their babies up above the multitude as if dedicating their blood to the Patria. From every mouth and every heart springs forth a loud, solemn cry, simultaneously a promise, a threat, a roar, a lullaby, and a paean of victory.

"Viva Mexico!"

And at that, the ocean of people spills out of the plaza into streets and avenues, following the various military bands that now play up-beat melodies. Tight knots of conversation form, many mouths drink from a single bottle. On the street corners, people dance to the rhythmless music of organ-grinders, and almost anyone might give the man next to him an abrazo, while reserving the right to quarrel with him and kill him shortly thereafter, when the overabundance of alcohol dims the conscience of both and drowns this rapturous feeling of brotherhood. Families picnic in the doorways of their houses, watching the crowd flow past, and, standing with his foot on the molding of a closed store front, a street singer plays the guitar surrounded by his buddies . . .

The coaches finally begin to move along with the people. In the one carrying Santa, el Jarameño, and the other couple, nobody says a word or smokes or chuckles . . . all of them are lost in reflection. Santa cries very softly, seemingly overcome in her sensitive femininity by the emotions of the moment.

"What're you crying for, gypsy girl?" El Jarameño asks her, leaning over to look in her face.

Santa cannot talk and instead points all around, indicating the plaza, what has just occurred within it, and the feeling that still remains in the atmosphere and in people's spirits. Then she puts her arms around the torero's muscular neck, pulls his head toward her, and between sobs, she murmurs:

"You told us that your Patria was a window with carnations and geraniums, no? Well, you're doing better than I am, because even though I'm in my own country, I can't call it mine. Right now all I've got for a Patria is Elvira's house, and later it will be another one, who knows where, and I'll always be a . . .

And she spelled the horrid, stigmatizing word on the window of the coach, as if spitting out something that had made her sick.

Four

Leaving aside the waiters, who are highly accustomed to the tumult, only a professional fighter would attempt to make his way through the tables surrounded by evening customers, or through the groups of men who down their drinks standing at the bar or elsewhere in bunches, not having found a seat, filling all available floor space in the three rooms that compose the Tivoli Central, a restaurant and bar, the city's well-known venue of risqué nightlife. After all, the fashionable establishment offers not just food and drink, no sir, but also a chance to dance, start a fight, and possibly get killed.

During the day, on the other hand, the place looks fairly deserted, with only a customer or two determined to eat the food that Tivoli employees serve reluctantly, at that hour, in dining rooms smelling of alcohol spilled on the floor, tobacco smoke that still clings to the walls and ceiling, and the faint scent of perfume that wafts by, informing us that a woman has been there, or who knows how many women or with whom. The perfume is, in fact, barely perceptible. The electric bulb that hangs from the ceiling sways very slightly because of the incessant comings and goings of so many flies that have made it their temporary home. The walls are covered with wall paper, scratched, wrinkled, or dirty here and there. The stained tables and the wobbly chairs maintain a strict silence about what, exactly, happened there last night or what will surely happen tonight. The whole establishment seems to be sleeping off the effects of its orgiastic exertions.

The sliding doors of the private dining rooms seem to yawn, as does the dance floor and the wide cantina. In the courtyard, the garden yawns with its sad, withered blooms, its flowerbeds trampled and muddied as if a herd of cattle had passed over them on its way to drink from the small fountain in the center. More than a fountain, the tiny dribble of water seems like a flood of tears provoked by deep, hopeless grief, and in the suspiciously-colored pool at its base float empty bottles, the butts of cigarettes and cigars, and occasionally, a lock of hair, a torn up photograph, or a comb hurled there by the anonymous hands of someone tormented by jealousy and hoping, by means of a sterile fit of spite, to achieve forgetfulness.

The morning passes slowly, heavily, and the afternoon, much the same. As sunset approaches, shadows begin to sneak into the garden like burglars who slip down from the tops of the enclosing walls, clustering initially in the corners so as not to be seen, and then, reinforced by many more shadows that come constantly slipping down the walls, advance together into the flower beds. There, they climb into the few, unhealthy-looking trees of the courtyard or bathe in the dirty water of the fountain before entering the restaurant and bar with a triumphant, menacing air, until suddenly, a lightning-like flash shatters them and sweeps them back into the corners in a large, black, shapeless heap. Their nemesis is the electric lighting: a powerful arc lamp hanging over the fountain in the middle of the courtyard, as if hovering on air, a profusion of electric bulbs in the cantina and the dining rooms, bulbs whose restless, luminous rays pursue their dark enemy determinedly out of every door and window into the night.

The interior of the building begins to stretch and awaken and—with the arrival of the waiters, who deposit their hats and look for their aprons in some dark cubbyhole, and of the chef and his assistants, who disappear into the kitchen and associated passageways without saying hello to anyone—the place comes alive once more. The bartender (a blond, blasphemous Italian, expert in potent punches) has put on his red fez and his starched jacket and, turning around to face the large mirror and the multicolored battery of bottles, he opens the cash register and begins to count the tokens that the waiters exchange for money. The waiters gather to do their own calculations, counting on their fingers or with a pile of coins in the palm of the hand, as the Italian piles the chips in rows, vomiting an oath every second. Clouds of dust and the rasp of a broom issue from the shabby dance floor, along with the loud yawns of the sweeper and the watchman who sleeps on the top floor of the establishment, which is also the location of the private dining rooms for the most important customers. The kitchen exudes provocative odors and, from time to time, crackles so loudly with flames that one might think the building had caught fire. The street doors stand fully open, replaced by grills that revolve to permit entrance or egress from the building. The street thrusts its noises in through the openings: the passing of coaches and streetcars, the clatter of horses' hooves, plenty of chatter and laughter and the cries of newspaper boys:

"Read all about it in *El Tiempo*! . . . The latest edition of *El Mundo*!"

And the great, lascivious city rouses and illuminates itself with excitement for another night.

The Tivoli Central commences its activities. The employees prepare for the battle that will engross them for hours as the various ground-floor rooms slowly fill with a public that is quiet and peaceful when the night is young, becoming gradually rowdier and more truculent as the night grows older and standards of comportment relax. Until midnight, everything remains orderly, customers eat calmly and drink slowly. At most, a woman may escape for a while from one of the private dining rooms to look for her lover, the one whom she does not charge for services rendered but who waits alone at a table in a corner, nursing an economical small beer. Urgent dialogue, interrupted by sickly caresses; she half sitting on his leg, he holding her fiercely around her uncorseted waist. She and he look into each other's eyes, their saddened faces quite close together, in mourning for the voluptuous pleasures that they have enjoyed together, but cannot enjoy tonight, because the girl has to rent herself to another, to anyone who pays. They beg for faithfulness and swear to be true. The woman rests her head on the man's shoulder, closing her eyes, and the man kisses her in the mysterious and variable place where he first kissed her on the night when he captivated her—the nape of her neck, her eyelids, her ear.

"You really won't dance with what's her name?"

"I swear I won't, I swear . . . but you've got to promise *me* . . ." and he whispers who-knows-what in her ear, something so depraved that not even a couple such as this wants to hear it said aloud.

Time flies, five minutes expire, and they must separate, putting an end to the scene. She gets up brusquely and hurries back to work, tearing herself away from the powerful magnet of his body, which she continues to contemplate from the doorway, hungering for him but resigned to not having him for now. Then, she runs away, hurling herself into the night, leaving the revolving doors spinning as if unsure whether to follow the fugitive or comfort the one left behind. Now, if this individual has a shred of decency, he will maintain a tragic pose after her departure, hat thrown back, hands grasping his hair, elbows on the table, gazing vaguely at the thin, snaking trail of beer that his beloved left behind when she escaped . . . If he is totally rotten, on the other hand, he will smile, not at the trail of beer, but at the wrinkled five-peso note that the woman has "forgotten" on the table.

The waiter (something of a philosopher, shall we say) approaches and begins to wipe up the spilled beer, taking orders.

"Another beer, small?"

Moments before one o'clock, the musicians appear in a compact line near the bar, holding their respective instruments, coats, and umbrellas. Several put their instrument cases on the bar, cases that because of their blackness and their odd shapes—containing a trumpet and a violin—suggest, perhaps, in this setting, coffins for deformed fetuses. The bartender who well knows what to serve them, jokes and smiles as he gets them their tequila, insulting them playfully, while the musicians no more than acknowledge him, calling him by the nickname that they themselves invented in honor of his nationality.

"How are you doing, Ravioli?"

The theaters have ended their shows and expelled their spectators. Here, too, incivility reigns. The employees hurry to turn out the lights and open the curtains of the spectators' boxes after only a few moments, releasing odors of humidity and various undetermined substances. They begin to close the outside doors, so that the laggards, leaving too slowly, will understand that it is all over. Did you pay to be entertained, and *were* you? Fine, then out of here, because nobody owes anybody a cent! People hurry out before the lights go off and the doors close, and the awaiting coaches swirl forward to receive them. Men whistle, horses snort, drivers shout. The police are there on foot wearing peeved expressions, giving directions more through gestures than words, which would not be heard anyway. Here one of them grabs a horse's bridle, there another one admonishes a driver or calls for help from his colleagues on horseback—who are stationed in pairs at every street corner—to come deal with the problem. Coaches and pedestrians, after a brief moment of jocular goodbyes, spread out through the streets of the city, headed for homes or cafés. The flow of people and coaches rouses sleeping neighborhoods, but their number diminishes quickly, as each person goes his own way and nocturnal silence regains its empire. The façades of theaters and places of diversion that once blazed with electric light stand in darkness.

Now Tivoli Central prepares itself. The waiters rub the marble tops of rows of empty tables that, like tombstones in a cemetery for ailing souls and sinning bodies, appear to await the fleeting epitaphs of fleeting loves soon to be inscribed on their shining surfaces in alcohol, tears, and cigarette ash by lovers who will come there to bury their money and dreams, their disappointments and invisible wounds. The chef loosens his apron, puts his hat more firmly on his head, turns on the backup burners, and grabs his frying pans. The blonde Italian bartender checks his stock and serving equipment. Entrance from now on is with cover charge. The sale of tickets starts—gentlemen for one peso, unaccompanied women free— as the musicians settle in behind their music stands and tune their instruments. A sign is hung over the dance floor to indicate the character of the first number, a danzón, and at exactly half past one o'clock, the place now packed, the danzón bursts forth like a tropical thunderstorm with the kettle drums and the trombone so loud that they rattle the window glass, trying to get out and reach passersby, who pause to turn their heads and smile, their nostrils dilating slightly in response to the titillating musical insinuations.

The police stationed inside the establishment glance at each other disapprovingly and, unable to arrest the irreverent harmonies, twirl the tips of their mustaches instead.

Santa, at the pinnacle of her personal ascendancy, the apogee of her firm, young flesh accessible to any man who wanted to try it, normally arrived last at these dances, escorted by a brilliant following of fashionable young fellows, the most select members of the city's Sport Club. She did not dance, but rather installed herself, surrounded by her court, at a table from which she enjoyed a perfect view of the spectacle. Her favorite table—which the waiters reserved for her against all comers and all fairness, their loyalty guaranteed by enormous gratuities—was just at the edge of the dance floor, with easy access to the bar, the garden, and the street door. Santa sat with her back against the wall, acting, looking, and sounding now like a woman of the world. One would say that not a trace of the village girl remained. Her style was impeccable, both makeup and clothing, her jewelry was of eighteen-karat gold and gems, and she smoked cigarettes imported from Egypt. She knew how to order a meal at a fancy restaurant, how to ask for Mumm champagne, extra dry, and how to reprimand the waiters.

She had gotten used—or rather, her customers had accustomed her— to getting up very late and taking a sponge bath, then having her hair done by a professional hairdresser, an old French woman who was also a manicurist and much esteemed by everyone from Elvira on down. Whenever she was sent for, a coach picked her up at the door: a closed coach at midday when she was invited for a cocktail at some bar with an excellent reputation that, nevertheless, discretely admits such women to closed dining rooms; an open coach when she went out for a ride in the afternoon, indolently reclining on the morocco leather seats, to breathe the pure air in the woods of Chapultepec, without any responsibilities beyond smiling from the seat of the coach as it passed at a trot by the door of the Sport Club, where all her admirers could see her with that day's beau. Wisely stoic, this fraternal group competed earnestly for Santa's favor, hanging on her every wink and glance, and alternating in her bed, rigorously keeping to one night for each fellow, utterly without conflict. Instead, the entire group of friends would go out together with Santa and whomever she belonged to that night. They enjoyed dinner in harmony and good company, and then went together to Tivoli Central or brothel hopping, with Santa as the trophy who belonged to all of them at once. At three o'clock in the morning, the hour at which such inveterate night owls typically begin to think of resting, they said their goodbyes, each giving Santa a kiss and patting her possessor on the back.

"Go and have a good time now, and I'll see you tomorrow when it's my turn," said the next in line, without any protest from her former or future possessors. And off they went in different directions or perhaps accompanied the couple to the door of Elvira's place, dark and quiet at that hour. The procedure resembled a primitive nuptial procession of ancient times, before women became a possession that men refused to share.

That is why Santa appeared nightly surrounded by an escort of wealthy champions wearing distinguished surnames and clothing tailored in London. Everyone knew that with her arrival champagne corks would begin to pop and the adjunct members of the party would begin to summon pretty girls from other tables, some of whom approached the distinguished group awkwardly, others, without any reservation, but all with the scarcely concealed resentment of their non-paying boyfriends, who almost did not let them go. Santa's party-within-a-party was just a little better behaved than most at the Tivoli Central, because, if it is true that even the most refined members adopted the generally wanton tone of the place, they did draw the line at physical violence, or at least bloodshed, making an effort to calm the confrontational impulses of Santa and her more pugnacious partisans, whose drunken insolence rivaled that of any other customers. Breaking glasses and plates was perfectly fine, in other words, but getting one's nose bloodied in a tussle with some nobody was not so good. Santa's free-spending group had Ravioli and the waiters on its side, as well as a number of the guardians of order, who found less inspiration in the faithful fulfillment of their civic duty than in the silver pesos of the gentlemen of the Sport Club.

The other customers looked askance at the phalanx of aristocrats around Santa, partly because they looked so longingly at Santa herself. The result was mutual antipathy and continual verbal sparring, loud (but coded) insults, and feigned, provocative laughter.

"Ravioli, send me a cigar in a tuxedo, 'cause it looks like they're in style," a troublemaker might shout, glaring in the direction of Santa's party.

"Ravioli, serve me a leg that doesn't stink of perfume, not like *those*," a girl might call out while looking straight at Santa, "a drumstick, I mean." (Her former client, now at Santa's side, had refused to acknowledge her that night, it seems, with so much as a nod.) Other times, Santa made fun of some professional colleague or other, garnering a salvo of gleeful guffaws from her various co-proprietors.

And on two or three occasions, so much accumulated alcohol exploded like a bomb amid howls of rage, knocking over tables, sending glasses flying through the air to shatter against the walls, splashing floors, staining clothing. Chairs were brandished over heads, and the vilest insults were hurled to and fro. On those occasions, as the waiters rushed to separate the gladiators, as the musicians watched from a prudent distance, and as the police struggled to restore order, Santa abandoned her recently acquired polish and sophistication, the tough country girl reappeared, and practically no force on earth could restrain her. Totally beside herself, she attacked the watchmen and even those of her own party, ignoring pleas, warnings, and threats, afraid of nothing. Using elbows and knees, she broke free from whoever surrounded her, twisting her provocative brown body, which acquired a steely hardness and the athletic curves of a Greek statue. Only occasionally did she fight with women. What had women ever done to her? Instead, her targets were men, whom she wanted to wound, to break, to mark and shame with her long, polished courtesan's fingernails, taking vengeance on whatever man stood within reach of her prostituted body, in repayment for the terrible blow she had received from the one who had abandoned her and escaped into her blurry memories of a violated virgin. Her fury was like the secret sediment of ancient, half-forgotten grievances that, when suddenly awakened from slumber, blindly topple, cruelly dismember, and implacably destroy whatever stands in their path, until finally, their energy spent, they lapse again into dormancy. In Santa's case, once a truce had taken hold and reconciliation had begun, she was the first to argue that nobody should be arrested and was the first to nurse the wounded warriors on every side. She usually ended up crying—half from exhaustion and half from sorrow—on the shoulder of the man to whom she belonged that night.

Only rarely did she dance, because she did not have a clue about the "Boston waltz" so much in vogue, nor had she gotten very far with danzones or related Caribbean rhythms that are danced with lascivious undulations of the torso, which the other girls tried to show her during off hours:

"You press your body really close to your man, like so, see? In the first part, there are lots of turns that you do almost in place, like so, see? Then, in the second part, you have to really relax your waist and let your hips go, like you're about to faint with pleasure and so you avoid your partner's advances by slipping from side to side and forward and back, like so . . . Come on, Hipo, play it right! We're teaching your sweetheart danzón . . ."

On certain afternoons when the band played at Tivoli, she had a wonderful time in the arms of one of her companions, massacring a waltz that the musicians dedicated to her, enjoying the enchantments of a danzón in the arms of some stranger. She laughed at her own ignorance, at her beginner's clumsiness, and at how the men gathered around to watch her, laugh with her, desire her, and applaud her.

"Bravo, girl! Bravo! You're ready for anything now!"

One thing she usually objected to, however, because she found it suspicious, was that on the nights when the partying at Tivoli lasted until dawn, blind Hipólito appeared in the bar at around four o'clock in the morning with the pretext of buying cigarettes or ordering drink that he then left untouched on the bar for hours, chatting on and on with Ravioli or the members of the band, ignoring the pleas of Jenaro, the boy who served as his guide and who could hardly stay awake due to the prolonged inaction and the lateness of the hour. Santa asked him point blank on one occasion, when she was particularly stimulated by the dancing and what she had drunk:

"Hipo, are you coming here to watch me? You know, I'd like it so much if someone took care of me like that . . ."

And the blind man, in a mocking tone, but squeezing her arm just above the elbow, answered her:

"Okay, how can a blind man be coming here to watch you? I come because I love this stuff, drinking, dancing, rowdy partying, I'm really into this stuff . . . right, Jenaro?" he added, interrogating the boy with at touch of the tip of his cane. But as the hands of avid partners pulled Santa back into the dancing and away from him, he added, whether in soliloquy or for the benefit of Jenaro, it is impossible to say:

"No I don't come to watch you, but to smell you and hear you and worship you, God help me . . ."

The matador, too, would put in an appearance in the wee hours of nights such as these, inevitably accompanied by a following of lesser toreros, who carried his sword or exercised other subordinate functions in the bullring, and, even at Tivoli Central called el Jarameño *maestro*, regarded him with singular awe, and served and obeyed him automatically.

The guys in pigtails had their own style, clean shaven, hat cocked to one side, pearls, coral, and rhinestones the size of garbanzos gleaming on the front of their embroidered shirts. They entered the place giving and receiving greetings, left and right, showing their teeth in rigid smiles, thumping the floor with their walking canes, many rings on their fingers, their pants tight, their boots shiny and black. Each sported a thick gold chain that sprouted from the vest pocket, swinging heavily and its emerald studs glinting in the raw, late-night incandescent lights. Their jackets were black and their eyes blacker, the expressive and passionate eyes of leisurely Arabs who live for women and weapons, horses and bulls.

Greeted and called from tables all around, admired by men and women, waiters and musicians, the toreros made of their entrance a kind of triumphal progress. Even Ravioli had a soft spot for them, and the police leaned against the wall to get out of their way. The toreros, haughty and boastful, accustomed to the applause of the bullring, basked in the warm welcome, and circulated through the bar and around the dance floor before taking their place at the round table in the corner, where they asked for cigars, served themselves glasses of wine, and began to converse noisily, knowing that they would be the object of everyone's attention, the center, pride, and splendor of the party. They never failed to be encircled by admirers, principally of the fairer sex. But how difficult it was to get them to dance! They sneered at the undulations of the danzón and paid scant attention to admirers of either sex. Instead, as they drained glass after glass of Spanish wine, their nostalgia grew, melancholy memories loomed in their Arabian eyes, and they felt the tender tug of their homeland in their hearts, dreamed of crisp dawns in the villages of Andalusia, of twilight conversations at the window grates of Andalusian beauties. They were not good singers, but at these moments one of them, the least tone deaf of the lot, would sing a song of home, and the others would vigorously keep time, with clapping hands, of course, but also by beating a rhythmic accompaniment with their walking canes on the floor and with empty glasses on the marble table tops, punctuated with shouts of *olé* and other expressions of encouragement:

"That's it . . . now . . . that's the way!"

And then, waxing sentimental and poetic, they all took turns singing verses, someone about his mother, someone about his sweetheart, someone else about prison. There was a death and a cemetery in almost every verse. They became increasingly absorbed in their song, for that reason paying scant attention to friends and lovers. They sang at first with a puerile desire to garner applause, a bit theatrically. Later, in the grip of their memories, they closed their eyes as they sang the intense lyrics, so better to see inside of themselves. El Jarameño stood on his dignity as matador, a headliner in the city's bullfight billing, and mainly just drank and announced judgments to which everyone else agreed.

"That's the way to sing a *malagueña*! No kidding!"

Aware that el Jarameño went to Tivoli to see her, and only her, Santa prohibited her elegant followers from approaching the matador.

"Go listen to them if you like, but I'm staying at my own table. I hate that weird flamenco singing!"

She lied, of course, when she said that she hated the toreros' singing. Why, if she hated it, would she hardly reply to the flirtatious comments of her rich-kid followers? Why would she become nostalgic and even sigh aloud, the way she did when the toreros sang, and forget she was holding her champagne glass in mid air? El Jarameño turned from time to time toward Santa, who, like a coward, refused to meet his gaze and slightly shrugged her shoulders to indicate that she remained unimpressed.

Hipólito, who rarely endured the entire repertoire, always left suddenly, without saying goodbye to Ravioli, whose assessment of the toreros' singing he basically shared. Together, they cheerfully and bitingly critiqued the singers:

"I'm from the land of opera, Hipo. This caterwauling isn't for me!"

"I've had it too—with the caterwauling *and* the caterwaulers, principally the caterwaulers. I'm out of here."

Irate, waving his cane, he grasped the shoulder of Jenaro, who stood sleepily, shivering without a coat, his arms crossed against the cold wind of the early morning.

"Did Santita see us, Jenaro?" Hipólito asked the boy in the deserted street.

"She sure did, from the time we got there."

"It would almost be better if she hadn't. What can she think of me?"

Jenaro fell silent, not understanding why Hipólito was so concerned about the opinion of a woman like Santa.

"Did the cat get your tongue?" insisted the blind man irritably. "I asked you what Santa must think of me."

"Figure it out tomorrow. What do I know about it?" concluded Jenaro, risking the thump on the head that normally rewarded answers like that one.

And wrapped in silence, both of them, they traversed the dark streets to the one called San Felipe Neri where they lived in a house with an enormous old-fashioned entrance way, a house that was slowly sinking into the sidewalk because of its advanced age, with short, habitable spaces, "between floors," in the colonial style, and balconies on the third story.

As Hipólito headed home, Santa began to look with greater favor on the singing toreros, who finally joined tables with Santa's young aristocrats and kept the party going long after the Tivoli employees locked the street door against the first hints of dawn and the curious gaze of early rising passersby. When the gathering began to dissolve, though, it happened quickly, as if the clubmen had suddenly become ashamed of their company or themselves. They broke and ran like an army suddenly convinced of its inevitable defeat. The toreros, on the other hand, took leave of their elegant new friends with the marked familiarity normal after an extended bout of drinking. Like the prostitutes, they were in no hurry, disorder and excess being their natural milieu. They said their goodbyes on the curb, their girls sleepily cloaked in men's jackets, reclining their heads on a strong shoulder from time to time, the toreros in knots, here and there, leaning against a storefront, disputing fine points of their art in thick accents close to each other's faces.

During more than one of these predawn farewells, Santa thought that she saw Hipólito—surely in a dream, though. It seemed as if he had been waiting for her to come out but, embarrassed to be caught doing something so silly, he hurried away into the shadows led by Jenaro, who trotted along, arms across his chest and trembling with cold, their silhouette etched in black against the pale gray light of dawn that sifted gently down on to the pavement. He could have saved himself the effort of fleeing! He was trying to hide his poorly clothed form, hoping to be taken for someone else, not suspecting that to be totally impossible for anyone with eyes, so much did he stand out with his guide boy and uncertain gait, his torso thrown back and his cane groping forward, his steps halting in spite of his obvious haste. Seeing him made Santa experience a deep commiseration that was not without touches of satisfaction and gratitude, and if, as often occurred during the predawn farewells, el Jarameño repeated once again his continual question:

"When, Santa?"

"Never!" she responded, with redoubled fervor and resolution.

Something happened during one of those stormy nights in Tivoli, when Santa had just installed herself with her escort of admiring gentlemen at the table reserved for them by prodigious gratuities. On this night, Santa felt really good, almost deliriously happy, and her court idolized her more devotedly than usual, fighting over the kisses that her red lips refused to no man, those tempting lips that allowed themselves to be crushed by dry, hard kisses flaming with lust. Her entire following was hungry for her—her beau for the evening, and last night's beau, and tomorrow night's beau all in attendance—and she considered herself queen and flower of the city's brilliant, corrupt nightlife. She felt herself to be the empress of the ancient, imperial metropolis bathed by lakes and guarded by volcanoes but steeped in sin, stained by the concupiscence of bygone races and dead civilizations that have left us precise but mystifying reminders of their primitive refinements, stained by the lust of brutal conquerors and later waves of blonde-haired invaders, all of whom have loved and slaughtered with equal energy, stained, finally by the complex and perverted sensualism of the modern age. All the male inhabitants of the city, it seemed— fathers, husbands, and sons—pursued and adored her, proclaiming themselves fortunate, indeed, if she consented to allow them access to her body, the universally sought location of true, if ephemeral, earthly delight.

On that night, a totally unexpected incident occurred.

"What's today's date?" Santa inquired. "I think I've never felt so happy!"

And at that very moment she saw Esteban and Fabián enter the bar dressed in black—her two brothers, whom she had not seen since the day they drove her away.

They saw Santa immediately, surrounded by her elegant court of young gentlemen in white ties and stylish dinner jackets. Despite the social supe-

riority indicated by the sartorial splendors of the clubmen, the two workers were not intimidated. They strode toward the glittering assemblage
without taking their eyes off Santa, who simply waited, pale and paralyzed, ceasing to pay any attention to the young men around her, her eyes
those of a frightened doe, growing wider than ever, her chest palpitating,
her mouth half open, her back against the wall . . .

"Santa," said Esteban dryly, "we've come to have a word with you."

Not a single protest was heard from Santa's elegant sycophants. The
only person to rise was their queen, clumsily, with a humble attitude,
bumping into the elbows and tripping over the feet of her half-dozen lovers as she made her way out from behind the table. In the middle of the
barroom floor, she hesitated between the two doors leading to the street
and the courtyard with its garden and fountain.

"Not here," she said to her brothers, "better in the garden where nobody will hear us."

And out went the three of them, Santa in the lead, covered with jewels
and silk, Fabián and Esteban behind, dressed in mourning clothes.

The three of them stand together, now, in the garden, well illuminated
by its arc lamp and by rays of light that escape from windows and doors
onto the wilted grass. From time to time, fast-moving waiters cut across a
corner of the garden carrying trays of steaming delicacies that leave their
spicy aromas in the air. Far away, two figures are conversing, and the echo
of their conversation floats by unintelligibly. Nearer is the form of a man
holding onto a tree trunk, probably quite drunk, bent far over and staring
fiercely at the ground. From the bar, the dance floor, and the private dining rooms, various sounds can be heard: drunken laughter, corks popping,
stray chords. And the central fountain blubbers softly its weak but steady
flow of uncontainable tears.

Esteban, the eldest, is the one who speaks, as Fabián nods and Santa
gazes at them both.

"Don't worry. We're not going to keep you long and reduce your profits too much. We've come here from the village because we think it's our
duty. We arrived on the 8:40 train and have spent hours looking for you
in all those disgusting dives like the one where you live, hussy . . . oh, excuse me, I forgot that we don't care anymore what you are and don't need
to insult you. Soon we'll leave you alone, all alone . . . So anyway, we're
worn out from looking and from talking to your . . . to those poor women
who keep asking for money for drink and I don't know what all else. In
most places they've never heard of you, but finally someone recognized

the description and sent us to the house where you live. They couldn't stop laughing at us there. If it weren't for a blind piano player who asked us if we are truly your brothers who work at the Contreras textile mill . . . how the hell does he know that? Did you tell him? . . . Why don't you answer?"

Esteban's tone softens somewhat as Santa continues to look at the ground.

"Well, anyway, he took us aside but wouldn't tell us anything until we swore, both of us, that we did not mean to hurt you . . . no Fabián? Then he explained to us about this place, Tivuli or whatever it's called. Who is that guy, huh? What's he got to do with you?"

Santa remained mute. Her heart would not calm down, nor was her throat prepared to utter a sound. She suspected that her brothers were about to tell her something extraordinarily serious, and she hardly dared to change her posture, hoping that if she stayed perfectly still and submissive, the news might not be so terrible, that it might hurt her, sure, but not so much as the news that she could not even bear to consider, even though she anticipated its horrible, inexorable, wrenching truth.

"Well, Santa," continued Esteban after a moment, suddenly feeling a bit sorry for her but delivering the news point blank, "mother died night before last, and we buried her today, there, in our cemetery, beside don Bibiano and Angela's little boy, to the left as you enter, under the flowering vine, right by the corner where don Próspero planted the willow, remember?"

It was not possible for Esteban to continue talking, nor for Fabián and Santa to continue listening. Unconsciously, they took each other's hands, and the three of them leaned against the wall, to which Santa pressed the bare skin of her back, left uncovered by her evening gown, and Fabián and Esteban inclined their robust, black-clad shoulders. The three of them wept: the two men, serenely, without handkerchiefs, allowing their large tears to roll slowly down their cheeks into their beards; Santa, like a woman suffering intensely, wracked by sobs, with a great profusion of tears that, having saturated her lace handkerchief, she wiped from her face with the quilted lining of her splendid silk jacket. One of her elegant admirers appeared at the door between the bar and the courtyard, wondering what had become of Santa, but after contemplating the scene from a distance, he quietly returned to the table. The drunk embracing the tree began to vomit noisily as the orchestra played another danzón, the dining rooms resounded with shouts and laughter, and the fountain continued to sputter in the center of the garden.

Esteban was the first to recover and, noticing that Santa was holding his hand, he withdrew it and obliged Fabián to do the same. Santa understood, and raised her hands to cover her face without ceasing to cry. Fresh from contemplating his recent loss, Esteban's thoughts had turned again to Santa, to what she had become, to what her luxurious attire made so plain and public. He remembered the sad end of old Agustina, who died disconsolate because her daughter was not at her side to comfort her during her agony. The memories revived Esteban's anger, and aware that certain onlookers had detected something unusual and were trying to discover the nature of their conversation, he turned to Santa and spoke quickly, hoarsely, with knitted brow:

"Mother, poor thing, did not curse you. She called for you. Understand? She called for you and told us that, if we saw you, we should say that she had forgiven everything . . . hear? Everything! And when she was dying and gave us her blessing, she asked God to protect you, too, just as much as the two of us who were there kneeling at her side . . . So now we've told you, and we'll go. But if our mother did not curse you, Santa, *we* do! Hear? Don't ever look for us or even think about us ever again. As far as you're concerned, we're dead, too . . . and may God help you . . . Come on, Fabián, let's go!"

And the two implacable brothers walked out of the establishment, solemn, erect, vengeful, without looking back at Santa, who found no words with which to defend herself but felt the impulse to follow them and implore them not to curse her, to feel at least, if not affection, then pity, a little bit of pity . . .

Without caring what her wealthy friends might think, Santa went out into the street, but she did not see her brothers. The great urban whirlpool had swallowed them up. And just as a few minutes before she had felt herself to be a queen, an empress, she now felt like what she really was: a bit of human mud, a clod of earth, pestilent and miserable, gradually disintegrating and dropping dirt as it gets kicked around. But why, dear Lord, does a lump of mud have a heart and a conscience? So miserable did she feel that, gripping the grate of a nearby window, she threw back her head and gazed at the stars in the heavens, the only place that might offer her some comfort . . .

But comfort came, in fact, from much lower down—from Hipólito, who, when he finished playing piano that night at Elvira's, went to Tivoli, and hearing from Ravioli about the arrival of the two men in black and the disappearance of Santa, began to imagine who knows what terrible scenarios and rushed out to search the neighboring streets and nearby houses of prostitution, the places that he was likely to find her under normal circumstances.

"Are you sure, Ravioli, that she left?"

"Yes, yes. Epigmenio opened the door for her about fifteen minutes ago."

"Let's go, Jenaro, my boy, and keep your eyes peeled!"

When they located Santa, when Jenaro recognized her at a distance and said so, Hipólito stopped short.

"Wait a minute and let me get my breath, you savage. You've been pulling me along at a full gallop!"

Jenaro laughed at the consternation of his bossy master, who had suddenly turned tremulous and tentative.

"Santita," murmured Hipólito as he approached the girl, "what has happened?"

"Oh, Hipo, I'm so glad you've come," she said, throwing her arms around his neck without the slightest hesitation, shaking anew with sobs, dissolving once more in a flood of tears.

"But, why are you so upset, Santita? What has happened?" replied Hipólito, without even putting his arms around her, despite the tempting opportunity.

And upon learning of the death of Agustina and understanding that Santa did not want to see—or sleep with—anybody, which might cause serious problems were she to return to Elvira's, he delicately suggested a course of action.

"Of course, you're right, Santita . . . losing your mother is . . . well . . . you shouldn't go back to the house tonight. Sleep tonight at a hotel, just you and your sorrows. Tomorrow, you can decide what to do next. Jenaro, look for a cab!"

Even more delicately, during the momentary absence of the boy, unable to restrain himself, Hipólito kissed Santa's hands—just a kiss or two, that's all—delicate, respectful kisses that barely brushed the silky skin of the luckless prostitute. Then he helped her into a coach, recommended a hotel, paid the driver tip and all, and sent her on her way.

"I'll pay, Santita. I'm sure you don't have change, and what does it matter?"

And he stood still for a moment after her departure, as if fastened to the sidewalk, his eyebrows twitching and his lips, too. Jenaro, who could not help being interested in these unusual events, even began to wonder whether the blind man might not be praying . . .

ONLY GOD KNOWS what went through Santa's mind during that seemingly eternal night of solitary grief in the Hotel Numancia, where she remained in bed, more drowsing than sleeping, until eleven o'clock the next morning. When she finally pressed the buzzer to call for a chambermaid, one quickly appeared in the middle of the room without taking off her cap.

"Should I bring up coffee? What kind of bread do you want with it?" inquired the chambermaid.

"I don't care. It's all the same to me. Bring me paper and a pen, though, and call a messenger. Oh, and open the door to the balcony before you leave . . . not so much . . . there, that's it . . ."

"I brought it from the Café Cosmopolita," announced the maid when she returned carrying a tray with coffee, sugar, and a piece of French bread split lengthwise and buttered. "It's the best, that's what the toreros who are always in there say, anyway. The butter is from Toluca and the bread is toasted. Do you want me to move a table over here? At the front desk they sent for a messenger, and I asked them to send up a pen. Do you want cold or hot water for the washstand?" She had finished serving the much-pondered breakfast and asked the last question as she lifted the pitcher that stood in the empty washbasin.

Santa paid little heed to the servant's chatter, nodding in absent-minded assent to everything. After awaking to rude remembrance of the scene last night, she felt even worse at noticing that, no matter how hard she tried to concentrate on the loss of her sainted mother, whose virtues she dutifully enumerated, her thoughts tended to go sliding away in every direction, even toward quite trivial and totally unrelated matters. Didn't they slide off, in fact, as the servant chattered away, toward el Jarameño? And in Santa's efforts to counteract that slide, she had to go where it had gone and naturally ended up thinking much longer than she intended to about that irksome matador . . .

When her melancholy returned, she wrote a few lines to her colleague la Gaditana:

" . . . I'm in a very bad, sad way. See you this afternoon, let Pepa know or Elvira. Please send the messenger back with the darkest dress you can find in my room and let me borrow a black shawl . . ."

She sealed the letter, made a bundle of the clothes that she had been wearing the night before, and slipped between the sheets. Returning to her mental solitude, this time she easily guided her thoughts to the place where she wanted them to go, down the road to her village, Chimalistac, and the little white house of her childhood, her mother and brothers, her birds and flowers, her morning communions in the crumbling little chapel with its worm-eaten bell tower and its string of swallow nests like mossy clay pots under the eves. She directed her steps from her own house through the gardens of relatives and childhood friends. It all seemed so fantastic, as if it came not from her own experience but from someone else's. Oh, it was beautiful, alright, but Lord how far away . . . somewhere far beyond good and evil, far from purity or prostitution, far, far away. In some ways, the distance pleased her, because it meant that, if she could not go back, it was not necessarily because she was being punished by an invisible, almighty power . . . But what if she *were* being punished, and what if she begged forgiveness, prostrated herself before that invisible power?

"No, no, I couldn't go there," she mumbled into her pillow, hiding her face, fairly certain that the invisible power was, indeed, watching.

The ensuing struggle was brief, the sort that occurs in ordinary people who do not think profound theological thoughts and let themselves be guided by instinct. And Santa's instinct told her to go to a church, light a candle for the soul of her deceased mother, and pray for her eternal rest— everything that she had been taught to do for the dead. She thought that it was mortally sinful for a prostitute to enter a church. But the deceased was her mother, and she had to pray for her. Was she going to pray for her mother's soul in a brothel or a hotel? How horrible, oh saints in heaven! No, she wasn't. And, anyway, she had begun to want to change her life . . . yes, change her life, and why not? Or was *that* the only way that she could make a living? Women made a living in all sorts of ways, after all, women abandoned by their seducers, just as she had been, women who sometimes had children, too. It was time to do like them and get to work, because she was plenty strong and healthy. What would she do? . . . Washing? Ironing? Housekeeping? . . . No, not housekeeping. She wouldn't be a maid for any amount of wages. But anything else, yes, whatever turned up . . . And she went on planning her future repentance and recovery, which she would accomplish much more slowly than her fall, admittedly, but which she would not waver in completing finally, by dint of sustained effort. True, the path would not be easy to tread. So thorny did it appear, even before starting out, that she felt somewhat daunted. And true, her meditations on projects of reform were occasionally interrupted by quick images of various not-so-disagreeable friends from her life of sin, men who might enable her to continue in an infallible health and wellbeing that only an already compromised mind like Santa's could ever believe in: Rubio, for instance, who had repeatedly offered to make her his mistress in a house of her own; the young fellow who treated her breathlessly, as if she were his fiancée; the old man who asked for very complicated indecencies that she thought were fun. Even the image of Hipólito flitted past for reasons that she could not understand, since the blind man offered nothing, especially in contrast to the other whose image crossed the path of reform most insistently and disruptively: el Jarameño. How annoying the torero was, with his relentless pursuit of her! . . . All right, then, so that's it? . . . That's it. A plan! Get rid of all of them, and, if necessary butt her head against the church wall!

Because she lay turned toward the wall with her eyes closed, lost in thought as she elaborated her plan, Santa did not hear when the chambermaid entered and deposited on a chair the dark dress and shawl sent by la Gaditana. When she found the clothes suddenly within reach, as if by magic, she took it as a sign to find a church immediately. She would go, yes, she would! Feverishly, she splashed the tepid water of the washbasin on her eyes, swollen from much weeping and little sleep. She dressed quickly, and, extracting a wad of bills from one of her stockings, paid the bill.

It was about four o'clock in the afternoon and the downtown streets were packed with vehicles and pedestrians, the pavement still wet from the sprinkling of water wagons provided by the city government in hopes of controlling the dust. Commercial employees hustled back and forth, drenched in the rays of the declining sun that angled down over the tops of high buildings into Revillagigedo, Independencia, and Tarasquillo Streets, in the direction that Santa was going.

Without thinking about what she was doing, she entered the pastry shop next door to the hotel, where the employees were clean, pretty, and friendly, and wore light-colored aprons:

"What do you want, señora?"

What did she want? She wanted to be just like them, or at least, the way that she imagined them to be: decent girls who worked long hours, lived at home, and loved their faithful boyfriends . . . Blushing, she bought candy because she thought she should buy something, and nothing else occurred to her, and, carrying the package, waited for an avalanche of streetcars to pass before going down Espíritu Santo and Santa Clara Streets to the church of the latter name.

Out front was a maimed beggar who extended his hand and Santa gave him a whole silver peso, put the shawl over her head, and walked up to the door, excited by the beggar's marvelous incantations:

"May Our Holy Mother of Guadalupe reward you, niña! Praised be the power of the divine sacraments!"

She set foot in the great doorway of the temple just as its bells peeled and the organ thundered a formidable hymn with something not quite human in its sober, imposing melody. Feeling overcome, Santa looked for a pretext to delay her entrance and went back to speak to the beggar, who was hurriedly about to leave in the belief that Santa had given him an entire peso by mistake.

"Wait, wait," Santa told him, "take this, too. It's candy." And she handed him the package.

Then, with a submissive air, her head bowed, her eyes half closed, making a supreme effort, she entered the church and ensconced herself in a corner between a confessional and the carpeted platform in front of a lateral altar. She would have liked to enter on her knees and had not done so only in order not to attract attention, so she kneeled now, in her hiding place, flustered by her emotions and the bells that the acolytes kept ringing and ringing, feeling annihilated, above all, by the organ that poured forth grave, trembling, sustained notes with otherworldly accents that reverberated in the nave and dome, producing in Santa both hopes of celestial pardon and fears of divine punishment. Either way, the very severity and majesty of the music made her feel miserable and unfortunate, feeble, tiny and alone.

The sensation made her want to pray even more.

"Prayer was made for us," she thought, "the miserable ones who were not able to resist temptation and have more need of mercy." She opened her eyes wide to look at the crucifix on the principal altar and listened with delight to the organ that seemed, now, to repeat the promise of mercy and pardon.

Lord God, what she saw!

She saw a priest standing with his back to the gilded altar that bristled with candles. He had raised the curtain of damask on the crystal and onyx tabernacle and held in his hand the monstrance with its sculpted rays so dazzling that they seemed forged of pieces of the same sun that entered the windows of the dome above him and sifted down onto the padre's gray hair and his embroidered vestments like golden pollen. The white humeral veil, glistening with gold thread, rested on his thin shoulders, and he had wrapped his hands in the ends of it so that impure human flesh would not touch the monstrance that contained the holy sacrament—the consecrated communion host—as he slowly lifted it up for the adoration of the faithful who had prostrated themselves before the altar.

Santa felt ecstatic, ready to die that instant, unmindful of her sins, face to face with the God of infinite goodness and mercy. And she regressed immediately to the practices that she had learned as a pious country girl, lowering her forehead to the church floor and kissing it over and over, with her fresh, full sinner's lips.

She was hardly aware when the organ and the bells fell silent, hardly registered the shuffle of footsteps when groups of the faithful departed from the temple or the scraping sound of benches and chairs being moved thereafter. Sitting up, filled with hope, she folded her hands and prayed fervently, with visions of her mother and her little white house in the village. So she did not notice at all the entrance of a battalion of little girls and half a dozen distinguished ladies—presidents, secretaries, and treasurers of some confraternity or lay association—who stared at her in disgust and pointed her out with angry whispers to a cassock-wearing chaplain. No, she did not notice these things, nor could she know whether these fine ladies had anything on their consciences, such as the adultery so common and so tolerated among aristocrats such as they.

The fine ladies, on the other hand, had recognized Santa for exactly what and who she was. Wasn't she the one who shamelessly bewitched their fathers, husbands, and sons with her firm, delicious flesh? Hadn't she exhibited herself enough in theaters and places of public diversion where señoras and señoritas (whom Santa ignored completely with the Olympian disdain of an empress without rivals) had memorized her face and her name?

Calling the sacristan, the fine ladies, the feathers on their hats atremble, raised their gloved index fingers in the air and issued an imperious order to the fellow, who stood with his hands pressing against his temples. The little girls looked now at their irate protectors, now at the kneeling woman, against whom the sacristan finally directed his vituperation:

"Get yourself out of here this instant!" he said loudly to Santa, who looked at him, dazed, from the depths her prayerful mysticism, without quite understanding.

"Get myself out of here . . . why? Do you own this church? Churches are for people seeking pardon, too!"

"Don't make me throw you out!" declared the sacristan, who knew that he was in a position of strength.

"Let me stay a little while longer, please," begged Santa. "I'm praying for my mother who has died and asking God to forgive me . . ."

"Oh, sure, your mother, I'll bet! Are you going, or should I call a policeman right now?"

The threat intimidated Santa. The police? No, no. The police were her terror and the terror of all girls like her.

"I'll go," she sighed. "You're right. Women like me shouldn't be in places like this . . . I'll go . . ."

Without crossing herself or putting the shawl back over her head, from which it had slipped, and followed by the sacristan who looked at her with feigned outrage, Santa walked out of the church and went to stand beside one of the columns in the atrium.

"No, not here, either," decreed the officious sacristan. "Out of here! Out in the street!"

Mute and obedient, Santa stepped into the street, where her stunned attitude attracted stares from passersby unaware of what had happened.

She alone knew why they had thrown her out, she alone. She was a harlot, a harlot who had lost her mother, now doubly and irredeemably an orphan.

Five

Like others of the guild to which it belonged, Elvira's house permitted illegal liberties that always redounded in the long run (when not immediately) to the detriment of the clients. For example, the house sold its alcoholic beverages at exaggerated prices, and the medical inspection that the girls were required to undergo each week at the municipal hospital did not occur there at all, but rather, in the comfort and tranquility of the brothel, where it was entrusted to the hands of very well paid private physicians who sometimes turned a blind eye to what they saw, or should have seen. Other examples abounded.

Santa, who had become Elvira's favorite because of the fat profits that she produced for the house, hardly came out of her room during the first few days after losing her mother and being thrown out of church, so she was permitted to skip her weekly examination, and the trusted doctor failed to write the word "healthy" beside her name in the official register. But after a week she reappeared in the parlor, slightly sullen, aggressive, and absent-minded, but apparently, in view of the abandon with which she surrendered herself to men and liquor, now resigned to her sad career and determined to drain the bittersweet cup to the dregs.

"Santita, slow down," Hipólito said to her. "If you trip and fall, it's going to hurt you a lot."

"If I fall, you say? If I fall . . . ? How much further could I fall, Hipo?"

"Don't be mad at me, Santita. Go ahead, then. I'm sure Pepa's thrilled!"

Santa did go ahead, in a sort of crescendo, never lacking opportunities or invitations. It seemed that suddenly, and in obedience to determining impulses from within, she began to lose the goodness that she had retained during the first months of her fall from grace, certain delicate attitudes and preferences, a reluctance to do certain things, that now died and descended into the depths of her desperation and disenchantment amid the stink of decomposing purity, dreams, and ideals. There was nothing to do but bury these items, because they were dead, and, condemned to be a provider of pleasure, she could not carry them around or hide them in her body brimming with life. She explained it to Hipólito, who now merited her entire confidence:

"I feel like I'm forced to do everything I do, like I'm a big rock and somebody stronger than me gives me a kick from the top of a high slope, and down I come crashing and nobody can stop me, and I bounce and bounce and a piece gets knocked off, and God knows what I'll be like when I get to the bottom, if I ever get there.

"Do you know why I think about rocks rolling down hills? Because I did that a lot when I was a little girl, in the Pedregal. I felt sorry for the rocks as I watched them go down the hill, smashing into bigger rocks and sharp outcroppings that spun them and split them but didn't stop their fall, bouncing on and on, through leaves and branches and over roots that didn't stop them either, getting smaller and smaller, becoming almost invisible, and I'd grab on to something solid and look and look and try to see them hit bottom, and then I'd lose sight of them and only hear the muffled blows continuing until . . . well, until I couldn't hear anything more . . .

"And I think about rocks because that's what people think *we* are, rocks without feelings or anything. You've got to be made of rock to do this job and bear all the insults and scorn that come with it. You saw what happened to me in the church!"

"Excuse me, Santita, but I already told you that wasn't right. How awful! If people didn't look down so much on your profession, I'd tell you to go complain. A sacristan can't throw you out of church just like that! Gosh, not even a bishop . . ." declared Hipólito, not very sure of where he was going. "But the church thing doesn't mean that you have to commit suicide the way that you're doing . . . because, Santita, listen to me, this life may be terrible and bitter and all that, but there's nothing else for it. Look at me, blind and everything, and I don't give up. Don't be so reckless," he added, starting to get upset and walking to the piano so that she wouldn't perceive it, "because who knows if your fate isn't to make some man happy, some man who needs you in order to be happy."

Santa's expression revealed little because, although she did understand the poor musician's discreet allusion to himself, she understood also that she did not love him, not at all. Oh, she did like him and pity him and feel grateful to him, but without anything like carnal interest. Physically, he almost repulsed her with those iris-less eyes of a bronze statue without patina.

Rubio, on the other hand, the man who had offered to make her his mistress in her own house, did appeal to her, and greatly. For him, although she did not realize it, Santa felt the fascination that people of plebeian origin naturally experience upon finding themselves on an equal basis with a social superior, the sort whom common folk regard with respect, and even awe, however unfounded—a liege lord who occasionally descends, because of a lifetime of vice, to the level of his vassal. In such cases, little remains of the previous lordship or vassalage, only the eternal desire that regenerates the world, that eventually pushes the two into each other's arms, obliging them to forget age and social distance. Rubio, moved by secret marital frustrations that related, not to matters of honor, but rather, to the temperament of his wife (upon whose fortune he depended totally, according to testimony rendered by other Sport Club members under Santa's intelligent questioning) had grown fond of Santa, but he did not really love her. He stubbornly persisted in his proposal to her because of insistent masculine habits of the flesh.

Santa did not let him lose hope, of course not! Instead, she asked for time, a few more months to try each other—as if she could be picky, with the life she led!

And as far as el Jarameño was concerned (this *did* bother her) the standoff continued, she denying herself to him, he becoming ever more ardent. He did not beg anymore, nor ask her "when." His new tactic was to try to spend as much time near her as possible. Spurred by an instinctive longing, an insatiable appetite, he appeared at all hours, seemed never to leave the brothel, courting Santa's prettiest colleagues, even sleeping with them without touching them, in an effort to awaken her jealousy.

How bitterly, from a distance, did Hipólito observe this amorous struggle! How quickly did he see, in spite of his physical blindness, that Santa was destined not only to surrender herself to the torero, but to adore him so much that the musician would have counted himself the happiest man on earth to receive half—no, a hundreth part—of her adoration. Because he could no longer doubt that he, Hipólito, loved Santa with all his four senses, with all his heart, and with all his unfortunate body. And what he suffered was a horror, because, even though he had never seen himself, he could guess just how unattractive he was. The human rags, almost undeserving to be called women, in whom he had vented his fiery desires, had confessed as much to him during the spasms of the carnal act, as if overcome by fright:

"Oh, Hipo, how ugly you are!"

And Hipo had gotten used to that verdict and wrapped himself in it, like a suit of armor, so as not to wince at the laughter and swear words that normally greeted the protestations of love that he made, now and again, to women whom he believed to be within his reach. Most of the time, if he insisted enough and they were capricious enough, he got what he wanted. With Santa, though, it was different. She was made of different stuff, he thought, despite her profession, and he regarded her as unattainable for him, a fairytale princess from a dreamy world of bliss. What an irony, then, that she seemed so delighted to belong to everyone but him, to whomever offered her a handful of silver coins. He knew that her arms—in which he would die a slow, incomparably delightful death if they would only hold *him*, without demanding anything more of them—her arms opened, embraced, and caressed anybody else, the first to arrive, almost in his presence! When he first began to feel what now consumed him, Hipólito failed to gauge the tremendous malaise that overcame him each time that Santa left the parlor accompanied by a random customer who, in all probability, did not even appreciate his luck. Now, he hated to be left sad and pensive at the piano while the whole disgusting program played out upstairs in Santa's room, the loveless coupling that he knew by heart for having done it and for having heard it described in detail a thousand times . . . In spite of himself, Hipólito spelled out that program in his mind, letter by letter, and envisioned it step by step, suffering unspeakably when, according to his highly informed calculations, the final step was about to commence . . .

"At this point, she's taking her clothes off," he thought. The thought made him tremble on the piano stool, as if ice water were running through the marrow of his bones, and his horrid whitish eyes—his eyes without irises and without the hopes of ever seeing that magnificent nudity over which the concupiscence of legions galloped with such demented fury—closed tightly shut, as if Santa's nudity possessed the prodigious power to dazzle and wound even the eyes of the blind.

He did not play the piano on such occasions, or rather, what he did hardly deserved the name. With titanic movements he made the notes howl and groan, improvising arpeggios and linking one to another in a weird dance that possibly ascended to the damnable room above to soothe the exhausted pair in their mute languor of satisfied flesh. And when Santa came down, and he heard her chat and giggle with the others girls and their clients—and with him, too—without giving any importance to what she had just done, as if it were insignificant, which, by dint of repetition, it had indeed become, Hipólito felt a serious urge to strangle her, no matter what the consequences.

Fortunately, these fits did not last long, and returning to his senses, he silently scolded himself and promised, at any cost, not to let it happen again, never to give a hint of a love that, with a cool head, he really thought to be madness. But his reformist intentions did not last long, unlike his resentment, which accumulated day by day. A time or two, he tried to turn the problem on its head, because, what the hell, Santa was not exactly the holy grail, either, so why shouldn't he try his luck, compete with her other suitors, use his own money, just as they did, to buy what was for sale, first come, first served? He was ready to pay, not just Santa's price, but a thousand times that—because Hipólito might be a poor devil, but he did not lack savings—in order to get rid of the obsession which was wrecking his peace of mind and gave no sign of abating. Wasn't it completely ridiculous, at his age, given his poverty and physical unattractiveness, given his experience, above all, to get stuck on one of these women and risk losing his job? Could he bear, in addition, the hooting derision of Elivra, Pepa, and the rest? Besides, he couldn't really think of how to proposition Santa, couldn't find the right words. The speeches that he composed in his head were always too chaste or too libertine, even though he considered himself well versed at such arts, even though women such as Santa are castles begging to be besieged. One afternoon, he went so far as to put twenty pesos in his pocket to purchase the girl's services, surely much less than she normally charged others who were not so frightfully ugly as he. Hopefully, his generosity would attenuate the repugnance awakened by his ugliness, or at least compensate for it. Jenaro, who would, of course, have to guide him, was surprised by the destination at that unexpected hour:

"We're really going to doña Elvira's house?"

"Why are you surprised? I've got to take care of some urgent business."

But upon arriving at the door, Hipólito hesitated pensively and, hearing footsteps inside, turned and plunged away, dragging Jenaro with him.

"Never mind. Now's not a good time. Take me to the bench where people will think that we're waiting for the streetcar or something . . . and hurry, idiot! If they open the door they'll see us. Look if there's anyone on the balcony . . . No? Good, that's good."

Once they were sitting down on the bench, their backs to the house and half hidden by the little garden, Hipólito breathed easier, lit a cigarette, and for the millionth time in recent days, interrogated his guide, listening carefully and reflecting on the boy's responses, which were not without spirit, color, and perceptiveness.

"Jenaro, *hijo*, tell me what Santa looks like . . ."

"Again, don Hipólito?" exclaimed Jenaro, who was barefoot and busy drawing letters and shapes in the sand with his big toe. "Well, Santa's real pretty, don Hipólito . . ." began the boy, not paying too much attention, for the moment, to the verbal portrait. "Imagine a woman a couple of inches . . . no, an inch, or a little more . . . taller than you . . . and strong, not with muscles, I mean, but . . . how do I explain? Firm all over, like you could squeeze her hard and not hurt her, almost like one of those statues in the Zócalo."

"How would you know? Have you squeezed her?"

"Gosh, no! Really squeezed her, no . . . but there's been times when I was waiting for you in the courtyard, and she's come by with a gentleman and kind of bumped into me and mashed me against the wall, like she didn't see me . . . on purpose, but just playing, you know, and laughing . . . She's good as gold to me, you know, always saves me some food from her plate, and on Saturdays she always gives me some coins and tells me to get cleaned up 'cause I'm always dirty. And I think she's going to buy me some clothes and, you'll see, I'm going to look cleaner than a bar of Puebla soap . . . And down at Tivoli, she has them give me those things with meat between slices of bread, what's that called? And sometimes cake, too."

"What do I care about all that stuff you're yakking about? I asked you to tell me what she looks like, in detail, starting with her hair and finishing with her feet. Okay? Now come on, Jenaro. Come on. We were saying she is very tall and very firm. Continue . . . and remember that you see her every night and I've never seen her at all. Draw me a picture of her, feature by feature, and talk to me slowly, so I understand and really get the picture . . . as if you were talking to a child . . . or, what am I saying, because almost all children can see . . . as if you were talking to a blind man. You've described a million things to me, right? . . . Well, okay then, man. Like that. Except forget colors because those don't mean anything to me . . . or, go ahead and describe her in your own way and I'll understand it in mine. Let's go . . . her hair?"

"Well, her hair," began Jenaro, quite serious now, looking for images that he could convey with his poor vocabulary of the street, images that his blind master would be able to comprehend, "her hair is the color that you see, who can't see anything . . . black, I mean. The color I see if I cover my eyes with my hand," which he did has he spoke. "Yeah, yeah, that's it. And when she washes her hair, every weekday, it hangs at least . . . how much? I don't know, *way* lower than her waist, and there's so much of it, don Hipólito, that it covers her whole back and keeps coming around in front, and she has to be pushing it back with her hands all the time, but the darned stuff won't stay there, and it covers her ears and piles up on her shoulders and tickles her neck . . . and the breeze blows into her eyes and her lips or tangles it up and annoys her, and she shakes her head . . . and wow, patrón, then it really looks like the black silk cloaks that the rich ladies wear to the theater, you know, the ones they carefully gather when they get out of their coaches to protect them from the dirty air of the street, and that look like pools of ink when they wear them under the electric lights . . ."

"That's what her hair is like?" burst out Hipólito, who had been lost in thought. "And her face? What does her face look like? I bet you can't explain . . ."

"You think I can't? Look, patrón, her face . . . is very pretty when she's not smiling, a little bit like the virgins and saints in church . . . no wait, don Hipólito, you haven't seen those, either. When she's not smiling . . . when she's not smiling . . . aw, crap, I can't . . . okay, when she's not smiling imagine that her face feels like a peach, and smells *that* good, and has that delicate, delicate fuzz on it, that just touching it makes your mouth water. Now are you understanding? And when she laughs these big dimples the size of lentils appear in her chin and both cheeks. And the light that comes out of her eyes is exactly like sunlight . . . okay, not that strong and not quite so much, God I'm dumb, but like sunlight, a lot like it, because it just makes you feel good. Even me, little and beat up and all, and I don't even go in the parlor . . . the light from her eyes reaches me out in my corner, and in my corner it cheers me up, and then even the cold drafts of night air that always make me tremble on the floor at night . . . they don't matter because the light keeps me warm, and I close my eyes and hold onto it so that it will go in deep . . . and I curl up with my head between my knees and I sleep so nice until you finish playing the piano and wake me up with your cane . . ."

"That's what her eyes are like?" Hipólito asked again, even more abstractedly than before. "If they're like that when they are just looking, Jenaro, what must they be like when they're full of love?"

"Jeez, patrón. Santa has the eyes of a doe, the size of almonds, and black, black, if you could only see them!"

"It would probably make me blind all over again," declared Hipólito in a prophetic tone.

"You love her that much, patrón?" asked Jenaro, for the first time outright, although this street-smart waif who never had a childhood, this pavement-pounding kid without parents had long since clearly recognized the signs of the blind man's passion.

Hipólito's head hung forward onto his chest, and his only answer to the direct question of the boy was a shrug of his shoulders, because he could not begin to gauge the intensity of his love, as if a seaman shrugged when asked to number the waves or an astronomer the stars. And he opened his arms measurelessly.

At that moment, the French dry cleaner's steam whistle thrust its anguishing shrillness into the air in its straight, white column of steam, and the workers there and in the other shops tucked in their filthy blue shirts and began to pour on to the sidewalk, obstructing it while they shouted their vulgar goodbyes to each other or the partiers, with arms around each other's shoulders, heading up the street, no longer to the Corner of the Magi, which had closed an hour earlier, but to cheaper eating houses and watering holes. The prudent workers headed to their distant, humble homes. Both partiers and prudent workers moved slowly, though; they were tired, tired of the work of the day, of the week, of the year, tired of the years and tired of their lives.

Neither Jenaro nor Hipólito paid attention to the parade of exhausted workers or the general exodus of the afternoon, which itself seemed exhausted, pale, as if struggling to get away over the peaks on the city's western horizon. They had not even noticed when, at five o'clock sharp, the public school opened its doors and inundated the street with children.

"Tell me about her body, Jenaro," murmured Hipólito after a prolonged lapse in their conversation, his chin still on his chest. "What's it like?"

Jenaro moved closer to Hipólito because a few couples of workers and maids—to judge by their clothes in the waning light—sat on the same bench, the men very close to the women, the men making all sorts of animated propositions and the women saying only "no, no" and keeping their suitors' hands under control with monosyllabic reprimands and occasional twists of the body. Jenaro lowered his voice, except that he had to raise it every two or three minutes when the streetcars passed, brightly lit and crowded, almost brushing the curb by the little garden where they sat.

"I've never seen her body to be able to describe it to you, patrón. But when she dresses up real fancy to go out, like to the theater or for dinner with those guys from the Club, I swear she gets taller, this much," he touched the blind man with his hands to indicate about four inches, "and her waist gets smaller and her breasts go up . . . ah, and her hips get fuller somehow, but that's about it . . . her dress and wrap cover a lot. The time to see her is when she's staying in and wearing that nightgown in which everything underneath makes some kind of mark. Oh, and when she's sitting down, her feet look really little, about the size of mine," he paused while taking a tactile measure of his feet, "and her leg, the one that she crosses, is real pretty, patrón, small at the bottom and big and round at the top. She always wears black stockings stretched real tight and shiny, without a wrinkle. But that's about it, that's all I've seen . . . But you want me to tell you what you notice most, and what her customers grab most when they sit her on their laps in the parlor? You won't get mad, patrón?"

Hipólito was about to declare that he would, indeed, get mad, very mad, if Jenaro continued describing Santa with that mixture of childish frankness and rascally wit, moved by the sickly desire that all true lovers feel to suffer somehow for the object of their affections, even though the loved one will never know of our actions or appreciate them. He finally gave a silent, negative wag of his finger, but then seemed to authorize and invite the information, by raising his head and gazing with his sightless eyes, his horrid whitish eyes without an iris, into the bright face of his young guide.

"It's her breasts, patrón," said the boy, drawing out the words for emphasis and lowering his voice further, as if that were the only appropriate tone in which to mention the hidden parts of our bodies. "It's her breasts that bulge like a couple of doves that are trying to peck their way through her dress and come flying out . . . but they never can get away, all frightened, that's how they look, anyway, when the men caress them so much you'd think it would hurt . . ."

"Enough!" roared Hipólito, sitting straight up: "Don't tell me any more or you'll get a thrashing! Now I can visualize Santa, now I can see her, and I thank God that I don't have to watch her the way you do."

After that night, the musician never again asked Jenaro to clarify or add further details to Santa's portrait. Nor did he again laugh like a lecherous fawn when he could hear, during the dances that he played at Elvira's house, how the excited customers examined the wares that the girls were offering for sale that evening. Now he sat stiffly as he played, lamenting his fate. One time he almost shouted "watch out" when he guessed that Santa was about to fall into the arms of el Jarameño, whose cause seemed to gain ground daily. And, in an effort to promote the lesser of two evils, he even tried to foment the mild affection that Santa felt toward Rubio, who clearly did not affect her the way that el Jarameño did.

"Santita," the musician said to her on one of those occasions, extremely rare now, when he could chat with her in the relative privacy that had once made him so happy and given rise to his crazy dreams. "Whatever happened to the idea of setting up house with that fellow Rubio, remember? I get the impression that he is still as interested as ever, right? Think about it, Santita. He's a gentleman, and if he said he loves you, he must have good reason . . ." Aside from el Jarameño, none of the others, including Rubio—for now at least—made Hipólito especially jealous, in spite of the continual possession of Santa that they enjoyed. Oh, they gave him an itch, all right, a bitter taste in the mouth, a foul humor—but merely that, and merely during the time in which he knew they were possessing his lady. El Jarameño, on the other hand, caused more intense symptoms, much deeper within him, making his heart and breathing seize up and bringing imprecise or incomprehensible acts of violence to his mind.

Even la Gaditana, who was also in love with Santa, bothered Hipólito much less than did the matador. Santa found the love of women abominable and, anyway, that love would not really make him jealous at all. Rather, he would chuckle indulgently, comforted by the idea that Santa detested men and could be easily cured of her life of prostitution, the way that one cures children of some undesirable habit with a stern wag of the finger. Everybody in the house knew that la Gaditana was in love with Santa, and they had told Hipólito because they viewed him as "one of the family." Santa herself had nixed it from the beginning:

"Hipo, I can't stand la Gaditana any more! She says she wants me to love her more than I love any man! Has she gone crazy? She was in my room all morning just kneeling by my bed and kissing my whole body with the most furious kisses I ever felt—and imagine how many I've felt! She wouldn't let me get up and was crying and saying that she can't feel anything for men anymore, that they make her sick, and she was moaning and sighing and saying 'you're so pretty, *hija*, so pretty' and that if I reject her she's going to do something really terrible . . . until finally I got tired and told her 'listen, Gaditana, I'm glad to hear it, now out of my room because I'm getting up.' I wouldn't have told her, Hipo, if I'd known how she was going to react. She rolled around on the rug, pulling her hair out and kicking her legs like she was having a fit, and then she begged to be allowed to stay . . . 'I promise not to bother you,' she said to me, sobbing, 'and I won't even talk if that bothers you, just let me stay while you wash and dress. If you want I'll help . . . or if not, I'll just sit right here.' She dragged herself into a corner between two pieces of furniture. And then . . ."

And then a number of clients interrupted her narration, demanding attention from Santa and music from the piano player, but as soon as Hipólito and the girl found themselves alone once more, he asked her to resume her story. But he perfectly understood the meaning of la Gaditana's behavior, the ancient sin against nature, the ancestral vice that so often germinates in brothels, then sprouts and flourishes there with the sickly exuberance of the Nile lotus. The voluptuous power of the ancient vice drove her toward Santa, who was still unfamiliar with it, who would possibly never practice it regularly, but only barely taste it before spitting and washing out her mouth, the way we do when an inexplicable curiosity leads us to sample an unappetizing dish.

"And then? . . . nothing, really. La Gaditana got in my bed where I had been lying before I got up, and she covered herself up with my sheets even though she was dressed. And whenever I threw a piece of clothing on the floor to put on something clean, she'd pull it off the floor and kiss it like a holy relic. What's all that about, Hipo? Do you know . . . or would Pepa? I don't know whether to slap her for being so filthy or call Elvira to give her some kind of cure. Tell me what to do!"

"Santita!" exclaimed Hipólito with a nervous smile as he played a few notes with his left hand on the keyboard. "You really don't know what la Gaditana wants? None of the other girls or Pepa or Elvira has talked to you about this? . . . I thought you knew, because you seemed to go along with it, and I bet that's what the girls think, too. You know since when? Since la Gaditana started teaching you to dance danzón and wouldn't let anyone else show you a single step . . . didn't you notice that at the time? Didn't you start to suspect something?"

"What on earth was I supposed to suspect? I still don't know what in hell you are talking about! . . . Don't laugh, Hipo! You think I'm lying? What's going on?"

"She's in love with you, Santita. It's love, and now you're going to think I'm the crazy one, but it is. Mixed up, twisted, indecent, whatever you want to call it, but it's love. Look, not all people are born the same. Just look at me carefully, if you haven't already, and you'll see I'm as ugly as sin, but Santita, I swear it's not my fault. If I'd had a choice, I'd have been real handsome, or just a little ugly, not like this . . . and with eyes that see everything, without this stinking ophthal . . . mia, or whatever the doctor said. Look at the babes that are born with too many fingers or withered legs or their heads swollen with water . . . well, the same thing happens with love. Sometimes it's born all healthy and the judge and priest approve, and other times, it is born in the wrong circumstances and brings disappointment and unhappiness . . . like you and that officer fellow, for example . . . and still other times, it is born deformed, like la Gaditana's love for you."

"But *love*, Hipo? Is it really love?"

"Yes, Santita, that's what the wise men say . . . Sometime when he's not too drunk, ask that poet who comes here. He'll tell you. It even has a special name that comes from some lady who drowned herself in the sea something like five thousand years ago . . ."

"So, a *woman* is in love with me? Yuck, Hipo, that makes me sick! And the next time that la Gaditana comes around I'm going to give her a taste of my body . . . with these fists. That'll fix her. It's fine that all the men want me, but . . ."

"No, not men, Santita," interrupted Hipólito, suddenly abandoning the kidding tone of their chat, "not *men* . . . but just one man who loves you deeply, down to the bones, who lives for you and loves you beyond death itself, a man who never taunts you because of what you are, who adores you and protects you and feels proud to deserve your affection, any of it, even a tiny bit, because he idolizes you so, so much. You need a man who is going to hold you up higher than the stars, bury you in his heart, watch over you when you sleep, and always know what you are thinking, a man that, even if he lived as long as Methuselah, would find the time too short to express his love for you . . . Ay, Santita, then you'd see how glorious life can be, and you'd forget all about tears and sorrows, and shame, and repentance . . ."

"Hipo," said Santa, turning as serious as he, "there is already a man who offers me something like that."

"That one," scowled Hipólito, "he'll never do all that, never in a million years! He is already happy. He's had nothing but good luck. What you need is somebody who's only had bad luck, you know what I mean? Somebody who will feel like you're doing *him* a favor . . . You've fallen in a hole, right? So be careful that you don't grab on to the first hand that someone extends from above, a hand that might get tired and let you go. No, no. Instead, look around you, look at you own feet, and settle for someone that you find there. Lift him up, and he'll help you get out of here. Then it doesn't matter where you go . . . The important thing is that he loves you, whoever it is, inside and out, that it's not just his whim, a matter of vanity, or because he likes you in bed. It's got to be a man who loves and wants all of you, they way you really are, blemishes and all."

"And where am I going to find that man, Hipo?" inquired Santa, impressed by his vehemence and already suspecting how he might reply.

"Where, Santita?" repeated Hipólito, short of breath, putting both his hands on the keyboard without playing a single note. "Well, okay then, I'm going to tell you, even if it makes you laugh, but you won't laugh, no, why would you laugh? . . . I'm going to tell you because I know that you already love someone else, the one we were referring to, and that you'll probably go away with him . . . I can just see it, even with these eyes that don't see anything else! . . . I'm going to tell you because you have got to know, and because this secret is going to kill me . . . Santita, come close because I don't want anybody to hear . . . Santita, I am that man! It's me . . . who's just an ugly worm that wants to follow you and follow you wherever you go and whoever you're with . . . me, it's me, the only one you'll ever find who will always be willing to . . ."

"Come on, Hipo! Play the piano, why don't you, and quit bending Santa's ear!" shouted la Gaditana, furious to see their conversation go on so long.

The musician played with exceptional inspiration, and Santa, without uttering a syllable, went to sit in the darkest corner of the parlor, legs stretched out in front of her, head resting on the back of the chair, arms hanging limply, eyes on the ceiling, and her mind thinking, thinking, thinking . . .

A pair of ordinary customers appeared at the door, and the girls greeted them, Hipólito fell silent, and Santa sat up. The customers were all business. They drank beer, served just so, without too much foam in the glasses, and emptied each bottle completely before beginning the next.

"Have a beer, girls, but watch your manners if you want more," they announced from the middle of the room.

Pepa set the good example, grabbing a glass off the tray with a wink to her girls, and everyone else drank, too, except for Santa. The two citizens chose two women and, after finishing their beer, went upstairs with them to the bedrooms.

Hipólito had long since stopped playing and turned toward the others. His pock-marked face with those horrid whitish eyes of a bronze statue without patina stood out from the black background of the piano the way that painted faces stand out on Japanese lacquer ware. Santa began to study his ugliness intently.

All of a sudden, Eufrasia, the maid, who only on rare occasions entered the parlor, walked into it angrily and addressed the manager:

"Doña Pepa, there's police out there, and they say they have a legal order, and I've told them that this is a bad time and the girls are busy, to come back tomorrow . . . but they won't budge!"

"Let them in, silly!" instructed Pepa, with the poise of a woman who knows that her accounts are in order, and who knows, too, how certain minor obstacles can easily be overcome.

It was a group of Sanitation Agents, the bottom rung on the city's administrative ladder devoted to the regulation of prostitution. Society had entrusted them with the direct supervision of the professionals themselves, ensuring their compliance with a list of requirements supposedly intended to safeguard the health of the community's male citizens. And because they somewhat resemble police, perhaps it is not surprising that they exercise their authority arbitrarily and commit countless abuses, even a few really scurrilous ones, like intentionally hauling in helpless, poorly dressed girls, who turn out not to be prostitutes at all and whom they finally release with a priceless smirk and an "excuse us, ma'am." On the other hand, as long as the professionals are careful to grease the agents' hands with money—because, after all, money is always useful in this life—even major infractions commonly pass unremarked. The only exception would be the ambitious agent who makes a show of his incorruptibility in order to rise in the ranks and harvest the benefits of larger graft in the future. At any rate, a visit from the Sanitation Agents must always be taken seriously, which is why Pepa went to greet them with a broad smile and Santa turned pale with the thought that her papers lacked a signature for the doctor's last visit. She quickly went to consult with Hipólito who, despite having so recently compared himself to a worm—and despite really believing it—stood up as soon as he heard mention of the agents' arrival and, turning his back to them, adopted an attitude of dignified nonchalance, resting an elbow on the top of the piano.

"Do you think they're here for me, Hipo? I haven't been inspected in two weeks."

"For you, Santita?" exclaimed Hipólito, incredulous at the notion. "For *you*? No way. They'd take away the whole house first, with all the furniture and me, too, before you. It's probably just some rumor or because they want a tip from Pepa . . . You know they're as corrupt as they can be . . ."

And he shook his head and laughed, signaling "no, no, no" with his hand in the air, as if Santa's fears could so easily be dispersed. He could hardly believe that she felt them, being, as she had become, in the eyes of everybody who was anybody, the most pampered, hotly pursued, best connected courtesan in all Mexico City.

The other women, their papers in order, half listened to the lengthy exchange between the agents and Pepa, who was gradually losing her imperturbable air. From the parlor, one could see that she gestured urgently, that she offered something repeatedly. One could hear bits and pieces of the conversation:

"Hey now, Saucedo, there's no call for that . . . I'll take care of it tomorrow . . . put away that order, you devil . . . it's not a bribe, it's a present . . . look, she just forgot, and we forgot to remind her . . . no? . . . okay, but you're going to be sorry . . ."

"Eufrasia!" she turned and shouted, "Go call a coach, and tell Elvira to come down! . . . Santa, go put on a shawl!"

It was as if a bomb had exploded. Hipólito turned whiter than Santa herself. The women milled around, confirming and reconfirming that the agents actually intended to leave with the brightest jewel in Elvira's crown. They physically had to restrain la Gaditana, whom the news converted into a mythical fury, vomiting toads and snakes at the agents in the hallway. Jenaro, amazed, took shelter underneath the stairs and peered out with one eye and half of his intelligent, picaresque little face.

"Bastards!" snarled Hipólito, feeling Santa beside him. "Promise them more money, Santita. What else can you do?"

But it was no use. The agents, puffed up by the odious exercise of their official functions, did not give an inch. Not for a hundred silver pesos would they let go of this particularly coveted prey, who, her pride notwithstanding, would always be at their mercy after the major fright they were giving her today.

"Better watch out," Hipólito explained to them off to one side and in solemn tones, "because this women has friends in very high places. You may be putting your jobs in danger . . . better just look the other way. I know what I'm talking about." And he moved his eyebrows and blinked expressively, just as if he were looking at them.

When the matter was reported to Elvira, she expressed little concern and predicted a speedy and favorable outcome.

"Go on down to the police station, Pepa, and don't be scared. This guy Saucedo is just in a bad mood . . ."

Elvira's confidence immediately heartened the girls and the piano player. She would know. Undoubtedly there had been some mistake, Santa and Pepa would be right back, and everybody would laugh about how worried they had been.

As a precaution, however, Hipólito sent Jenaro to the police station, too.

"Find some way to listen in, and if you notice signs of anything serious, run back and let me know!"

Under Elvira's direction, the regular operation of the business got back under way. The music of the piano and the laughter of the girls again resonated throughout the house, as did the sound of corks popping and clients demanding this or that. The girls began to go upstairs again with the customers who hurriedly chose them, and money again flowed into the small leather bag that Pepa had turned over to Elvira, who did not hesitate to hang it on her wrist and descend from her lofty status as owner, rather than lose a single peso of profit by leaving the interim management of the business in hands less careful and expert. Only Hipólito's hat did not resume its normal circulation because Santa did not return to pass it around, much to the dismay of both the piano player and two or three potential customers who sat for a long while buying beers for the other girls as they waited. Elvira separately "explained" the situation to each of them:

"Santa's going to be a while. She's in her room with some big shot and . . . you know . . . Why don't you go up with this other one? Don't you like her?"

Yes, yes, they were all pretty, young, and adorable, but the men wanted Santa. And so they opted to wait patiently, impelled by their insatiable desire, in the little parlor, spending their money on liquor, speaking politely to each other, and even chatting amicably if they were already acquainted. Those who did not know each other gradually struck up ephemeral friendships, the kind that arise spontaneously when men drink together and last only as long as it takes to drain a glass, a few minutes, friendships that disappear completely when the conversation ends. The girls took advantage of the wait, flaunting their attractions with unerring instinct in the faces of their impulsive interlocutors, who finally—one by one, pushed by Elvira, by the piano's obscene harmonies, and by the lecherous atmosphere of the house as a whole—resigned themselves to accept a substitute.

"It doesn't matter. Next time I'll get Santa."

There were a few holdouts, one or two who were determined to have Santa and nobody but Santa:

"Elvira, another round of beer for us and whatever the girls are drinking . . ."

But as objects of intense yearning and desire tend to do when so long awaited, Santa failed to appear.

Her inexplicable delay in returning now really began to alarm Hipólito and Elvira. What was Santa doing? Had they dared to detain her at the inspection? And Hipólito stopped playing, supposedly because he was tired out. Later, he'd play a bit more, after he had smoked a cigarette. And Elivra walked back and forth, back and forth, between the parlor and the front door. Finally, she saw Jenaro come running with his straw hat in his hand.

"I beat the coach here, wow!" he panted. "Doña Pepa's coming back alone, because Santa's been detained and they're taking her to the hospital." And he wiped his sweaty brow with a ragged shirt sleeve that hung from his arm in tatters.

In an instant, Elvira made up a lie to preserve her business reputation and Santa's, and to get rid of the obstinate customers who were still waiting for her. Santa had gone out to dinner without informing her:

"It's those club gentlemen who won't leave her alone for a moment! Just goes to show . . . So there's nothing for it but to come back tomorrow, good and early."

Hipólito asked for his hat and his cane and left without saying a word amid the general panic that the news had produced:

"Take me to the police station, Jenaro, and fast!"

At the door, he was stopped by Pepa and el Jarameño, who were arriving together, having met at the curb where Pepa was climbing out of her coach. The bullfighter had come for his daily visit, and, on the way inside, as they skirted the small park area, Pepa told the bullfighter the news, which, at first, he did not seem to think very significant. What was the fuss about? But as soon as Pepa explained in grim and highly dramatic detail that it meant jail, suffering, detention, the hospital, he got the picture. And then, in the manner of someone who removes a disguise that no longer matters, he practically declared his love for Santa:

"I don't know stuff about justice or nothing, and I really don't like to deal with the authorities, all I need is a Bible to get married, as they say, but if someone can take me to Santa, I'll get her out of there, by God, I will!"

Elvira and Pepa, neither of whom gave a thought to recent rumors about the piano player's feelings for Santa—a passion that nobody took seriously, anyway—simultaneously designated Hipólito with gestures of their heads and hands.

"Here's Hipo, who can take you . . . Hipo, take el Jarameño, you know where . . ."

Imagine the anguish and revulsion that coursed through Hipólito's body upon receiving such inhumane instructions. How could he . . . how could he take his abhorrent rival to Santa and become the tool by which el Jarameño would finally win her? The blind man actually took several steps back, as if he had suddenly lost his balance. He raised his hands to fend off dangers that sighted people around him were unable to discern, as they watched him and waited anxiously.

The struggle was over quickly, lasting only seconds, each of which seemed to Hipólito as interminable as a year. It was his love for her that forced his decision, his love that in spite of all the torment could still, with a little encouragement, spill through his veins in a simulacrum of happiness. And the decision shattered his insides, paining him to a degree unimaginable before this moment—his mouth bitter, his legs trembling, and his heart . . . his heart totally out of control. It beat wildly, with stabbing pains that made him raise his hands to his chest involuntarily, though he disguised the reaction by pretending to look for something in his vest pocket . . .

In a fit of heroic self-sacrifice, preferring to suffer himself if it kept his loved one from suffering, he muttered sullenly:

"Let's go in a coach. Jenaro can ride with the driver, because I'll need him to guide me when we get there."

Neither he nor el Jarameño said anything as they sat side by side in the vehicle. Whenever the rough ride jostled them together, their mutual revulsion quickly separated them. Perhaps the torero already had intimations of the piano player's intentions regarding Santa and treated him with hostility for that reason. Perhaps he had been alerted by the mysterious magnetic field that alerts us in a café or a theater, at a dance or in whatever public place, that someone there, one among thousands, ardently desires to have the woman whom we love, who belongs only to us. And at the moment of mutual recognition, a current of homicidal hatred flows between him and us. Expressions of defiance flair on bloodless faces. A minute more, and the hatred could explode, annihilating everything. Hatred for love, ancient, incurable, eternal . . .

Because Hipólito was blind, and because, even had he not been, nothing was visible inside the dark coach, they could not look at each other, and their bodies reflexively repelled each other. Meanwhile, the only light inside the coach came as they passed under the electric street lights and a few rays entered randomly through the small windows in the doors, like dirty water thrown from a second story window by bare, anonymous arms, that wets only a small area of pavement and is quickly absorbed.

The inspector was not in. That night his deputy was on duty instead, a sleepy, unshaven fellow of indeterminate age and with a high opinion of himself. He wore a wool scarf around his neck and, stuck to his forehead, one of those visors often used by watchmakers, jewelers, engravers, and people with an illness that necessitates protection from electric lights. He was reading a periodical or pamphlet of some kind.

"Good evening to you, gents," said el Jarameño upon entering the office and approaching the wooden grill that divided it in two, separating the public from the employees who worked there.

"First, take off your hat, my friend. You're in a government office," spat a clerk who approached the grill from the other side, curious to see what chance had brought them a bullfighter, as el Jarameño's small braid and accent indicated him to be.

"Well . . . er . . . ," began el Jarameño with a frown, removing his hat and giving his pigtail a little flip as he rubbed the nape of his neck in a gesture characteristic of toreros, "it's that a couple of agents of . . . er, public order, I guess . . . have brought you a girl as healthy as a ripe peach . . . which has got to be a mistake, right? Because . . ."

"Man alive! It's el Jarameño!" announced the deputy inspector, just then, with recognition and excitement as he put aside his reading, got up from the desk, and eagerly stepped over to the grill. He was an avid fan of bullfights.

El Jarameño reacted with the habit that matadors have of smiling automatically in any direction from which they are called, even when they are fairly sure, because of a poor performance, that the caller may be an unhappy fan intending them insult or hurling something injurious at them from the stands.

"Come on in, man. Come right on in!" continued the deputy inspector, personally opening the way for him to enter beyond the grill. "And tell me what's wrong . . . You know, I hadn't recognized you! I thought it was one of those second-rate troublemakers, the kind we see in here night after night . . . Hey, what a coincidence, no? I mean, I was wanting to meet you, and here you are! We'll talk in the other room where nobody will bother us . . . after you. It's usually not this quiet . . . Cedillo, let's have some light in here!"

As soon as Cedillo had illuminated the adjoining room, el Jarameño, puffed up by the adulation, entered it with a swagger.

It was a bare and ugly room, dusty and uncarpeted, with a desk in the middle, a calendar on one whitewashed wall, and on another, a map of the city divided into its various police precincts. There was a sofa and, hanging over it, a lithograph of the independence hero Father Hidalgo, its frame in deplorable condition. In a corner was a cabinet fixed to the wall that contained a newfangled telephone terminal bristling with shiny metal parts, gear wheels, bells, a receiver, and also many wires with tiny metallic labels indicating the connection provided by each—Fire department, District government, Inspector's Office, and so on. On the table lay an enormous pearl-handled Colt 45 revolver, standard issue, and leaning against the walls were four large, closed cabinets, black and funereal looking. In the air, a smell of disinfectant, the bitter odor of miserable, dirty people, the sound of distant, disagreeable voices, of heavy footsteps and horses outside in the courtyard and, coming from behind a movable screen, the loud, rhythmic snoring of an exhausted man.

"Man, Jarameño! It's good to meet you. Word of honor! . . . Hey, how about a little shot of tequila? I keep it for, you know, when I can't sleep . . . during the day I don't touch a drop," explained the deputy inspector, pulling a couple of scratched-up glasses, a bottle, and a salt dish out of the desk drawer. "Look, you drink this with a little salt, so it goes down easy . . . Yeah, that's it, the salt first, on your tongue, that's it . . . to your health!"

And both drank the good tequila of Jalisco.

El Jarameño, in a hurry and not at all comfortable, deep down, in a police station, went straight to the point. He was there for Santa. He would be responsible for what happened, he would pay whatever, and he would bring her back whenever they required. But he did not want her to spend the night there . . .

"Do me the favor, please. You have the authority to do it, and you're a nice guy. And the girl's delicate. It could be the death of her, I swear."

"Santa, huh?" replied the deputy with a sparkle in his eye. "I know who she is, and I compliment your taste. You old dog, Jarameño! You hanging around with her? Tell me the truth!"

El Jarameño shrugged:

"Hanging around with her? No . . . well . . . yeah, I guess." He stopped, truncating his answer.

"My dear matador, I'm sorry but you're too late. Santa has already gone to Morelos Hospital for the night."

The bullfighter jumped up, muttering a curse. He was going straight to the hospital then! Santa was not going to spend the night in a hospital . . . "Moleros" Hospital or any other.

With benevolent superiority, the deputy calmed el Jarameño, explaining the intricacies of the administrative mechanisms involved, enumerating a list of reasons why the hospital would not only refuse to let him rescue Santa, but would, in fact, refuse to let him see her or even open its doors to him. It was risky to even try.

"Jarameño, no lie, if you knock on the door there more than once, a cop, or a bunch of cops, will grab you and throw you in the slammer . . . Don't go off half-cocked, man! . . . And if you promise not to tell anyone, I'll give you a way to get Santa tomorrow morning, no matter how sick she may be . . ."

He was interrupted by a complex of noises, people simultaneously entering the office and the courtyard outside. In the office, suddenly, a child was whining and a woman sobbing. One could hear policemen struggling to restrain someone, insolent protests from whomever they were restraining, and the precise questions of clerks. Horses' hooves echoed in the courtyard, where several men breathed heavily after depositing a stretcher and its groaning occupant on the pavement. One heard imperious orders given, quick footsteps, matches striking.

"Sir," said Cedillo through the door, "we've a girl beat up out here, several fellows under arrest and one bleeding."

"I'm on my way, Cedillo. Wake up the medic." And to el Jarameño: "See? You can't even have a conversation here. Where was I? Oh, yeah. You go down tomorrow and offer to withdraw Santa from prostitution by making her your mistress. Hear? Your *mistress*! That's the magic word. Then you pay a doctor to cure whatever she's got, if she's sick, I mean. And then you take your sweetie wherever you want . . . How's that for a solution?"

The tumult inside the office was increasing, although less than the tumult in the courtyard. Cedillo stuck his head in again, without excusing his interruption.

"The wounded guy is dying, sir! He's refused to make a statement. The woman wants him to confess. Do you want to question him?"

"Okay, we're going to interrogate him. I'll be right there." And turning to el Jarameño, who was stupefied by the proposed solution to Santa's problem, impressed by the talk of wounds and confessions, and intimidated anew at being in a police station, he added: "Another tequila, Jarameño? This stuff won't hurt you, even if you have a little too much. It's nice, know what I mean? Doesn't give you a crude one . . ."

"What do you mean, a 'crude' one?" asked the torero, already standing up with the smoky aftertaste of tequila on his tongue.

"It's what we call the sickness you have the next morning after you get drunk, you know, a hangover! Oh, and before you go, is it true that the bulls you're fighting come from Spain, and also, how much are tickets for seats on the shady side of the bullring costing?"

"For you, pal, they're on the house! The bulls are from Mexico, but they're so smart, they could have studied at the University of Salamanca . . . Now, point me the way out of this joint, friend, 'cause you've got stuff to do, and me too."

The deputy inspector opened the door to the courtyard, bumping into the stretcher with the dying man on it, so that el Jarameño had to squeeze past on his way out. And, much as this victim of gypsy superstitions tried to look the other way, he had plenty of time to absorb the lugubrious scene: the shape of the wounded man, swathed in shadows, jerking in his death throes; the medic to one side, his services grotesquely useless, slowly unfurling his rolled-up sleeves dotted, here and there, with human blood; and kneeling close to the stretcher, a woman, her infant asleep in her left arm, its dirty little face moving palely in the half-dark as she bent over the wounded man, devastated to see that he was dying. The woman kept repeating "Longinos! . . . María Santísima! . . . Longinos!" as if she knew no other words. A priest in black held a crucifix in front of the dying man's face and prayed very quietly, as if in secret, prayers that floated away over the bowed heads of the clustered employees and police.

"Who did this to you?" asked the deputy inspector, placing his hands on the sides of the stretcher, his face very close to the dying man's. "Tell me. Come on, make an effort! Who was it? Was there an argument, or was it in cold blood?"

From the stretcher issued a horrifyingly stricken voice, struggling to pronounce a last request:

"Water . . ."

And then he must have died, because el Jarameño, who had been tip-toeing by, his hat still in his hand, heard the woman cry out, and someone said "that's it." Meanwhile, the deputy inspector went to remind him of his offer:

"Jarameño! About those seats . . . right up front, okay? Near the judges!"

The matador was so affected by the scene that he hardly understood what the corporal on guard duty said to him as he left building:

"That blind guy, the one who came with you, went away when he heard that the woman had been taken to the hospital already. He left you the rental coach."

The next morning, el Jarameño went to the hospital and carried out the deputy inspector's instructions to the letter. All went as predicted, except that it took most of the day. El Jarameño declared in Santa's presence—and signed a written statement to the effect—that she was his mistress and that he intended to withdraw her from a life of prostitution. The delay was caused by the list of bureaucratic procedures that the torero was required to fulfill at the hospital, the police station, and who knows where else, racing back and forth in coaches all afternoon. And when they gave Santa to him, when the last coach finally started home with the two of them inside, they were so eager for each other that, without talking, unable to wait a moment longer, driven by a long-denied reciprocal need that finally exploded inside both of them, their lips and bodies came together in a prolonged kiss. The vertigo made them close their eyes, their nostrils flared with the need for air, and then they pushed each other away, arms rigid, in order not to go mad with delight.

"See, Santa? See that you're mine? Now hold me like you'll never let me go!" sighed el Jarameño hoarsely.

Santa snuggled against his throat and put her arms around him voluptuously:

"It's you who's mine, silly . . . every bit of you. Don't you feel how much I hug you? More than you!"

And, forgetting everything around them, what had just happened and what might happen, they held each other's hand and spoke of their life together, of their certain and endless happiness. Santa did not owe a cent to Elvira. She was free! First she would go by for her clothes (you'd better believe it!) and her jewelry (that's for sure!) and to say goodbye to the girls who remained there, at whose side she had been enchained . . . Poor things! She felt profoundly sorry for them now, but what could be done? Supposing that a lover appeared out of nowhere to rescue each of them that very night, there would always be others: the girls of nearby houses, those of more distant ones, those who worked alone, a legion of slaves, teeming, never ending. A brigade that endured persecutions, cruelties, and affronts, closing ranks without wavering, without pausing to evacuate its wounded or even bury its dead. On they go, living personifications of Love, Desire, Temptation, and the Flesh, charging ahead, without more of a shield or weapon than their naked breasts!

Once at Elivra's, what with all the farewells, the packing of trunks, and el Jarameño's delirious, ceaseless invitations to visit, they lost track of the hour, until eventually Hipólito showed up for work. All the girls together blurted out the sensational news.

"Hipo! El Jarameño's taking Santa out of here! Tonight!"

"I'm sorry for her, but he must be thrilled," pronounced the musician sententiously. He had seen this coming since the day before, having well understood the mutual passion that the torero and the girl had tried to resist and conceal. Since the day before, Hipólito had said goodbye to Santa, not because he expected her to disappear forever—to the contrary, he expected that she would eventually return to Elvira's house—but because he knew that the torero had captured her heart, and he, Hipólito, might never come close to it again.

In his lodgings, he had cried as much as is humanly possible to cry, witnessed by Jenaro, who, despite his sleepiness and his toughness, said more than once:

"Master, don't cry like that anymore, because you're going to use up all that's left of your eyes . . . Go to sleep . . . Rest . . ."

But he didn't cry there in the brothel. Not on your life! He went straight to his piano, tried out the keyboard, and wished with all his soul for two things, both of which happened: there were a lot of customers and Santa did not appear in the parlor.

That was no coincidence, because what could be more discouraging to Elvira's clientele than the spectacle of Santa's departure? So Elvira escorted Santa and el Jarameño out a private door with only a few indispensable things in a suitcase carried by Eufrasia. The rest of the things would be sent along in the morning.

Outside, as Elvira said goodbye to them beside the sad little garden, they heard the sound of the piano, and Santa felt a chill run down her spine. She was so happy that until that moment she had forgotten all about the blind man and how much he adored her.

"Elvira, say goodbye to Hipo for me, tonight, will you?"

"Sure, honey. Don't worry. I know he's going to whine, though, when he finds out you're gone."

El Jarameño arrived at the coach first and opened the door for Santa.

"Let's go, my glory. It's late!" he practically shouted, radiant and hungry for her, his clean-shaven face illuminated by a lamp.

Santa stood close to him and, before climbing into the coach, she turned to look at the brothel, which looked from the darkened street like a house on fire inside.

In both the downstairs windows, those of the parlor, most of the up-stairs windows, and those of the bedrooms, the glass shown with light, so much, that one expected to see flames come licking out of them at any minute, like purifying dragons' tongues that would gradually, tenaciously, voraciously envelope the entire building and fuse twenty flames into one fantastic, swirling mantel of fire and sparks, glowing ever brighter, rising to the roof, twisting in demented, infinite fury, devastating and consuming everything.

Envisioning that righteous fire about to burn down the brothel, Santa stood transfixed and immobile on the sidewalk.

"What are you looking at, my Santa?" inquired el Jarameño, already ensconced inside the coach and leaning out the door.

"Fire. Look. It's like the house is burning."

Truly, it was burning, but only as it did every night, on fire with bestial lust, with nauseating sexual traffic. The flames of lechery and howling perversion, had they been visible, could have enveloped the building in just the way that Santa envisioned. But no . . . imprecise shadows occasionally moved across the panes of window glass, probably cast, downstairs, by people dancing to the piano music, and upstairs, by celebrants undressing.

"Come on, Santa," insisted the torero desperately. "It's me who's on fire. I'm burning to love you . . . now, come on!"

Returning to reality, Santa looked again at the house, this time with the melancholy affection we always feel when leaving a place that once gave us shelter from the storm.

"Come on, Santa!" implored the torero, reaching out his arms to her. "Come to me!"

And Santa went to him.

Part Two

Six

"Well, I can assure you that you are, in fact, drinking an infusion of eyelids."

"How revolting, Ripoll!" His tablemates vociferated their unanimous disgust as they stirred their tea to cool it.

"You come up with the most awful jokes!" added don Mateo, the pawn-broker, with indignation.

"Jokes?" insisted Ripoll, half seriously, half mischievously. "Well, let's just see who knows what he's talking about." And he got up from his chair, putting his napkin to one side, and went into his darkened room. The others heard him strike a match, twice, and shuffle through a pile of papers.

He returned to the table triumphantly, armed with a book that lacked a binding, which he deposited on the mantel, holding out his hand to keep the others away from it:

"Now you will hear, noble sons of Spain, now you will hear the words of a Frenchman, translated in my own fair homeland, Barcelona, which is to say, *outside* of Spain . . ." The others, all of them Spanish, immediately began to protest this assertion of Catalonian nationalism, provoking Ripoll's firm insistence: "Outside of Spain! The Frenchman is named Goncourt, for your information, and he affirms that he learned what I am about to read in a book about Japan . . . just around the corner here, so to speak."

He drained his cup of tea, rolled and lit a cigarette, and flipped through the pages of the book until he found what he was looking for. The keeper of the boarding house acted as if she were about to leave the room until Ripoll indicated with an expressive gesture of his hand that there was no need of that:

"No, doña Nicasia, your modesty will not be offended. Stay and listen. All right, here it is. Please don't interrupt . . ."

And, with a long drag on his cigarette and a rather Olympian glance over the heads of his audience, he began to read:

"The Legend of Tea. Dharma, a holy ascetic of China and Japan, decided to deny himself sleep, considering it too pleasurable and worldly. One night, however, he went to sleep and did not awaken until the next morning. Indignant at this demonstration of weakness in himself, he cut off his eyelids — two pieces of flesh whose contemptible weakness impeded his quest for superhuman perfection — and flung them away. And the two bloody eyelids took root in the ground upon which they fell, growing into a bush the leaves if which the local inhabitants have harvested ever since to make an aromatic infusion that banishes sleep."

Not one of his listeners applauded or evinced even the slightest interest in what he had read. Ripoll's voice disappeared in a silence of utmost indifference, and the poetic legend was lost in an absolute void. The resident priest, don Práxedes Luro, known to the group for his Carlist conservatism, who had been rolling breadcrumbs into twenty little balls with which he amused himself by throwing them at an empty glass, spoke without looking up:

"Ripoll, my friend, that's the stupidest thing I ever heard."

This comment, unlike the reading, garnered applause from everyone, including doña Nicasia, who had begun to clear the table and reflexively reprimand the serving woman. The boarders filed past Ripoll, who blew smoke their way, patting him on the back, laughing at his failure, and repeating the curate's put-down with various additions of their own.

"Nice one, Ripoll!"

"Whoops . . . there go the eyelids!"

"Our engineer's such a funny guy!"

"Ripoll, a bit annoyed, shrugged and bombarded them with insults lightly veiled in jest:

"Bunch of ignorant savages! I should have known . . . You'll never understand anything but money. Jackasses! Not so much you, curate, as the rest of your countrymen here. Jerks!"

In response, the supposed savages and jerks laughed louder than ever as they went to their rooms. The curate settled into one of the less worn-out corners of the sofa to sit and doze while he waited for the evening card game with his regular adversaries: Mateo Izquierdo, the pawn broker; Anselmo Abascal, an employee of the Covadonga clothing store on Espíritu Santo Street; and Feliciano Sordo, who always talked about "losing his money, his youth, and his best energies" in the mines of San Luis Potosí, but who nonetheless paid his rent with extreme punctuality, carried a gold watch, always had cash on hand, and was the only one among the boarders who drank an expensive beer like Carta Blanca of Monterrey. It was whispered that the cash on hand, the gold watch, and the Carta Blanca all derived from the generosity of doña Nicasia, with whom Sordo had an understanding—it was also whispered—so that the two slept quite comfortably together every night just as if they were legally married. In public, however, both of them kept up appearances. She addressed him in the same tone she used for everyone else, without noticeable familiarity or any noticeable preference when serving food at table. The Spaniard called her *tú* with characteristically Spanish familiarity, but not greater than the familiarity that he applied to his fellow boarders, excepting the curate and el Jarameño. The one detail that more or less gave away their secret was the location of their bedrooms, contiguous one to the other, with a connecting door. The furniture that blocked the door on each side offered an exceedingly weak barrier: on doña Nicasia's side, a light sofa, and on Sordo's side, a small writing table, its ink pot completely dried out and its pens rusted and useless. It had been a long time since Sordo had written any letters to his problematical business contacts in San Luis Potosí.

Doña Nicasia's story, which she told now and then for the benefit of her boarders, inspired their respect and sympathy. She was the proud widow of a Spanish military man who had been killed in 1881 fighting against Cuban rebels, and she pronounced her married surnames, Aspeitia de Flores, slowly, with emphasis, to invoke the full luster of the Aspeitia family of Calatayud—her own clan—and of the possibly better-known Flores family of Segovia, her husband's. She assured them that she had distinguished, even noble, relatives on her mothers side, who had objected to her marriage with Flores, a mere lieutenant. But she had insisted, oh yes, being madly in love, and had said goodbye to everything and come with him to América. América, this heartless place that holds so many painful surprises for the decent people of Spain who incautiously take up residence here! Cuba, and everything about it, she knew by heart, especially Havana, which she described mixing its horrors and marvels indiscriminately: How money had rained from the sky at the time when she and her husband had first arrived, how hard times had ruined trade until little was left of the festive commercial city and until the entire island, once so prodigiously rich and so prodigiously indolent, had become a shadow of its former glory. By her account, the godless, unruly, and above all extremely ungrateful Cuban independence fighters had ruined the island's tobacco and sugar plantations, depriving it of fruit and flowers, impoverishing it, and decimating its rural population, burning and denuding its tropical countryside, leaving its ports depressed and its cities silent. The Cuban earth, insatiably thirsty, had been soaked in the blood of the damnable black insurgents and the noble Spaniards who had traveled there to give the place a brighter, more splendid future.

"People like us, men like my unfortunate Santiago, who wasn't just anybody, no sir . . . a Flores of Segovia, no less!"

All the tenants of doña Nicasia, from the curate on down, then waxed indignant. Illuminated with holy rage, they menacingly shook their fists and belched to the four winds insults so foul and resourceful that the small group gathered in the humble parlor of the boarding house seemed to have studied the dictionary for hours in order to create each one. It was the bitterness of disappointment, the incurable illness that afflicts Spaniards who, after a brief residence in the continent that had once been their colony, inexplicably fail to become very rich. América, they snarl, this América that now only tolerates them without distinguishing them from other outsiders, this América that actually requires that they labor, and sometimes, do dirty work in order to live! And in their bilious envy and ire they exaggerate the defects of Mexico (already great enough and numerous enough without exaggeration), the natural product, in their view, of Indian savagery, past and present, while the county's rare virtues, on the other hand, were mere importations for which they take immediate and full responsibility. And to think that this petty republic actually denied its debt to them, pretended not to recognize it, refused them fair compensation!

They sighed, and their spirits became still bitterer as they turned to the nostalgic contemplation of their distant homeland, to the towns and provinces where each of them had been born. Now the ancient local rivalries and hatreds of the Iberian Peninsula burst forth in full force: Navarre! No, Valencia! No, Santander!

Doña Nicasia, because she was from Aragón (to her mind, an obviously superior part of Spain) considered the dispute that roiled around her to be beneath her dignity, and because she was the owner of the boarding house, the boarders generally left her out of this curious melee that so divided and so incensed them. This town, that village, this city, that province! Each was an example, a disgrace, or, to the contrary, an exception! Rivers, forests, mountains, crops were brandished like weapons in attack, held up like shields in defense. And the same people who, moments before, had joined in disparaging América, now turned on one another and tore apart Spain, their beloved homeland.

"You people," shouted each of them at the others, "don't contribute a thing to the country!"

"Well, if you ask me, the all the products of *your* province don't amount to a hill of beans!"

But once they had insulted each other quite thoroughly, once their hands had fluttered in the air for emphasis and landed with a thump, like birds shot dead in the air, on the backs of chairs, on table tops, and on each other's knees—calm gradually returned. Four or five unsteady cigarettes were lit in the flame of a single match, and those accustomed, in normal situations, to address each other familiarly as *tú*, did so once more. Together, they recovered the spirit of unity and solidarity that makes them strong in this foreign land, the spirit that every Spaniard carries latent within him, ready to express itself in the service of every other Spaniard. Calm returned, and two thousand leagues away Spain continued to be Spain, its rivers running the same as ever, its mountain ranges in their place, the lion and towers on its coat of arms, all wrapped in a mantel of fleurs-de-lis, flowers of glory and greatness, still alive after so many years, across so many centuries, like the light of a star of the first magnitude that, even after it has burned itself out, continues to shine for millennia in our heavens.

Only two boarders did not participate in the tremendous daily disputes: Ripoll, the Catalonian engineer who believed himself to be a moral and intellectual entity vastly superior to the others, and Isidoro Gallegos, an unemployed comic actor, and, more to the point, a boarder without funds to cover the modest cost of his room and board. Isidoro's good humor did much to compensate for this shortcoming, however, and his sharp tongue (and it was sharp, indeed) made him dangerous and much feared among the other boarders. The man was capable of saying anything about anyone, and, because of certain allusions, doña Nicasia suspected that he knew about her relationship with Sordo. For that reason, she did not press him on the occasions when rent was due, and she generally tried to limit his power of coercion by making a face whenever he began to administer a tongue-lashing, which was often, indeed, because Isidoro understood the human comedy like the back of his hand, and whenever he lacked specific information about any particular individual, man or woman, he quickly invented it in order to complete his critique and maintain his legitimate reputation for being well informed.

But the daily disputes over which Spanish city or province was superior to all the others made him impatient. He left immediately when they began, so as not to offend the stubborn contenders, shutting himself in his room or going out earlier than he had intended to. He had already told them that such disputes were a waste of time and needlessly offensive:

"We're all bad and all worse off for coming here to seek our fortunes, yes sir, both the winners and the losers in América, this godforsaken place that never missed us when we pulled out and never invited us to come back. I'm really talking about you, though, because my case is a bit different. I came here in pursuit of Art, in pursuit of that great Art that none of you can even name properly. My talent put the competition in the shade even back in Madrid and Barcelona, can you imagine? Here in Mexico, who can compete with me in the realm of light musical theater? My word, nobody can touch me in any genre! Just name someone! And they're all so jealous, naturally, that they detest me and plot against me and have ostracized me, leaving me penniless . . . Isn't that right, doña Nicasia, that they've left us both penniless? . . . But the rest of you loafers have problems of your own making! Didn't you want to make a fortune in América? Well, then, get out of the city and into the countryside, where there's need for men to work hard, to fertilize it with their labor and water it with their sweat! Do those things, and the harvests will become silver pesos, and the pesos, ounces of gold, and the ounces, the fortune that you dreamed about in Spain . . . Get out from behind the store counter and you'll see. In a decade or so, you'll return to Spain as big shots, eating beef and sausages until you burst and waving your fork in the air, knowing how to read and write, wearing shiny shoes and a top hat, paying for a construction of a new church in your home village, and sending your nephews to América! You'll still be ignorant, but fat and sassy . . . whereas I . . ."

"Whereas *you*, always *you* . . . first, last, and always, no?" protested his listeners indignantly, and the curate let him have it with both barrels:

"Leave him alone, poor man. Let him vent. It's just histrionics . . ."

"Histrionics! Theater! And proud of it! Careful, father curate . . . don't mess with me . . . And here's another way," he continued, turning back to the others. "Want to get rich quick without working a single minute? Well, then, just marry some ugly rich woman! I'd do it, but I love my freedom and doña Nicasia too much for that. I'm a free man, a republican, an artist, an anarchist!"

"A moocher is what you are!" said the moneylender and the Covadonga employee at almost the same time. Both had lent the actor money some months previously, and both despaired of ever seeing it again.

Such conversations would normally be terminated by Ripoll, shouting from his room that he needed a bit of quiet in order to study, or by doña Nicasia, more maternally, with a wave of her arms and a few hoarse and not too courteous admonitions to Isidoro Gallegos.

The actor normally withdrew, at that point, although not before helping to set up the card table. Pulling his mended wool cape off the coat rack in the hall, he went out, first to the theater, where he entered gratis in the name of professional solidarity, then to a café, and after that, to any of various nocturnal watering holes, inveterate night owl that he was. The departure of Gallegos brought the boarding house some tranquility, though the calm was still only relative, since it included various disagreements of the card players, which are inevitable in such games, and all the more so among Latinos. The game might go until midnight if one of the players were enjoying extraordinary luck, but if not, the session would conclude at ten-thirty or eleven, when the players calculated their winnings and losings and doña Nicasia, who sat by the lamp reading all evening, had already gone to bed. The consensual signal occurred when Sordo pulled out his gold watch—which attracted the converging gazes of the other players more because of its monetary worth than because of its power to tell the time—and commented that it was almost eleven o'clock, whereupon everyone settled up and trundled off to bed.

The Guipuzcoana Boarding House (so-named according to painted signs in the entry stairwell) then advanced into the night like a great frigate: lights out, hatches battened down, wrapped in silence and darkness, its intrepid Spanish crew undaunted by the great distance to shore or the treacherous waves that rocked them all, both the strong and the weak, cradling both their ambitions and their disappointments. The fragility of their vessel did not concern them overmuch. Life is always fragile, and yet, think of all that conquerors, pilgrims, and poets can achieve before they arrive at their final destination.

From outside, only one small light could be detected, as if belonging to the helmsman on watch alone through the night on the sleeping ship. And appearances were not completely misleading in this case. The light came from Ripoll's room, and the engineer's concern was, in fact, a vessel, though not the "frigate" Guipuzcoana, but rather, a submarine that he had invented and that he had come to América with the intention of selling to the Mexican government. Ripoll sat surrounded by blueprints and drafting tools, facing, on the table in front of him, a perfect scale model of his invention: a beautiful contraption of aluminum, replete with towers, railings, skylights, torpedo tubes, and even a pair of masts that could be erected when the submarine was on the surface and taken down when it submerged into the oceanic depths. The Catalonian inventor spent hours and hours with his papers and numbers, calculating velocities and resistances, determining defects and advantages. Armed with a variety of tools, he reinforced a screw here, removed a plate there, changed the position of the smokestack, and moved a ladder from the starboard to the port side, and then back. His precious invention filled his heart with hope but also tormented him. The boilers were just not right, and the clumsy revolutions of the propeller drove him to distraction.

Doña Nicasia and her boarders had a superstitious respect for the engineer and his invention—and even some superstitious fear of the kind that illiterate people sometimes feel for books and words and numbers. Ripoll had read much, he let fly words in foreign languages, and he opened large technical volumes as calmly as the curate opened his missal to say mass. He had a magical ability to execute arithmetic operations in his head: doña Nicasia's queries about the expenses incurred at the market, Izquierdo's requests for interest calculations on objects left in pawn. Gradually, Ripoll became the pride of the boarding house, displacing, at least in secular matters, the sway formerly exercised by the curate, Práxedes Luro, which was based on no more than the prestige of his priestly cassock. Ripoll was a wise man, and he was Spanish—yes, Spanish, of course he was—and his wisdom validated their pretentions to have come to América to civilize it, demonstrating once again the universal and absolute supremacy of Spain. Because the inventor was temporarily impecunious, doña Nicasia actually consented to lend him money following a sort of plenary session in which the other boarders gave their endorsement, expressed by Sordo:

"The important thing is, don't give up on the submarine. When the government buys it, when they pay you for it, above all, you can pay us back. But in the meantime, forget it, you just tell us what you need . . . okay?"

It was, indeed, okay with Ripoll, and that's how things stood. His living expenses and the sale of his invention, once linked, remained equally insoluble. He became accustomed to living on credit, just as he got used to finding the doors at the Ministry of Defense permanently closed to him. The key was patience, and more patience, as doña Nicasia patiently demonstrated by never reminding him of his constantly mounting debt to her. Everyone at the Guipuzcoana Boarding House became interested in the submarine, the workings of which (precisely because they remained utterly incomprehensible) represented something not only otherworldly, but also, a source of future honor and advantage for each and every one of them. The curate rarely had an opportunity to say mass as he waited in vain for an appointment to a rural parish near the capital, promised to him by a well-placed member of the Spanish community in Mexico, but when he did say mass, he always included the invention among his petitions for divine favor. And on one Sunday, the boarders emptied their pockets to buy cider and walnuts and held a naming ceremony for the submarine, which, at the suggestion of Sordo and in tribute to doña Nicasia's regional origins, was baptized as the *Aragonés*. Nicasia danced a jota, the curate blessed the contraption, and Isidoro Gallegos sang, by himself, both parts of the duet from a fashionable zarzuela of recent years:

"Oh, the progress of the sciences is awesome to behold . . ."

The other boarders began to regard both inventor and invention with reverence, always speaking softly when at home and taking his every pronouncement as scripture. Arriving at the building late at night, they would look up at the engineer's lit window and smile to themselves, proud to live so close to a true genius who was bringing life to a fabulous creation, a submarine, that belonged somehow to the entire boarding house and that they therefore embraced with fierce adoration, even in its current state — tiny, imperfect, unfinished. They would adore it more fiercely yet on that great day, soon, when it splashed into the Gulf of Mexico and swam off like a whale to blow the most formidable armored battleships right out of the water! Olé!

Alas, the reign of Ripoll, inaugurated with such tender yearnings, did not last as long as he needed it to last. The arrival of the noted matador, el Jarameño, was the end of one era and the beginning of another. When el Jarameño entered the boarding house one fine day with a letter of recommendation from Spain, fistfuls of money, a pile of suitcases and trunks, and a personal valet, Bruno, rich in Andalusian lore of all kinds, Ripoll was instantly eclipsed in the eyes of the other boarders, and the *Aragonés* was just as instantly forgotten. In a kind of atavistic, ethnic instinct, everyone turned avidly to the torero and, driven by a secret, irresistible force, they welcomed and pampered him, as if his presence brought with it a miraculous blessing that they had awaited for years and years. El Jarameño won spontaneous, enthusiastic, unanimous approval with little effort on his part, but one thing he did have to do was produce plenty of cash, and quickly. With no offense intended toward doña Nicasia, it must be said that the Guipuzcoana was sailing straight into bankruptcy. El Jarameño, who was good at sniffing out such matters, applied a radical remedy, offering to pay double to be well taken care of and forking over the first two weeks' worth on the spot:

"Transparent accounts, *patrona*, and milky chocolate," he said. "Here's enough to tide you over for now, and later . . . there'll be more where that came from!"

Doña Nicasia squealed blissfully, Sordo squeezed the torero's hand firmly, the pawnbroker admired his gold jewelry, and Gallegos stepped shoulder to shoulder with him, applauding. Everyone praised el Jarameño's generosity.

Ripoll did not appear for lunch and only reluctantly rejoined the group when he got back to find them still sitting around the table, digesting an extraordinary meal with the help of countless drinks of anisette and manzanilla.

El Jarameño completely replaced Ripoll in the collective estimation of the boarders. He was the horn of plenty, the life of the house, an inexhaustible font of jest and good humor. The curate confessed frankly that el Jarameño was "a real man," and doña Nicasia always addressed him as *hijo*. With spontaneous consensus the house adopted the honorific title used by Bruno and the other toreros who were becoming frequent visitors—*maestro* is what they called el Jarameño, so doña Nicasia and her boarders followed suit. By coincidence, their adoption of this honorific term occurred just when the ministry finally notified Ripoll that his submarine design was unacceptable, that they did not want it at any price, or even as a gift. The news naturally plunged the engineer into a depression that he had to hide to avoid doña Nicasia's finding out and cutting off his food supply, as she was very likely to do if she discovered that, because of the ministry's decision, she would likely never recover Ripoll's debt to her, except perhaps on Judgment Day, if then. It must be admitted that Ripoll's intent was honest, that he clung to the notion of selling his submarine to somebody, to anybody, to private interests, to China, maybe, thereby paying off the immense mountains of debt, as high as the Pyrenees, that he owed to the owner of the house and to others. Resentment and fatigue soured his spirit and yellowed his skin. At the table, he sat sullenly, scowling and refusing to pay the customary homage to el Jarameño, blasphemous, aggressive, and irascible, growling insults that nobody except Gallegos understood at all, and he, only a word or two.

"Why don't you tell us anything interesting anymore?" asked the actor on a certain occasion.

"Because I've become an anarchist—really an anarchist, unlike you, who just pretends to be one. Any day now I'm going to alter my invention so that, instead of just sinking ships it will blow cities and entire nations to kingdom come! Oh, yes! Don't laugh! Entire nations with all their inhabitants . . . boom! To the clouds!"

"Aw, you don't want that," replied el Jarameño benevolently. "What did all those innocent folks do to you?"

Ripoll shrugged and let loose one of the incomprehensible terms that he had gleaned from his extensive reading and scholarly dealings:

"They have done me harm, immense harm," he said to the torero. "You still believe in innocent people, although arguably Herod eliminated all of them ages ago. I believe in other things. I believe, for example, that you and I and everybody on earth all descend from Anthropopithecus . . ."

Ripoll might have fared ill had he not immediately explained that Anthropopithecus (which no one, not even the curate, could pronounce) was a prehistoric ancestor, something akin to the great-great-grandfather of humankind, because the boarders surrounded him demanding a translation of the offensive word. The prehistoric ancestor more or less completed Ripoll's precipitous decline and fall. Doña Nicasia indicated that his rent was far overdue and required payment. Sordo avoided his gaze, the curate stopped saying hello to him, the group began to mock him to his face, and the maid began to leave his room uncleaned for two or three days at a stretch. Isidoro Gallegos, on the other hand, tried to remain his friend, visiting him in his room to give lessons on how to endure bad luck and derision with proper stoicism.

El Jarameño surprised everybody by defending Ripoll. Attracted and impressed by the engineer's fancy pseudoscientific language, by his bearded and virile countenance, and by his undeniably terrible fortune, the torero calmed the storm, paid doña Nicasia a month's worth of the rent in arrears, and, acting as absolute monarch against the curate's affirmation that Ripoll stank of heresy, el Jarameño lifted the decree of ostracism and tried to restore a bit of the man's former reputation.

"He really knows plenty," proclaimed the torero. "Can you imagine how many grammar books and universities he's messed with? Look, I stick up for him because I want to. Some afternoon, I'll dedicate a bull to him . . ."

The matter never went that far, though the amnestied party put aside his rancor and antipathy and showed himself to be undeniably grateful. But, go to the bullring? Him? A man who never attended a bullfight in Barcelona or Madrid?

"No, Jarameño, you'll have to excuse me, but I can't do that. Bullrings make me ill. Seriously. Don't dedicate anything to me there, because you've already done enough for me here. I hate bullfights and, usually, bullfighters—just let me continue to esteem you greatly as a friend and human being . . ."

That night el Jarameño did not come home for supper, which surprised nobody because, despite the culinary feats of doña Nicasia and the beaming faces with which the boarders normally greeted his arrival, he was not uncommonly absent at that hour. But everyone, even those deeply absorbed in the evening card game, did take notice when the matador's valet and sword bearer, Bruno, stuck his head into the parlor at about ten o'clock.

"The maestro needs a word with you, *patrona*."

"Is he sick?" asked doña Nicasia anxiously.

"No way!" Bruno replied, smiling. "He's healthy as he can be, but he's bringing someone with him . . ."

The card game stopped instantly. Gallegos, who had been about to go out, did not do so, doña Nicasia followed Bruno down the hall to his room, and the card players crowded against the near side of the screen that divided the parlor from the street door and the hall, each of them still holding a handful of cards. Nothing was heard from Ripoll's room, though he was there, with the light on. Apparently el Jarameño had gone directly to Bruno's room, half closed the door, and lit the oil lamp inside, because the light passing through the glass panes of the door finally clarified matters for the curious onlookers in the parlor.

"Darn," murmured Gallegos, stepping into the middle of the hallway for a better look, "the maestro's got himself quite a woman!"

"Doña Nicasia," said el Jarameño at that very moment, getting straight to the point, "here you have the woman who has captivated my heart and agreed to come live with me so that I don't die from lovesickness . . . She'll be the queen here . . . yours, mine, everybody's . . . So, that's it . . . If anybody doesn't like it, they can just leave, and if everybody doesn't like it, everybody can leave, because I'll pay for the whole house and the whole world, too. The lady's name is Santa, doña Nicasia. Will you take good care of her? Santa, come here my glory, come meet the *patrona*."

In the way women have of never forgetting certain gestures and expressions that suit them particularly well, Santa instinctively recovered the superb air that had adorned her in better times, her captivating air of country candor. All she had to do, in order to win over doña Nicasia utterly, was step into the lamp light and smile. Although the *patrona* did not, at that moment, welcome Santa as enthusiastically as she might have (despite already guessing what enormous and sorely needed benefits might accrue if she were willing to avert her eyes from the irregularities of the situation) it was only because she wanted to avoid irritating Sordo or incurring the ecclesiastical wrath of the resident priest. She quietly returned Santa's greeting and left the room.

Then, quickly and discretely, doña Nicasia convened an executive council meeting—Sordo, don Práxedes, and she—in her bedroom, and they speedily arrived at an agreement.

"Don't you think, father, that there's no problem as long as those involved are respectable people? Wouldn't you agree?" insisted Sordo, who took the initiative.

And, in the face of the evident assent on the part of both doña Nicasia and don Práxedes, who expressed his approval by raising his arm as if distributing blessings to his parishioners, the two male councilmen rejoined the gathering in the parlor while the *patrona* tried to get el Jarameño to open the door of his bedroom.

"It's me, Jarameño," she shouted. "Open the door. It's me! Both of you can stay, just like you wanted . . ."

No answer emerged from the darkness behind the locked door, and nothing could be seen through the keyhole, either. The only faint sound was that of kisses and mutual caresses, the awesome, triumphal hymn of the Flesh.

El Jarameño and Santa were finally offering to one another the princely gift of their bodies, their youth, and their beauty. The ceremony took place in silence and shadow: the silence interrupted only by the diffuse echo of lips meeting lips or exploring sweet and silky skin, long adored at a distance; the shadow attenuated only by the glow of their burning desire, long repressed, although life and love are short . . . The entire Guipuzcoana Boarding House gradually filled with, and was transfigured by, the love that seeped out of the bedroom through the cracks in the door, as if calm, invisible hands were quietly distributing incense throughout the structure, banishing envy, vulgarity, covetousness, and the other unworthy emotions that one commonly breathed in its rooms. Santa and el Jarameño were not, at that moment, merely a prostitute and bullfighter who, spurred by crude, lewd desire, had shut themselves in a shabby, rented room to satisfy themselves. No. They were the eternal pair, intoning the sacrosanct, eternal duet. They were love and beauty personified, and this was their consecration.

Doña Nicasia stepped gravely, respectfully, away from the door, her head bowed, with the attitude that we always adopt in the presence of the mysteries of birth, love, and death—the august, sacred mysteries of life itself.

The news circulated first among the boarders gathered in the parlor, and later, among those who were absent during this turn of events, upon arriving at their rooms later that night. The word spread that the curate had posed no opposition, that Sordo had given his approval, and that doña Nicasia was extremely pleased. There was a general shrugging of shoulders: what did another woman in the house matter? At the most, there was an eagerness to see her, a vague idea that she might somehow prefer one of them to the torero, the vaguely titillating disquiet that the presence of a pretty woman awakens in men of whatever age or walk of life. Corroded by disappointment, Ripoll shrugged even more than the others, upon hearing the news from Gallegos, who every morning installed himself in the engineer's room, wearing slippers and a ragged jacket, to chat and smoke half a dozen cigarettes:

"How about it, professor? A real invasion of skirts, if you ask me . . . and, I'm pleased as punch! She's a first class woman, if you ask me . . ."

Ripoll, bent over his numbers, refused to be excited: "Women? Bah! They're the same, all the same, no matter how much each and every lover may claim that his woman is exceptional . . . An entirely subjective judgment. If fact, they are all cut from the same cloth, women, with the same quirks and flaws, imperfect and imperfectible mechanisms. And because there is no other kind, and because we need them, we swear that we'll improve whatever woman we manage to grab for ourselves in the perennial scuffle . . ."

Gallegos chuckled at this philosophy: "If we kill ourselves for them and spend our lives chasing them—imperfect as women are—what if they were perfect? That would be the end of the world, professor!"

He told Ripoll that the boarders had acted that morning as if el Jarameño and his girl were real newlyweds, married the day before, eating breakfast in silence and tiptoeing off to their daily routines with a sidelong glance at the closed door:

"Go figure, man! Even the kitchen maid was careful to make as little noise as possible when she whipped the hot chocolate and washed the dishes. It's even better than the five acts of *The Lovers of Teruel*..."

Not a single boarder missed the midday meal which, according to house rules, was served at one o'clock sharp. On the other hand, there were some innovations: spotlessly white napkins and a table cloth, for one, and a centerpiece, too, containing a huge bouquet of flowers, a silver peso's worth, at least, that brought a smile to everyone's face. Gallegos floated a few risqué double entendres that the others carefully ignored and that soon evaporated amid loud throat-clearing from Sordo, a stern look from doña Nicasia, and a severe frown from don Práxedes. A large serving bowl of delicious-smelling soup preceded "the lovers of Teruel" to the table.

"Today I cooked the meal myself," proclaimed doña Nicasia. "There's cod, garlic soup, scrambled eggs with tomato, and potpourri."

"And the wine is on me!" shouted el Jarameño, arriving, radiant, hand in hand with Santa, who was blushing, if you can believe it, *blushing*, and secretly worried. Would they figure out what she had been? Would they see it in her face?

Fortunately, the round of applause that exploded at that moment bolstered her spirit and gave her confidence, even though they were applauding mostly for the dishes announced by doña Nicasia and the wine, promised by el Jarameño, that quickly materialized in a basket carried by Bruno: two dozen clinking bottles of real Spanish red wine from la Rioja.

Without difficulty, Santa captured this bunch of two-bit fortune seekers in her man net, the tool of an elegant and experienced prostitute, a net she had refined and expanded in numerous expeditions, and even mended in places where it threatened to wear out with incessant use. Ripoll succumbed, in spite of his contemptuous theories about women, and Isidoro succumbed as well, although he was trying to remember, as he stared at her, where he had seen this girl before.

The next Sunday, however, el Jarameño had a bullfight, and the scene changed considerably. The crew of lesser toreros who served el Jarameño, their matador, visiting him daily, were used to his periodic, stormy involvements with women, and they treated Santa unquestioningly as his temporary wife, but beginning on Saturday evening, she noticed a change in them. They had lost their accustomed boisterousness and did no laughing nor singing that night, but instead, at any point in the conversation, and especially when it seemed about to recover its characteristic gaiety, they became taciturn, removing the ash from their cigarettes with pensive meticulousness and sighing very, very softly, as if mechanically trying to conceal their mood even from themselves. They gazed fixedly at their "maestro" as if internally lighting votive candles in favor of tomorrow's performance in the bullring, where his skill might bring renown to all of them, but where an error might be fatal.

"Behave yourselves tonight, and tomorrow early, everybody to the bullring to take a look at the bulls we'll be fighting," el Jarameño said to them when they left.

Santa saw clearly that they went away worried, and that Jarameño, too, was worried as he walked back to the room. At their late supper, he ate soberly, without tasting the wine, and in their warm bed with the light off, he did not embrace her. Surprised and alarmed, she reproached him:

"Don't you love me anymore?" she asked, pressing her body against him in an unmistakable offer.

The matador trembled with temptation, but quieting his fiery temperament, he said to his mistress, as if begging for an enormous favor:

"No, I don't love you anymore. Now I *adore* you. I'd give my life for a single hair on your head . . . and for all of you, well, I'd give the life of my whole hometown. And for you to be always faithful . . . I'd give all the kingdoms and empires in the world. And there's a lot of kingdoms and empires out there, too! If I don't hug and kiss you and eat you alive right now, I miss it more than you, I swear by the cross!" And he held up his crossed fingers, unseen in the pitch blackness. "And you better believe that if I'm still alive tomorrow night, I'm going to, too! And I'm not afraid, neither, because you should see me pushing that sword into the bull, with my hand just as calm and steady . . . It's that, if you get too stirred up the night before a fight—hey, it may be gypsy superstition—but you run the risk of being gored . . . and loving you like I do, I can't let that happen, right? No way! . . . So don't touch me or tempt me, please, in the name of your blessed mama that bore you, because if you touch me I can't be responsible for what happens because I feel flames in my veins right now, and they're flaming your way, and I'm trying to come after them, and I could so easy die on top of you and feel nothing but the desire to stay with you, dead, and stay buried right there, until the end of the world, a million years, our whole lifetimes, and our kids' and grandkids' lifetimes, too, all added together . . . Santa, my darling Santa!"

Contrary to his usual habit, el Jarameño did not drink coffee in bed the following morning. Instead, he received the breakfast tray from Bruno at the door and served a cup to Santa, who had now become impressed with the gravity of the day and drank her coffee unhappily, propped up on the pillows. Even having just opened her eyes, she was ravishing. Her rebellious black mane cascaded over the pillows, followed by a round shoulder and then a superb hip rising like the principal mountain on the wrinkled landscape of blankets, flanked by many grottos and canyons, and continued by the long, gentle slope of her extended legs. Dozens of trails led away from the human mountain range toward the edges of the bed, though some of them turned under the sheets and led, innocently enough at first, in the direction of the courtesan's warm, velvety brown skin.

The sun, the sun up in the sky—that had bathed the room when el Jarameño opened the wooden shutters of the balcony, invading like repressed waters that suddenly burst a dike and flood a field—flooded over Santa, spraying her with brilliant light and golden motes that floated in the atmosphere, painting her shadow on the wall behind her, also penetrating the tiny gaps in the front of her nightgown and silently kissing her breasts with its astral lips.

"This afternoon is going to be great," predicted el Jarameño, turning to admire so much sun in the room. And lingering on the image of Santa, who motionlessly awaited the double bath of heat and light, he growled between half-clenched teeth, as if talking to himself:

"You're sooo pretty . . ."

And then, remembering that this was not a time for tender feelings, he put himself in the hands of Bruno, whose straight razor shaved the maestro with the skill of a professional barber's, leaving it smooth and bluish. As he dressed the matador in street clothes for the time being, carefully brushing his broad-brimmed hat, and handing him his walking cane adorned with tortoiseshell and gold, Santa began to insist that she be allowed to attend the bullfight:

"Take me with you, Jarameño. Just imagine what I'll go through if I sit here alone all afternoon. Should I get ready?"

Not in a million years. El Jarameño did not smile as he repeated the negative reply he had given earlier when Santa had asked to see him fight, referring again to his presentiments, his "gypsy superstitions" as he called them:

"No, no, my Santa, not on your mother's soul, don't ask for that! I feel in my heart that the day you see me fight, something terrible is going to happen to me . . . You stay here and pray and keep me on your mind and in your heart, and before night falls I'll come back to you."

Bruno had meanwhile set up a sort of imitation altar on a dresser top: in front of a colored engraving of the Virgin of the Remedios, two votive candles that would burn during the period of imminent danger. El Jarameño himself would light them upon leaving and put them out upon returning, whether returning safe and sound or carried by his men, as had occurred that time in Bilbao, when a bull gored him in the groin, a wound that still bothered him.

All the boarders at the Guipuzcoana restrained themselves, not giving free vent to their excitement with the maestro in mind, making the early midday meal, which would be served during his absence at the bullring, quieter than usual. El Jarameño himself had only the light breakfast prescribed for toreros before a fight—two soft-boiled eggs and a shot of dry Jerez—because his stomach needed to be relatively empty to fit the tight suit he would be wearing and to maximize his agility and speed when facing the bulls. Santa had no appetite and ate no more than a mouthful despite the urgings of doña Niacasia, who was showing her singular affection. Santa experienced nervous palpitations. She felt like crying and resented the others' tendency to check their watches and give each other knowing looks. The phlegmatic Ripoll, who did not share the general mood, ate with gusto, while Gallegos, a true fan, delirious with enthusiasm, particularly because of the excellent seats that el Jarameño had arranged for him, tirelessly augured favorable circumstances and outcomes of all kinds. There was going to be an enormous crowd at the bullring, with lots and lots of pretty girls:

"All rooting for you, man! So do your best to show the flag! Artists like you and me owe it to . . ."

A hail of insults and crumbs of food shut him up. How could a worthless comic actor compare himself to the likes of el Jarameño . . . ? The only risk that an actor runs is a few boos, a stray kick in the head from the can-can dancers, or possibly the loss of a contract, whereas toreros risked their lives! They could die or be crippled. Bruno entered to tell the maestro it was time to go, breaking the funereal silence that followed these observations. To die . . . and yet, no matter how easily lives are lost, nobody present really expected that it might happen, including el Jarameño, who walked confidently out of the dining room that afternoon with Santa by the hand.

Bruno preceded the lovers into their room, and once all were inside, he locked the door.

On the large double bed was the sparkling matador's "suit of lights," the jacket with its open sleeves, the knee-length pants, the other pieces, all carefully laid out, awaiting the wearer. Still holding Santa's hand, el Jarameño went to light the candles, kneeling and contemplating the image of the virgin for a time, lost in thought. If he prayed, he prayed mentally, because Santa failed to note the slightest movement of his lips. He looked pale.

"Sit down, country girl, and learn how to dress me. It's complicated," he said, sitting back so that Bruno could pull off the tight pants of his street clothes to begin the dressing operation.

The sun now shone so brightly in the street outside the window that its reflection from the sidewalk below was enough to fill the room with friendly, vivifying light.

El Jarameño stood up, almost naked, and Santa silently admired the classical beauty of his virile physique. The muscles, the tendons, the steely hardness that one sensed in the biceps, the pectorals, the shoulder blades, the broad back, the massive neck, and the wiry, solid calves of his legs—all harmonized with one another. The matador possessed the athletic perfection of an ancient gladiator or discus thrower, a potent, total male, born and bred for manly contests that require boldness, bravery, and strength, like the ancient Olympic games in which the contestants died facing the sun, in a noble pose, smiling at the female spectators and the heavens, their feats celebrated by warlike music, their funeral bed splendid, indeed. Lying on the sun-drenched sand of the arena, the hero expired surrounded by the blood of beasts howling in their death throes, covered in the purple shroud of his own blood, caressed by gentle breezes, and hearing from the colorfully attired audience a mad clamor and applause, the panting, tremulous breath of the multitude fascinated by the near presence of a danger that cannot reach them but that subjugates them and sends shudders through them, awakening their deepest and wildest passions. Oh, how Santa admired her man!

She recognized intuitively that he was made for this. On the other hand, she knew that he was also made for love, for *her* love, and she adored him in her adaptable way, for his gypsy oaths, for his strong arms that crushed the breath out of her in savage caresses. She could not bear the thought of losing him so soon, the thought that a bull might kill him on an afternoon like that one, that seemed made more for intimacy than carnage . . .

"Now watch, my dark one, watch how a matador is prepared for the arena," said el Jarameño as he lowered himself into a chair and put himself in Bruno's expert hands.

First, short linen under-breeches, then the tight binding of the ankles against sprains and dislocations, then cotton stockings, then, over these, silk ones stretched so tight as to eliminate even the hint of a wrinkle, and finally, the slight, shiny black shoes. Now, up, on your feet! The breeches are next, and the showy, ruffled linen shirt, with four buttonholes in its starched collar.

"My button chain, Bruno," ordered el Jarameño as he slipped the silk necktie under the collar, fastened his suspenders, tucked his shirt into the breeches and buckled them, ready for the sash that Bruno bound and cinched tightly around his waste before stepping away to prepare the hair extensions.

El Jarameño was about to button his collar when he saw in the wash-stand mirror, his saint's medal—glistening with sweat and tangled in the thick, black hair of his chest—and devoutly raised it to his lips, kissing it softly.

"The hair extensions, Bruno. Quickly!" he commanded, sitting down again and unbraiding his pigtail.

At that very moment, a coach could be heard stopping at the curb in front of the Guipuzcoana, and doña Nicasia and all her boarders (except Ripoll) were instantly outside the bedroom door:

"The coach is here, maestro, and it's almost two-thirty! Shouldn't we be going?"

"I'll be right out," el Jarameño reassured them. "You go on ahead, and remember to let me hear you in the bullring!"

Bruno braided in the hair extensions and tied everything with the regulation oval bow. Good! It looks good . . . okay, the vest. Now tighten it there. That's it. And the jacket . . .

"Careful with the shoulder pads, man! Straighten them out. No, pull hard . . . not so much . . . there," directed el Jarameño as he fit his arms into the narrow sleeves.

Then he placed the distinctive matador's cap on his head, firmly, so that the front bit into his eyebrows and the chinstrap clearly bisected both cheeks from temple to chin. With hands and elbows, he checked to see that the two handkerchiefs protruded just the right amount from his jacket pockets, and bending slightly forward, he permitted Bruno, with the reverence of a sacristan handling the priest's holy vestments, to drape his shoulders gloriously with the large green and gold street cloak.

"Open the door, my jewel! And tell the coachman to put the top down," el Jarameño ordered Santa, still admiring himself in the mirror, his left hand on his hip so that the cloak hung off the elbow, egotistically in thrall to his own image and studiously cultivating it for the benefit of spectators, the way that star performers do.

The open door to the balcony admitted diaphanous waves of light interspersed with the cool auras of a tropical winter. Both waves and auras played splendidly over the matador's green suit of lights, encrusted with gold embroidery. Santa experienced an unexpected and instantaneous jealousy, understanding why toreros awaken such enthusiasm from the crowd as they parade into the bullring, why even high-society ladies fall passionately in love with them, or rather, with their image. The toreros' vices and defects do not become apparent until later, much later. In the bullring, they are pure art and power, simple color and curve, all agility and mastery. Their faces are smooth and pale, their eyes dark. Bloodstained, they fight, kill, wound, fall . . . and sometimes die. And always, they love, one woman today, another tomorrow.

Bruno gazed at him like a faithful dog, idolizing him, attentive to his least gesture, proud to dress and care for him, yearning to satisfy even his passing whims. The sword bearer and valet calmly bundled together the matador's equipment, the three fighting capes, stained with bull's blood and mended here and there, the three rods that el Jarameño would use to extend the capes and incite the charging animal, and the large leather case emblazoned with the matador's monogram, containing three straight, heavy swords of Toledo steel, their tips as sharp as needles.

"Are we ready?" asked el Jarameño.

At the sword bearer's affirmative response, he then went quickly to Santa, put his arm around her waist, and whispered in her ear. He whispered promises and desires, quickly renewed declarations of boundless love, renewed demands of impossible fidelity, the kinds of things that people demand and promise in the face of separations that may be eternal, to somehow buttress themselves against fate and overcome the dangers through sheer willpower, their blind confidence in their reunion itself becoming a kind of poetry.

"See you later, my Santa, I swear that I'll see you later! Pray for me now, and love me, love me a lot."

It was a scene from a Goya painting, until el Jarameño and Bruno finally walked out of the room. Santa went to the balcony and watched the open coach pull away from the curve, Bruno, with his bundle and a serious expression, riding up front beside the driver, el Jarameño the lone passenger, his upturned face sending her thousands of kisses, so unabashedly that passersby looked up as well, interested in the target of such a bombardment. As the coach went around the corner, el Jarameño stopped blowing kisses and made hand signals indicating that he would be right back, that she should wait for him . . . Would he be back? Ha! You had better believe it!

"May we come in, dear?" Santa heard someone say behind her as she closed the door to the balcony. Doña Nicasia and Ripoll, neither of whom was going to the bullring, had agreed to keep her company and try to distract her with a little conversation: a bit whiny and vulgar on the *patrona*'s part, a tad angry but more amusing on the naval engineer's part.

El Jarameño's coach was not yet three blocks away, however, when the maid appeared in the room to tell Santa that someone had come to see her.

"Come to see *me*?" she asked, shakily. "Who can it be, if I haven't told anybody I'm here?"

Still, she could not resist, even in the presence of Doña Nicasia and the inventor, giving the automatic response, learned in her recently abandoned profession, of making herself available to anyone who sought her.

"Excuse me, then . . . no, no, doña Nicasia, don't trouble yourself! I'll go see who it is . . ."

It was Jenaro, Hipólito's guide boy, who smiled at her from the stairs, barefoot and ragged, with his rumpled straw hat held firmly between his knees.

"Jenaro, are you looking for me? What's going on? How did you know I was here?"

"Gee, Miss Santa, going off with el Jarameño like that, where else would you be?"

"And what brings you, who sent you?" said Santa affectionately moving closer to the boy and already knowing the answer.

"Well, who do you think, Miss Santa? Hey, don't act dumb! It was my master, don Hipólito, who doesn't know what to do with himself, seems like, since you left. He is *sad* . . . I swear he's sad. And he said to me this morning, he said 'now Jenaro, go over to the Guipuz . . . the Guipuzco . . .' whatever it is, 'and when the other fellow leaves . . . and I hope a bull gets him, too . . .' he said this now, not me, okay? 'When he leaves, you go in and talk to Santa, but without saying anything about me, like it was your own idea. Go on now, be a good boy, go and see her for me.' So here I am, and I've seen you, and now I'm going, but I'll be back next Sunday. Today I came at one o'clock and watched from the pulque shop across the street while I waited for el Jarameño to leave. I saw you on the balcony! I'll bet you saw me, too, what do you bet? And Miss Santa," he murmured shyly before saying goodbye, "could you get me as seat at the bullring? It wouldn't need to be a seat in the shade . . ."

Santa explained that she had no tickets to give, that the ticket sellers had them all:

"But how about a two-peso bill?"

"A two-peso bill," repeated Jenaro, stunned, as she gave him one. When it was his, he smelled it, rolled it up like a cigarette, and stuck it in his waistband through a hole in his shirt.

"With a couple of pesos, even the policemen on the corner respect me!"

He half turned, ready to fly down the stairs, but Santa stopped him:

"Wait, Jenaro. What are you going to tell Hipo?"

"What else? That he's right to love you, that he should love you even more, blind and all, the way we all love you, all of us who see you."

And he plummeted down the stairs without seeming to mind the pounding of his bare heels on the stone steps, and, passing through the courtyard, he could not resist kicking over a soapy basin full of socks belonging to Sordo and the curate . . .

SANTA'S LIFE AS A MATADOR'S MISTRESS was tranquil, indeed. One week slipped quietly along after the next in the insipid atmosphere of the Guipuzcoana Boarding House, amid Gallego's jokes, Sordo's wheedling, Ripoll's rages, and the curate's constant, if elastic, moralizing. Santa started to laugh as soon as Gallegos seemed about to speak, asking him to sing music from zarazuelas and listening for hours to stories, true and fabricated, from his bohemian life as a comic actor. In the presence of don Práxedes, true to her country upbringing, Santa kissed the priest's hand, and with doña Nicasia she talked about her village, her Chimalistac, at once so near and so far away, with its fruit trees and little white houses, between the villages of San Angel and Santa Catarina. Ripoll interested her, without her knowing why; Izquierdo, the pawnbroker, frightened her because she thought that one day he might try to make off with her jewelry, which he studied intently at the table whenever they shared a meal; and toward Abascal, the retailer, who sighed for her behind el Jarameño's back, she was utterly indifferent.

Her love for the torero seemed to wear away with the passage of the weeks, each so like the next, so featureless, so without parties or excitement. They would go for carriage rides some afternoons, attend the theater and dine out occasionally in the evening, wandering the shops together and buying things that, afterward, once brought home to their room, seemed totally out of place.

That the man loved her cannot be doubted. What frenetic caresses and extremes! What lightening glares when they spoke of the sordid past, what sweet humility of an indomitable beast restraining itself when they spoke of a future without pain or shadows, there in his Andalusian home, very soon, just as soon as he finished his contract. Nonetheless, if not for the weekly alarm of Sundays, and the danger that a bull might rip el Jarameño's belly open, if not for the drunkenness of his weekly homecomings, safe and sound, smelling like a goat and falling insatiably on her gorgeous body, that he took and took until he hurt her, begging her to bite him hard—if not for all of this, Santa would have tired of him. She would have left him without hatred, but it would not have been hard for her to do.

She had imagined it differently, this life he promised during his visits to Elvira's house. She had envisioned a continual party, guitars and toreros, Spanish wine and the bullring, Santa there, highly visible, el Jarameño dedicating his kills to her, the public learning of their love, applauding Santa like the poor cigarette girl Carmen, who loves a bullfighter in Bizet's eponymous opera . . . And what a contrast with reality! El Jarameño was jealous about the past, jealous about the present, distancing himself from old friends and new admirers, excluding third parties in the carriage rides and dinner outings, as selfish as all men when they are in love and really believe they can fulfill all a woman's heterogeneous and unguessable aspirations by themselves. No, the perpetual and monotonous "I love you" is not enough, or at least it was not enough for Santa. She had heard it so often and from so many! One Sunday she even told Jenaro, who never failed to appear in the matador's absence, that she missed her old life . . .

It was true. The experiment with a decent life had bored and displeased her, probably because her fall was irreparable. The damage had gone to the root, so to speak, because the two months that the charade lasted should have been long enough for Santa to reacclimatize herself. Besides, el Jarameño really did terrify her. She felt him capable of carrying out the grisly threats that all lovers formulate but few actually execute: the idle death threats that we utter without thinking when a pitiless instinct tells us that love has ended. How can the flesh we adore, the soul we thought incorporated into our own, abandon us, the flesh going to join with other flesh, the soul to another's soul, with no power on earth that can stop them?

"If you stop loving me someday, I'll kill you . . . I swear I'll kill you!" all lovers say, but few carry out the threat.

Maybe fear itself had something to do with Santa's apparently motiveless infidelity. Maybe it was the voluptuous attraction that danger exercises on feminine temperaments, an unhealthy desire to defy death, to tremble in its presence and breathe its icy breath with delicious terror.

However that may be, one Sunday when the bullfight was unexpectedly terminated halfway through by an enormous scuffle, a protest at the poor quality of the bulls resulting in the armed intervention of the authorities and the broken heads of a number of fans—one treacherous Sunday, Santa betrayed el Jarameño, surrendering herself to Ripoll, who even resisted at first. No, no, it wouldn't be decent, he owed the torero favors, he'd given him his hand in friendship, and so on. But Santa insisted, el Jarameño was far away, he'd never know.

"And I like you, silly! You're a real hard luck case . . . so let's go!"

Enflamed by the temptress, Ripoll gave up and gave in, allowing himself, in accord with his socialist theories, to destroy the property of someone else almost as a lark, taking the happiness of a happy man, a man to whom he owed a debt of gratitude.

Suddenly, el Jarameño entered the room, a bolt of lightening frozen into a statue at the sight of the ignominious deed. Ripoll made an instant, miraculous escape, leaving only the echo of his hatless, breathless sprint down the stairs and across the courtyard. Then, a second later, came the volcanic eruption, the blinding rage, the need to destroy, to repay harm with harm.

Wobbling slightly, el Jarameño locks the door of the room and tears off the restraining suit of lights. He looks for something in the dresser, then in his street clothes hanging up, and when he finds it, he growls a sinister, guttural sound, as if his Bedouin ancestors were reawakening inside him.

At the balcony door, which stands ajar, enters pallid late-afternoon light and the sounds of Sunday on the street.

Santa thinks her time has come. Quickly, solemnly, tragically, she kneels, looking at the image of the virgin with its two candles, their untrimmed wicks now flickering and hissing. Candles like those placed around a corpse, she thinks. Meanwhile, like a tiger that is about to pounce on its prey, el Jarameño gathers himself and opens his pocketknife with his teeth. It squeaks as it opens, a promise of mayhem. The curved blade glints as he violently extends his arm far back to deliver the most devastating blow possible, to stab the deceiving heart straight through, to sink his hand into guilty blood and splintered bone . . . and so powerful are his movements that when the blade catches and embeds itself in the dresser behind him—the dresser with the image and its candles—it lodges itself deeply in the wood.

El Jarameño pulls and pulls with wild anger, but it takes him how long to free the knife . . . a minute? A century? In the process, he knocks over the candles and the framed image of the virgin, and the glass in the frame shatters with a crash. El Jarameño obeys his gypsy superstitions, drops the knife, picks up the image, and brushes it off. He says to his mistress hoarsely, without looking at her:

"The virgin in heaven has saved you. She's the only one who could . . . Now, get out! Get out, and don't let me see or hear you! Get out! Because if you don't . . ."

Seven

Straight as the flight of an arrow, without a hint of hesitation or vacillation, like a swallow that returns to the dusty eaves of a roof where its nest has awaited, empty, resisting the rain and frost during the season of the bird's absence, Santa directed her fugitive steps to Elvira's house. She did not reflect that she had abundant access to other resources that were safer and, above all, more respectable. She did not remember the projects that she had imagined a few months before, when the death of her mother had so shaken her spirit and offered, if she could abjure a life of prostitution, the promise of resurrection for her body and soul. She thought of none of that.

Pursued by the terrible look of el Jarameño, a look pregnant with homicide, that had made her think her time had come, she fled from the Guipuzcoana Boarding House, humiliated, trembling, her lovely head hanging, her eyes on the ground, her heart intimidated and beating irregularly, now with great haste, as if she were escaping from jail, now very slowly, as if she were attempting, in her panic, to make herself invisible. She knew that doña Nicasia and all the other denizens of the Guipuzcoana were watching her from doors and windows, immobile and aloof, indicating that they all knew of her filthy behavior and all condemned it. She lifted her skirt in order not to trip, and not feeling safe with even one foot in the Guipuzcoana, she took a few steps away from the broad entrance of the building onto the busy sidewalk, hoping that she would not attract too much attention there in her house dress, without a hat or coat. Fortunately, it was getting dark and because it was Sunday, few stores had lit their show windows. Shadows had begun to gather in the downtown streets, resting here and there on the cobblestones, nosing their way into open doors, hanging down the sides of tall buildings, catching on balconies, splitting on signs and other protrusions, like a very old curtain that the wind has whipped to tatters. Santa found a pool of shadow on the sidewalk and stayed in it until she was able to hail an empty rental coach and direct it to the well-known brothel.

"Hop right in, my *patrona*," said the coachman, lighting the lamps as he listened to the address. "Okay, I know where, Elvira's house."

The strangest thing. Now that she was alone in the coach, going by Plateros and San Francisco Streets where the cafés and hair-cutting establishments were open, brightly lit and crammed with customers; now that she was part of the slow-moving traffic that snaked in luminous slow motion through the center of the great city, now that she was amid the multitude and yet felt more isolated than in the Guipuzcoana—now Santa was sorry that she had cheated on el Jarameño. Why betray him when he loved her so much? Why give up the planned trip to Spain, a trip that would have been something like a honeymoon? And why in the world do it with the inventor, who had never pursued her, instead of with Abascal, whom she mesmerized? And the infinite sadness that sometimes presages the slow onset of an incurable disease, long before there are any apparent symptoms of it, came over Santa for just an instant—an intense instant that forced her to recognize the running sores she had within her, like a fruit that rots from the inside, bored by a worm, while it still looks good on the outside, so that people buy it, taste it, and admire it, but then throw it in the trash as soon as they find the internal decay. How had she become so perverted so quickly if yesterday, just yesterday, she had been so pure? . . . She did not, could not, answer this question, and she did not want to. She accepted *what is* with the passive resignation that comes over both the wise and the ignorant, both the humble and the powerful, when facing the secret forces and unfathomable purposes that sweep us like dry leaves down the twisting paths of life. She began to recognize the evil, felt its contours, and accepted the fatal consequences. On the other hand, escaping the ire of el Jarameño filled her with the instinctive happiness that makes us touch and caress our own bodies after a near brush with annihilation. It seemed a miracle. If that knife had not buried itself in the wood of the dresser . . . why, it would have buried itself in her flesh, in the turgidity of her silk and marble breast that men sought so deliriously, perhaps . . . or at any other point, any superlative curve or dimple of the myriad that covered her dusky body like resting places for lips that, somehow condemned to madly kiss every inch of her, must stop occasionally to gather strength to go on, and on, and on . . . What luck to have escaped! . . . But what if el Jarameño saw her again . . . would he try to kill her again? . . . No, he wouldn't try it again! Those things happen the first time or not at all. If the attempt fails, that's it. Both parties are usually happy to leave it at that. Now that the link between them had been broken and she was no longer his mistress, the torero was unlikely to act violently and throw away everything on her account.

And distractedly, the girl began to look carefully at the windows of beauty shops that displayed masks, wigs, and other disguises. Today, Sunday, was the first day of carnival.

Eufrasia's reaction when she opened the door and saw Santa surpasses description. She hugged her, lifted her off the floor, caressed her cheeks, her waist, her clothing. She was so, so happy that the pride and happiness of the house had returned! Doña Pepa, doña Elivra, and the girls would be astonished, too, because no one expected her!

"And don Hipólito, the piano player, might just recover his sight when he hears! Doña Pepa! Doña *Pepa*! . . ." shouted the ecstatic servant from the bottom of the stairs in a rush to convey the glad tidings. "Good news, doña Pepa! She's back! Santita is here again! . . . They're having supper," she explained to Santa.

There was a true uproar in the dining room, a sound of spilled dishes and falling chairs, then many hugs and kisses for the returnee, curiosity in glances and salutations, some sincere jubilation, some renewed envy.

"What has happened to you, woman?" asked Pepa when the din diminished. "Have you had supper?"

Before she could reply, Santa's nerves let loose. The jumbled and repressed emotions of the afternoon awoke: happy feelings because of the warm reception, but bitter feelings because she saw how far she had sunk, that being in a brothel comforted her. The emotions choked off her voice, and, instead of words, what came were tears as she sat beside Pepa at the head of the long, noisy table.

"What's that about?" asked Pepa, absently fondling the wisps of hair at the nape of Santa's neck. "Dummy! He'll change his mind, and if he doesn't, who cares? This world is full of trousers, but not full of pretty things like you. What did you quarrel about, anyway?"

"It's a miracle that he didn't kill me today, Pepa!" said Santa, finally, sitting up in her chair. "And I'm afraid the he still may try to kill me."

"What did you do to him?" asked Pepa neutrally, chomping on her habitual cigar.

So responsible did Santa seem to feel for what had happened, that she could not confess it even there, *there*, where indulgences and pardons in such matters are easily obtainable. Instead, her eyes on the tablecloth in order to better dissimulate her lie, she answered merely:

"Me? . . . Nothing! It was jealousy, the damned jealousy that girls like us always get from men!"

Pepa, incredulous and quite expert in sniffing out infidelities, did not insist. Instead, she waved her lit match in a vague and expansive gesture that seemed intended to illuminate, with the tiny flame, a vast assortment of deceptions and other failings that play havoc with love. It was probably just as Santa claimed, she appeared to indicate, lighting her cigar with the meticulous care of a connoisseur and the phlegmatic calm of a philosopher unfazed by irremediable human frailties.

Nor did the other women swallow Santa's story. Jealousy? True, jealousy might occasionally be without foundation, but more often, and most especially with women like them, who, in order to continue their unhappy existence, make of deception a habit, of infidelity an incentive, and of forgetfulness a necessity—with them jealousy was almost always well founded. Consequently, if the torero had tried to kill Santa, he probably had a reason, and if some of the women tended to excuse her behavior, others censured it out of pure envy. What more could Santa ask than to live with a man who offered her both love and money? How presumptuous of her!

Santa noticed the absence of la Gaditana. What had happened to her? Oh, she had gone off with a customs official who took her more or less to the ends of the earth, Nogales or Tapachula, some place like that near the border, a remote corner of Mexico, a countless days' journey away.

"And you've lost the room you had," said two or three of the women, "right, Pepa? Now you'll live on this floor, in the room beyond the small parlor."

Pepa nodded, giving no importance to the change of rooms, urging Santa to eat:

"Doesn't matter what it is, a few sips of broth, whatever, to get rid of those dark circles under your eyes. Are you going to the masked ball tonight?"

The girls all talked at once, wanting Santa to go with them. Some were going with clients, some in a group, some disguised, some not. Santa didn't have clothes? No problem, she could cover herself completely in a hooded cloak, the perfect costume for the situation. Nor was there any reason to fear el Jarameño, because supposing that he went and looked for her there, she'd be fine as long as she kept a mask on and left before it got too late.

"If you want, don't come to the parlor tonight," offered Pepa, "I'll let you off and won't charge you nothing. Go lie down for a while and try to sleep, if you can, to get your strength back, and later on, when the gang is ready to leave for the ball, you can decide if you want to go . . . Oh, and do you want poor Hipo to come say hello? He's going to go crazy when he finds out you've come back."

Santa said yes to everything. She told the girls she'd go to the dance wearing a hooded cloak and mask and told Pepa she'd take some broth and rest and say hello to Hipólito . . . really, poor guy!

From her closed room, minutes later, she listened to the sounds of the parlor, so familiar to her, and even recognized the voices of a few old clients, the regulars, who have transcended the category of mere customers (who come to pay, do their business, and leave) to enter the category of friends. The regulars ask about the health of each one of the girls, call them by their real names instead of their professional monikers, take an interest in all the house gossip, and sometimes enjoy a card game and a free glass of anisette in Elvira's room. In the relative quiet of her new bedroom, Santa felt a total calm that reconciled her with herself and with others. Nobody had really been so perverse, not even she. At bottom, she didn't love the torero, but she didn't hate him either. To the contrary, she still liked him a lot, and even hoped that it might cheer him if she told him so. They could still be friends, sleeping together whenever their respective bodies asked it of them. Santa would not admit that she was the guilty one. She hardly ever analyzed actions, whether those of others or her own, and she was driven by cosmic, elemental forces of nature that are sometimes blind forces of invincible destruction. Woman, it has been said, is a microcosm of nature, the matrix of life, and for that very reason, the matrix of death, too, because life is constantly reborn out of death. Blind forces of destruction, unopposed by Santa's facile logic and debased values, drove her to absolve herself, not only for what she had recently done, but also for what she would do in the future, some things more benign, some less, so many things she would do, given her hunger of flesh and sickness of heart.

The only thing that she really wanted, her purity, her honor, the totally clean conscience of an immaculate virgin, trusting and gullible, who knows nothing of sin and is pitilessly sacrificed just because she loves . . . that was gone, gone forever, and it wasn't coming back. Was it so far away? . . . Neither near, nor far, but rather somewhere for which there are no words, somewhere invisible, where death is, for example. That was it, death, which she had just escaped—never near, because it might be far, but never far, because it might be near. The idea intrigued her. What she wanted was *there*.

Santa abandoned herself, mind and body, to what she supposed to be forces beyond her control, and finding herself back in the brothel, she breathed easier and wrapped herself in ignominy as if wrapping herself in cashmere and silk. She would not try to change; she would continue being bad. Her plan, since she could not resist being bad, was to use evil as a weapon, willy nilly. So it is, always, with forces that are beyond control, such as the river by which she had grown up in Chimalistac, she reasoned. When it flowed gently, it was a blessing, and when in flood, it tore up tree trunks, drowned livestock, and ruined fields without caring one whit if people cursed and shook their fists or cried and begged it to stop. What were their threats or entreaties to the river? Nothing! She would behave the same way. With her caresses she would calm the men who thirsted for her body, calm all who wanted it. There was enough for everybody. And if she happened to deceive and cause grief, what of it? They could kill her or let her be, nothing in between!

Convinced of her own perversion, dizzy at having gazed into a moral abyss, Santa twisted her face in the dark and sat bolt upright in bed. It was not her fault. It was not! Let them inspect every moment of her girlhood, let them dig through the rubble in her heart if they could bear it, the rubble of innocent castles in the sky that had crashed silently to earth in a world of pain. But they wouldn't take the trouble to dig, would they? They'd be happy enough rubbing and kissing her breasts, without wondering whether the heart that beat underneath were happy or unhappy. And if all they wanted was her body, that's all she'd give them, until they couldn't take any more, or until they'd made her sick, as normally occurred, as had occurred with various of her predecessors at Elvira's house, as would occur with those who came after her. Who cared about her heart, anyway? Not her! She'd almost forgotten about it. Maybe she should look for it and dedicate it to el Jarameño!

No, what had happened was enough. As long as she loved the torero—because without any question she had loved him—she had been faithful.

But that afternoon, she had wanted the inventor, and so what? For that he's going to kill her? . . . Again she felt the pure, physical pleasure of having escaped a near brush with death, and she ran her hands over her lovely body automatically, as if needing confirmation that it was still intact.

Just then, guessed Santa, they told Hipólito that she was back, because the piano fell silent abruptly, notes left hanging, and the footsteps of the blind man sounded in the courtyard, his cane tapping incessantly on tiles and walls, his voice softly but urgently alerting the sleeping guide boy:

"Jenaro! Jenaro! Santa is here! This time it's true because Pepa told me . . ."

"Come in, Hipo!" shouted Santa from the bed as soon as the musician knocked on her door.

And despite the darkness of the room—much less dense and absolute than the darkness inside his horrid, whitish eyes of a bronze statue without patina—the blind man advanced across the floor, exploring it with his cane, until he reached the bed and sensed Santa's presence, whereupon he let go of the cane and lowered his two hands together slowly, slowly, until they rested on one of the girl's shoulders. There he held them, exerting no pressure, in a light caress that was at once idolizing and innocent, before starting to tremble and exclaiming by way of welcome:

"Santita . . . Santita! But is it possible that you changed your mind so quickly?"

Santa protested that she had not changed her mind, that she still loved the torero. It was *he* who had repudiated *her*.

"He threw me out, Hipo, he threw me out! And he came that close to killing me! He was going to stab me . . ."

Hipólito's silence, as his legs continued to tremble against the edge of the bed and his hands pressed convulsively for just a moment against her soft shoulder, reminded Santa of the blind man's forlorn love and of the cruelty she was committing by telling him the details of what had happened. And because she did not want this admirer of hers to suspect the truth, she agilely played the victim, indirectly (but in a way that Hipólito understood immediately) casting him in the role of possible future aggressor.

"You see what I get for loving one of you? I can't trust any of you, can I?" she said. But as she said it, distractedly or calculatedly, she took the piano player's hand as if to reinforce her point, and Hipólito, smothered in delight, his dreams reborn, leaned over her and answered in a way that only she could understand:

Chapter Seven 153

"It's different, Santita, I tell you that it's very, very different . . ."

All the poetry of his immense affection—immense as only hopeless love can be—was contained in those few, almost indecipherable words.

"Hipo, for the love of your mother, go play! They're getting impatient in the parlor," declared Pepa, stepping hurriedly into the room.

"Well, I'll please them, then, even if I have to play all night."

Hipólito searched a moment for his cane on the floor, found it quickly, rose smiling, and stepped nimbly to the door, where he added:

"Pepa, tonight I'm even going to play Verdi for you! You just wait!"

That night a substantial number of customers filled the establishment, but no matter. The women were much less interested in business than in the impending costume ball, which exerted a powerful attraction on the rental bodies and atrophied minds of these poor social outcasts.

For a few hours of a few nights a year, they inherited their kingdom, so to speak, at carnival balls, as if these were dances in their honor, in honor of the timeless scourge without antidote, the perennial temptation of the flesh, the devouring, avenging she-wolves who howl with pain and howl with pleasure. These dances are like ancient rites to Pan, the terrifying horned god with a goat's cloven hooves, whose name brought us the word *panic*, and who played the flute for dancing nymphs. Carnival balls likewise belong to the nymphs, who reign supreme there, and only there, where men never belittled them and even the police do not harass them. Men who have attended such events well know who rules over these ephemeral kingdoms, a wine glass for her scepter, magnificent semi-nudity for her mantle, and a halo for her crown. Supreme vice, like supreme virtue, creates a kind of an aureola around the semblances of both cloistered virgin mystics pallid from prayer and aging courtesans withered from a life of coupling. And the courtiers who wait on these blasphemous queens? The men they actually accept without charge on these occasions? Young men who have not yet learned good behavior. Grown men who have forgotten all about it. The fathers of daughters who dream innocent dreams in the chaste bedrooms of perfect homes. The husbands of wives who lie awake in those homes thinking black thoughts, obliged to embrace adulterous disappointment in their abandoned marriage beds.

Santa allowed herself to be persuaded and went to the dance in a dark, all-concealing hood and cloak, with a silk and velvet mask. It was nearly two o'clock in the morning when the gang from Elvira's house entered the Arbeu Theater, where the dance was held, an already ugly structure that transformation into a cheap dance hall had made even uglier. Of the half

dozen women, four had escorts, and the other two were Santa and a tubercular colleague who dressed as a witch because her sickly thinness suited
the disguise. Jenaro and Hipólito brought up the rear, the latter having insisted on accompanying the group because he and Jenaro were domiciled
across the street from the Arbeu. A childish pretext, obviously, because
what the piano player wanted was to be wherever Santa was, to take care
of her, blind and all. He had exhorted Jenaro to exceptional vigilance:

"If you see that pigtailed bastard, take me close to him and don't take
your eyes off him. Not for an instant! And if, God forbid, he tries to do
something to Santa, push me on top of him, hard, and run get a policeman.
Okay? I'll make sure he doesn't go anywhere in the meantime!"

Each couple bought its own tickets to get in, which is to say, the girls
paid for themselves and for their consorts. Santa paid for herself and for
the tubercular witch, and Hipólito temporarily disappeared in an attempt
to avoid paying altogether, but finally decided to buy a ticket for himself,
at least, refusing to pay anything for his young guide, however.

"He's an innocent little kid!" he added in protest.

The man at the ticket window, who knew the musician, stuck his head
out to inspect Jenaro, saying:

"Are you kidding? This little angel shouldn't even go in free, because it's
against the law, could amount to prostitution of a minor or something . . .
but . . . okay, guy, go on in. But you got to buy me a drink sometime, and
seriously, keep that kid out of sight, would you? He's too young and too
beat up. Hide him in the hallway or the cantina or something . . . Let the
blind guy in without a ticket!" he called to the men who were guarding the
entrance.

Hipólito and Jenaro entered the theater, where the seats had been removed for dancing, by a side entrance, with the boy hidden between the
blind man and the wall.

"What do you see?" asked the musician. "Do you see Santita?"

"From here, no. There are tons of people and tons of noise. Hear that
ruckus? Let's sit down. I saw some empty seats."

With lots of elbowing and "excuse me's," left and right, they managed
to make their way down a few steps and ensconce themselves in two seats
at the edge of the improvised dance floor.

The ruckus that Jenaro had mentioned was a formidable clamor, a ca-
cophony of fictive glee. The orchestra, which had been installed in three
spectator boxes well above the dance floor, showered its deluge of notes
on the crowd below. From farther up, in the gallery, descended shouts of

laughter and the raucous commentary of inebriated artisans observing what was, for them, an unusual scene. In several boxes lower down, one saw police and municipal officials surrounded by various uniformed police, the one chilly note in the festivities. The seats around the floor seemed occupied, in their totality, by vulgar loudmouths, both the older kind who no longer dance but cannot do without their favorite bacchanalias, and the younger kind, who may have money but do not hesitate to rub elbows with the plebeians wearing disguises on the floor. They lean over the rails to engage in conversation, taking care to greet acquaintances who might otherwise take offense, inviting some of them to join private parties. They toast continually with champagne that bubbles in the glass and spills on the floor, amid the jostling, covering it with patches of foam that are absorbed, soon enough, by the parched boards, if not immediately erased by the shoes of dancers or the edges of the women's long dresses. From the floor rise transparent clouds of dust; a pronounced odor of perfume, alcohol, and sweat; the sound of giggles, oaths, and kisses; and a potent feeling of multiplicitous desires unleashed. The heady amalgam ascends to the lofty ceiling where it whirls around the opal-colored electric lights like a swarm of dazed butterflies floating in the gray atmosphere. On the floor, the packed mass of humanity sways to the pulse of the music, mouths meet, hands grope and find what they are groping for, dancers press their bodies together as if planning never to let go. An unhealthy jubilation seizes both men and women, and one can observe the onset of alcohol-fueled madness, such as the lightning looks and tragic expressions that signal the death throes of love . . .

A "staff bearer" supervises the dance floor, and he carries himself with the dignity of an ambassador, both in his courteous manners and his irreproachably correct formal attire. He leans on his staff, which is tall and decorated with flowers, ribbons, and bells, like an island of peace, an eddy in the churning flow of humanity. Even the staff bearer vibrates, however, in unison with the entire theater, the structure of which can scarcely withstand the swirling stampede of males and females who squeeze and bruise each other, declaring their love, and, at least for now, believing in what they declare. Suddenly, the staff bearer raises his tall staff even higher over the heads of crowd, and for an instant its ribbons flutter there like the colors of a sinking ship or streamers above a pagan feast. Then he brings the butt of the staff down, hard, on the wooden floor, and all its bells jingle shrilly. The music stops, the entwined couples release each other, their intimate dialogues interrupted, and the mass of humanity breaks, like a fleeing herd of cattle, in the direction of the cantina with its limited number of tables, craving the alcohol that promises consolation, conformity, oblivion, and every variety of bliss, at a bargain price!

It is the intermission.

Standing on tiptoe in his chair, Jenaro surveyed the room and bent down to report to the attentive ear of his master, who clamored for information. There was no sign of el Jarameño, although there were various toreros—the Lizard, the Bishop, and so on, all by their nicknames—but not el Jarameño.

"Look carefully, Jenaro, my boy. Look carefully. And you don't see Santa, either?"

No, he didn't see her, either . . . until, yes, he thought so, but had to wait until she turned his way to make sure.

"Yeah, now I see her, *patrón*. There she is. She's in a box with those fancy rich guys from the Sport Club . . . She's got her mask off, and now she's lowered her hood to drink a toast. They're climbing all over her, *patrón*, like she was a honeycomb and they were flies."

"That's enough, Jenaro. We've seen enough. Let's get out of here. At least she's safe with those guys, because they won't try to rob her from me."

The orchestra had begun to play a mazurka to attract people back to the dance floor, and taking advantage of the tumult, Hipólito and Jenaro sneaked out through interior corridors where the coat checkers slept, inveterate smokers puffed secretly on cigarettes, and a man whose entire face was covered in white greasepaint softly begged a woman in a particolored costume to be faithful and love him at least for this one night.

The blind man and his guide walked in silence across the vestibule, clogged with tables. All except for a few stood deserted. At the few sat stragglers from the dance, quite drunk at this point, like the lone, exhausted-looking harlequin doubled over in a corner, singing softly to himself and soaking his mask in the little lakes of spilled drinks on the well-worn table top. They squeezed past a policeman and heard, back in the cantina, the sounds of a fight beginning: vociferations, someone running, a scuffle, the sickening thud of a well-landed punch. They kept walking and were soon outside.

Who knows where Hipólito got the nerve to do what he did the next day. What he did was show up for work a bit earlier than normal and make a formal request—through Eufrasia, who carried the message—to see Santa:

"Ask Santita if she'll talk to me a moment in her room, alone, about a certain matter."

Santa granted the request and, after Hipólito settled onto the couch, she continued curling her hair, seated with a curling iron (which she heated with an oil lamp) at a vanity table imported from the United States. She was scantily dressed, her robe and other clothing still spread out on the bed, and had just washed herself, as was evident from the soap-filled basin on the floor and the perfumed fragrance that floated in the room.

"What did you want to tell me, Hipo?"

"Well, Santita . . ." said the blind man, and told her, unburdening himself of his troubles once and for all, waxing eloquent and even imperious at moments, asking not only that his affection be recognized and tolerated, but that it be returned, not in identical measure, of course (because what cannot be, cannot be), but in a lesser measure that he, Hipólito, would cultivate like a delicate plant that requires unstinting care for years to bloom and reward the dedicated gardener with its perfume. He couldn't captivate her with metaphors and fancy talk, he said, and if he compared her to a flower it was only because, even though blind, he loved flowers. They were really all he loved, and he loved them almost as he had loved his mother, who had taught him to smell them and tell them apart by their aromas:

"But I learned to love my mother all by myself. No one taught me . . . and imagine, Santita, that the love I feel for you, too, is in my bones, and I can't get rid of it, because I love you against my will, I really do! So incredibly much . . . you have no idea!"

"But Hipo," said Santa, interrupting him, and one hand holding the hot curling iron and the other twirling a curl from her temple around her finger like a pet snake, she turned to look at him, her posture putting the dark patches of her armpits on display.

"No buts about it, Santita," insisted Hipólito, "the only things that matter are my sentiments and yours. And I do understand yours, Santita, as if you'd told me yourself. You feel surprise, repugnance, and, hopefully, a little bit of pity, no? . . . Don't deny it! I'll be the first one to confess that it makes sense. I must be as ugly as a monster, but here inside, Santita, I'm not so ugly, and there may even be some nice things in there that not everyone can offer you . . . Love me a little bit, Santita! It's not so hard. Look," he added, standing up, "and just imagine how much I love you, that right now I know you're almost naked and I could grab you and not let you go, holding you in my arms"—he tightly embraced the air in front of him—

"until you couldn't breathe and had to say yes, yes to anything! Oh, I know you'd cry out and they'd come and carry me off, all tied up, to the insane asylum to be with the other crazy people. But look how I control that wild beast that roars inside of me. I keep it on a short chain, and it chews and chews my entrails, but I'm satisfied as long as it doesn't hurt you and you're not afraid of me. And look how I just sit down and how still I am, so that you don't kick me out of here."

Santa, who had at first felt threatened and had gotten up and retreated across the room (without worrying that her nightgown slipped almost off as she did since Hipólito obviously could not see her) relaxed as the musician sank back onto the couch and sat there, submissive and imploring, with the humble attitude of a poor devil who knows that he has overstepped his bounds and fears a reprimand. At the same time, she read in his horrid whitish eyes, in his entire being, a deep and overpowering affection engendered by her, nourished by her. And for the first time, he did not look so ugly to her. He was no Adonis, admittedly—all right, he was ugly—but not a monster. Ugly on the outside, then, but what if, on the inside, he really was different from the men who possessed her daily and made her feel inferior and degraded? What if Hipólito actually thought she was perfect and better than him? What if he actually made her happy?

No, no that was crazy. Hipo was a real monster, all right: a piano player in a brothel, filthy, poorly dressed, and utterly destitute, an individual possibly worse off than herself. She imagined what the girls would say if she left the house to live with him. No way on earth!

"You don't have any response at all, Santita?" gently inquired Hipólito, still slumped on the sofa in an attitude of defeat.

"Yes, Hipo, I'm going to answer you," replied Santa, who, searching deeply, found inside her a shred of decency that she was pleased to confer upon him, doing so with the righteousness of a person who gives her last coin to a beggar.

"I know that you love me. You've proven it to me on various occasions. And, for right now, honestly . . . I don't love you . . . but you don't make me sick or want to throw up or anything, I mean . . . no, no! And it would even make me real sad, Hipo, if I found out you didn't like me anymore. Go figure, huh? I kind of feel like your affection protects me against stuff that could happen to me, stuff that probably *will* happen. And I feel like"— here she became solemn and sincere, glimpsing something dark in her future—"you and I will never be separated. How can I say? Like you and I will be together in hard times to come. And I'm sure that one day I will love you . . . I don't know when . . . someday! Who is it?" she barked in annoyance at a knock on the door.

"It's me, *señorita* Santa," answered Eufrasia from the other side of the door. "A coach is here to pick you up. That gentleman, Rubio, sent it, and he says he's waiting for you you-know-where."

"Okay, tell it to wait. I'll be down in a minute."

Santa began to dress in great haste, unhindered by modesty that she no longer possessed and had no need for, at any rate, in the presence of her blind suitor.

Hipólito's unseeing eyes had closed, meanwhile, his chin had sunk into his chest, and his arms dangled limply from his shoulders as if belonging to an empty shirt on a clothes hanger.

All one heard in the room was Santa's agitated breathing as she hurriedly dressed and the complex sounds that each garment made as she put it on. The blind man's expert ear completely compensated for his absent sight, translating each small noise into an exact mental image of what Santa was doing, almost as if he were touching her or helping her dress. That is why, like a little child who wants adults not to notice his presence, Hipólito remained totally immobile, hoping that Santa would not ask him to get out and leave her alone. And in his mind, with his blind eyes tightly shut, he saw everything when Santa took off her house blouse, standing briefly naked before donning a nicer silk one that announced its quality by rubbing crisply and noisily against her clean flesh. In his mind's eye, Hipólito saw the girl sit down to wrestle on her tight silk stockings, making the chair creak; he saw her lace up and buckle her corset, making its cords hum in the eyelets as she pulled hard to narrow her waist; he saw her drop a slip over her underclothes and saw her take a dress, a hat, a coat, and gloves out of the wardrobe.

"Hipo," exclaimed Santa with her back to the piano player, "to prove we're more than friends I'm going to tell you a secret. Depending on something that I'm about to find out, I might leave the house to go with Rubio. We kind of made up last night at the dance and he wants me to live with him. He insists. And you yourself told me it was a good idea, remember? So if I do, you won't hate me, right? I mean, if something happens to me, I can still count on you, can't I?"

"Santa, you can always count on me. You don't have to ask your dog or your slave if you can count on them. But one condition, or I guess it's a favor. Let me know where you're going to be so I can visit you, just every once in a while . . . every week, maybe, or every month. Will you?"

"Yes, Hipo, don't worry, but careful you don't say a word about this, okay? You can't imagine how jealous they are of me since I came back. Tomorrow we'll talk, okay? By the piano, like before, with you playing the dances you made up for me . . . Got to go, or my man will get impatient!"

They were walking out together into the courtyard when Santa, giving in to a sudden impulse, grabbed the blind man's hand and pulled him back into her room.

"What's going on, Santita? You forgot something?"

Instead of replying, Santa overcame her revulsion, shut her eyes, and fulfilling a charitable obligation, kissed Hipólito right on the lips. Then, grabbing her skirt, she bustled out of the room, leaving the blind man petrified and breathless, his squalid, ill-clad body leaning against the wall, his eyes wide open, his arms rigid, as if a firing squad had just executed him but his body was taking a long time to fall.

As he played and played the piano, the dazzled musician began to notice that Santa was not mistaken. The other girls, and even Pepa, gave indications that they had grown tired of Santa's status as Elvira's pet. They wouldn't tolerate it any more. No longer content merely to list her defects and criticize them, they exaggerated her defects in spirited conversations dedicated, more or less, to eating Santa alive. It was the kind of unrest that undermines thrones of "queens." A good thing, then, thought Hipólito, that he was there, ready to protect Santa against any secret threat by foiling the plans of malevolent plotters. Sitting quietly at the piano, feigning distraction, he cocked an ear and soon confirmed the seriousness of the conspiracy, which had spread to neighboring brothels no longer disposed to tolerate Santa's irritating and still-increasing hegemony among the clientele. The plan, as Hipólito was able to discern by assembling fragmentary evidence, was to circulate a rumor saying that Santa was sick, rotten, in fact, that she had bribed her way out of the hospital, that her innards stank like Brazilian swamp water, and who knows how many other infamous lies they would tell! They would say whatever it took to scare away the customers, the perennial procession that until now had never tired of tasting the dubious attractions of the arrogant village girl, whatever it took to bring her down a few notches and divert the stream of silver pesos that accumulated ceaselessly in her bed alone. Weren't the other girls worth something too? Of course they were! Worth as much or more!

Hipólito was alarmed, indeed, that he had failed to sniff out the conspiracy at the outset, and he swore to make up for it by giving Santa an exact and thorough report on the enemy forces that had revealed themselves to his intelligence.

What with the fruits of Hipólito's information gathering, on the one hand, and of Santa's dinner discussion with Rubio, the two allies had a lot to report the following evening. They chatted at the piano, in their old way, as he played her his "Welcome" and her other favorite tunes. And it was to the amorous strains of pieces composed in her honor, that Santa announced her big news:

"We're all set, Hipo. Rubio made me a great offer, and I accepted it. So unless some big problem comes up, let's see, today's Tuesday . . . day after tomorrow or Saturday at the latest, I'll be in my own place, with furniture and two servants, on Ayuntamiento Street. Do you know where that is?"

Hipólito knew the location of every street in Mexico City, and he reluctantly accepted this second abduction of Santa with the thought that, even if it lasted longer than her stay with el Jarameño, and he suspected that it would, she would be less at risk than if she were to remain at Elvira's house. The prospect tore at his insides, but yesterday's kiss, with its lingering aftertaste of unearthly wellbeing, a taste that he had savored ever since with solitary and silent enjoyment, kept him from opposing his idol's plans in any way.

"You go on, Santita. It's the right thing for you to do. I'll wait for you . . ."

He would gladly sacrifice himself! Let her go to the places that her sovereign beauty could carry her! Let her enjoy the good things in life, things he could not offer her even remotely! Let her get everything that money could buy from someone else. But when, disenchanted at last, Santa asked for love, he'd be ready, and that would be his ultimate triumph, to wrap her in the love that had been swelling and swelling for so long inside his poor body. Hipólito confidently believed in Santa's prophecy of the day before, in the postponed consummation that she had promised him. Yes, it was their destiny! Someday, necessity would throw them together, yoking them side by side to pull the heavy load of their shared misfortune. Yes, that promised "someday" would come! It *would*. And then Santa would make it up to him, after suffering with other men and realizing that her true happiness, lay in her being at his side. That day would dawn someday. Hipólito, with his blind eyes, could see it far away, on the chimerical horizon that we scan for the arrival of things we long for. On that day, he and Santa would walk together holding hands down a wide, wide road, lit by the sun, clear of thistles and clouds, without perils or iniquities, their respective sufferings combined into one. And they would confide in each other, as if in prayer, all their sorrows, all they had been through in their long journey through sin. They would reveal to each other the wounds made by life's roughness, the wounds that so horrify the Pharisees of this earth, and calm their aches reciprocally with chaste and solemn kisses. Yes, that day would come, and upon its advent their former cares would disappear, their spirits would heal, and their tears would evaporate. Someday they would be together in love. It was their infallible destiny, and it was merciful, because everyone, everything loves, even the most miserable beings, even tiny particles like atoms. The world only exists because of love. We are born because our parents loved each other, and then we live in order to love, and ultimately we die because the earth loves the mud we are made of, needs it, and reclaims it . . .

Hipólito said all this to Santa deliriously as he played "Welcome" and the other melodies he'd composed for her.

Yes, that day would dawn with beautiful colors, the sun would ascend in a golden haze, and finally it would set in an opal, evening sky. What would it matter that his body was deformed or that hers had withered under a thousand lascivious hands? Love would straighten his body, cleanse hers, and redeem them both. Together their souls would enter the Promised Land, without remembrance of the past, leaving their flesh behind, now worthless, cast away to be consumed by wild beasts . . .

Hipólito went on and on deliriously, speaking very softly, his horrid eyes without irises wide open, turned upward, and somehow luminous.

Evil did not exist, and if it did, would not rule forever. Repentant, Santa would bathe in the waters of the Jordan River and emerge as white as the whitest ermine. It was already happening. Already she was not an impenitent prostitute, nor he a miserable blind man. Already she was out of the brothel. No, now there were no brothels anymore! What could this mean? The day had come! They had started down the road of redemption, freed from the infinite evil of life on earth . . .

Hipólito's vision was rudely interrupted by the arrival of a group of drunken, frock-coated revelers. They waved money and gave the other girls a squeeze, then asked for Santa and vociferously demanded a bottle, glasses, and a waltz.

"Don't worry, girls, it's just us, and we come in peace, to have some fun and shake a leg! Let's hear it, piano man!"

The party was neither better nor worse than usual, four or five "decent" gentlemen, regular customers, full of tipsy high spirits, addressing each other familiarly like old buddies, ready to keep drinking deeply, keep spending freely, and perhaps stay all night. They were warmly received and immediately served.

"I'm about to run out of steam," declared one of them, collapsing on the sofa and looking pale.

At that point, more visitors walked in. Well dressed like the others, they too were regulars at Elvira's house and not unknown to the first arrivals, whom they greeted with friendly handshakes and, one or two of them, by name. Pepa, alert to potential frictions, judged that the two groups would get along fine and consented in their mingling, with no notion of what was going to happen. Such chance encounters are frequent in establishments like Elvira's, and frequently profitable, too, because they stimulate spending.

How did the quarrel begin when the party seemed to be going so smoothly? There is simply no telling. Apparently, though, it began when Santa, who had been sitting on the sofa when the "out of steam" fellow sat down beside her, got up without asking his permission and went to inquire something trivial of one of the new arrivals. The seated fellow resolved not to endure her egregious misbehavior, and he found enough steam to rise and approach Santa boorishly:

"When you're with me, you don't talk to some other jerk, because I'm not a pimp, hear?" he said, brusquely pulling her arm.

"Who are you calling a jerk?" asked Santa's interlocutor evenly, in hopes that the aggressor might take back the insult and avoid trouble.

Santa intervened more loudly:

"Hey, let go of me! That hurts! . . . What's wrong with you, anyway? I'll talk to anybody I want. Since when do you give me orders?"

Fortunately, the rest of the gathering, and most especially Pepa, became aware of the incident, and the friends of the troublemaker—whom they called Rodolfo—struggled to calm him down while Pepa and Santa convinced the other man to pay no attention to insults proffered by a drunk.

The only way to ratify a peace treaty made in a brothel, however, is to drink more alcohol—that great enemy of the mankind that constantly spurs us toward our own undoing. The men ordered more drink and drank it. They managed to get Rodolfo and the man he had insulted to shake hands and clink their glasses together. In view of the cessation of hostilities, one member of the first group to arrive put his arm around a girl and disappeared with her up the stairs. Rodolfo, who was still very pale, collapsed again on the sofa, sullen and taciturn. The dancing started once more, and at the piano, Santa decided in consultation with Hipólito to retire to her bedroom alone. What was she doing there, anyway, exposing herself unnecessarily to insults and unpleasantness on the eve of her departure to set up house with Rubio?

Meanwhile, the flow of alcohol continued its silent, implacable, destructive work, cascading into stomachs and surging through veins like a river of fire, saturating the drinkers' bodies cunningly and inescapably, wrapping around and around their brains like the web of a poisonous spider, more densely and inextricably with each drink. At first, the river brings excitement, hilarious jubilation, joy of life, the need to love. The entire world acquires a rosy tint. The heart becomes a cheery gravedigger, busily burying sorrows, and the mind becomes a provident midwife, bringing to light a series of deformed impossibilities: plump, vigorous desires and ideals that logically ought never to be born at all. Life smiles at us, all men are our friends, and all women eagerly await us. Alcohol is not the great enemy, but rather, a blessed elixir, and we ask for more . . .

The invasion continues, and the enemy advances. It sweeps away the reticence and self-respect which even the most uncouth individuals have somewhere in their makeup. We lose our shame, our ideas of good and evil become confused, and we blithely absolve ourselves in advance of the most reprehensible acts with a fatally dismissive "what do I care." Dignity fights a losing battle, ceding ground drink by drink.

The enemy advances, the invasion continues, and the ultimate defeat is almost consummated. Dignity wobbles, and, out of ammunition, finally succumbs. The invader throws open internal prisons of conscience, and the prisoners emerge armed to the teeth. Trampling the will to resist, shattering the brittle chains of duty and morality that have kept them in check, the escaped prisoners rampage freely: perverse instincts, criminal intents, the primitive, bestial inheritance of our prehistoric ancestors that composes half of our being.

The enemy has triumphed. The will to resist lies paralyzed, the brain is shutting down, no sort of judgment remains, and the result, as in all invasions run amok, is savagery: rape, murder, degradation, the extermination of the weak. The invaders profane the household deities, give no quarter, raze everything that is beautiful, sow evil in everything good, abuse the young and the elderly, and raise their blood-red flag over the ruins. Time has been turned back, and the Stone Age has returned. All good intentions and efforts are now useless.

"You know wh-what? I think your clothes are pr-pretty ridiculous . . . hey, what did you say your name is?" stammered Rodolfo, looking glassy-eyed at the same fellow whom he had recently insulted and who now sat by him in an arm chair.

"You really do want a fight, don't you?" replied the other man, much less conciliatory than before, thanks to the extra liquor.

"Trouble with *you*? No way, I fight with men, not sissies!" replied Rodolfo, with emphasis on the last word.

It all happened quickly. First, verbal insults that, in their way, cause more damage than the blows that follow. Next, defiant attitudes, the fighters on their feet, sizing each other up, their looks cold and steely, full of abhorrence, crossing like sword blades, with a thirst for blood that surprises even them. Then, the blind homicidal impulse, the physical need to kill for killing's sake, Cain senselessly slaying his brother who had done him no harm, the murderous action that, once initiated, takes on a life of its own. Rodolfo, with a fateful glare, brandished and cocked a revolver.

When the others tried to intervene it was too late. The piano fell silent, although Hipólito could not see what was happening. Those who were laughing or talking or singing fell silent, as well. The dancing stopped, and the kisses and caresses, and the intimate tête-à-têtes. Everyone understood that something tragic and definitive was about to occur. The revolver oscillated quickly up and down almost as if aiming itself, the rays of the overhead light glinting off its nickel-plated cylinder and barrel, the yawning black hole at its tip spewing fright, quickly, quickly, before spewing death.

The victim, already covered in a funereal pallor, crouched and writhed in a useless attempt at evasion, tripping over the furniture, his hands fluttering crazily over the seat backs, his bulging eyes fixed on the black hole at the end of the barrel, oscillating with it, up and down, all his love for life, pleading eloquently, humbly, poignantly, revealing his conviction that he was about to die.

The revolver moving quickly, quickly, left no one time to intervene.

Hipólito now on his feet, leaning on the piano, trying to see the drama that was unfolding before his sightless eyes without irises, his whitish eyes of a bronze statue without patina.

Cain standing erect, adjusting his aim to make sure that the bullet would not miss its target. Abel, losing hope, dying healthy, strong, and young.

Quickly, a loud, fiery shot, then another, quickly, quickly . . .

Then, the dying man on the floor, returning his soul whence it came with a pious exclamation, invoking the divine name:

"Jesus!"

The killer does not want to look in the direction of the dead man. He gazes at those who surround him, stupidly or lucidly, depending on the flow of alcohol now gradually draining out of his brain. His fratricidal arm, as if repenting its crime, seems about to release the weapon that continues to yawn and oscillate, pointing only at the carpet.

In the atmosphere, a languorous odor of sulfur of the sort that floats in the air over town squares in the wake of public celebrations. The witnesses, behaving in accordance with the dictates of their individual temperaments. Pepa, unable to speak or flee, wanting to do both. Another woman sobbing and covering her face with the edge of her petticoat.

Santa, who has unconsciously moved to Hipólito's side, stands there holding his hand. The eyebrows of the blind man twitch spasmodically. Jenaro's face appears briefly at the door to the courtyard, then disappears.

At first, no one speaks, stupefied in the presence of the irreparable. When death enters the scene, it brings a hush to everything.

Then comes indignation, as everyone looks righteously at the killer, and the dead man's friend throws himself on the fallen body. Once and again and again, he places the palms of his hands over the still heart, and despite feeling that it no longer beats, he lowers his bloodless face over the fallen man's and speaks in his ear, stubbornly hoping for an answer:

"Benito! Benito . . ."

After waiting an instant or two, he looks up at the killer and says to him slowly:

"Why did you kill him?"

The killer lets go of the revolver, which falls to the floor with a heavy thump, and the police, called by Jenaro and Eufrasia, finally enter the parlor.

The yellow light of the oil lamps goes to kiss the face of the unfortunate victim, melancholically, reverently . . .

Eight

The courtroom, in both the gallery with seating for the public and the narrow section reserved for the press, was totally packed. Around the doors leading outside and to the jury room clustered curious onlookers happy to endure uncomfortable postures, sharp elbows, chilly drafts, all sorts of pushing and shoving, and the foul-smelling heat of so many compressed bodies, just in order to have a view. Quite a crowd, indeed!

Outside, the overflow milled around or sat along the edge of the courtyard turning their eyes and ears toward the courtroom inside. Police stood guard in front of the grill-covered windows of the main courtroom and the room where witnesses waited to testify, but that did not stop frustrated spectators in the courtyard from crowding around those windows as well. Outside the main courtroom, one could hear bits of the proceedings, such as stray statements from the witnesses, the fulminations of the attorneys for the prosecution and the defense, and portions of the official record occasionally read by the official court reporter in monotonous, nasal tones like those of a priest saying mass. At the window of the witness room, people gathered simply because they had read in the newspapers—which serve at least for this—that testimony would be taken at this trial in the austere Palace of Justice from each and every one of the occupants of Elvira's well-known brothel.

The crime, of course, naturally piqued the prurient interest of a hypocritical society that desires avidly to learn the most sordid and repugnant details of such affairs, the more sordid and repugnant the better. In fact, the more the mud gets stirred up, the more the witnesses describe indecent behavior explicitly, the more we taste the spectacle of a fellow being who has fallen into what we ourselves have avoided, the more we contemplate the poor devil's isolation and disgrace—why, the more we like it! The more we then hurry to the trial and fight for a good seat to hear all the juicy details. The more we then rejoice in being merely spectators when, in a different situation, we might have been actors in this courtroom drama. And at the hour of the verdict, when the bloodless lips of the judges and the gray pages of the legal codes rain a storm of imprecations—and many years in prison—on the heads of the delinquents, when we observe the righteous anger of those who maintain their innocence and copious tears of those who love the condemned, when we hear the death sentence and observe its impact on participants and onlookers—then a thrill of selfish satisfaction gives us gooseflesh and fills our hearts with relief because it did not happen to us. In the darkness that has been revealed in those poor, condemned souls, we have glimpsed the darkness that resides in our own, identical weaknesses, analogous perversions. But the condemned will suffer for it, and we will not. We will be free to withdraw at the conclusion of the drama, free to express our sympathy for the defendant and his fate!

At first, Santa and the other girls of the house regarded the matter lightheartedly, as a kind of farce, and the lawyers among Elvira's customers coached them on how they should behave in court and just what they should say on the witness stand. Why condemn the killer if it wasn't going to bring the dead man back to life? Hipólito, who was also to testify, disagreed. Perjury implied risks to the perjurers, and he thought it inhumane to absolve someone who had murdered inhumanely.

"Let's tell the whole truth, Santita, without playing favorites, what happened and what we saw . . . I mean, what you saw. Otherwise, that friend of the dead man's is likely to protest and get us in big trouble, and then who will we appeal to? You are about to leave Elvira's, so why get mixed up in this at all?"

That afternoon, when the whole crew was marched into the witness room and the doors closed, they initially remained silent and composed, as was to be expected. The Palace of Justice—with the presence of so many police, judges, and court officials—always makes a strong initial impression. The bolder members of the group rehearsed the upcoming situation for the more pusillanimous among them: "You just walk right in and look the judge in the eye and say . . ." Pepa smoked one cigar after another.

Hipólito, for his part, tried not to appear too thrilled by this opportunity to spend so many hours at Santa's side, talking to her about whatever he wanted without having to fear the interruption of impatient customers or the other girls.

The piano player's chattiness was carefully graduated, bland and indifferent at first, increasingly entertaining as he and Santa reviewed their recollections of the night of the murder. They spoke of the presentiments that one always imagines having felt before important events, harbingers invented ex post facto, for the most part. They said what they had thought at the moment of the crime, what it later brought to their minds, how poorly they slept afterward, and how they had felt the imminent possibility of their own deaths. She had thought she was wounded by the first shot! He had heard the second bullet whine close by! They spoke of what haunted them subsequently: Hipólito, of the brief, hoarse groan of the dying man in his agony; Santa, of the glassy-eyed stare of the cadaver. Finally, a mutual confession, softly uttered, followed by an expression of philosophical acceptance:

"How low we have sunk in life, Hipo!"

"Low, Santita, so low . . ."

Persuaded of their reciprocal lowness, they moved closer together, sitting side by side in a corner of the waiting room, without anyone to hear them except Jenaro, who hardly seemed an outside presence at all. As the conversation gained color and flavor, Jenaro could have sworn that the hands of Hipólito and Santa clasped and unclasped as if of their own accord, unconsciously. The blind man was determined to find out whether Santa loved Rubio, or rather, intended to become his mistress for merely practical reasons. Santa insisted that Hipólito declare whether, no matter what she did, his love for her was really eternal. Neither of them was willing to put all the cards on the table, however, and instead preferred to talk about past unhappiness, each hoping that the other would confess having suffered less. Their obsessive inspection of wretchedness and melancholy experience seemed a way of establishing a claim on future happiness. In plain language, they were saying: "If you love me, let it not be for my deserving, for I deserve nothing. Love me, instead, because I have suffered so much in this life!"

Outside, the public continued to mill around, standing on tiptoe to get a better eyeful and earful, and the policeman who stood near the window continued to shoo away the occasional nosy onlooker who approached the window grate to wink at the woman flesh in the witness room.

Inside the main courtroom, the trial continued, interminable, bound by the plethora of formalities and mandatory procedures of a trial by jury—that highly imperfect, sometimes hare-brained institution of justice. At one point when a bailiff entered the waiting room to see if "the girls" needed anything, Santa and Hipólito could hear various garbled phrases corresponding to the prosecution or the defense—"conscientious, upstanding gentlemen of the jury," "public retribution," "a mother who must now weep for her son"—phrases applicable to both killer and deceased, phrases that might be intoned with equal plausibility by the prosecutor or the defense attorney. Santa and Hipólito returned to their conversation as Jenaro dozed.

The people who milled around outside the courtroom could read the large sign on the wall that announced the barbarous precept contained in Article 134 of the Penal Code: "The law does not specify how a jury is to arrive at its verdict." So innocence or guilt could be decided on the basis of subjective impressions alone? And the flaming final words of Article 134 seem designed to finish undermining the Justice they pretend to serve, dulling sentiments of clemency, sweeping away all pity toward the innocents that the most hardened criminals leave behind, blinding the jury to the gallows that stands grimly behind the formulaic speeches: "Members of the jury shirk their principle duty if they take into account, during their deliberations, the punishment stipulated by the penal code if the accused is judged to be guilty as charged."

Impatient groans began to be heard in the witness waiting room. Were they going to be called to testify or not? The room darkened gradually as the light that entered from the courtyard through the window grill made subtle preparations to withdraw for the evening. The bailiff again. This time accompanied by the man whose job was to light the oil lamp hanging from the ceiling while, outside in the courtyard, at the same moment, a colleague lit the lamp that swung suspended over the central fountain. Pepa and the girls surrounded the bailiff. When were they going to get out of there?

"We have a job to do," affirmed Pepa without blushing.

The bailiff had a good laugh, indicating that he knew the nature of the job, and told them not to get their hopes up, it was going to be a while, probably into the wee hours of the morning, according to the message that the judge had sent to his wife:

"They want to get this thing finished," he added. "Imagine . . . it's been only a month and a half since the crime. We've been working hard!"

Pepa got indignant, but the girls were secretly delighted to think about Elvira back at the house all by herself, confronted by the frustrated clientele, pulling her hair and demonstrating her mastery of the very foulest Spanish.

In the meantime, Santa explained to Hipólito why she had not yet set up house with Rubio. It was his capricious wife. She had returned unexpectedly from the thermal baths at Puebla, where she had gone in pursuit of the maternity that would probably continue to elude her. Santa also reiterated just how well Rubio treated *her*. In fact, Rubio already considered her his responsibility, and he had offered, of course, to pay all the costs of renting and furnishing their love nest.

"He sends me letters and telegrams every day. He's a perfect gentleman! I really think I've hit the jackpot with him, don't you, Hipo?"

"Santita," replied the musician, "I don't know if he's that much of a gentlemen, but what I do know is that it seems like he's got money, a big pile of it, too, which recommends him for sure. What matters is that he gives you what you are worth, what a poor guy like me would give you if he could . . . what I *will* give you someday, I swear. Rubio's got to hide you, but I'd never do that. You know what I think about guys like Rubio who get to be with you but have to sneak around to do it? I feel sorry for them! The idiots! What more do they want than to be with you? As far as I'm concerned, Santita . . ."

And he was back to his old refrain, building castles in the air, planning an idyllic future, drawing imaginary floor plans, even blueprints, for their enchanted dwelling, with this piece of furniture here, that one over there, and they'd do this in the morning, that in the afternoon, something else in the evening . . . the dream.

As she always did when the blind man gave free rein to his passionate visions and these, in turn, soothed her feminine sensibility like a flock of cooing doves and mitigated the sting of her shameful profession, Santa averted her eyes from Hipólito's ugliness in order not to break the spell and let her hand float between his. The piano player held her hand as if it were a sacred relic, caressing it lightly with his fingertips, and occasionally, very infrequently, lowering his head to kiss it slowly, more than respectfully, devoutly, without ceasing to speak.

Every once in a while, Santa would ask something like:

"And after that, Hipo? What will we do after that?"

"After that? . . ."

Why, after that they'd start all over again, doing the same things all over without ever getting tired of it, without ever needing to seek entertainment because they'd already had enough of that to last them a lifetime.

"All we'll need to do is the simple natural stuff, Santita, and we'll be astonished that you can be happy with so little. Okay, but when we finally get tired of all that, because they do say that you get tired of anything sooner or later—not that I necessarily believe it, mind you—well, *then* the big surprise will be . . . but I'm not going to tell you because I bet you ten to one you'll never guess . . ."

Several of the girls indicated that they were hungry. Pepa consulted her watch and saw, to her astonishment, that it was close to eleven o'clock. No way! They had to let the girls eat and had to let her reprovision herself with cigars. With some difficulty and the offer of a fat tip, the bailiff was made to reappear. Couldn't they have something to eat?

Why, of course they could. What did they want? They made a list: sandwiches, beer, coffee with shot of liquor for Hipólito, Banqueros del Destino cigars for Pepa. The girls went to the window to watch the bailiff go off across the courtyard, deserted and gloomy at this hour, carrying the list and a five-peso note.

Nighttime darkness and emptiness had restored to the courtyard—and to the entire Palace of Justice—a strong resemblance to a converted colonial convent, which it is. During the day, that resemblance is much diminished by the hustle and bustle of litigants and lawyers, heirs and executors, prisoners and police, the impromptu conferences in the corridors, the men gesturing threateningly on the stairs, the continual buzz of a wasp nest, and occasional shouts and laughter that rise above the din to echo in the domed ceilings of the ancient building. During the day, the convent blurs and disappears behind a total disguise of paint, plaster, and disrespectful renovations. Who is likely to think, when entering the chambers of the Supreme Court, or any of the inferior tribunals, or the Registry of Deeds—who is likely to think of the austere cloisters and oratories, the silent passageways, the bare cells where nuns once slept? Those who go there now do not recognize or think about it because, after all, they have other business to attend to. They have to litigate, to steal legally, using laws as their tool, to fashion the intricate deceptions of which lawyerly reputations are made. Too bad for whoever believes in true Justice, because such candor has no place here. In the palace dedicated to her, the goddess holding scales and a sword rarely shows her face, and when she does, seems to shrug her shoulders. The assault on justice is incessant; the continual scuffle, deafening; the doctors of laws, notaries, and scribes are numberless; the claimants, both honest and dishonest, never ending. Greed and venality hangs so thick in the air that one can almost reach out and touch it. Christians are as good at this as Jews. And as if these hawks and hyenas spitting articles of law codes were not a sufficient plague in themselves, the authorities, in their wisdom, have chosen the right courtyard of the ancient building for the location of jury trials, whose Solomonic deliberations crown the magnum opus of human justice!

Nonetheless, in the quiet of the night, the building recovers the feel of a convent. The files slumber in the filing cabinets; the long desks and tables, as black as coffins, sink into the shadows that fill each room and become invisible; partition curtains billow softly like misshapen, satanic owls; the ceiling rustles infinitesimally as worms, spiders, and bats move about unseen. The Supreme Court, the inferior tribunals, and Registry of Deeds vanish, and the old oratories light up, the bare cells are repopulated, and through the austere cloisters file ghosts of the convent's inhabitants of centuries past. The watchman swears—and one should always heed what such persons say—that voices praying and singing psalms can often be heard in the building at night, that many have glimpsed figures clad in the old habits, carrying tall yellowish candles with frail yellowish hands, gliding along noiselessly on bare feet. He says that a soft, dull sound of bones accompanies the spectral procession on its way to the main sanctuary of the convent, which is still a church and where the specters are doubtless awaited because—and again, the watchman guarantees this and cites testimony—the old organ can be heard playing on those nights, though the sound is muffled as if it were coming from underground. And before dawn, the procession returns and dissolves through closed doors, going who knows where, so that, when the sunlight spills into the building the next morning and the janitors arrive, they find everything in its place, and it appears that nothing—not a table or chair, not a sheet of paper or a cigarette butt, not even a spider web—has budged during the night.

"What an awful place, Hipo, and scary!" said Santa, turning away from the window.

"And a good thing, Santita, that neither you nor I will have reason to come back," declared Hipólito, feeling his way toward their pleasant corner with his cane and holding Santa's two hands in his.

The bailiff returned at around midnight with his arms full of food and drink, and needless to say, was immediately mobbed, as if by a band of starving castaways. The trial continued in the main courtroom, and they had still not been called to testify. The guests at the meal were the bailiff, who did not need to be invited twice, and the two police guarding the door and window, who politely refused the first invitation, but finally gave in, tempted by the smell of food and exhausted by their long vigil. The two had to eat standing and using only their left hands, but everyone else could spread the food out and sit where they liked, which the bailiff assured them was routine practice when a trial went on for so long. For a few minutes, guards and the guarded fraternized unselfconsciously with their mouths full. To disguise the pop of beer bottles being opened, they all pretended to laugh or cough at once. Santa put sugar in Hipólito's cup of coffee and liquor and stirred it.

"Give it here," she said to Jenaro. "You're going to spill it and I want to fix it for him."

Santa and Hipólito bumped into each other clumsily as she insisted on stirring too much and he tried to make his gestures less tentative and blind.

Suddenly, Santa felt a powerful chill and began to tremble uncontrollably, despite her efforts to control the shaking and despite the wraps that they gave her.

"Why are you trembling, Santita? Do you feel bad?" asked Hipólito, alarmed.

"No, not bad. I must have caught a chill . . ." she replied with difficulty, so severely did her teeth chatter. "Feel how cold I am!"

A cold draft pushed the half-open door, making its hinges creak unsettlingly.

Just then another bailiff entered with another police guard and interrupted the meal with brusque ill-humor:

"Josefa Córdoba . . . time to testify!"

"Thank God, *hijo*," said Pepa, getting up sluggishly, stretching, and taking five or six consecutive puffs on her Banquero del Destino. "Okay, let's go."

The other women gathered around Santa, who continued to shake. They put various wraps around her and agreed that something was wrong. Dismayed by this turn of events, all Hipólito could think to do was blame the draft and curse it. One of the girls confused and worsened matters by making a perfunctory examination and declaring that the pain was in Santa's ribs.

"Look, breathe in, breathe in . . . deep! Now, don't your ribs hurt?"

Fortunately, Santa's turn to testify appeared to be among the last. In the meantime, Pepa returned to the witness waiting room—although this was strictly against the rules—and the other girls were called one by one.

Hearing her name called, each of them got her face ready, smoothed her hair, and, standing, adjusted her long skirt at the waist using both hands. Those who had brought a hat put it on and those without gave a little flair to their scarves before swaying out the door, smiling and provocative, knowing that they would cause a sensation and enflame the appetite of the men who packed the courtroom, many of whom had patiently endured the claustrophobic conditions for hours just to see Elvira's girls. The girls knew that the magistrates and functionaries of the court awaited them no less eagerly than the spectators in the gallery, to say nothing of the guards and police officers who gently escorted them the short distance to the witness stand, offering them an arm, walking very close, and breathing with flared nostrils the whole way, subjugated by the presence of their defenseless, disquieting flesh.

And what a commotion they caused when they stepped into the courtroom! A wave passed through the male audience in the gallery, and a lesser, but still perceptible, movement could be observed among the members of the tribunal on the platform at the front of the room. A general phosphorescence smoldered in the eyes of old and young, married and single. A tangible, palpitating desire was visible on the faces of all of them as the prostitutes appeared, one by one, to take the witness stand. There stood each to give her testimony, resolutely, holding herself erect behind the varnished wooden bars of its railing, where she lowered her head scarf to make sure that her corseted bust stood out clearly, showing the provocative protuberances of the captive breasts that seemed about to escape from the low-cut blouse. Each put one hand on her round hip and used the other to gesture or take hold of the railing, her eyes surveying the entire courtroom, a slightly smiling expression of triumph or disdain playing over her face and lips, apparently (but not truly) indicative of supreme self assurance, seemingly full of promise to each of so many eager spectators, but promising nothing specific to any of them. Each awaited questioning with an expectant, placid, and innocent look, feigning ignorance in spite of all the sordid things that each of them had seen in her time.

The commotion reached its apogee when Santa presented herself. The chill had passed, but her physiognomy still recalled it, with her cheeks flushed and her eyes bright, with pronounced dark circles beneath them, as if she had wept copiously and recently, making them look even larger than usual.

The entire courtroom, including functionaries, jury, and audience, was sick of the proceedings. For ten or eleven hours, they had sat uncomfortably, stealing out occasionally to smoke a cigarette or drink a glass of water, and now they were starving, dying to talk and move around, get out of that choking atmosphere stinking of sweat, bad breath, and the fumes of candles and oil lamps. They knew by heart every detail of the evidence. The accused, who initially had inspired sympathy in some, now elicited universal abomination. When was this trial going to be over? Let the fellow be absolved or convicted, but get it over with! The attitude of the entire assembly implored relief. Heads rested on chair backs or against the wall. One of the defense attorneys leaned forward on his desk, drawing pictures of animals and houses, and the court reporter seemed to doze, his elbow on the judge's desk, covering his closed eyes with his hand, as if screening them from the light. The judge himself watched a guard yawn and struggled not to do so himself, drumming with his fingertips on the desk and practically pulling his mustache off, so incessantly did he stroke it. Only the accused murderer remained grave, concentrated, and unblinking, curved forward on his backless bench with his arms crossed on his chest, feeling the apparatus of justice tug disconcertingly at his hide.

Therefore, the much-anticipated parade of prostitutes worked wonders as the priests of Temis, god of justice, welcomed the priestesses of Venus, goddess of love. The tedium, the drowsiness, the stiffness of tired joints evaporated as the entire courtroom turned with utter unanimity toward the witness stand. One or two nearsighted spectators could be observed wiping their eyeglasses hurriedly with handkerchiefs or jacket linings. Many noses sniffed like those of bloodhounds on the trail, delighting in the smell of the girls, a delicate mixture of expensive perfume, well-washed flesh, and the very slightest hint of perspiration.

Each new witness further warmed the collective spirit and undermined the professional seriousness of the scene. Faces accustomed to maintain an official frown relaxed and opened up. Jurors elbowed their neighbors and winked at others father away, and the judge, his face notably red, fidgeted uncontrollably in his chair. The public prosecutor—a furious positivist, a reader of Brocca, Ribot, and Lombroso, a paragon of modern criminology—leaned on the railing in front of the witnesses and studied them carefully with the benevolent smile of a wise scientist examining specimens of insect life. It was whispered in the room that the prosecutor possessed a much greater familiarity with such specimens than he was likely to admit, that he was a regular in the city's houses of ill repute, where he perhaps went to gain deeper insights into certain processes of inevitable degeneration and decline.

Santa, so accustomed to awaken and provoke the carnal appetite of men, did nothing on this occasion to elicit such a reaction, not even taking the same care as the other girls to show off her charms, which more than one of the spectators had actually tasted. She simply replied to what she was asked about, what she had seen and heard, the whole truth that Hipólito had urged her to tell. She wanted, above all, for them to let her leave as soon as possible, suspecting, because of the chill that had shaken her so, that she might be seriously ill despite her apparent good health, like an oak tree that loses its leaves too easily in a cold wind.

Indeed, Santa's testimony threatened to be so brief, so contrary to the collective wish of the courtroom to ogle her, that one of the defense attorneys was forced to cross-examine her. He addressed his petition to the judge in the appropriate legalese:

"May it please Your Honor, the defense would like to direct a few questions to this witness."

General noises of approval greeting the request of the defense attorney, who rose to face Santa:

"You said that you thought the two men had reconciled their differences when you saw them conversing calmly, isn't that correct? . . . What did they say to each other? Repeat their exact words!"

Santa did not remember the words, nor did she really know anything about the relationship between the two.

The defense attorney, in with a purely professional reflex, challenged her veracity. Santa listened with knitted eyebrows as he twisted her earlier testimony:

"You seem to be contradicting yourself. Earlier you testified that you saw the two men being introduced after their first argument. They obviously did not know one another if they had to be introduced. How can you now testify that you knew nothing of their relationship?"

Cornered and confused, Santa did not answer. Instead, she looked the attorney up and down, as if waiting for him to provide the answer that he wanted. Then she bowed her head to formulate a new statement, and finally she said clearly, with a shrug of her shoulders:

"I just don't know. It's true that I saw them introduced, but I don't . . . I really don't know . . . what you're asking about their relationship."

Connoisseurs of forensic technique were no doubt preparing to applaud the questioner's shrewdness and agility, which seemed to have fatally compromised this witness. They were disappointed, however, when the defense attorney, inexplicably satisfied, gave Santa a slight, ominous nod and indicated to the judge that there would be no further questions.

As Santa left the witness stand, she had another chill, this one less harsh but more persistent than the first, and she was obliged to spend another long quarter hour in the witness room as the court decided whether, in view of her sudden indisposition and flagrantly contradictory testimony, she should be given permission to go home.

She did not utter a word in the dilapidated rental coach between Cordobanes Street and the door of Elvira's house. Pepa, who rode with her, thought that Santa had a fever, and she let the girl lie in her lap, comforting her and cursing the authorities who gave them such a hard time:

"As soon as you have a good sweat, the fever will break and you'll feel better, my dear . . ." And had the other two women in the coach seen the airs that old So-and-So put on tonight? A grand official of the court, the idiot! "He's in big trouble the next time that shows up at the house!"

Straight to their wide, empty beds, untouched in the cool dawn owing to the total absence of clientele, went the witnesses. Meanwhile, Elivra cursed like a cart driver. How dare those cretins at the Palace of Justice! For no good reason at all, in order to supposedly clarify events that required no clarification, they keep her girls all night? And she has good, paying customers, including el Jarameño, waiting patiently for nothing? Well, the customers finally went to satisfy their need for a woman in one of the rival houses of the neighborhood! Standing in front of her submissive livestock, the irate madam examined them one by one, slapping their flaccid thighs and inquiring of no one in particular:

"And who is going to indemnify *me* . . . huh? Who? They've cost me two hundred pesos at the very least . . . the *very* least! Nobody better kill anybody here from now on! If somebody has got to kill, let them do it in the street, where they kill dogs, and let *us* earn a living! . . . Tomorrow night, I'm taking a double cut at parlor time, hear? You've got to help make this up, too! Get more from your clients. You know how . . . as if you didn't! . . . And you, Hipo . . . no music, no money, hear? . . . Pepa, get this one upstairs, give her a drink, and pile blankets on her to make her sweat."

Elvira continued to bellow as she climbed the stairs, and those still in the parlor heard a loud bang when she entered her bedroom and slammed the door. Hipólito, still extremely upset, got Pepa's permission to stay with Santa that night in case her illness worsened and someone needed to go to a pharmacy or bring a doctor:

"If she lets you, it's all right with me," decided Pepa as she sorted through various bottles in the cabinet to prepare the potion that Santa was to drink.

Santa, who had gone up to lie down as Elvira finished her tirade, signaled her own permission with a shrug of her shoulders. The chill had returned and was shaking her hard underneath the mountain of quilts and blankets. A high fever was making her groggy.

The girls entered her room on tiptoes to say goodnight, touching her cheeks and forehead, pensive and superstitious in the presence of their wounded comrade, feeling vulnerable, all of them. When would a soft, treacherous little draft, or something else infinitely trivial, cause them to get sick when least expected? Disparaged and alone, a sick prostitute is quickly judged useless for the sad art of selling sex, and she is shunted first to the hospital and finally to a trash heap if some charitable soul does not intervene and secretly claim the corpse that once served as an urn of temptation and delight, to return it to its holy mother Earth, which will accept and cover it, just as it accepts and covers the righteous who, if they sinned, did so no more than seven times a day.

And, more to cheer themselves than their sick comrade, after sensing her fever, they said:

"Don't worry, honey. It's probably nothing. I bet you'll feel fine in the morning . . ."

Getting to go to bed alone, even for just a few hours, tempered the melancholy that Santa's illness inspired among the other girls. How wonderful to belong to themselves! To be able to roll in the fresh, clean sheets, adopt any position, extend an arm, bend a knee, obey nobody, not pretend what they do not feel, recuperating, if only for a while in their indefinite captivity, a little bit of liberty! For that short while, they did not have to overcome revulsion or sleepiness or tolerate breath stinking of alcohol or worse things. With the exception of a pair of lesbians who went to bed together with all the repressed excitement of a couple of newlyweds, the rest of the women entered their perfumed bedrooms with the placid attitude of a prisoner who has been allowed temporarily to remove his shackles and chains. They looked at their deserted beds with the thrill of a kid unwrapping candy, and they laughed with glee. To really rest, without suffering filthy, painful, degrading demands! Tomorrow, things would return to normal, and nothing could be done about that. But tonight, for a few hours, they were free! Eager to enjoy their precious freedom, they undressed as quickly as possible, regretting only the absence of their boyfriends with whom they slept willingly, at no charge, whom they had not been able to notify of this rare and unexpected good fortune.

Hipólito installed himself on a chair by the head of Santa's bed after putting a pillow on the floor for Jenaro, who had almost fallen asleep on his feet. Santa had mechanically swallowed the potion and continued drowsing.

"Santita," whispered Hipólito, "do you know I'm here. Do you know it's me?"

"Yes, Hipo. I know it's you. But it's hard to talk . . . I think I'm going to die, Hipo . . ."

The piano player spent some very dark hours by the bed of his beloved, while the day dawned for everyone else. For him, dawn never came. Ignorant and blind, all he had with which to counter Santa's fate was his aching, obligatory resignation to it, so he crossed his arms and entertained a host of heart-rending possibilities.

What did Santa have? It had to be something serious, really serious, because minor illnesses do not attack with such sudden intensity, and especially not with such a high fever. How long would she be like this? Would she get better, and if she did, would she suffer permanent harm? He simply could not imagine that she might die. No, no, she couldn't die . . . of that he was certain, though without basing his certainty on any firm evidence. But even if Santa was not going to die, the unanswered, unanswerable questions that kept repeating behind his unseeing eyes were enough to devastate and terrify him. Stirred to the very core of his being, he appealed to prayer, the supreme last resort, but prayer, somehow, was not available. Random fragments of it rambled through the wrinkles of his heart, through the gray hair of his soul, but only broken, faded, inefficacious phrases reached his lips, the remains of the magic formulas that he had memorized and that had brought him peace as a child, when he had babbled them with indestructible faith, first at his mother's side, and later, in memory of her. His disorderly life of a piano player in a brothel had separated him from spiritual exercises that he believed himself unworthy to practice, and now the old prayers would not answer his call. They were no longer his friends, no longer a soothing balm for his anguish. Let him try to reconcile them! He felt paralyzed by insignificance, suspecting that he and Santa—and even the strongest and healthiest of people—were mere ants, diminutive, defenseless insects that could be crushed instantly and for trivial reasons by a shoe they were never aware existed. We are born, live, and die without understanding any of these three mysteries, and yet with what vain airs, how continually, and how knowingly we speak of birth, life, and death!

Then Santa began to prattle in the delirium of her fever, creating tragic, swirling reconstructions of her childhood and youth, confusing dates, people, and events: el Jarameño in her family's little white house in Chimalistac; Rubio, a dashing young second lieutenant of the municipal guard, trying to seduce her at Elvira's house; Santa herself, married to her brothers' co-worker from the Contreras textile mill, the fellow who played the guitar and sighed for her when they were both so young; Jenaro, transformed into her son; and Hipólito, divided somehow into the two brothers who had repudiated and scorned her:

"Fabián, bring me some cool water from the well! . . . Esteban, don't let Cosme gallop the chestnut horse! . . . The sun, my God, the sun . . ."

Hipólito panicked. He had not expected this and had never heard a delirious person. All he could think to do was awaken Jenaro, who sat up startled and bleary-eyed on the carpet where he had been sound asleep, his eyelids drooping stubbornly in spite of his astonishment at Santa's incoherent rants. She lay facing the wall, her head buried in the pillows and her frame totally motionless, as if immobilized by the weight of the blankets. Occasionally her blathering ceased, and then she panted as if she were trudging up a steep slope or arriving, fatigued and mewling, from a long journey on foot.

Neither the boy nor the blind man said anything. One might think that Jenaro (now wide awake) was the blind one, to judge by his fixed stare, which seemed directed less at Santa's person than at her words, her wandering nonsense, that acquired an other-worldly resonance in the predawn silence of the darkened house. Hipólito, by the same token, seemed more like the terrified child, moving close to Jenaro, his hand fumbling silently for physical comfort and moral support on top of the boy's tousled head. The two of them sat hushed, their faces turned toward Santa's bed, frightened by the sudden, disturbing disarray of her thoughts and words, which suggested intoxication or madness.

"Could there be a spell on her, *patrón*?" Jenaro was finally able to ask, very softly.

"Who knows what she has, Jenaro, but it's bad! . . . Do you think she might die?"

"Do I think she might die?" repeated Jenaro. And after a long, thoughtful pause, he concluded: "Only God knows . . ."

At that moment, the sick woman interrupted their whispered conversation with a coughing fit. Turning away from the wall she threw off the covers, raised her head, and leaned toward her two anxious caretakers with a searching look. She seemed not to recognize them.

"Santita," pleaded Hipólito, lunging to her side as if he were not blind, "don't uncover yourself! Tell me what you want . . ."

"To spit," stammered Santa, trying to keep it off the sheets.

"Quick, Jenaro, get her something to spit in."

Jenaro did so, and Santa spit and coughed more, sputtering feverishly and looking at Hipólito, then at Jenaro, then at the long, tremulous flame of the candle that had almost disappeared into the candlestick. Finally, she let herself fall back onto the pillows, briefly tried to fan herself with a handkerchief, and slipped away into her somnolent delirium:

"Oh, this sun . . . my God!"

"Blood, *patrón*. Santa is spitting blood!" announced Jenaro, carefully examining the puddled liquid in the dish.

"Get it out of here, Jenaro!" ordered the piano player, as if he couldn't bear to see. And then, in a soliloquy intended for the ears of nobody in particular, he added: "Blood! So she *is* going to die!"

But no, she did not die, in spite of her full-blown pneumonia. Whether it was her youth and her sturdy peasant stock (that contributed much, clearly, to aid the strong medicines that they gave her) or whether, on the other hand, it was merely the demonstrable caprice that governs the course of grave illnesses that fade when expected to kill and kill when expected to fade—whatever it was, Santa had gotten so much better seven days after the onset of the disease that the doctor pronounced her cured. He did recommend extreme caution during her convalescence. "A relapse," said the doctor in so many words, "could well be fatal."

And yet, Santa's recovery, her figurative rebirth, took place under auspicious circumstances, indeed. For the second time, she was leaving the brothel and its anti-hygienic slavery, ignorant of the risks that she had run during her sickness, ignorant, too, of the heroic role played by el Jarameño, whom she would in fact never see again. She was convinced that Rubio, her new lover, really loved her and would satisfy her every whim. Overnight, she became the mistress of her own little house, with her own servants and her own furniture, her own everything, with plans to acquire a bird cage to hang in the courtyard with songbirds to gladden the house and bring her pleasant memories of her former life. Even the season was propitious, summer. The torrential rains of mid-July were refreshing and cleansing everything. Delightful afternoons were followed by soft, pensive nights, clear and sparkling, perfect for sitting outside in the open air, chatting with the stars and promising oneself never to repeat the errors of the past. In addition, she again experienced the instinctive joy of having escaped death, a sensation that poeticizes the whole world for those who feel it, and Santa felt it deeply. She felt generous toward everyone she was leaving behind in the brothel, even Pepa and Elvira, not to mention Hipólito and Jenaro. The shabby little garden that grew in front of the brothel, half-concealing it, appeared to her eyes as an enchanted sylvan grove when she observed it now, from her convalescent window, still bundled in blankets, gradually recovering her health. From her high vantage point, the street looked cheerful, the neighborhood admirable, the entire city grand, life itself incomparable.

Santa made her farewell early in the day to avoid being drenched in transit to her new abode by a menacing thundershower. The brothel was tranquil and silent, with no nosy customers around at that hour, and the coach sent by Rubio was of the better class, with shock absorbers and an expert driver who pledged to avoid potholes. Weak, pale, and thin, Santa walked out slowly, holding the arm of Hipólito, whom Rubio (not daring to appear in daylight with his new mistress on such a busy street) had commissioned to escort her. The women, their hair uncombed, wearing slippers and robes that occasionally came brazenly unbuttoned, went out to the curb to say goodbye to the escapee. Eufrasia cried like a baby, and Elvira made jokingly dire predictions:

"Go on, *hija*, and the best of luck . . . but don't get too stuck up, and don't let this one go. Hold on to the money, and try not to lose your looks in case someday you need to come back to the brothel . . ."

Hipólito could hardly resist telling Santa everything she did not know! He managed to contain himself, however. If she did not hear the good news, she could more easily forget the torero, who would soon return to Spain, where distance and the passage of years would eventually erase all memory of his love affair with a Mexican girl. If she did not hear the bad news, it would not spoil the start of her new life.

Hipólito would not forget, however, how a steady stream of telegrams had arrived from Rubio, who was in Puebla during the worst of Santa's illness and who, in the absence of any response, began to think himself betrayed. Or how Elvira had opened the telegrams, discovered that Santa was planning a second escape from her clutches, and determined to toss her out of the house immediately. Did Santa imagine that Elvira would keep her around indefinitely, in bed by herself all day, without working for her room and board? To the hospital, the ingrate! Elvira had been un-moved by all entreaties, quarreling savagely with Pepa, shaking her fists at the girls, coming very close to ejecting poor Hipólito with her own hand. What a beast!

The good part of the story was personified by el Jarameño, no less, and whether or not Hipólito wanted to admit it, he had to give credit where credit was due. Explain it any way you like. Perhaps the matador just had to see her. Perhaps it was the approach of his departure for Spain that made him wish to part with his ex-mistress as friends. The only thing certain is that, without knowing of Santa's illness, he had appeared at Elvira's on the night following the trial to inform himself, so he claimed, of whether the girls had all become jailbirds or had remained on the loose and returned to the trenches. In reality, he was looking for Santa, about whom, though he did not even inquire about her, the girls soon provided detailed informa-tion. She was really, really sick with pneumonia and the doctor could not guarantee she would survive. El Jarameño's first reaction was incredulity and indifference:

"Is that right? Well, I'm sure that she's got something in her bag of tricks for the pneumonia, for the doctor, and for the doctor's mother, too. Don't pull my leg . . ."

He did not believe it, not when Pepa confirmed it, not when Hipólito corroborated the testimony of everyone else, not when he saw how the musician, in order to avoid bothering the sick woman but still obey Elvira's command to play, had put half a dozen newspapers on the strings inside the piano to mute the sound. The clients actually liked the result.

Jarameño only became convinced of the truth of Santa's illness when he went into her room (which smelled of medicine), felt her burning fore-head, and witnessed her delirium. She fixed her wide, feverish eyes on him and did not recognize him at all. For an hour he sat by the foot of her bed, without smoking or drinking, taciturn and motionless. He listened long and attentively to descriptions of her symptoms, asked about the doctor who was treating her, and also asked, four or five times, if she needed any-thing. He was back the next day, and the next, and the next, quietly with-drawing to a corner of the room to watch her get treatment, afterward returning to sit at the foot of her bed, still taciturn and motionless. On the fifth day, when Santa seemed to be a bit better, Elvira had announced her inhumane determination to evict the girl and send her to the hospital. The matador had risen, forced the madam out of Santa's room into the courtyard, and there, in front of "her girls," Pepa, and all the servants, he had blistered her with a hail of colorful terminology, no doubt considered Spanish in Spain, but mostly incomprehensible in Mexico, except that it was quite clear he was saying nothing good. His listeners did catch the terms *bitch* and *harlot*, along with many apparent synonyms, applied in this case not to Santa but to Elvira herself, along with an obvious threat of violence, a generous offer to pay all costs, and the strict injunction to keep his role in the matter a secret. Let her live with anyone she wanted, and be happy, and never again be a prostitute—that part they understood.

As Santa got better, el Jarameño visited less often and stopped going to her room. He simply got an update on her condition, asked if she needed anything, and left. When she was almost well and herself again, he did not come back.

Hipólito, no dummy, was not going to tell Santa about all this! And, to square it with his conscience, he decided not to tell her about Elvira's behavior, either. Hushing up the bad might somehow compensate for hushing up the good, or so he hoped. So he talked about how sick she had been and how much he had worried about her:

"Can you imagine what it was like for me to think I might lose you? That I might never again smell you, or hear you, or see you the way that I see you, inside?"

Rubio was waiting at the rented love nest and emerged to help Santa get out of the coach, almost carrying her and setting her down unsteadily on the sidewalk. Knowing the Hipólito must be in agony, she made a point of thanking him and insisted that Rubio do the same.

"Don't forget to come visit me, Hipo, because Rubio says it's okay. And bring Jenaro, Hipo. Be sure to come with Jenaro!"

The dawn of the time that Santa and Rubio lived together was like sunup on a day without clouds, bathed in a powerful celestial light that lifts the spirit and beautifies everything—fields, houses, streets—makes diamonds of common stones, fills muddy puddles with molten gold and inanimate objects with an inner life, the kind of sunlight capable of turning black into white, old into young, and illness into health, capable of cleansing the discoloration of centuries from the ancient bells in church towers and the pockmarked façades of the oldest buildings, a sunshine that lovingly warms the flowers in the city parks and the wretched beings who shiver there, kissing the half-naked children of the half-built outskirts, allowing them to forget their wretchedness, smile, and laugh. They were happy together for just one month, a month during which Santa could forget, smile, and laugh. She forgot all the things whose memories could hurt her (which were many) and smiled and laughed at all the gratifying things of the present (which, for a time, were even more). It was less a convalescence, less a progression of pains, residues, and worries, than an ineffable rebirth, the start of new existence, wonderful and previously undreamt of. Not only did her still beautiful but not-so-immaculate body, quite used to the company of elegant lovers like Rubio, gradually recover a semblance of its former vitality—a vitality now borrowed, however, on an account owned by death—her soul gradually recovered a bit of the innocence that vice, veiled now in the cobwebs of forgetfulness, had sullied. It was like getting a new body and soul, fashioned by an expert, that fit her perfectly in all ways, without a wrinkle of any kind, the precise measure of her needs and desires.

Rubio was not what you call madly in love with her, of course . . . she knew that. And so what? He wasn't exactly a kid, and she was still getting her bearings. We can see what happens . . .

But, oh my, how the developments of months two and three disheartened Santa! The dawn of her sunlit day, with its powerful celestial light, simply evaporated, as often occurs on gorgeous spring days that sudden, unforeseen storms transform into something lugubrious, and rain falls implacably like a wet blanket on the spirit, a transparent funeral veil that covers fields and towns, closing the horizon and imprisoning our desires. In just such a momentary transformation, all Santa's castles in the air came crashing down. Not only did Rubio not love her, he ridiculed her. Each time that the prostitute took a step toward the unreachable Promised Land and felt herself almost there, each time that her convalescent soul spread its clumsy wings, numb from neglect but growing stronger day by day, trying to launch itself in flight once more—Rubio took it upon himself to bring her down with vicious terms of scorn.

"Prostitutes don't get into the Promised Land. Can you imagine? And the souls of fallen women can't fly because they don't have wings. They're wingless souls!"

Rubio's behavior, no matter how mystifying to Santa, was actually commonplace and easily explicable. Stuck in a loveless marriage, not unlike the great majority of marriages, he had supposed that a lover of Santa's caliber would ease his pain and deliver some of the sweet pleasures he believed that he was owed. So, instead of trying to fix his marriage, thanks to the comfortable and accommodating moral code by which such things are easily excused, he headed straight for a brothel like a sick man going to a pharmacy, in hopes that money would provide a cure. The ultimate store-bought treatment—more palatable and, hopefully, more efficacious than the brothel—was his expensive mistress with her own house. And at first, it worked. He absorbed the idea that Santa belonged only to him and set about trying to kiss away the indelible marks of so many thousands of kisses that fallen like hail on her voluptuous body. There was even something provocative about how much she had been kissed and caressed by others, about how her docile, bought-and-paid-for flesh resembled a coin that has forever lost its pristine shine by circulating in fairs and markets and accumulating the fingerprints of countless rough hands. It did not take long, though, for Rubio to decide that all the brothel's medicines are inefficacious—even Santa, from whose skin the deep impressions of others' kisses and caresses could never, never be erased. The perennial human desire to be the first and a horrendous retrospective jealousy broke the bond between them. Exasperated with his wife, Rubio became just as exasperated with his mistress. He went back and forth between them, hoping one of them would change and suddenly give him everything he wanted until, faced with a double disappointment, inconsolable, he became enraged and cursed them both, although with different language and manners. He told himself that he still respected his wife and that his relationship with his mistress was simply carnal. Two distinct and compatible sorts of affection, according to the hypocritical rationalization of middle-class men like Rubio. The two women, on the other hand, treated him much the same, which made him even angrier. As if they knew and advised each other, as if both were formed of the same stuff and necessarily approached their sentimental conflicts in parallel ways, though separated by a vast gulf, and though one was of alabaster and the other of common clay, they had similar reactions and opinions, the same reticence and silences. Their greetings and goodbyes seemed identical to him. And so he quoted an idea that he had read somewhere, he had forgotten where, by which he was pleased to insult them both at once:

"Among women, there is no hierarchy of moral quality, only hierarchies of social class. Inside, all women are alike!"

Because love is alloyed with hate, it starts with desire and concludes, not with the satisfaction of that desire, but with disgust. This disgust does not reveal itself directly, but rather, in a certain tortuous twist of word and deed, or sometimes, subdued by the power of suggestion, it expresses itself only as silence or as a repetition of the carnal act, in which we engage not so much to possess our lovers a second time as to convince ourselves that we really love them. At the edge of the pleasure of sensual delight lies satiation, and at the edge of the carnal act lies violence, although most men fortunately do not reach that point. All men, however, without exception, no matter how in love they may be, experience occasional moments of repugnance toward their adored one. Momentary repugnance aside, though, almost all reflexively defend their mates from other males, just the way wild beasts, whether in their lairs or at the zoo, ferociously defend the flesh that lies at their feet, torn by their claws and half-devoured, long after they are satiated.

Rubio passed through all of psychic states, each of them aggravated by the fact that he had never really loved Santa. The tenderness of the first days, during which lovers happily divulge their deepest secrets and swear eternal fidelity, now filled him with embarrassment. Feeling degraded and delinquent in this relationship with a lowly prostitute, he turned on his confidant and vilified her in revenge. He had told her everything, relieving himself of the bile that his wife had unloaded onto him, the lethal, colorless melancholy of a loveless marriage. Dismayed to find that his mistress was just another woman, he vilified her, not because she was a prostitute, but because he had been weak and indiscreet:

"Don't get too stuck on yourself because I've told you things I shouldn't. And don't think you can use those secrets against me, either. Nobody would believe you because of what you are!"

There was the horrible affront that she hated most, the cursed name, fluttering in the air, written on the walls, the furniture. Santa saw it everywhere and sometimes read it aloud . . .

Santa began to despise Rubio. And to think that she might have been able to love him if he had taken advantage of her previous sympathies! She did not leave him immediately, with all his pesos and all his coarseness, because she refused to return to Elivra's house, where she now felt unwelcome, and because she was equally unwilling to go to a similar or an inferior house, where she would be admitted because of her queenly reputation but would also be resented for that very reason and would be at the mercy of that resentment.

And there was another problem, too. Santa felt the insidious attack of the illness that had signaled its onset with her pneumonia. Strange and alarming symptoms, atrocious hemorrhages accompanied by a heaviness in her abdomen, pain radiating from her kidneys and the musculature of her groin and lower pelvis.

"What could it be, Hipo?" she asked the musician, who had no idea of her unhappiness, despite the frequency with which he and Jenaro visited her. "I haven't been to the doctor because it would give Rubio the wrong idea, and I don't want to go back to Elvira's house."

Hipólito clarified nothing. He promised to get her miraculous herbs supplied by folk healers in the marketplace.

So Santa began to drink more, much more, than the moderate intake of alcohol recommended for her convalescence, gradually upping the daily dose of everything from fine cognac to corrosive raw rum. She slipped into alcoholism, or rather, she threw herself intentionally into the river of forgetfulness, regarding it as the only balm adequate to her need and within her means.

Because of her deeply rooted habit (and who can blame the ex-prisoner who persists in dragging the foot that was attached for years to a ball and chain?), because of the alcohol, because she was sick, and because she was desperate, she also cheated on Rubio. She cheated on him frantically, constantly, wherever she could, in the street, in rental carriages, even in the house that he rented for her. And after each event of her recidivism, she drank and drank and, occasionally, cried out with the pain of her strange, alarming symptoms.

When Rubio eventually learned of her activities and, after several rounds of drinking with and pardoning her, on the day when he threw her out of the house, brutally, pitilessly, once and for all—Santa was drunk. The coach driver recognized her and proposed to take her to Elvira's house, but she just staggered and laughed:

"No, not there . . . another one. There are so many . . . but make it a house where the girls cost at least eight pesos. I'm still worth at least that!"

Nine

Like decay or an infestation that has established itself and cannot be halted by anything or anybody, Santa's inevitable decline had begun, and it was to be rapid, frightful, and devastating.

She circled down through the city's shadowy circuits of cheap prostitution, one after another, pausing in each only long enough to taste its infinite bitterness, not long enough, even, to draw breath and brace herself, after a brief repose, to continue her descent, in fits and starts, falling and then stumbling to her feet, over and over, sick, alcoholic, and pitiable. To look at her, one would say that she felt her way along, timid and shrinking, the way one walks in darkness, not knowing where she would end up, trying to hurt herself as little as possible, because hurt was unavoidable, apparently resigned to her fate. The outward appearance of resignation was surely deceptive, however. Who knows what curses she growled to herself through those lips trembling with drunken hiccups, lips that spoke more openly only when the alcohol granted her relief enough to remember happier times in the past, in better days that were now gone forever . . .

From the night when Rubio repudiated her, indignant at her flagrant infidelity, Santa went down, down, down. Much more than simply canceling their apocryphal love nest, Rubio's repudiation sent her tumbling as if launched by a superhuman force, into the city's bottomless pit of corruption, its dark, pestilent sewers of vice and poverty. Down she went through the city's intestines, she and the rest of the effluvium, the cloudy, stinking waters that can go in only one direction, no matter how much they may resist, protesting and whirling in the foul concavities completely unknown to the people on the street above, roaring and foaming uselessly before descending, again, with a sinister glug glug glug, into pipes that will strangle them even more. Down go the sewer waters, gathering volume as they blindly go to they-know-not-where, gurgling against the slimy walls of the tubes in which the incessant torrent of waste gradually etches marks like unblinking leprous eyes that are condemned to stare perpetually in the dark. Down go the sewer waters, mysterious, without a glint of reflected light, full of microbes and detritus, lethal and nauseating, unknowable, unnamable, emitting a heavy odor and a mournful, tired whisper that rises through the drains to the street above. And finally, out of the city they flow, away from its busy denizens, expelled through the iron grate into the rivers that will carry them to die in the sea, their shroud and tomb. The sea alone remembers that these waters were born, crystalline and pure, in the mountains where they quenched thirst and brought forth crops from the fertile countryside, where they were dew, perfume, and life itself.

So it was with Santa!

But, on the night of her breakup with Rubio, she foresaw none of this. Habituated to the easy triumph of her delightful, sinful flesh and emboldened by the alcohol that softened the aches of her ailing body and her disastrous lifestyle, she gave the event no importance. Her quasi-imprisonment with one man had ended? Bravo! That was fine with her! It had lasted too long already. Another man would come along. And if another individual didn't, a crowd of them would—eager, supplicating, humble, patient, and ridiculous, all with like offers and similar foolishness, seeking the same thrills, imploring her to let them love her. Men? Ha! She scoffed at all of them, the whole sex. Remembering their macho expressions and attitudes, unable to contain herself, she laughed aloud in the grubby interior of the rental coach as it lurched along in the stream of traffic. For an instant she thought of looking for Hipólito to tell him about the breakup and about her decision not to return to Elvira's house, but her thinking had been so addled by dipsomania that she rejected the idea and even chuckled at the thought of his dismay at finding that she had flown the coop. She would let him know later.

The coach halted at a place that Santa failed to recognize.

"What house is this?" she asked the coachman when he opened the little window and looked in.

"It's an expensive one," he replied, turning his eyes to the house. There's a bunch of *gringas* here that speak in their language."

"Americanas? No way, idiot! You couldn't force me in there at gunpoint! They don't like us. Take me to la Tosca's house." She started to explain where it was.

"I know where it is," said the driver, climbing back up to his seat and cracking his whip. "It'll be just another minute."

But la Tosca, Elvira's competitor and enemy, and Spanish like her, refused to admit Santa to her establishment, informed, no doubt, by the sisterhood of the brothels, that although Santa had been in high demand she had a tendency to leave with individuals, something that annoyed the regular customers, who preferred more stability in the staff, even when not so pretty and stylish. It was known, as well, because of the anti-Santa conspiracy that had started at Elvira's house, that the girl had been in the hospital without a clear explanation of the reason. Supposedly, she had then gotten pneumonia, but who was going to believe that? It was known, finally, that she was currently mixed up with a rich fellow who had rented her a house and who would certainly not approve the impertinent departure of his mistress following some inconsequential spat. And, above all, why didn't she just go back to Elvira's, which seemed the logical thing, when her stay there had been such a gold mine? Something wasn't right with Santa, that was for sure!

La Tosca offered her a drink of anisette and, alone with Santa in her bedroom, with its tacky decorations typical of a brothel's madam, she sweetly took the girl's hands and with a tranquil smile explained the reason for her refusal:

"Look, *hija*, here's why. What I said about not having room, well, that's not true, because we could always find you a nook somewhere, right? But I don't want trouble with Elvira. She's always after me for something. And just imagine what she'd say . . . and what she'd do, no? Just imagine! And anyway, you're mixed up with some rich guy, right? . . . Of course, silly! You think I don't know? And don't tell me you've quarreled, because that doesn't last. No, no, no. He'll come looking for you, you'll make up with him . . . and then I'm out of luck."

Santa tried to reply with counter arguments, but the madam wouldn't let herself be interrupted. So Santa just sat there downing glass after glass of anisette, with the dirty words she wanted to say tussling with each other in her throat.

"Don't say a word, girl. You're not well, believe me, I can see it in your face, honey. And you're drunk as a skunk, too. You just run on home and don't be a fool. Go home and make up with your sugar daddy, and tomorrow you'll thank me, okay? Did you already send the rental coach away?"

Irate at what she had heard and wobbly because of what she had drunk, Santa stood up and let fly the dirty words that had been tussling in her throat. No way would she listen to such-and-such from any old so-and-so.

"I came to your house to do you a favor, hear? I can go anywhere I want. I've got lots of options, no matter what you think or how mad it makes you. But that's it! I don't care how much money you offer me now. And I'll pay for my drinks!" she concluded, tossing a couple of silver pesos on to the tray.

And, more inebriated than when she arrived, she lurched into the street. It was too late to go to another house, since at this hour everyone would be "working" rather than contracting new girls. Although she believed that she would have no trouble finding a place, la Tosca's rejection had injured her pride. The coach was still waiting.

"Hey, what time is it?" she slurred, struggling to open the door of the vehicle.

She did not really understand the coachman's answer, but climbed shakily in anyway, then stuck her head out the window and added:

"To the tavern on Las Ratas Street. I'm starving. And if you make these nags jump, I'll buy you supper!"

When they got there, Santa refused to go inside the lowly eating house, a place that she had gone several times at the whim of her rich friends, who went there to taste the food of the common people, expertly done at Las Ratas, which is the only positive thing about the otherwise dirty, crumbling, and germ-ridden little establishment, with generally the worst sort of clientele that shows up half drunk on pulque and leaves completely drunk on it. The rich boys go there "slumming," when they go out in a bunch to "paint the town red" with their hired girlfriends. They have a good meal and, often enough, share a glass with some humble artisan at the big common table, a shy fellow who politely accepts the offer of a drink and may even reciprocate. The same polite artisan is capable of impressive violence, however, if he perceives the slightest hint of condescension or fun at his expense, so the slumming clubmen behave with moderation. Therefore, and also because the place shuts its doors at eleven o'clock sharp, rarely does loud quarreling disturb the neighborhood. There may be the rowdy sound of a popular dance, admittedly, or of a romantic ballad that seems less melancholy when mixed with noisy carousing and the occasional belch. Otherwise, it is an almost-respectable little dive, far superior to its multitudinous competitors, the pulque shops that spring up like nettles in poor neighborhoods, teeming anthills that one positively cannot venture into without risk. The owner of the tavern on Las Ratas Street, a fat and jolly fellow to look at him, has been around the block more than once. He knows the weaknesses, vulnerabilities, and vices of the clubmen. He truly feels sorry for them, but since he can do nothing about these characteristics of theirs, he has resolved to exploit them quietly and systematically. The man formerly waited tables in restaurants and he retains certain attributes of waiters: the clean-shaven face, the ready smile, the unreliable math. He stands behind a counter and presses his distended belly over the money drawer that nobody ever opens but him. Just to his right stand the three barrels of pulque that steadily transform liquid into money. The waiters are supposed to show him every dish they serve, and though he affects not to pay attention, nothing escapes him. Directly in front of him is the door to the kitchen, and not a single enchilada comes out of it without his knowing. His chin in his hands, he watches placidly over the clientele, drowsing with the jaded air of an old cat who allows the mice to squeal and play, within limits. His earnings are assured. He smiles at everybody, extends credit to nobody, and reads the newspaper, *El Imparcial*, in the early evening. The poor customers respectfully call him "don," but the clubmen address him casually as "*tú*," the way they are accustomed to do with waiters.

"Have them send the food out to the coach," Santa ordered the coachman. "Get it good and spicy. You can eat yours up on the driver's seat."

Santa never could remember how that night ended. Where did she find the young guy in whose arms she awoke in a third-rate hotel after noon the next day? The guy, whose appearance and behavior suggested a young man of fairly good family, was dressing quietly with the windows still shuttered as if he meant to slink out embarrassedly. He saw Santa open her eyes and froze, blushing and holding the towel in the air where he had been drying his dripping neck.

"You're awake now?" he asked, looking into Santa's wide-open eyes and calling her *usted*, with awkward formality.

"No kidding," replied Santa impatiently. "Who *are* you? Why am I with you? And where are we?" She addressed him as *tú*, a professional habit.

The agitated adolescent—who was sixteen years old at most—responded in a fit of boyish sincerity. Standing in the middle of the room wearing only his underwear, with his freshly-washed hands and face still glistening and unconsciously waving the white towel as if asking for a truce and parlay, he explained everything.

"I'm gong to tell you the 100-percent truth. There's no way around it, and I don't want you to get the wrong idea. If you want to call the police, okay."

"*Me* call the police? Really? . . . So what did you do to me?" asked Santa with new interest, lifting herself up with one elbow on the pillows, so that her silk blouse sagged to expose a shoulder and the beginnings of a breast. "What did you do to me? 'Cause you don't look too scary . . ."

Still blushing bright red, the kid confessed his feat.

He was an impoverished preparatory student whose family did not live in Mexico City. It had been some time, at least a year, since he had first set eyes on Santa at the theater. Elegant, bejeweled, and beautiful, she was with another girl and with two nicely dressed fellows who sat at the rear of their box trying not to be noticed. Infatuated with her, he had asked around and learned where she lived and how much it cost to visit her—also that a visit was hard to arrange because of so much competition, even were he to be able to raise what was, for him, an intimidating purchase price. Nonetheless, by dint of relentless economies and privations over a period of months, he was able to save ten pesos in small change from the living allowance sent by his family. He exchanged the coins for a brand-new ten-peso note and carefully hid it in a human skull that belonged to his roommate, a medical student, hoping the cleaning woman would not dare look inside the grisly conversation piece. But the money just sat there, in spite of his rabid desires, because he could not make up his mind to act on them and, instead, simply daydreamed about how fabulous it would be to visit Santa when the desires finally overpowered his shyness, a shyness that seemed inexplicable in a young man whom his school friends regarded as bold and resourceful. He had a girlfriend, and a pretty one, and on the evenings when he was able to talk with her at the window of her family's house, he got a goodnight kiss between the bars of the window grill. And he had enjoyed more substantial loves with a couple of humble girls, a seamstress who worked on Plateros Street and an employee of the American place with large mirrors on the walls that serves soda and ice cream on that same street. Both had been receptive to his initial flirtations, delighted to receive his bouquets of violets, and willing to accept his invitations to go out alone with him at night to see the lights, only until ten o'clock, of course . . .

"But with you, I don't know. I just never could make a move!" he went on, sitting down on the bed where Santa listened with rapt attention. The bed groaned weakly under the double load.

"I just never could. I'd hang around in the little garden in front of the house, and I even went in once. There's a blind piano player in the parlor, right? . . . See, that proves that I really did go in! But when I tried to ask for you my tongue stuck to the roof of my mouth, my legs trembled, and all I could do was get out of there. I kicked myself all the way home! And . . . I'm sorry Santa, but I finally spent the money on something else. Mexico City is no place to try to economize! So I've had to be content, since then, to dream about you and look at you whenever I can. Don't I look familiar? . . . Anyway, last night I was coming out of the Arbeu Theater, and I saw you in front of the pharmacy on Las Damas Street, the coachman was trying to get you to take some mineral salts because you were really out of it. I recognized you, and I couldn't believe my luck! Right then I spoke to you by name, and you answered, just like that, calling me *tú* and inviting me into your coach. You didn't have to ask me twice, let me tell you! I was in there beside you before you finished asking, and you put you head on my shoulder. The bad thing was . . ."

And he fell silent, twisting the towel in his hands, redder than ever.

"What was the bad thing? Tell me, dummy! What was it?"

"Yeah, okay," said the student after a moment's reflection. "The bad thing was that the driver got mad when I ordered him to take us to the house where you live. I told him how to get there, but all the jerk did was laugh in my face and tell me that he wouldn't go anywhere unless I paid him right then. Well . . . I didn't have any money, but I did have my pocket watch. It's nice and big and made of nickel and runs great, so I pulled it out and offered to leave it with him as a guarantee, saying I'd find him today to pay what I owe and get my watch back. So the guy looked at it and listened to it, and I swear he almost bit the metal, the suspicious jerk, but finally he brought us to this hotel. What else was I going to do with you, all dizzy and almost asleep in the middle of the street? But . . . the room hasn't been paid for, and we've got to do that when we leave . . . Look, if you'll trust me more than the coachman did, I'll go and be back in five minutes with the half-peso room rent. Okay? And then I'll pay you in installments whatever you charge for a night, because I couldn't resist looking at you and . . . undressing you," he concluded softly.

For long minutes, Santa had delighted in the charming confession of her star-struck young lover, and at this point she threw herself on top of him like a she-wolf, and, embracing, they rolled together in the wobbly, creaking bed.

"You didn't do anything bad, dummy! You did real good, in fact. Take your clothes back off and forget about your little seamstress and your girl-friend, nobody but me. Just think about me, you little darling, because I'll give you all you can handle, and free, hear? So that you dream about Santa from now on!"

Like a starving ogre, Santa dined on the youth, who seemed to sprout sharp canines and a wolfish appetite of his own, devouring her in return. How he bit and chewed her succulent flesh, with all the natural gluttony of his sixteen years, without the depraved refinements of the more experi-enced lovers whom Santa was used to.

"Oh, Santa! Santa!" he sighed, exhausted, during the moments of truce. "You're so beautiful!"

Santa had no need of recourse to her professional arsenal of erotic tech-niques, the ones she used to stimulate her more phlegmatic customers. All she had to do was look at the boy, move a little bit, just breathe, and he attacked again with ever greater ardor, partly following the reflexive im-pulses of his almost-virgin organism, partly in a calculated attempt to satu-rate himself, as much as possible, with a much-sought-after woman far be-yond his ordinary means. Probably, he thought, he would not enjoy such a woman again for many years, until he earned lots and lots of money.

Santa actually surrendered before he did, a new experience for her, and a sweet one. Pulling a roll of bank notes out of her stocking, she shook her finger at him: This is on me now! A servant brought food and beer from a cheap eating house down the block, the most delicious banquet they had ever tasted.

Both of them felt saddened by the entering light when they finally opened the shutters, having forgotten that everything in this life must come to an end, even life itself. For a while, they had remembered nothing, nor had they made any promises, which was best of all. Without memo-ries, there was no return of the sorrows that always cling, like dust, to even the most pleasant recollections that we keep stored away in the chests and drawers of our reminiscences. Without promises, no deceptions were required, and they did not feel the foreboding of inevitable future disap-pointments. Their festive sexual conjunction had been unencumbered by baggage from the past or apprehensions about the future. They simply kissed and loved, and they lived many years in a few fleeting minutes. And when sheer fatigue finally separated them, both beamed placidly with satisfaction, pleased to have held nothing back.

Their conjunction was also a twilight, and doubly so. For the student, with his sixteen years, it was the twilight of dawn; and for Santa, the twilight of dusk, a delicate harbinger of night, not yet alarming, but rather, comforting, promising rest and a relief of pain and sorrows. It was beautiful, as twilight always is, for both of them. The lad repaid the woman's splendid gift with his youth and his kisses. Neither owed the other anything, so they parted without demands of any kind, as carefree as frolicking shepherds and shepherdesses, the Daphnes and Chloes of Greek literature. They did not even arrange another meeting. What would be the point? . . . Love does not set a schedule. Birds and flowers do not chain themselves to anything. They simply meet, with a flutter of wings; some feathers flutter to earth, and songs fill the air. Or stems bend with pollen on the corollas of their luminous blossoms, a few leaves fall, and perfume fills the air. And that is all. Nature rejoices, the earth lies amazed, and the world simply loves.

Poor Santa! How often she later recalled every detail of that gratifying day! One could say that her casual encounter with the student had been analogous to a match that we light in the darkness. It flares up briefly, and though it sheds little light, its illumination is infinitely precious. Because, from that day onward, Santa's decline became a freefall—rapid, implacable, something that, once begun, no one and nothing could slow or stop. Only one thing happened even faster than her fall: the progression of her disease. The pain that had been, at first, infrequent though sharp, became regular, racking, pregnant with dreadful implications. Santa attributed the pain to syphilis, the nemesis of all prostitutes, the scourge that terrifies them and that almost always gets them sooner or later. To combat it, she adopted the standard procedure of the profession: absolute secrecy, which, when the pangs become terrible, requires superhuman endurance to maintain. The tears come in silence, the women laugh uproariously so not to howl, they squirm in agony when alone, and in public they suffer the torture of a tightly laced corset. The rough embraces of the customers become like tongs that rip the flesh of holy martyrs.

In addition to absolute secrecy, the profession seeks the application of folk remedies, the herbs that may cure or may kill, powders and ointments with unintelligible names, sold in semi-clandestine circumstances by soothsaying old women who live in remote, horrid dwellings on the outskirts of the city, where the streets give way desolate, open country. The old women also sell talismans, foretell the future, and cast spells: "Get the blood of a rooster, the fur of a black cat, the eye of a deer, the skeleton of a lizard. Put a container of water in the light of the waning moon. Burn incense and kiss a baby's bottom." They deal in magical instructions, diabolical incantations, portentous mysticism, heretical sacrilege—things that further sicken the spirit without alleviating the flesh. Santa did it all, and the disease persisted, unstoppable, insidious, ever progressing, steadily undermining her organism with cruel, incurable torment, like a punishment sent from above as retribution for the most obdurate sins. Miraculous remedies and drugs could do nothing against the advancing illness, as the pain spread to various regions of her body, lacerating, ulcerating, gnawing away like a small, invisible animal impossible to trap. Unbearable crises immersed Santa in a true hell of pain, only to recede, leaving her face, her color, and the lines of her body unaltered. She did notice that she felt physically worse and worse each time she finished providing pleasure to the men who bought it from her, but she refused to consider herself wounded and out of combat. Instead, she exercised prodigious feats of pretense, endurance, and dissimulation.

Another thing, her jewels. How carelessly the gorgeous temptress had kept the jewelry given her by her rich lovers, accumulating a considerable quantity of precious gems that she had enjoyed spilling out of her hand, on occasion, to watch them tumble, glittering, into the plush interior of her carved jewelry box. Her jewelry—like her health and her rich protectors—now disappeared quickly and quietly into the hands of Spanish pawn brokers or, more directly, into the clutches of the women who often scout for them in brothels, paying merely a seventh or an eighth of the true value. In the blink of an eye, Santa's expressive eyes, still large, velvety, and bright in spite of all the tears, still defended by her silky, curled eyelashes, were the only jewels that remained to her. She looked away for barely a moment, it seemed, and the coffer stood empty. How was it possible?

While the jewels had lasted, their gradual sale had produced enough money to sustain the situation. With money, she could bribe the Sanitation Agents who never left her alone anymore, who stuck to her like burrs, impatient as grave diggers, sensing that this bird was sick and not long for this world. A bit of money allowed her to keep her legitimate pride and resist, or at least, protest against the inhuman demands of the madams and change houses, or even rent her own place for a short time. When the jewels were gone, she sold her costly dresses and other things that she had not previously deemed to be of great value, the hats and wraps and accessories of which she once possessed dozens. But no more. Incredible how everything just vanished! And as her former elegance diminished, her illness worsened and, increasingly, the word got out. Even the cheap brothels did not want her now. The more her former colleagues said about her, the worse her plight. The clients of the houses began to warn one another about Santa. They never considered trying to help their former idol and simply counseled each other to shun her. She was a danger, a threat. One of them proposed denouncing her to the authorities in order to get her out of circulation and control the infallible and imminent contagion.

Perfectly aware that she was sinking, Santa only continued to sink. To lessen the pain, she frankly embraced her last faithful lover, the bottle. Alcohol could at least dull her consciousness of what was happening and, with its viscous embrace, offer her illusions so seductive that she filled her glass repeatedly to keep them in view. And in the leaden sleep from which one awakens pounded to a pulp, the alcohol carried her back to her village, Chimalistac, to her little white house with its chickens and orange trees, to the lap of her mother, and to the esteem and affection of her two honorable brothers. Waking in the dungeons of reality made her weep, but soon enough she began again to sip the poison and laugh a hoarse, lugubrious, alcoholic laugh that her comrades in arms respected with quiet commiseration without quite understanding.

During all of this, Hipólito suffered more, if possible, than did Santa herself. At the beginning of her precipitous decline, which is to say, from the moment when la Tosca turned Santa away, Hipólito could smell the disaster that his blind eyes could not see, and he even predicted it using a thousand euphemisms when he talked to her. His long, grim experience gave him full knowledge of what would happen in the brothels to a girl stigmatized by disease, and he well knew what Santa could expect if she did not leave the city immediately to live somewhere else while the storm blew over.

"Take a rest, Santita. Rest will do you good, and you've got to do something to erase the impression that people have gotten from your breakup with Rubio and from the way that la Tosca treated you. If you need money, don't worry, I've got some, and it's all yours . . . Above all, you need to get treatment, starting tomorrow, starting today if possible. We don't really know what is causing that pain. You think you don't have a man who wants to give you his name and take you out of this blasted business? Well, if you're not embarrassed by it, take my name. It's free, and you won't owe me anything."

At the beginning of her decline, Santa did not view her prospects with the piano player's pessimism. To the contrary, she kept stubbornly optimistic, possibly as a way of maintaining her fighting spirit, as well. She even claimed to see some benefits in the recent turn of events:

"I've had a chance to learn something I've been curious about for a long time, Hipo," she commented to the disbelieving musician, "which is how poor prostitutes manage to get along. If I decide I don't want that kind of life, I can always go back to what I was doing before. I'm practically rich, you know, Hipo. Don't worry! And once I've satisfied my curiosity, why, I'll go back to some high-priced house or maybe move in with you. How would that be? You'll get what you've dreamed about, and I'll settle down and regain my health . . . But for now, don't stand in my way or predict horrible stuff that's not going to happen. Let me try this, just a few more days, okay? I'll finally get fed up with it, and then I'll really turn over a new leaf and become your faithful woman, okay? . . . You won't get mad? You'll still love me?"

And finally, influenced by the alcohol and her progressive debasement, Santa even overcame the physical repugnance she had felt toward the blind man and caressed him with feline cunning. Hipólito lost all self control, at that point, kissing her face and neck and hugging her so tightly that she could not breathe, as if Santa's concession gave him the right to do it or as if his pent-up passion had finally overflowed and streamed out of his every pore.

On one occasion, he almost possessed her, spurred by the power of his repressed animal desires and by the growing intimacy between him and her. These days he usually visited her in one of the fleabag hotels where she bedded her anonymous customers, after her temporary owner had exited the scene, leaving in payment the standard fee, a handful of coins that shimmered on a bed table in the half light of the shuttered room, with a lazy hint of tobacco, liquor, and male sweat wafting gently in the atmosphere, an odor similar to, though much fainter than, the smell of a stable where many cattle have spent the night, once the animals have gone out to pasture and sun has begun to stir the manure with its entering rays. Hipólito would show up, guided by Jenaro, and give free rein to his fears, supplications, and dire prophecies. The stink of the place would drive him crazy, make his heart seize up, drive the rivulets of tears slowly across the white globes of his eyes without irises, seeming to wrinkle them. How many mornings did he enter her room and weep helplessly, unable even to say hello, standing in the middle of the room and waving his cane like a sword that he eventually lowered without punishing the harlot, much less thrashing his own despised weakness, a weakness that brought him back, day after day, to witness this ignominy. She made him want to die, but still he adored her! And day after day, he proffered the same protest and the same oath:

"If you don't change, Santita, we're through! I swear that I'm not going to come after you anymore or even care what happens to you!"

To eliminate witnesses, he often sent Jenaro out for coffee with a shot of liquor, the only breakfast that the girl's disordered stomach could tolerate, and once, when he was alone with Santa, he threw himself at her deliriously, menacingly, unrecognizably:

"Me! Me!" he shouted, "When will it be my turn? I'm dying for you! Me, Santita. Take pity on me. If I wait any longer, there won't be anything left for me. Everybody steps on you as if you were a cobblestone in the street ... And here I am, adoring you, and listening to it happen, and what do I get? ... No, Santita, whatever happens, today it's my turn!"

There were a few moments of struggle, actual wrestling. Santa's only advantage was her sight, still healthy and sharp, while Hipólito flailed randomly in the pitch black of his blindness. Santa finally broke free of him, put the bed between them like a parapet, and, breathing very hard, she declared:

"No, Hipo, for God's sake! You're a good man. You deserve better from me than to have me the way I am now. No, I said ... no!" she continued to protest, running away from him, semi-naked and totally terrified by the blind man, whose appearance at the moment was more horrifying than ever: his eyes enormously wide, his nostrils flaring and his mouth compressed, crouching like a tiger ready to pounce, his cane gone, his arms opening wide and desperately, repeatedly, closing around nothing, huffing and puffing like a caged beast.

"No, Hipo, no!" repeated Santa, fleeing back and forth from one end of the room to another, Hipólito gaining on her little by little, his arms outstretched ahead of him like the antennas of a monstrous spider, wordlessly, frenetically pursuing the fugitive body that he could not see, the body whose whereabouts he detected with a blind man's acute hearing, the body whose nudity he smelled with his unreasoning, long-suffering frenzy, the body toward which he stretched his trembling arms in a supreme quest for relief . . .

The struggle became fierce and implacable, as if between sworn enemies. Gone were adored and adorer, gone the adoration that had bound them. Instead, there was only the primitive, eternal combat between the male pursuer and the female who rejects his advances. Now and again, one could hear the soft, rasping protests of Santa—"No! No!"—confused with the sound of Hipólito's feet dragging on the brick floor . . . Then Santa slipped and fell, and two cries followed—her cry of terror and his cry of victory—and then . . . then, merely panting, and the wrestling began anew, the blind man on top, bruising the idolized flesh that belonged to everyone but him, forcing himself on her like a gorilla, Santa surrendering, dominated, awaiting his furious attack with the silent passivity of her sex, physiologically constituted to absorb such defeats . . .

And at that instant, Jenaro, returning from his errand, brashly entered the room and stood petrified at the sight of the writhing knot of bodies on the floor. He dropped the tray of coffee and, a child, after all, sobbed in protest:

"*Patrón*! . . . Don Hipólito! . . . Miss Santa! . . . What's going on?"

That was the last time that the blind man sent Jenaro for breakfast. If the employees of the hotel could not bring it, Santa preferred to skip her coffee and everything else in order to avoid being alone with Hipólito. No matter how depraved she had become, Santa truly did feel an odd kind of modesty in relation to the piano player. Rather strange, no? But that is the way it was. She did not want to give herself to him all stained and dirty, straight from the arms of others. She hoped that there might be an end to her degraded lifestyle, followed by a decent interval that might purify her at bit, make her more or less worthy of the piano player's love, a love that, when all was said and done, shone in the darkness of her life like a beacon, a celestial light, a lodestar that promised rest, oblivion, and forgiveness. So why did she, nevertheless, not initiate the indispensable interval? Why did the resolutions that she had made yesterday always fall apart today? Why did the resolutions of today fall apart tomorrow, as she continued to roll down hill?

The interminable delay finally drove Hipólito to summon all his strength and follow through on his threat to abandon her:

"Santita," he told her one day with determination, "goodbye! You've never loved me, and you never will. If you did, you'd never leave me in this purgatory . . . I tell you that I just can't take it anymore. Day after day I come to get you out of these devil's lairs, and I have to drag you, and you say 'later,' later you'll go with me, and 'later' never comes. That blessed 'tomorrow' that I've waited for for so long, you know how long . . . never comes. It looks to me like you delay on purpose, because you like the darkness of the night and hate the sunshine. Ay, Santita, if you were blind like me, you'd be ready for the light. I can tell you don't really want to come with me, that you'd bring the darkness when you came. So you just stay here, then . . . and God help you, because I'm tired of waiting. I'm going! . . . Jenaro, say goodbye to Santita," he commanded, hoping that this would be her cue to ask him to stay.

But Santa was so drunk that morning that she hardly listened to the blind man's pathetic explanation and simply allowed him to leave, murmuring in response to Jenaro's goodbye:

"Yeah, yeah, go on, because I've got a splitting headache, and I'll see you tomorrow . . . or tonight at the café on Escondida Street. You know where . . ."

"No," answered Hipólito, coming back to the door. "Not tonight, and not tomorrow . . . Goodbye, Santita!"

When a river floods destructively, it can drag even enormous boulders with it, and massive tree trunks will ride the green flanks and foamy crests of its bellowing torrent, tumbling, submerging, and reappearing helplessly in demented flight toward the sea, despite their proud weight and strength. An insignificant bit of straw, however, torn from its roots, may wrap itself around a snag as insignificant as itself and survive the flood in place, as if the river pitied the weakness of both straw and snag and respected their solidarity. Eventually the waters subside, the current returns to its gentle, beneficent course, and the boulders and massive trunks are nowhere to be seen, but behold the bit of straw bent around its snag, trembling now in the breeze, weak, humble, and insignificant as ever, still ringed by foamy kisses from the passing torrent, kisses that, like the ones left by lips, fade very quickly, no matter how eternal the act of kissing may have seemed. But take away the snag, and the straw will be swept away infinitely faster and more completely than the boulders or tree trunks.

So it was with Santa. With Hipólito out of the picture, she plummeted toward the abyss at a vertiginous rate, wretched, ridiculed, friendless, and hurting. Descending the slope bristling with thistles, lurch by lurch, her disintegrating body finally landed in a stinking hole where each trick sold for half a peso: a snake pit, a stronghold of hoodlums and criminals, a factory of diseases. She landed in a room that was itself malformed, mis-shapen, two of its crumbling walls seeming to collide at an odd angle, forming a corner in which both walls threatened to collapse, or rather, had already commenced to do so, to judge by the handfuls of dust and chunks of material the size of fists shaken down from the edge of the ceiling by the rumbling passage of heavily loaded trucks that filled the streets of the peripheral neighborhood, busily coming and going like monstrous, industrious ants during eight hours of every day.

Santa landed here after a thorough tour of the very worst that the great city has to offer, the infectious social rot, the itchy rash that only the police dare to scratch. The well-off residents of luxurious neighborhoods feel the itch, and it keeps them from resting easy, but they fear contamination. Scratching the itch can spread the contagion. If the itch becomes unbearable and the police scratch the infection, they will rouse and scatter the social lepers who shelter there, and the famine-racked frames and delinquent physiognomies of these pariahs will soon be seen in the neatly paved streets of the city's central district, ogling its sumptuous constructions and fancy shops. The bare feet, suspicious looks, and hesitant gestures of the social lepers mark them as refugees of the recent police raid on the outskirts of the city, totally out of place here, like lice that one happens to see on an expensive garment worn by a well-washed person. Feeling exposed, the human lice move quickly, silently, singly rather than in groups, never stopping, families dissolving in fear, the mother over here, the father over there, the children wherever. They all know where they are going: to some other poor peripheral neighborhood, back into the lonely shadows on a different side of the city. The important thing is not to be noticed as they traverse the light. They hope to pass anonymously, concealed by the noise of the traffic, by the hustle and bustle, praying that the owners and masters of all this will be distracted by the daily concerns of work and diversion. Woe to him or her who fails to escape attention and gets detained by the authorities. No friends or family members will stop to find out why, or try to help, and possibly share the same fate. No. They continue furtively toward the distant endpoint of their flight.

Santa experienced all of that, and more. She became familiar with social types and circumstances that many city dwellers live their entire lives without ever encountering firsthand, no matter how faithfully they may have read newspapers, fulfilled their jury duty, or cultivated relations with the police and authorities. Santa experienced it all as a requisite of her profession, because cheap prostitutes often function as discrete, natural intermediaries between criminals and the law.

Her current domicile, located on the far southeastern outskirts of the city beyond the old monasteries of Monserrate and San Jerónimo, had a staff of no fewer than seven harpies, not counting Santa. The room with the crumbling walls was therefore divided by a number of partitions: two main ones down the middle with a narrow passageway between them, and various lateral partitions that created a series of cubicles on each side. The lateral partitions were tacked precariously to the main ones and to the crumbling walls with bits of wire, wood, and greasy cord. The furniture of the establishment consisted of dark, rickety, sagging beds with withered, half-empty mattresses and pillows, and a wobbly chair or two, their cane seats sunken and broken through. Fixed invariably to the wall of each cubicle like an icon of the barbarous religion practiced therein, one could observe a dented platter, made apparently of pewter, the metal hidden by stains and crusts nothing could ever remove, and on the platter, a nauseating towel the hanging tips of which oscillated slightly like a noose on the gallows whenever one of the women or their visitors closed the door. At the end of the narrow passageway between the two main partitions, on the wall above a small table with an oil lamp that flickered there day and night, was a photograph of a saint's image that seemed almost sacrilegious in that setting, tacked up by its four corners and surrounded by paper flowers and a few votive offerings.

Here Santa ended up after she was thrown out of everywhere else, racked by pain and poverty, half drunk, glassy-eyed, her splendid body swollen where her bones did not protrude, ragged and ruined.

"Do you have room for one more?" she asked the old woman who opened the small, worm-eaten, much-mended door when Santa knocked on it. The old woman was wrapped in a shawl, with bits of soap stuck to her temples as a cure for headache. She puffed on a cigarette butt and reeked of cheap lavender perfume.

For a moment, she did not reply. Meanwhile the sun bathed the sidewalk and generously entered the doorway of the poor establishment as well. The old woman submitted Santa to a visual inspection, somewhat impeded by the puffy eyelids that half-closed her eyes. Then she extended hands reminiscent of clusters of knotty vines, revealing forearms so thin, with skin so parchment-like, that they could have belonged to an Egyptian mummy. The hands unfolded themselves like trained tarantulas to explore Santa's hips, thighs, and breasts through her dress, then lifted her skirt slightly before their owner finally spoke again:

"Come on in . . . There's some breakfast if you haven't had any, and if you have, get a broom and sweep. But be quiet, because we've got a customer still asleep in here."

The old woman did not think to ask if Santa's sanitation documents were in order, nor did Santa explain that she had none. What for? The Sanitation Agents rarely showed their faces in fleabag establishments such as this. And even if they should be seized by the rare desire to initiate an investigation here, documentation enough to satisfy them could always be found somehow. Nothing else mattered, because the clientele of this den of iniquity had compelling personal reasons not to raise a stink if someone got them sick. At most, they would find the responsible woman and give her a good thrashing on one of the scary nearby streets or in one of the horrible little taverns where the women ply their trade. But they won't go to the police, no way, because that would be a losing proposition entirely for the customers who frequent this sort of establishment, an impressive crew, to put it mildly: professional thieves who hide what they have stolen in the brothel; deserters from the army who make a business of selling their uniforms and equipment there; carters, muleteers, and merchants of all stripes, all of them contrabandists; bankrupt businessmen whose tiny stores—more loaded with debts than merchandise—have been closed by the court; and shifty tough guys, the kind you see watching over a pulque shop, with no job at this stage, but plenty of money, a pistol, and lots of people they hate. Among the customers one might even encounter, though only exceptionally and by special permission from the owner, some poor convict recently emerged from Belén Prison, tired of waiting to find out if he would be executed or let off with a twenty-year sentence, waiting now in the brothel while his friends arrange the next step of his escape. It is a world apart, one that simultaneously distresses and fascinates us; a world without morals, or at least, of stunningly confused ones, where the very dregs can sometimes show surprising self-abnegation. But those are few against the many whose consciences gape cavernously empty; those who know only crime and speak only the argot of the streets. They are the scum that floats at the edges of the great cesspools of humanity called cities, the antisocial elements, as we say.

After closing and locking the door, the old woman demanded of Santa: "What's your name?"

"Santa."

"Santa . . . yeah, right! From now on it's Loreto."

And even her enchanting name disappeared in the muck.

As far gone as Santa was, this inferno, surpassing anything she had expected or imagined could exist, completed her annihilation. What nights, what afternoons, what mornings, and what agony! When not in the embrace of some bandit, she was in the throes of the agony that ripped perpetually at her insides, or in the clutches of the cheap booze that she gulped by the bottleful, seeking unconsciousness, sprawled snoring in complete stupefaction on the sagging bed or even on the floor. And she watched what was happening to her, astonished and unresponsive, without protest or resistance, the way that we all do during our worst nightmares, the ones that seem never-ending and continue to make us tremble even after we awake from them, praying to God that such a thing should never, ever happen to us in real life.

Her only consolation in these dark days was to leave the brothel and spend some free time at the "Siesta for the Tired" tavern on Regina Square, that did not close until after midnight. It was the refuge of a multihued crowd of all kinds of folk, shiftless veterans of life on the street, who were in there drinking for at least six hours every night, from the hour of evening prayers to twelve o'clock, when the joint was jumping. Was it here, at this tavern, or was it from the convict who had escaped from Belén Prison, who stayed up all of one night with her, that Santa learned the dance lyrics that she sang so ceaselessly for a time? Who knows, because people sang plenty at the tavern, with guitars and everything, and the murderer (the world is like this) treated Santa with an almost feminine tenderness, confessing why he had killed, and even telling her about a woman he loved and about a child, a little baby, whose whereabouts he did not know. The couple on the other side of the partition from Santa and the convict later told how they heard crying and the whispered sharing of confidences all night, and how, at one point, the guy just burst into song, overcome by the liquor or his sorrows. So it is not known where she learned the popular dance melody that she hummed stubbornly, repeatedly, tonelessly, as if in supplication, as if she hoped that the sweetness of the melody and the magic of the rhyme might guarantee the truth of the lyrics. Our popular dances provide a suitable musical accompaniment for dying individuals and disappearing races!

One verse promised such sweet mercy in heaven ("They say the dead always rest in peace /'Cause there's no suffering beyond the sky") that Santa repeated it a thousand times, obsessed now with death and certain of the peace that the lyrics promised. She sang the rest of the stanza without much conviction, however, merely to complete the rhyme: "Our bodies die, but our souls live on / And my soul is yours, oh why, oh why?" And sometimes, when she got to these last words, or even more often, to the mention of "blind passion" in another verse, Santa saw the image of blind Hipólito, looking at her with his horrid whitish eyes of a bronze statue without patina. The apparition always dissolved before Santa could tell what it meant. Did her soul want Hipólito to rescue her, or was her soul already in his power somehow?

Before she had solved this riddle, her illness progressed to its final and most intense phase. Truly in its grip, she could not make a movement or take a step in the hellhole where she lived without emitting wails that no amount of attempted muffling could conceal from the other women and their customers, or from Santa's own soul. There were times when, unable to walk, she dragged herself across the floor to the bed and lay their pulling and tearing at her soiled clothing, crying, imploring clemency from the men who still wanted to rent her body:

"Don't touch me, please! I'm dying! . . . But don't tell the old lady, because she'll run me out, and I don't have anywhere to go . . ."

Some of them, like infernal, rutting goats, forced themselves on her nonetheless, in the belief that she was faking it. A few paid her for nothing and even recommended this or that remedy. Most simply called out, from right in her room, asking for a replacement:

"Hey, what's-your-name, send another girl, because this one's no good!"

The old lady tolerated this for about a month, and at the end of that time, she fired Santa, using the same imperious tone as when she had admitted the girl:

"Pull yourself together, because tomorrow you're out of here. Forget what you owe me for the shawl . . ."

Nothing could make matters worse than they already were for Santa, so she simply assented to each of the old woman's three peremptory admonitions:

"Okay . . . okay . . . okay, I'll be out tomorrow . . . You bet I will!" she added, without knowing why.

That afternoon the pain was so powerful and unrelenting that she did not drink a drop. She sweated profusely, her eyes sunken deeply in their sockets, the circles underneath them so dark that she appeared to have been severely beaten. She was getting really sick, really sick . . . Rolling around in the bed she looked helplessly in all directions. Something was moving, the train, the ship, whatever it was . . . was moving, for sure . . . taking her away . . .

At dusk, she felt a little better, not much, but enough to do something. She would send for Hipólito, and Hipólito would come, right away, generous and loving, to get her out of there, help her have a good death, and above all, forgive her. She asked the administrator for one more coin to pay a messenger:

"The gentleman who will be coming to get me will pay you back," she asserted confidently, and in the face of the old woman's obvious incredulity, she added: "And if nobody comes, what's the difference?"

Her message to Hipólito was brief and to the point, like a telegram announcing a funeral:

"Go to such-and-such a house on such-and-such a street and tell a blind man who plays the piano there that Santa—pay attention—Santa is dying and wants to see him. That's it. And he should come back with you. Now go!"

If the old woman, her girls, and the clients of the house had been the least bit impressionable, they would have been amazed at what happened shortly thereafter, when a horrible, ill-dressed blind man and his ragged, barefoot little guide appeared at the brothel in a rental coach and went straight inside:

"Santa! . . . Santita! . . . Where are you?"

And hearing Santa respond, the blind man went into her cubicle, and there was the quiet sound of crying.

"Hipo," said Santa softly to the piano player who devoutly touched and smelled and kissed her. "They've tossed me out of here, out of *here*! Nobody wants anything to do with me anymore. It's all over. I'm dying!"

"I love you, I . . . I'm going to take you with me . . . Because you can't die. You can't!"

And he paid what she owed and took her with him.

The disbelieving inhabitants of the brothel followed them out into the street.

The blind man put Santa into the coach and climbed in after her. Jenaro climbed up beside the driver, almost like a liveried servant. The evening twilight completed the spell, and Cinderella's coach pulled away from the curb in triumph.

Ten

The bells were ringing ten o'clock at night when the coach stopped at the house where Hipólito lived, so the large iron-bound street door of the subdivided old structure was already closed. That pleased the piano player, because it would spare him the curiosity of other residents, who would go crazy if they saw him taking a woman to his room.

On the other hand, the Arbeu Theater, which stood right across the street from Hipólito's house, was totally lit up, all its batteries of exterior lighting ablaze, its doors wide open, the spectators pouring into the street for a breath of fresh air during the intermission. The theater's illumination stretched across the street, bounced against the façades of the houses opposite, and glinted on their windows. One heard talking and laughter, and one saw matches flare up and go out, identifying groups of smokers, the red tips of whose cigarettes made small circles in the air as they gestured in conversation. Along the edge of the sidewalk in front of the theater stood a row of tables piled high with sweets, pastries, and bread with sardines, each table identically lit with a candle inside a paper screen to keep the wind from extinguishing it, each table guarded by a vendor alert to defend his wares from the circling urchins, emperors of the crowded pavement, whose specialty was reselling tickets and snatching an occasional bite to eat without paying for it. Parked coaches lined the curb to each side of the theater's doors; their waiting drivers, having put out the coach lights for economy's sake, stood around conversing in bunches to pass the time.

Many of the horses were dozing, their necks stretched out, their heads sometimes resting on the gear that harnessed them to the coach, sometimes sinking gradually with each breath that the animal exhaled, as if the distance between its head and the cobblestones indicated how deeply it slept.

Jenaro leapt like a monkey from his place beside the driver, opened the door of the coach, and asked for orders:

"Should I go get supper?"

Hipólito first paid the driver of the rental coach, then fished in his pants pocket for the big key and opened the street door of the house. Jenaro in the lead, guiding his master, and his master holding on to Santa, the three of them entered the tiled courtyard of the silent, enormous old house. Everything was dark, save a few glimmers of pallid light that emerged timidly from underneath and around the closed doors on all sides and a few curtained windows on the upper stories. The only sounds in the courtyard were the soft, monorhythmic blubbering of the fountain and, here and there, from behind doors and windows, the distant voices of restless children and of their mothers singing them lullabies. In a shadowy corner, attached to two walls of the building, a softly swaying clothesline gave a sinister impression, its shirts and pants dangling like dismembered bodies or outstretched like startled ghosts about to take flight.

Hipólito's rooms were on an upper floor, to which they climbed in silence, except for Jenaro, who knew about all the possible hazards and announced their approach:

"Look out for that pipe! . . . Miss Santa, don't hold on the banister here, because there's a piece of it missing . . . Single file, now, around these broken floor boards. That hole's as big as me . . . Okay, we're there!"

Santa, now accustomed to living in complete squalor, could not help but admire the building. Leaning on the railing, she looked at the courtyard from above as Hipólito fumbled excitedly with the key to his room.

"What a nice place this is, Hipo. So big!"

The piano player's little apartment had three rooms and a bit of terrace. The first room was midsized, with wallpaper (although streaked and torn) and a ceiling (although full of holes and covered with stains where the roof leaked). The second room, windowless and dark, belonged to Jenaro and the pet dove that had arrived one day from the skies, of his own accord, and had become so tame that he came when called by his name, which was "Jaws." Jaws was the most attractive thing about the whole place. He followed them around like a dog, toddling across the floor with his tail fanned out, and flew confidently from room to room. Jaws ate while sitting on Hipólito's shoulder, taking food from Jenaro's lips, and his cooing and burbling cheered them up. The last room was the kitchen, with a place to cook, long unused, and a cupboard populated with dust, damp, mice and spiders. Jenaro's room, however, boasted a bed devised by the resourceful guide boy himself: a set of wine crates in a row with straw stuffed between them and a sleeping mat spread on top, plus several faded pieces of old carpet and a hand-me-down blanket that had belonged to Hipólito. The kid slept in the lap of luxury! The *patrón*'s room, of course, was the best furnished by far with its nice store-bought bed, a mattress with springs and wool padding, sheets, quilt, and pillows, and a store-bought dresser with a mirror that did Hipólito absolutely no good. The apartment had everything you need: a night stand and a dinner table, a cheap sofa, a wardrobe that actually locked, four chairs, and a quirky array of plates, glasses, forks, and spoons. There was a lamp, missing some parts, that did not illuminate much even when lit, and a half-burnt candle in a candlestick that previous candles had decorated prodigally with overlapping layers of melted wax.

They opted to light the candle instead of the lamp, and when informed that his house was now illuminated, Hipólito removed his hat, took both of Santa's hands in his and, kissing them, he exclaimed solemnly:

"Look how little I can offer you, Santa, but it's all yours, everything, even Jenaro and me. Here you'll get better and be in charge, and here nobody—nobody you don't want, I mean—will come to disturb you. Are you happy?"

Santa threw herself into Hipólito's arms, blinded by the flame of a love that, far from dying out, seemed destined to last until death, the death of the person in whose heart it burned or the death of the person who inspired it, or possibly beyond.

"You really love me so much, Hipo?" asked Santa, wondering how anyone could idolize her so infinitely now that she was sick and despised. "You don't think," she continued softly, "that maybe, because you can't see me, you imagine me differently from what I am? . . . Don't you know," she went on almost in a whisper, "that my beauty is gone? Didn't I tell you? Didn't I tell you that nobody wants me now, not even vagabonds off the street? . . . Don't you feel disgust? Don't you just feel sorry for me and want to do me a favor in the little time that I have left?"

There was a long, portentous pause. The musician gently extricated himself from Santa's arms, asked Jenaro to go bring something for supper, and pacing around the room with assurance, as if he were not blind at all, he stopped at her side and said:

"Listen."

There was another pause. Hipólito bowed his head as if examining the floor. In reality, he was examining his feelings, looking back at how much he had suffered, at the long, lonely desolation of his heart. And finally, he spoke:

"I myself don't know how much I love you. Some things are impossible to know! . . . But, just imagine that they chopped me up in little pieces, know what I mean? Tiny, little pieces, and that a lot of men, a lot, scattered my pieces around in handfuls, all over creation—a handful here, another in China, which they say is far, far away—so that the bits of me were separated by mountains and forests and rivers. And say that you were in the middle of a desert, a thousand times sicker and poorer and uglier than now, so ugly that even the wild beasts were scared of you . . . well, Santita . . . if you were to call me the way you did today, and you swore you loved me . . . I'd come, just like today . . . the pieces of me would go back together, all by themselves, in a great miracle . . . and I'd come to you, to bless you and adore you, just like today, and I'd be with you until we die!"

"Yes, Hipo, I do love you, I swear that I do!" truly captivated, at last, and truly loving him. "Believe me, please! Tell me that you believe me!"

"You have no idea," said Hipólito, turning away, without answering whether he believed or not in what she swore, completely transported. "You have no idea what it's like to live a whole life without love. God spared you from knowing what that's like. Be thankful! To the contrary, you received more love than you wanted. You toyed with love at first, then ground it under your shoe, but you never took it seriously, like a child that laughs when it breaks a toy or destroys a flower that can easily be replaced. You've been lucky . . . And I think you're still good inside, despite what you've been through. That's why you've finally decided to come with me and love me, something that nobody else has done, except my mother . . . How ugly can you be, compared to me? How much have you suffered, compared to me? I'm good, too . . . I mean, I'm no saint, but I'm good, and the proof is that I've never blasphemed against God, and I've made the best I can of this endless night that I live in . . ."

As he said this, the blind man turned toward the candle, and its light illuminated his pockmarked face and his horrid eyes without irises, which seemed to gaze vaguely at the very sorrows he evoked, at the accumulated pain that he detailed, at his whole melancholy, loveless life. Deeply moved,

Santa looked at him, paying no attention to the ugliness of this last lover and, to the contrary, discovering something beautiful in his face triply marked by childhood fever, lifelong suffering, and moral and material poverty. He had drunk his bitter cup to the dregs, uncomplaining and alone, like a martyr.

A great wave of pity swept her toward Hipólito, and she knelt at his feet, embracing his knees. At that very moment, the pet dove flew in from one of the other, darkened rooms and landed on the shoulder of its master. And in the weak candlelight that flickered against the clouds of shadow that filled the room, the blind man stood stock still, like a statue symbolizing irreparable, eternal human suffering, a statue abandoned somehow at one of life's many crossroads, weathered by time and the elements, but standing firm, finally attracting to itself the living signs of winged and earthly love, the dove on his shoulder and the woman at his feet.

Jenaro arrived carrying their dinner and, with his buzzing vivacity, restored motion to the tragic tableau. Without asking permission, the boy lit the lamp, set the table, opened the window to let in a few stars, and clapped his hands to seat Hipólito and Santa. He served them with the precise movements of a professional waiter, crumbled some bread for Jaws who, with outstretched neck and tail, threaded his way across the table between glasses and plates to eat them, and, at the moment when Jenaro opened the large bottle of inexpensive beer with a pop that he had assured by giving it a little shake, he poured the foaming brew and announced with comic flair:

"Champagne at ten smackers a bottle, from Elvira's house, the former employer of us all!"

The boy was as thrilled by the new state of affairs as was his *patrón*, the piano player, who dined with a dreamy expression, his face turned toward Santa, exactly as if he could see her. That was what most surprised Santa. Why, every time she looked at him, did he seem to know and "look" at her as well? Nor was that the last wonder of the evening. When supper was over, as if he were a mind reader, Hipólito asked for the bottle of brandy and said tactfully to Santa, who was dying for a drink:

"Have a little sip of this. It's what I have after supper, and it wouldn't be right for you to let me drink alone." And with amazing accuracy, without spilling a drop, he poured two or three shots of liquor into the bottom of a large glass.

Then, in order not to mortify her with his presence, he got up and called Jenaro out to the apartment's homely little terrace, where the two had an animated conversation of which Santa was able to catch only bits and pieces:

"No, that's too early, Jenaro . . . even seven o'clock is too early . . ."

Santa hurriedly drained her ration of brandy, because her pain was beginning and she needed to lie down. But it was not too bad yet, and she watched with a smile as Jenaro cleared the table, putting the best of the uneaten food on his own plate, for he had not yet eaten. He lowered Jaws gently to the floor, and then, with his dinner held high in one hand, the boy raised the other to his mouth like an imaginary bugle and walked out of the room blowing the call to mess. Jaws trundled quickly after him, his little head oscillating from side to side and his little breast inflating and deflating with each step. After Jenaro disappeared and his bugle call faded, Santa was surprised to hear his voice continue speaking with undiminished enthusiasm.

"Who is Jenaro talking to?" she asked Hipólito.

"With Jaws," explained the piano player, well acquainted with the habits of his guide, "and with the mice and spiders in the cupboard. He's giving them their dinner."

A little while after that, Jenaro was quiet, asleep, no doubt, and his animals, too, as Santa made a mighty effort to overcome the pangs of pain that soon took hold of her and shook her, under the sheets, like a ragdoll. She bit on a fold of bedclothes to muffle her involuntary groans so that Hipólito would not hear them, and with all her heart she desired that they give her at least a brief truce now, even if only to throttle her even worse later. She wanted, above all, to be able to give herself to Hipólito, to give him pleasure with her body at least once, to let him possess what nobody wanted anymore, nobody but him, who desired it like nothing else on this earth, and who deserved it more—oh, so much more—than the thousands who had bruised it with their clumsy caresses and their revolting, despotic lechery! But as Hipólito, for his part, undressed with the excruciating slowness of someone who wants to prolong a sublime moment of anticipation, both to savor that moment as long as possible, and because he cannot quite believe that the anxiously awaited consummation of his desires is really at hand, about to be converted from dream to positive fact, and not about to vanish into thin air—just then Santa's pain swarmed through her body like asps and vipers, curling around muscles and nerves, biting, ripping, and tearing at her body most where she wanted them least. Santa chewed harder on the bedclothes, racked by the unbelievable intensity of the pain and by the growing awareness that she could not—that she physically could not—reward the immense love of the blind man who now moved toward the bed with the reverent attitude of a person entering a church, his head bowed in supplication, his arms outstretched eagerly to begin, with the very tips of his fingers, the communion he had dreamed about for so long, with the woman whom he idolized so passionately, and who, time and time again, had seemed lost to him forever.

His blind eyes did not tell him that the candle had burnt down into the candlestick and was about to sputter its last gasp, but his instincts told him that he was almost there, that Santa was almost his, that one more step was all that stood between him and his ultimate triumph. He controlled his eagerness and, timid as a newlywed, slid softly into the bed . . . but as soon as he felt Santa's warmth and the multiple contacts of her body, the volcano inside of him exploded. With strident fragments of exultant laughter and intermittent, truncated, barely audible murmurings he launched himself onto Santa, whose pain had become so horrendous that, despite all her resolutions to endure anything for Hipólito's sake, she reared up in the sheets wet with tears and perspiration, and pushed him away.

"I can't, Hipo, I can't . . . It would be better to kill me!"

Miraculously, the same limitless love that had exploded inside the blind man now calmed him in an instant. Through a heroic act of sheer willpower, he tamed the charging horses of his desire and, kissing Santa's forehead serenely, it was he who explained the terrible reasons why they must go no further:

"You're right, my Santa, I was forgetting that you're sick. Forgive me and rest, poor thing! For me, it's enough just to have you here with me . . . That's it, rest on my arm . . . that's it, Santa, that's it . . . rest . . . sleep . . ."

That night had to be among the purest and most chaste of Santa's life, purified by her pain, which did not let up for hours, and saturated with the love of Hipólito, who did not dare move at all in his determination to provide her the rest required by her ailing body and spirit. Neither of them slept, although both simulated sleep with their immobility and their closed eyes. Occasionally, she felt a pang of pain and he, of desire, but both resisted firmly and wordlessly. Santa's thoughts rambled through the bright future that we all want and need, a recompense for her long suffering; Hipólito's thoughts went there, too, in recompense for his long and patient waiting. The day that she had promised him had finally arrived!

They felt happy together, sharing the warmth of their bodies, covered by the same blanket, a blanket as humble and ragged as both of them. They were sure of each other at last, bound together by the indissoluble bond of common misfortune and misery. So their thoughts naturally rose up—along the same path, unbeknownst to them—to the destination of all such mystical confluences. Their spirits arose to give thanks, remembering guiltily en route all they had to be thankful for, that Santa could easily have died in the squalid last stop of the descent from which she had just been liberated, that Hipólito could have died almost anywhere along the way, with only darkness in his sightless eyes and his yearning soul. Certainly, they had been forgiven, they thought, precisely because they had been allowed this moment of love, which they swore to honor and knew would salve their wounds and soothe all their accumulated resentments. Love was leading them back to God! And their thoughts continued to rise, white as ermine, thoughts that knelt as if in communion. They forgave everything that they had suffered at others' hands, in the conviction that they themselves would be forgiven. And Santa's pain was dulled, transmuted into something that she could bear, and Hipólito's desire diminished, transmuted into sweet, chimerical delight . . . Little by little, they moved until their bodies touched, without evil appetites or twisted temptations, in the immensely pure promise to belong to one another as soon as they could. And they heard a slight flapping of wings, that they believed to signify not the restlessness of Jenaro's pet dove, but rather, the affectionate Guardian Angel that each had known in infancy, sent back to them now from far, far away. The angel took pity on the motherless two of them, without wealth or health or happiness in their lives, and it folded its immaculate wings to stand guard over them through the night, watching over the only sort of sleep worthy of watching over, the sleep of chastity, that finally descended on the poor prostitute and the poor blind man.

Thanks to that sleep, the next morning Jenaro was able to fulfill exactly the instructions that he had received the night before. Before seven o'clock, he tiptoed out the door, locking it behind him to make sure no one disturbed the sleep of his *patrones*. The boy felt so jubilant that he could not help provoking the cacophonous cries of the parrot belonging to the woman who managed the building, cries to which the manager added her own. Her cartload of abuse did not dampen his mood, though, and it even pleased him to have annoyed someone whom he regarded as a personal enemy. He was back in less than an hour, accompanied by a carrier with a large covered basket that greatly intrigued the neighbor women at their doors and the ragged kids who played in the courtyard. Jenaro carried another basket with two restaurant breakfasts steaming like a pair of coffee-fueled locomotives. Arriving at the apartment's little bit of terrace, he paid the carrier after directing the man to pour the contents of the large basket into the sink for washing clothes, a contents that turned out to be a load of fresh flowers of all scents and colors. Hipólito, who never saw anything, could not imagine anything nicer for Santa than to cover her humble little house, and principally her bedroom, with flowers:

"I want her to open her eyes, Jenarito, and see flowers, lots of them! And then when she sees me . . . maybe I won't look so ugly."

Jenaro hardly breathed so as not to wake them up! The sound that his agile bare feet made running back and forth was almost imperceptible. He imprisoned poor Jaws in his own room to keep the dove from loudly cooing or flying around, and he set about decorating the terrace and the room in which the lovers slept. His method lacked rhyme or reason, order or concert, and obeyed only the impulse of his turbulent fantasies, but the truth is that a professional florist probably could not have made the bedroom more beautiful. It was a joy to the eye, delightful to the scent, a bit like a garden, a bit like a church, most of all like a village festival. At about nine o'clock, he put the final touches on his work and threw open the door and window of the room to let in the sun and Jaws. The breakfast coffee had been served on the table bristling with flowers.

Santa was the first to awaken, and in the pleasant somnolence that follows sleep, she probably imagined that she was dreaming. She inhaled deeply with an expression of satisfaction, opened her eyes, took one look at the flowers, and shut them fast, grinning at so unexpected a spectacle.

Jenaro launched Jaws at the bed, where he fluttered to rest on the pillows, and, knocking loudly on the already open door, the boy announced with excited shouts, that breakfast was served:

"Here's your coffee with milk!"

Hipólito, too, lifted his eyelids, but calculating that Jenaro's boisterousness meant the flowers had made a big hit with Santa, he closed them again so that his horrid whitish eyes would not spoil things. And although he did feel that Santa was sitting up, he never imagined why. How, after all, could one imagine anything so delightful! Santa sat up and, without the slightest hint of disgust or repugnance, she took hold of him, held him in her bare arms, profoundly moved and crying, and she kissed his blind eyes—the eyes that were condemned to never, ever see her—and they opened wide, trying so hard to see, just one instant, sweet Lord! . . . And the tears of Santa, whose face was suspended over his, rained into his eyes, and they were immediately absorbed, the way raindrops are absorbed into barren earth that has been thirsty for years.

That moment inaugurated a dreamy existence that lasted only days, during which they did not so much live as resuscitate. Santa's feminine instincts came out through her pain, which did not let up; Hipólito did not need sight to count himself a happy man; and Jenaro leapt and frolicked like a carefree lamb. Those days just flew past, full of planning and projects for the future. Santa would sew, sweep, and cook—she was already doing so in her eager imagination—Jenaro would run errands, and Hipólito would continue to work nights at Elvira's house.

Hipólito approved all the plans with the unconditional acquiescence of those who know themselves to be truly blessed, occasionally catching hold of Santa's arm or waist or dress and kissing it with the gluttony of a stray hound that has managed to snatch a delicate morsel in the street.

For now, Santa and Jenaro started to give the apartment a good cleaning, raising a dense cloud of dust that made them cough, cry, and laugh. Santa cooked in the long-unused kitchen, producing results that were more enthusiastically applauded than eagerly devoured, because the truth was that despite her much-publicized culinary abilities—which she really had possessed during her village upbringing—even her simplest dishes did not come out too well. So they simply added the enjoyment of sumptuous meals to the uncertain future that they never doubted lay around the corner. They postponed anything presently impossible, which was almost everything, for some day soon, tomorrow or next week, the brief postponements of people who carry a heavy load of miseries and yearn to rest.

But why, every time they announced a plan or proposed a project, did the pain return to sink its claws into Santa, collapsing their house of cards, saddening Hipólito, doubling her over so that she had to lean on the wall or the furniture, disfiguring her face? With both hands, Santa pressed hard on the places that hurt, Jenaro tried to comfort her, and Hipólito frowned, muttering who knows how many protests and oaths under his breath. When the pain became so great that Santa had to lie down, the piano player declared darkly:

"The first thing is to get you cured! Tomorrow we'll bring a doctor to see you, and if he doesn't work, another and another, until one of them finally makes you feel better!"

One was enough, an associate of the doctor whom the girls at Elvira's house normally consulted and to whom Hipólito appealed in his tribulation. Santa's illness was at such an advanced stage and had become so pronounced that the physician needed only one examination to diagnose it, with its terrifying name and its grim prognosis, which he believed would play out very quickly, indeed. After the examination he called Hipólito out to the little bit of terrace, still strewn with petals, leaves, and stems from the day before, and without prologue or euphemisms he delivered the news point blank:

"She's got a cancer, a tremendous and incurable one. Absolutely incurable. We could perhaps prolong her life with an operation, although there are no guarantees. The operation has its own risks, and it's extremely expensive."

"How much?" asked Hipólito, pale and shaking, determined to do anything rather than lose Santa.

"Well, at Béistegui Hospital, for example, where they've got all the modern equipment—because forget trying to do it here," replied the doctor, alluding to the ratty apartment, "it could cost a hundred pesos, not including what they charge for a room while she recovers from the operation. I'd have to take a colleague with me, and an anesthetist to administer the chloroform."

"Did you say that without the operation the patient will die soon for sure?"

"For sure and soon, yes."

"When do want to operate?" asked the blind man, making his decision without further discussion of costs. "I'll pay in advance."

"Day after tomorrow, in the morning," answered the doctor after glancing at his schedule. "Tomorrow I'll have her admitted, and she'll spend the night in the hospital."

"Can I watch the operation?"

"Hmmm . . . if you insist . . . and if you promise not to move or make a sound."

"What is the operation called?" Hipólito asked his final question, contorted with grief.

"A hysterectomy."

The strange and sinister-sounding name was the last straw. It had a terrible, dangerous, inhumane ring, and he accepted it with the passive resignation of someone accustomed to absorbing the evils that had washed over him incessantly for a lifetime.

"What did he know! Nothing! Nothing but how to paw a piano keyboard to stay alive. So if the doctor said that without the hystect . . . or whatever the devil it was . . . Santa would die—his Santa!—there was only one thing to do: the operation, as soon as possible, with all its risks and dangers, that could not be more intractable, after all, than certain death.

Hypnotized by the proximity of death, Hipólito was not fully aware of the doctor's departure, even when the fellow shook his hand. He saw death courting Santa, sleeping with her, superceding him, the person who had waited patiently until everyone else had had his fill, everyone else before him, who finally rescued her and adored her from her thorn-bloodied feet to her hair crowned with dew and roses, with scorn and infamy. And just as the pack of slathering, howling machos turned away from her and descended instead on her prostituted replacements that come from everywhere, like an endless herd of cattle to feed the insatiable slaughterhouses, the brothels of the great urban centers—just as he stooped to lift her up, cancer came to close forever the door that had been open to everyone but him, and behind the cancer was Death, who would take Santa away from him and possess and enjoy her itself, charm by charm, bone by bone. He couldn't fight against death the way he had fought against his earlier competitors, with his only weapon: patience.

So, had the new girl's debut been a big success, and was she the new queen of the night? So much the better! He had contemplated her initial triumph in the confidence that darker days lay ahead. Was he a perfect monster of ugliness and she a portent of beauty who gradually acquired refined, if decadent, tastes? No matter! He would be there on the day of her ultimate disillusionment, when the refined, elegant clubmen spurned her, and she would love him ugliness and all. He had gotten worried, though, when Santa became el Jarameño's mistress—now *that* was a close call! But after that, he again felt sure that Santa would eventually be his, and so he took a lover's cruel delight in each step of the decline that brought her closer to him. Let her tumble and scrape herself up, sure. Let an illness sap her beauty or a cut on her cheek disfigure her in some jealous rage! Let her suffer the disdain and derision of everyone else, so that she would finally, finally remember him . . . Hipólito. Finally call him. Finally love him.

And he would be there, no matter what. He was in love, which meant he pardoned her automatically. No, for him there was no uncertainty, ever, only patience and waiting, as the injustices and iniquities of the world did their job on Santa . . . In the end, he would be there—blind, ugly as a monster, poor as Job, and all—to lift her up and soothe her with the balm of his infinite adoration.

But death is invincible, stronger than everything good and everything evil. Death pulverizes the strongest individuals and the best laid plans. And it was death that appeared at the precise moment when Hipólito began his star-struck rehabilitation of Santa, his waiting had finally come to nothing.

In a demented fit he raised his curled fingers to his eyes without irises, with the impulse to pull them out because they had never been good for anything. Since they were never going to see Santa, let them rot in the garbage and all of him along with them, because next, he was going to tear out his heart. Without Santa, it wasn't good for anything either.

"Hipo, what are you doing?" said Santa, coming out to see why he lingered on the little bit of terrace. She took hold of, and quieted, his convulsive hands.

"Me? . . . Oh . . . I think I've got something in my eye. Do you see it?"

For Santa, this was the decisive test. She had never had such a close look at those horrible whitish eyes with their wrinkles, their networks and knots of colored veins like tangles of hair, those gray tear ducts with disgusting little accumulations of mucus. Without having to overcome anything, but rather, like women in love, she kissed his eyelids, eyelashes, and eyebrows! How he moved them, then, and how quickly they were all dripping with tears! With what gentleness the blind man lowered his face onto Santa's shoulder!

In that posture, she brushed his bestial ear with her lips, the lips that had been so enchanting and full, juicy and red as a pomegranate, fresh as a mountain spring, lips that now, swollen here and sagging there, inspired only indifference or even pity, and she asked him:

"I'm going to die, right? The doctor said I'm dying and you can't accept it and don't know how to tell me . . . Tell me, Hipo, tell me because I already know! . . . I feel like something's tearing me apart to pull out my bones . . . But I don't want you to get like this. Hey, what's the big deal? Don't you know that we all have to die?"

Trembling, Hipólito squeezed her, touching now her waist, now her flank, so thin and unprovocative, so unlike just a year ago, as if he were trying to protect all of her, shield her from harm with his hands and arms. Wrapped in each other's arms, they went in to the sofa and stayed there for a long time without talking or letting go of one another, enjoying the simple pleasure of each other's attention, accepting together, in loving, silent resignation, the unjust fate that threatened to separate them for all eternity. Holding hands, they floated high above the mire and mud in which they had lived, their bodies in chaste, intentional, intimate contact, their mutual offering to each other at the edge of the abyss, the gesture of two unfortunates wounded by life, no longer attempting to oppose the inscrutable forces that doom us all, but instead accepting impotence, loving each other, and moving tearfully closer together, so that a single bolt of lightening could destroy them at the same time.

And in that dramatic quietude, the night came upon them. Jenaro, forlorn, did not dare disturb them, and Jaws hardly flew at all, but instead, landed near them and stayed, seeming to look at them sidewise with his palpitating, red little eyes. They did not eat any supper. When Jenaro offered to go bring it, they took the opportunity to begin the many little confessions, reminders, and requests that precede definitive goodbyes.

"Tell Elvira that I'm not going to play tonight, and here . . . take this and have supper wherever you want and come back late. Take the keys . . ."

When they were alone, Hipólito lit a cigarette, Santa refused a glass of liquor, and both of them, employing infinite tact, dedicated themselves to the unpleasant but urgent task of retrospection.

Good Lord, how many hidden tribulations they unearthed, how many scars and open wounds, and how much common suffering! In their rush to tell each other everything, it all came out in an incongruent jumble of serious things and childish things, experiences that mark one's soul and experiences that make one smile to remember. But no matter how distant the topic, Hipólito returned obsessively to a single idea, which animated questions and answers, rectifications and ratifications, determined to convince both Santa and himself of its truth, by dint of constant repetition:

"That's why you don't have to die of that cancer stuff, because that's what the operation is for, so you'll get better, and when you're completely well, then we're going to . . ."

A million projects, leaving death out of the question, even though death buzzed around their ears again and again, like an insistent fly, hushing them with its invisible presence. Between those occasions, they regained their confidence. Yes, they would have a life together! Why on earth shouldn't they? They weren't in anyone's way! Just a couple of wrecks that no one wanted . . . And during those fleeting moments of confidence and victory, they felt the powerful instinct of self-preservation that makes us hang on to dear life even as we feel it slipping irremediably from our grasp, and they spoke of pleasant things, of their childhoods and their mothers, and of how Santa got her unusual name. She had been born on the first of November, All Saint's day, but her godmother, an Italian woman who was married to the administrator of the Hacienda de Necochea at San Angel, did not want her to be called Santos, the name that corresponded to that birthday, explaining that in Italy women were commonly named Santa, to which was added a diminutive — Santuzza or Santucha, something like that — she didn't remember exactly.

For his part, Hipólito confessed a big secret to Santa. He really wasn't so penniless, after all. He was a man of substance, with four hundred pesos saved up.

"What did you think?" he said, getting up to pull a little bundle from under the mattress, "You figured me for a beggar? Wrong, my Santa, wrong! I have a bit of capital! Here, count it!" he exclaimed, putting his nest egg on the table.

They lit the candle, and Santa counted coins and bank notes amounting to four hundred eleven pesos and change — their future assured for an entire year, at least! But the fictitious happiness soon evaporated, and they went back to their places on the sofa, took each other's hands, and pressed their bodies together. The miserable little room was illuminated now. Jaws was pecking at the coins and bank notes on the table. What good would they be, anyway, with no one to spend them?

It had to be late, because the old building was so silent.

Santa spoke nervously, all of a sudden, her gaze apparently fixed on the money, though in fact, she was looking far beyond, at the gloomy distance:

"If I die . . . don't interrupt me, Hipo, it's not what I want, either . . . but if I die, swear that you'll bury me in the cemetery of my village, in Chimalistac, just as near as you can to my mother . . . Do you swear?"

And the blind man swore, with a clear voice and firm intonation, but protesting with his expression, pulling Santa into his lap and hugging her furiously, as if he were already locked in combat, one on one, against forces emanating from the earth that wanted to swallow her up.

Unable to remain upright because of the pain, Santa lay down on the bed, and Hipólito said he would lie down in a minute.

"Give me your hand, Hipo, don't leave me alone," Santa begged him from between the sheets. And Hipólito went to the bed, knelt at the side of it so that he wouldn't make her uncomfortable, and buried his monstrous face in the covers. Neither spoke any more, but both of them thought the same thoughts, keeping totally still, squeezing their hands, oh, so tightly, so that neither of them could go anywhere without the other. The candle was almost gone, and its dying agony produced an intense alternation of light and dark. On the table, Jaws had fallen asleep, nestled in Hipólito's pile of useless capital, the dove's little head tucked under one wing.

When Jenaro got home with a pair of sandwiches so that they would have at least something in their stomachs, the scene saddened him so much that he felt the urge to kneel as Hipólito had done. But he noiselessly slipped into his own room where, for the first time in his life he was visited by insomnia and lay there sweating without a wink of sleep all night. The imposing silence of the night, of the house, and of his *patrones* made a powerful impression on him, and he even imagined for a moment that Santa and Hipólito had both died, and he along with them . . . that everyone was dead.

What a cheerful looking hospital! Its new, modern façade, accented by the old church to one side of it, the tranquil plaza in front of it, the sunlit gardens of its first courtyard, and the extreme cleanliness that one can smell as well as see throughout the building—everything about it contrasted with the melancholy appearance of other hospitals. Santa, who was gravely ill and facing major surgery, naturally arrived with her heart in her hands. She had only seen one other hospital, Morelos Hospital, a sinister-looking place, indeed, and the bright appearance of this one raised her spirits:

"Hipo! Hipo! This doesn't look like a hospital at all! It's so nice that it makes me think I really am going to get better."

After the paperwork of admissions and, of course, prior payment, Santa was installed in bed number eleven in a ward located near the operating room. Like the rest of the hospital, the ward was as clean as could be, with a total of twenty beds arranged symmetrically down both sides, each bed flanked by a varnished nightstand that contained various prosaic necessities of patients' bodies, such as bedpans.

At one end of the long room, a table with various other utensils and books, a couple of rooms for the nursing staff, and, hanging on the wall, a large sculpted crucifix; at the other end, a large, unfinished automatic washer of nickel and marble. A subtle odor of disinfectants. Perfectly graduated ventilation. Clarity and spaciousness. People speak automatically in a soft voice, and their shoes do not clump on the floor. Various patients, all of them women, raise their heads to look curiously at the new arrivals, then plunge them back into the pillows. From a corner, a muffled, rhythmic moaning. A dressed woman seated on the edge of one of the beds coughs, spits into a receptacle that she herself raises to her mouth, wipes her lips with a handkerchief, and starts to cough again. Propped up on the pillows of another bed, one can see the thin frame of another woman, with angular shoulders and arms as thin as a child's. Her hands rest on the folded sheet above her swollen belly, and her fingers move the beads of a rosary as, with sunken eyes and bloodless lips the color of dry dirt, she recites the litany without quite forming the words, as if she were ruminating on their meaning.

Santa has been describing all this to Hipólito—who holds tightly on to her—from their entrance into the hospital to their arrival at her bed. There they say goodbye. He'll be back in the afternoon.

He and Jenaro are told, on their way out, that the operation will be at seven o'clock the next morning. They tremble to hear it. Without saying a word, they exit the hospital under the curious gaze of its employees and staff.

"Where are we going, *patrón?*" asks Jenaro as they cross the threshold of that painful place.

"To hell!" vomits the blind man, with a cracked voice.

And the insolent word echoes in the small, quiet plaza.

Without a fixed plan, they wandered through indifferent streets brimming with the life of the immense, unfeeling city.

The visit that afternoon was less a comfort than a torment. They could hardly talk in that room full of suffering and witnesses. They could not even mention their love, which had been converted by this unjust contrary alignment of stars into a cruel joke. They could not risk revealing that they were not brother and sister, the false family relationship that Hipólito had declared so he could visit and be present during operation. So they just held hands and never seemed to tire of that simple contact, so innocent and so loving at the same time.

Very few words. Santa looks at Hipólito and finds him decidedly handsome. Hipólito tries to get his eyes to see Santa and, failing, he shuts his eyelids and presses his chin into his chest tightly enough, one would think, to bore a hole. Jenaro, sitting on the floor, watches them both.

It took every ounce of Hipólito's willpower to make himself go play piano that night at Elvira's house, but in view of the nights he had already missed, he could not afford to stay away again and thus lose the job that provided his livelihood. There were too many nocturnal pianists with whom Elvira could easily replace him. Once he was there, though, it was not a bad way to kill the time. What would he have done in his apartment without Santa there, counting the minutes that had to pass before the moment of supreme danger? So he just stayed up, willingly playing on for additional hours on the upstairs piano that the police could not detect from the street, until, at five o'clock, with the dawn, with Jenaro, and with fif-

teen pesos extra in his pocket, he finally stepped back into the street—
dragging his feet, as if by walking slowly he could retard the arrival of the
fatal moment. Mostly for Jenaro's sake, he consented to stop at a recently
opened little place for two steaming bowls of coffee with milk, which they
drank without either of them touching the bread they were served. And
there on the filthy bench where they sat having this breakfast, they heard
church bells ringing half past six o'clock.

As they rounded the corner to enter the plaza in front of the hospital,
Hipólito halted and, timorously and innocently, as if his guide held the
keys of life and death, he asked the boy:

"Is Santa going to die, Jenaro?"

The boy, never suspecting that he was addressing one of the great mysteries of creation, answered simply:

"Why should she die, if she doesn't hurt anybody by living?"

Surrounded by doctors, nurses, and aids with their sleeves rolled up
and wearing surgical aprons, Santa was about to receive the anesthesia.

"Hipo, thank God!" was her greeting. "I thought you might be too late!"

White as a sheet of paper, disoriented as a blind man, and unsteady as
a drunk, bumping into this fellow and that without excusing himself or
even saying hello, Hipólito let go of Jenaro and ran to the bed. Santa's
arms caught hold of the piano player and guided him to her lips, to the
great surprise of those who stood around them observing the emotional
display of this "brother and sister." The surgeon finally separated them,
handed to the anesthetist the mask through which Santa would inhale the
chloroform, and told Hipólito:

"Calm down, my friend. If not, you can't be present for the operation.
Remember what you promised . . ."

They placed the mask on Santa's face and began to administer the first
drops of anesthetic. One could still hear her murmur, inside the mask:

"Goodbye, Hipo! . . . I'm going!"

"Go to sleep, my Santa . . . go to sleep and don't be afraid. This is going
to cure you. See you later . . . when you wake up. I'll stay right here with
you."

It was not true. The doctors hustled him away, and Jenaro, frightened
by the unfamiliar proceedings, moved close to his side. Administering the
anesthesia took abnormally long on account of the advanced alcoholism of
the patient, who soon began to blather incoherently, mixing fragmentary
truths with partial fictions, a concubine's sordidness with a maiden's innocence, the experiences of her short life with the ambitions she had never

achieved. Only Hipólito understood, paid attention, or felt moved. Then she shook twice—a laugh, a sob, a cry—and hushed utterly, her inhalation almost imperceptible, her exhalation like a small bellows: puff . . . puff . . .

"Ready to go," announced the anesthetist, without removing the mask or suspending the drop, drop, drop of the chloroform, that permeated the immediate surroundings with its sickly sweet odor.

At a signal from the surgeon, the male nurses lifted Santa's sleeping form and carried her feet first, her legs bent at the knee, swaying limply as rags, doctors and their assistants walking at her sides, the anesthetist with his drops of chloroform at her head. Hipólito, guided by Jenaro, brought up the rear of this solemn, early morning procession as it proceeded down the central aisle of the ward, attracting the attention of the recently awakened patients in the row of beds on either side, who sat up with foreboding to watch it pass.

The somber procession went down a corridor and through a door. Hipólito felt his heart lurch, and Jenaro's whole body trembled. This must be the operating room, because as soon as they had put Santa down—on some sort of table, it seemed—the surgeon gave orders for the door to be closed, and he pushed Hipólito in the direction of a distant chair. In a routine voice, he told Hipólito that the surgery was about to begin, that he must not budge because everything was sterile except for him and Jenaro, and that, above all, he must not speak or interrupt them for any reason.

"The operation itself is extremely delicate and requires our utmost concentration. Stay right here, the two of you, because here you're not in the way."

How on earth could they get in the way? They felt so fearful they could hardly move! Hipólito dropped into the chair, and Jenaro crouched between his legs, both of them softly clearing their throats. The sulfurous stench of caustic disinfectants made them feel nauseous. And it was so hot, too! The cause was the newfangled autoclave that sterilized instruments and bandages using steam, with its pressure gauge like one in the cab of a locomotive.

They heard the conversation of the doctors without understanding it, a series of questions that the surgeon directed to his helpers, and their respective replies. Were the patient's extremities covered and secured? Yes, doctor. Was the drip—with its life-giving serum, a mere saline solution—inserted and ready? Yes, doctor. Had the sponges, cotton, clamps, valves and whatever else been inspected? And when all the affirmative answers had been given, the team suddenly fell silent, and the battle began.

Chapter Ten 233

The wall clock, with its large pendulum and sonorous mechanism, took charge of the operating room at that point, it seemed—firm, deliberate, and tireless, an almost human presence:

"Tick ... tock ... tick ... tock ... tick ... tock!"

The clock's ticking alternated with the squeal of surgical scissors slicing living flesh and pincers clamping their little steel teeth into it. Only the voice of the surgeon challenged the dominance of the clock, when he raised it to request or command what was urgently needed:

"Curved pincers! ... Clear the blood! ... Cotton! ... Tie this off! ... Another scalpel! ... Sponge!"

The silence returned, and again, because the surgeon's audible breathing was rapid but quiet, the clock took charge—firm, deliberate, tireless, and almost human:

"Tick ... tock ... tick ... tock ... tick ... tock!"

Santa was letting out a very soft, continuous, hoarse little sound with occasional louder cries and groans when the scalpel and scissors bit into delicate parts of her, as if, no matter how anesthetized, no matter how obliterated her consciousness and immobilized her muscles, her nerve endings could still feel what was happening and lament what they were suffering.

Hipólito, who could not see and only hear the clock, began to hallucinate. At first, he was able to identify it as a wall clock with a loud pendulum, but gradually it seemed to him a giant rodent gnawing diabolically at the structure of the building. It fell stealthily silent when someone spoke, then immediately renewed its destructive labor:

"Tick ... tock ... tick ... tock ... tick ... tock!"

Then, he perceived it as a clock again, but one that gnawed at lives rather than marking the hours. A gnawer of lives, that's exactly what it was! It would destroy Santa, and him, too, and the doctors, and the whole world ... simply because we don't pay any attention to it and just let it gnaw and gnaw, day and night, whether we are awake or asleep, whether we are happy or sad, gradually reducing us to nothing:

"Tick ... tock ... tick ... tock ... tick ... tock!"

Then it happened. The patient's respiration stopped just as the brilliantly executed operation was reaching completion.

"Doctor," blurted the anesthetist, "the patient isn't breathing."

Then ensued the agitation and confusion that accompanies all catastrophes: running, agglomerations, hushed urgencies. First, they tried the modern scientific procedures for resuscitation, pulling her tongue out of the way and administering artificial respiration. Then, the traditional methods, such as pressure on the ribcage, prescribed in the old treatises. All in vain! Now, they threw open the doors and windows that had been closed to maintain a sterile environment, and the outside air rushed in to hear the news. The trees in the courtyard swayed outside the windows, as if shrouding the deceased with the whisper of their leaves in the breeze.

Santa, who had gone to sleep hoping for health and life, had crossed the last, awesome threshold.

Not remembering Hipólito's blindness, the doctors permitted him to approach her corpse:

"Your sister has died. I'm sorry. You can look at her, if you want . . ."

And the clock, sounding above the funereal hush, continued to gnaw— firm, deliberate, tireless, and almost human. Santa represented one more down, but there were many more to go, and so on it went:

"Tick . . . tock . . . tick . . . tock . . . tick . . . tock!"

There are some states of consciousness that cannot be described, and Hipólito's, during the coming days, was one such. Sometimes it bordered on madness; other times, it calmed him to wail and cry; other times, he seemed to descend into imbecility. But he made good use of his lucid moments, calling on the well-placed acquaintances that he had acquired during his many years of playing piano in brothels characterized by a certain egalitarian intimacy and frequented by men of authority in the government of the Federal District and in various ministries and offices. He went to them now for the special permissions that he needed: permission to hold a wake over Santa's body in his apartment, which would not normally be allowed, and permission to bury her according to her last request, in the cemetery of her village, near her mother.

Aside from them, he told no one about the mournful event, least of all Elvira and her girls, the only ones who might actually have attended. Suffering, love, and death had together purified Santa, according to the blind man's judgment. He believed that inviting the impure to her humble burial would be like inviting strangers, and he refused to do so. Only he had any say over Santa's remains. They belonged to him alone, and he hid them even from the curiosity of his neighbors who wanted to see the body and be at the wake to accompany the widower and orphan, which is what Hipólito and Jenaro seemed to them to be.

"Very kind . . . thank you, but no, no . . ."

Hipólito and Jenaro shut themselves in the apartment to watch over the deceased with flowers and candles, just the two of them, or rather, the three of them, because Jaws participated, too, not flying to sit on Hipólito's shoulder as he normally did, nor pecking at Jenaro in pursuit of crumbs and leftovers. Probably the sputtering and light of so many candles kept him awake, because he did not tuck his head under his wing all night, but rather, sat on the table cooing and never seeming to take his beady little eyes off Santa.

And there in the cemetery of Chimalistac, the village of Santa's honorable birth and upbringing, there Hipólito and Jenaro buried her: in the pretty little ruined cemetery that is always open and always peaceful, with its softly crumbling adobe walls where lizards scamper and warm themselves in the sun, where ants and bees live and labor, and where cows enter to graze and moo, shaded by ancient trees with leafy branches in which the resident warblers give stupendous concerts at morning and evening. The rain and grass gradually obliterate the names of the disappeared and the dates of their disappearances, and the boys of the village play among the heliotropes and bellflowers that sprout profusely and lovingly interlace among the graves. From there, one can hear the murmur of water spilling over the bigger of the village's two mill dams into the river, after flowing quietly through the orchard of the old Carmelite convent, as if the water sprites were singing their faint, sweet ballad to comfort the dead in their eternal slumber.

To this cemetery, the blind man and his guide directed their steps one afternoon after another, staying until the fireflies began to flair and the crickets began to sing. Then Jenaro would approach Hipólito, who lay face down on the tombstone, and shaking him gently, as if he were awakening him from a heavy sleep, the boy would repeat:

"Patrón . . . it's night already."

The visit was repeated the following afternoon, with an identical duration and an identical script, including what seemed an identically heavy sleep.

Hipólito had ordered for her a wide, smooth slab, and in the middle of it, he had them carve the name Santa, without any other words or epitaph, only those five letters very large and deep, so that the rain and grass would never obliterate them and he would always be able to read them, over and over, the only way he knew how to read, with his fingertips . . . Time passed, Santa had been buried for months already, and Hipólito still never missed a day, lying for hours face down on the tomb, his monstrous face pressed against the slab as if his useless eyes could see through it, his hands caressing the name-poem that his lips pronounced as his fingers spelled it out:

"San-ta!"

Jenaro, who was just a kid, after all, quickly tired of the cemetery, and after about a week, as soon as Hipólito entered into his ecstatic trance the boy would slip away and romp, play marbles, or go after fruit or honeycombs with the village boys. At dusk, he returned to awaken his master, who had been unaware of his absence and asked no questions.

And the day finally came when Hipólito felt that he no longer had anything to say or give to Santa, not even tears, because he had already given them all. But it so happened that, from reading aloud, over and over, the name graven on the slab—"Santa . . . Santa"—a prayer came spontaneously to his lips, and prayers were the one thing that he had never given her. But . . . could he? His being what he was . . . her being what she had been . . . would the prayer be valid?

On his knees beside the grave, he still did not pray. What had they been, the two of them? Ah, it was now only too clear: a prostitute and a miserable piano player in a brothel! She had tasted everything forbidden, been stained by the worst perversions and concupiscence, and induced others to sin and go astray. He had not been much better. The two of them had abandoned the duties of righteousness and wallowed in the mire, in darkness and immorality, despised and despicable.

If she were to come back to life and, taking his hand, ask the world forgiveness for everything, it would be no use. Men and women would cover their ears, so not to hear, their eyes, so not to see, their consciences, so not to forgive. Their love and what they had suffered together would earn them no earthly pardon at all. None!

God alone was left to them. God is always there! He takes the humble and the wretched, the despised and the despicable, all into his divinely merciful arms, the whole numberless, infinite procession of those who hunger and thirst for forgiveness. Love and suffering do not win earthly pardon, but they are a road that rises to God.

Hipólito was gesturing and speaking aloud, as if someone could hear him.

Transfigured, his horrid face turned toward heaven and his whitish eyes opened very wide. Delivered from evil and vice at long last, believing at long last that true health, the supreme solution to all problems, lies up there, he kissed the name engraved on the slab again, this time as an eternal farewell, and he repeated it many times:

"Santa! . . . Santa! . . ."

And radiant with confidence in the supreme solution, his arms folded and his face turned toward heaven, he prayed for the soul of his beloved Santa, whose name had placed upon his lips the simple, sublime, magnificent prayer that our mothers teach us when we are children, the prayer that not even all of life's accumulated vicissitudes can make us forget:

Santa María, Madre de Dios . . .

He began very softly, and word by word the rest of his supplication rose to lose itself in the glorious firmament, the colored lights of the evening sky:

Holy Mary, Mother of God
Pray for us sinners . . .

Guatemala City, 7 April 1900
Villalobos, 14 February 1902